Death to Spies

A Tom Doherty Associates Book New York

Death to Spies

QUINN FAWCETT

DEATH TO SPIES

This book is printed on acid-free paper.

Book design by Jane Adele Regina

A Forge Book
Published by Tom Doherty Associates, LLC
175 Fifth Avenue
New York, NY 10010

www.tor.com

Forge® is a registered trademark of Tom Doherty Associates, LLC.

Library of Congress Cataloging-in-Publication Data

Fawcett, Quinn.
    Death to spies / Quinn Fawcett.—1st ed.
      p. cm.
    ISBN 0-312-86930-4 (alk. paper)
    1. Fleming, Ian, 1908–1964—Fiction. 2. Nuclear weapons
information—Fiction. 3. British—New Mexico—Fiction.
4. Intelligence officers—Fiction. 5. Los Alamos (N.M.)—Fiction.
6. Novelists—Fiction. I. Title.
PS3556.A992 D43 2002
813'.54—dc21

                                    2001058279

First Edition: July 2002

Printed in the United States of America

0 9 8 7 6 5 4 3 2 1

For Guy

Death to Spies

Chapter 1

"OH, NO," said Ian Fleming, stretching out his long legs and crossing his ankles. "I'm retired. No more of that snoop-and-mischief business for me. Talk to my brother. He's still in the game." He lifted his drink to his visitor. "Chin-chin."

"I'm not asking you to do anything official, Fleming," said his visitor, looking uncomfortable in his Bond Street pin-striped wool suit and waistcoat on this tropical afternoon; the sun was flooding the island with warmth and light as opalescent as Bombay gin. Even his signet ring, a massive knot of gold with a couchant wyvern cut into it, was too heavy for the tropics, suggesting Tudor or Victorian architecture and over-stuffed chairs under baronial displays. "That would be the point of it, old son. Nothing on the books. The essence of covert. No one would know. You'd be quite safe."

"Perfect deniability, you mean," said Fleming with a quick, hard smile as he reached for the packet of Players on the table and proceeded to light up. "No. I don't see how I can do it, not without knowing a great deal more. I'm sorry, but I have other work to do." He was wearing a light linen shirt and khaki trousers, more in accord with the warm, humid weather than what his guest had on. He was limber and lean, a good-looking man in his late thirties, well-mannered, properly educated, charming, perfectly at home in his Jamaica estate down a narrow private road on the edge of this cove that gave privacy as well as a spectacular view. "I have a great deal to do around here, as you are undoubtedly aware. I can't leave the island johnnies to tend to it themselves—you know what they are; well-meaning but lazy, most of them, and needing supervision. I can't walk away and hope for the best. You can see the place needs—"

"Someone must undertake the work, and do it circumspectly. This is not the same as Churchill's missions to rid the world of Nazis who escaped Nuremberg, this is a more immediate and less settled problem, needing discretion as well as careful investigation," said his visitor more sternly. "Like it or not, I know you are the very man for the job."

Fleming angled his head to the side. "Yes? And how is it you came to this—wholly unfounded—conclusion?"

"Your record, of course. I had a squint at it last week." His guest, who had remained standing since his arrival at the isolated house, now allowed himself to lean back against the nearest cabinet, a tall mahogany one with louvered doors. It had a matched fellow at the other end of the lounge where the two men were conversing and taking in the fine afternoon. "I have been looking over the secret files for almost a month and you are clearly the most qualified of any I have reviewed."

"You mean the official file, or the unofficial one?" asked Fleming, his face showing no trace of emotion as a wraith of smoke curled by it and was gone.

"The most revealing one, of course; the one no outside eyes will ever see," said his visitor. He pointed out beyond the open French doors to the verandah and the view of the water. "It was providential I had occasion to visit an old colleague on Jamaica—it has given me an excellent cover for my visit, and an opportunity to speak with you without drawing any attention to my presence."

"Do you think that's necessary?" Fleming asked.

"Precautions are always necessary for a man in my position," said his guest with a faint, self-deprecating smile. "I can find it in me to envy you, Fleming. You have a wonderful place here. I don't blame you for not wanting to leave."

"Then why did you bother to come here? I'm a newspaperman now, and it suits me down to the ground; I am happy in my employment. I haven't the least inclination to go back to that kind of work. Grubby, nasty, and dangerous, spying is. I made that clear enough after the war, I thought." He set his glass aside. "A pity you had to come so far, but there it is."

"I completely understand, my dear fellow," said his visitor, his bland, square features turning ruddy from the heat. "But I fear it is rather beyond you. This isn't a case where just anyone will do. England expects, and all that: just now, England expects of you. In this instance, I am very much afraid that your qualifications require you to return to field-work. It is very important. I cannot stress that enough." He sighed.

"How important?" Fleming asked with an innocence that hid his purpose. "You keep hinting but you tell me very little. Don't, for God's sake, ask me to take your word for it, or accept what you say on trust. I'm not still wet behind the ears, you know. Explain what you mean by important."

"Important enough that you will have authorization to kill if necessary," said his guest, the gesture of his hand showing off his signet ring as if the mythical beast on it was adding its support. "This is no minor matter, Fleming. It is, in truth, deadly earnest. You must be prepared to kill when you take on this assignment. I have been given leave to grant you the protection of the authorization. In fact, I have the authorization for using deadly force with me."

"You mean what they're calling a license to kill?" Fleming asked, expecting an answer in the negative.

"Yes," said his guest flatly, repeating, "We are in earnest, Fleming."

"Good Lord," said Fleming, doing his utmost to conceal his shock. "This must be of the first order of—"

"Yes, yes," said his guest, making a gesture to show his determination to go on. "It won't take long, and then it will be all over, unless the bloody Americans try to muck about. You never can tell how they'll jump these days. You'll have to deal with them as you think best when you're in their country, as you will have to be. They could bring undue attention to this mission, if they get wind of it before we're ready. Not much chance of that, though. President Truman wants to get rid of intelligence gathering as much as possible—that CIG bureau of his is hardly up to the job—and that maniac Hoover wants all such agencies under his control. So long as they bicker, we should not have to dodge them."

"And why would I have to go to America?" Fleming asked.

"It seems some of the problem is centered in America. So you will have to visit there. If you can deal with them." The flare of his guest's nostrils suggested that he could not.

"They did their part," said Fleming, giving credit where it was due. "It would have been difficult without them. You cannot deny that."

"That they did, but tardily. And now it's time they leave the field to the experts. Besides, these are British secrets being compromised. The Americans should stay well out of it. It's too delicate for their style of espionage." There was a hard glint in the visitor's eyes.

"We didn't despise them eight years ago," Fleming pointed

out, mischief in his attitude. "We asked them for their help, as I recall."

His guest nodded slowly. "Well, that was different. And I must say, General Donovan did well enough during the War, all full of sneakiness and derring-do; it appealed to his sense of heroism, I believe. He had excellent men, and women, working for him, I'll say that. He needed all the exuberance he could engender during the War, but this is different. The business of covert missions has no place for so reckless a man as he."

"I couldn't help but like him," said Fleming, smiling slightly as he put out his cigarette. "Only met him briefly, of course, but he struck me as too enthusiastic. Rather like a very clever, dead-set hunting dog—thoroughly American, when you look at western films. Still, I take your meaning. His—um—cowboy hero approach to dealing with certain sorts of actions is ham-handed." He studied his guest over the rim of his glass, thinking that this Whitehall bureaucrat was not as engaging as General Donovan had been.

"He is out of the picture, in any case," said his visitor. "Though you can give the devil his due."

"All right," said Fleming. "We are agreed that this is not an ordinary case. We are also agreed that it is internal, and not to be bandied about beyond our immediate company. Am I right on that score?" He saw his visitor nod. "How much can you tell me about it?"

"I thought you were dead against it," said his visitor. "Could it be that you are changing your mind?"

"Only insofar as I am curious," said Fleming. "Perhaps I can advise you in some way that would be useful, without actually participating."

"That is not enough reason to show you those files," said his visitor stiffly. "Not if you only want to peruse them. You are, as you say, a newspaper-man now, and the secrets contained therein are not for unauthorized eyes."

"It is the only way you will persuade me to change my mind. I don't know what you expect me to get involved in, and I will not agree to anything until I do," Fleming said, still at ease but with steely purpose under his facade of bonhomie. "If you will not provide me the information, I must suppose I am being hoodwinked. Sorry."

"Must I do this?" His visitor was clearly flummoxed by the impasse. He twisted the golden couchant wyvern around his little finger.

"If you want my participation, you must," said Fleming with a vulpine grin. "I will keep your confidence, if that's your worry."

"Yes, you will. You signed the Official Secrets Act, didn't you, Fleming?" he asked, knowing the answer already, for everyone who had done covert work had signed it. He saw Fleming hold up his right hand and went on, "It is still binding on you, as you must know. You will have to hold everything I tell you—and the fact of this visit—in utter confidence."

"I understand," said Fleming. "I'll abide by the terms, never fear." He finished his drink and set the glass down again. "Everything you tell me will remain secret."

"Very well," said his visitor. "Then I want you to understand that we have been busy working on developing atomic weapons."

"That isn't very secret. They're all hungry for A-bombs. Everyone who can is doing it. The Russians, of course. The Americans want to make theirs bigger and better. Probably the

French, and the Chinese may be trying. Who knows, perhaps Canada is working on an A-bomb." His mild sarcasm was met by an unfriendly scowl. "They all want one, since the War."

"That's as may be," his guest said, dismissing Fleming's flippancy. "The problem is, we seem to be losing some of our work to the Russians. I'm sure you've kept abreast of events at home, haven't you? Russian spies everywhere. And not only them, which is the most distressing."

"The Chinese?" Fleming suggested.

His visitor shook his head. "We need to determine who is doing the most damage, how much damage has been done, and stop it from happening again, preferably with as little public outcry as possible. This could be a very dangerous development, concerning atomic weapons and other military secrets." He paused to stare at Fleming, as if the force of his gaze could provide persuasion. "You do see the importance of this situation, don't you?"

"I should think so," said Fleming, and whistled slowly, a single alarmed note that was rapidly lost on the soft Jamaican air. "Is any of this confirmed, or is it all rumor and innuendo?"

"Confirmed, I am sorry to say," his guest told him. "I have the information with me if you care to look at it."

Fleming let out a long breath. "You still mean you will show it to me only if I agree to undertake this venture, I assume?"

His guest gave him a wintery smile. "Something like that."

Chapter 2

"MY POSITION is unchanged. I must see what you have before I can give you a decision. There must be some underlying reason for me to be involved in this, and so far, you haven't shown me what it is." Fleming studied his guest with a degree of skepticism that revealed his many reservations about the project. "Why should I do this? Pray, don't wave the flag and expect me to leap into action without enough information to do the work you want done."

"It isn't what I want, it is what the British Empire must have in order to remain secure." There was a wary light in his eyes. "We're very vulnerable, if only people knew. There are forces in the world that didn't exist a decade ago, and they are growing stronger the longer they remain undefined and undetected. Anyone might take advantage of this peace and turn it to his advantage. And there are men in the world who are committed to just that end. Britain is a sea power, and anything that compromises that harms Britain."

Fleming shook his head. "If that's the case, don't you think you should have more than one man on the case?"

"I don't want to bring undue attention to what is happening. It would be most unsettling if anyone should stumble upon what you are doing. Those enemies I spoke of will not be looking for one man, and that should provide you a degree of cover that will prove invaluable." His visitor coughed. "You know about covert activities and you have enough experience to do what we need. A single man can do what a dozen cannot."

"So you mean to use me as a coal-mine canary," Fleming said. "I can find out how these enemies are working against Britain and then you will know what you have to put in motion to stop their nefarious plans. If this turns out to be nothing more than a minor dust-up caused by jumpy nerves, you won't have any red faces around Whitehall. You would rather have one unaffiliated man out there than three or four established agents until you know what's actually going on." He chuckled. "Rather lose one independent man who can be disavowed rather than risk all those men who are still part of MI5."

"You don't think that this is the only reason I've come to you, do you?" His visitor smoothed his waistcoat. "As there may be travel required, you can do it with less attention brought upon you than someone departing from London or Southampton."

"That seems likely," said Fleming at his driest. "Is there some reason I should pack my bags on your behalf that your agents cannot employ?"

"As a newsman, you have a broader entrée to the world than many others do," came the uncomfortable answer.

"How do you suppose I can find something you have not? I cannot be the first man you have approached about this, not with a killing authorization in hand. I suspect someone has gone before me. What happened?" It was a last-ditch effort to avoid the whole thing and both of them knew it.

His visitor didn't answer the question. "You have been away from the milieu for long enough that you are no longer caught up in the . . . ambience. You will be able to assess matters more independently. You will not be noticed the way many of our agents would be. Remember: many of those you worked with are aware that you're no longer in the game, and they'll tend to overlook you, assuming you're on journalistic assignment." He paused briefly. "And I know you are reliable, and you are not likely to play favorites."

Fleming pursed his lips. "What about my brother?"

"What about him?" The visitor kept his demeanor of calm unconcern.

"Is any of this apt to—"

Before Fleming could finish, his guest said, "No. You will not be putting him at risk any more than he already is. What an odd notion. I would not place you in such a precarious situation: it wouldn't do you or the country any good. Your brother is not among those who we consider to be part of the conspiracy, if there is a conspiracy." He paused. "The last man who tried to get us the information we seek went missing."

"Stealing atomic secrets *and* a conspiracy? And a missing spy?" Fleming stood and strode to the bar to refill his glass.

"Perhaps two. There may be an accomplice, which is one of the things we would like to know." The visitor looked about as if he expected to be overheard. "That accomplice may be here—on Jamaica."

Fleming gave a little shake to his head, not quite smiling. "This is becoming more complex by the moment."

"Do you think so?" His guest laughed, a brittle sound.

"I do, and well you know it. You are tantalizing me with just enough to set my curiosity going. That has been your intention since you came here. I know you mean to pique my interest so that I'll be willing to do as you wish, just to satisfy myself about what you are hinting. I am journalist enough to know the sound of a major story." He poured out gin and added a bit of tonic. "You are certain this will not compromise my brother. I won't undertake anything—no matter how fascinating—that could put him at a disadvantage."

"Yes, I am certain of it; in fact, if this case is successfully concluded, it will probably help him," said his visitor with as much conviction as he had shown at any time since his arrival. "Good Lord, man, I wouldn't want you to be divided in your loyalties. What good would that do anyone?"   .

Fleming nodded. "I take your point."

"And what do you say about it?" His guest waited. "If you will undertake this for the government, you will find that we are not ungrateful."

"An implied bribe?" said Fleming.

"I wouldn't put it that way—not with so much at stake," said his visitor. "I'd say rather that I am appealing to your devotion to duty."

"Of course you would put it that way. You have reason to ask for my help out of your patriotic concern, and you rely on mine to support your request."

"You have shown yourself to be reliable and patriotic," said his visitor. "Unlike many who served the country for the duration of the War and now want nothing more to do with the defense of the Empire, you know that the war isn't over, and the battles we won have continued in another form. You appreciate how much more perilous our victory has become in the last year." He leaned toward Fleming. "You can't imagine peace, can you? Not peace without danger, without threat."

"I know many problems remain from the War," Fleming allowed, weighing his thoughts carefully. "I tell you what, Sir William," he went on, using his guest's name for the first time, as if he finally was willing to acknowledge his purpose. "I will look over the material you have brought with you, and I will give you my advice and my decision after I have seen for myself what you have on hand. I cannot offer anything fairer than that."

"You're being very autocratic," Sir William complained. "I would rather you give your commitment to the project before I show you any of it, but—"

"Yes. But. Give me a little credit, Sir William. If I do not comprehend what the mission entails, what sort of assurances can I provide in regard to my abilities to carry out what you need me to do?" He offered a predatory smile, one that hinted of strong emotions beneath his cool exterior. "I know what kind of a snake-pit this may turn out to be, and I am in no hurry to be dragged into it needlessly, with or without a license to kill."

"And what should I do while you are busy here?" Sir William asked.

"Perhaps you can return to the friend you were visiting earlier," Fleming suggested.

"That might not be wise," said Sir William, tapping the side of his nose with his index finger. "It wouldn't be prudent to have it known I've been here, if you understand me? I rely upon you to keep my visit confidential. It may be of the utmost importance that my role in all this remains clandestine."

Fleming nodded. "You would prefer not to go into Kingston for the same reason, I take it? You don't want to be recognized."

"Yes." Sir William looked about. "Have you any other suggestions?"

"Relax; this is a wonderful place, and so long as you are here, enjoy it," Fleming recommended, the intensity gone as quickly as it had appeared. "Is there something you would like to do? Somewhere you might go and not have to worry about your security?"

Sir William snapped his fingers. "I think I'll walk on the beach." He stared in the direction of the window. "I'll give you an hour or so with the material I've brought you. I'm sure your cove is a pleasant place for a stroll."

With a knowing glance, Fleming said, "A good idea. By the look of you, you could use a little exercise. I'm sorry we haven't a generator. Only kerosene lamps when the sun goes down, and candles, of course, but you can be comfortable enough if you don't set your expectations too high." He took a long sip of his gin-and-tonic. "Considering what you have told me, you shouldn't begrudge me a night to review your reports."

Sir William shook his head. "I wanted a faster answer. Shall we say two hours, as a compromise?"

"That is hardly a compromise, if you don't mind my saying so. You are forcing my hand." He managed to keep a cordial manner, but there was an edginess in his voice that made him seem more formidable than he had intended. "If you mean to have an ill-considered answer, then it would have to be a refusal. But as it is a case of some delicacy, as you have said, then I should think you would prefer I take my time and acquaint myself with the particulars before I make up my mind. You would not like me to underestimate the problems to be faced, would you?"

"Of course not," said Sir William grudgingly.

"Very well, then," said Fleming, doing his best to mollify Sir William. "If you will hand me your files, I will begin at once. I'll review them as quickly as possible; two hours is a bare minimum—I will do what I can in that time. I may have more questions for you when I've done."

"I shall endeavor to answer any you may have," said Sir William, sounding exasperated.

"Sir William," Fleming said patiently, "you do not want me to jump at this as if I were a mere tyro. You say there is a great deal of danger, and I wish to see for myself what you mean by that before I agree to take on any of the work. If I gave you any other answer, you would not believe I comprehend the nature of the work, and you would not want to entrust the mission to me."

"You have a point," said Sir William.

"So enjoy the sunset. No one will disturb you. The sky is beautiful here; you won't see its like in England. Two hours, Sir William, and I will give you my assessment of the project, and my decision about participating." He reached out for a cigarette.

"If you insist," Sir William said. "I must admit that duty compels me to stay near at hand—I truly don't wish to be observed."

"I'm very much afraid that I do insist; you needn't go onto the beach, but you must let me make my review in private," Fleming said. "I won't tell you I'm not intrigued, because I am, but, Sir William, I am not a reckless man. I've had too much experience for that. I will not jump at this simply because you tell me that it is necessary." He paused and smiled. "I can offer you a tolerable evening, if you have no objection to remaining about for an hour or two beyond my reading time. Dinner at seven-thirty, drinks at seven. I believe there is a tolerable conch chowder tonight. My cook knows his work."

Sir William shook his head. "What a time to be fussing over food."

"It is just the time," said Fleming. "If this is the last decent meal I am to have, I want it to be truly enjoyable."

Chapter 3

CESAR HOLIDAY, Fleming's houseman, rang the bell for drinks at ten minutes to seven. Hearing it, Fleming rose from the chair where he had been sitting for the last two and a quarter hours. He stretched, put the papers back in their thick file-folder, and tucking it under his arm, went off to his room to change into his dinner jacket and a proper pair of trousers. His expression was thoughtful, a frown hinted at by the angle of his brows. As he passed Cesar in the corridor, he said, "Is Sir William dressing?"

"I don't know, sah," said Cesar in his musical Jamaican idiom. "He went down to the beach more than an hour ago. Shall I send Joshua to look for him?"

"No," said Fleming. "I'm sure he'll be along directly. It's still light out." He continued on to his room, slipping the file of top-secret material into the safe at the side of his bed, and then began to change, slipping off his sandals, setting his linen shirt aside to be washed and pressed during the night, and hanging his light-weight khaki trousers on the Silent Butler. He poured water from the ewer on the dresser into a flowered basin and gave himself a quick rinse, rubbed his face, arms, and neck with a hand-towel, then emptied the basin into the potted palm in the corner of the room, disturbing a gecko and a small herd of spiders in the process. He donned his boiled shirt and dark, tropical-weight wool trousers, then his dinner jacket, taking care to smooth the front of both shirt and jacket.

That done, he ran his brush through his hair, and fixed his tie in place, making it match on both sides. Hardly grand enough for Mayfair, but more than acceptable for Jamaica. It had taken him just nine minutes, and as he put on his shoes, he wondered if he would arrive in the lounge before Sir William did.

To his surprise, the lounge was empty. Fleming looked around, taking stock of the place as he poured himself another gin-and-tonic, adding a slice of lime. He lifted his glass in a silent toast, and took a small sip, not wanting to get too much ahead of Sir William.

The clock struck the quarter hour, and Fleming became impatient. It wasn't that difficult to get from his house to the beach, and the path was well-marked. The sun was just above the horizon, smoldering over the sea. He scowled at it, as if suspecting the sun of behaving rudely. "Cesar!" he called out.

Within the minute, Cesar appeared in the door, his black face shining from his work in the kitchen. "Yes, sah, Mister Fleming."

"Where is Sir William?" It was an abrupt question, but for once Fleming did not apologize for his tone.

"I haven't seen him, sah. I set his bags in the room off the verandah. There was just the one, and a valise. I thought he would want to put on something less heavy before you ate." He gave this as a kind of explanation for Sir William's unaccountable absence.

"Do you mean you think he has gone out to buy luggage? Or a shirt?" Fleming laughed aloud. "Why should he?"

Cesar shrugged.

"You told me he had gone to walk on the beach," said Fleming. "Which is it?"

"He went toward the beach, Joshua says. I can send him to fetch him." Cesar lifted his head, sniffing the air. "I must tend to the chowder, sah, or it will scorch."

"Go on, then; can't have scorched chowder," said Fleming. He began to pace, anticipating the fast-approaching night. He disliked the notion of having to search for his guest, but he realized it was necessary. "I'm getting a lantern," he called out as the clock struck seven-thirty. "He may have lost his way coming back."

From the kitchen, Cesar called out, "I'll send Joshua with you."

"No need," said Fleming. "I'll manage." There were lanterns hanging in the entry-hall. He took one and lit it with his gold cigarette lighter, adjusting the flame with care. He knew Sir William would be annoyed if he were led back to the house by a half-grown black boy in canvas shorts; Sir William was too much of a stickler for such relaxed standards. "Keep the chowder warm," he added as he went out of the house.

The lantern gave off enough light to make going along the pathway easy. He strode easily, swinging the lantern from side to side in order to provide more illumination as well as an obvious target for Sir William to fix on. As he made his way toward the beach, he heard the sound of a motorboat some distance away, and he wondered who might be out at this hour, for the day-time fishermen had all returned to port and the night-time fishermen had not yet left the harbor just beyond the point of land at the west end of the cove. There weren't many tourists on this part of the island, which was one of its major attractions to Fleming. He walked a little faster, rehearsing in his mind what he would say to Sir William in regard to what he had read, for clearly the trouble was internal and Whitehall had real trouble: there was a traitor somewhere in Military Intelligence.

Preoccupied with his thoughts, he walked out onto the fine white sand, and shaded his eyes as he scanned the beach. Seeing no one, he lowered the lantern and looked for impressions in the sand, and saw a line of footprints going off to the left toward the bend in the cove. Cursing slightly, Fleming set out, keeping to the right of the footprints, still swinging his lantern. Why on earth should an English bureaucrat take it into his head to venture so far from the house? And with such purpose, for the trail was a direct one, as if Sir William had a specific destination in mind. An uneasy feeling had come over him, one that he told himself was nonsense, the result of his reading material and the hint about a possible spy on the island, not of anything more immediately sinister. There was no reason for Sir William to be in any danger, not here.

He crested a slight rise in the sand that was hardly enough to be called a dune, but more than a hillock, and the rest of the cove came into view. The white line of the spent waves marked the water's edge, and the intense blue of twilight faded land and sea into a single wash of sapphire. Fleming blinked and stared out toward where the horizon had to be. The only difference between sea and sky was that the sea was shinier. Fleming could feel sand in his dress shoes, and it aggravated him. "William!" he called out, hoping for an answer; he deliberately did not use the man's title, in case his call was overheard. "William Potter!"

The silence that followed seemed ominous. Fleming shook off the apprehension that was turning his body cold. "Absurd," he said aloud, as if that would increase his conviction. He made his way toward the water, following the footprints by lantern-light.

The first evening breeze sprung up, skittering the sands ahead of it and beginning to obliterate the trail Fleming was following. "Bloody hell!" Fleming swore, but kept going toward the water. He swung the lantern more vigorously, and called out "William Potter!" again, and again, was answered by silence.

The sand underfoot grew firmer, damp. Each step left a spray off the toes of his shoes. The tracks were only oval impressions now, and as the sand turned wet, they disappeared altogether, succumbing to the great equalizing force of the spent waves. Fleming stood just beyond the limits of the water and stared along the beach, looking for something—anything— that might tell him where Sir William had gone. In the gathering darkness, his lantern seemed more and more minuscule against the night. He began to walk westward, toward the edge of the cove, hoping to use the outcropping of rocks there as a vantage-point.

As the sand gave way to stone, Fleming noticed the cuffs of his trousers were wet. Cesar's wife, Bathsheba, would be furious with him; she took care of his clothes and this was more than she would tolerate. He kept on, trying to decide what to do if he could not find Sir William.

Then his lantern picked out something dark on the rocks, a heap of cloth that proved, on closer inspection, to be a jacket of dark, pin-striped wool with a Bond Street label sewn into it. There was a deep slash on the front of the jacket, running from the left shoulder to the lapel, and the dark shine across the fabric of something that could only be blood.

Fleming picked it up and looked it over. Sir William's dip-

lomatic passport was in the inner pocket, along with a small
leather slip-case containing a key. There were two shillings and
a threepenny bit in his outer pocket, and a stub from a West-
minster cinema, but nothing else but a small leather sleeve for
business cards, empty but for one of Sir William's and a small
wedge of stiff paper with a linen finish, quite unlike the cream
laid texture of Sir William's card. His handkerchief, which had
been so correctly placed in the outer breast pocket, was gone,
and Fleming could see nothing on the rocks that was even
suggestive of the pale-grey linen. A bit of lint in one pocket
had nothing out of the ordinary about it. Fleming held on to
the jacket and began to look around, hoping to find something
more.

For a quarter of an hour, he walked back and forth along
the rocks, checking in crevices, trying to look deep into the
sea for anything that would reveal Sir William's whereabouts.
Once he scrambled down under a stone overhang. All he found
there was an old ring where sailors could tie their dinghies. He
recalled the distant sound of a motorboat and wondered if the
ring had anything to do with it. He scrambled back to the
beach and walked along the water's edge, studying the waves
with care. The tide was going out, and it wouldn't turn for
another two hours. If he put Cesar and his nephew Joshua to
work, they could make a very good search before the water
rose and obliterated any evidence that might be left behind.

He thought about the conch chowder and knew it was a
pleasure he would have to forgo until late that night, for as
soon as his search was complete, he ought to get into town
and place a call to General Lord Peter Broxton, who ran the
military mission for HM's government in Kingston. He took a
deep breath, already preparing for that call. Lord Broxton was

a self-important martinet, one of those men who had learned his place in the world before World War I and was still convinced that nothing had changed since then. Fleming had avoided dealing with him in the past, but now he would have to. Perhaps he would wait until morning and approach Broxton in person, and spare himself the chore of running his lordship to earth by telephone tonight.

He returned to his house a few minutes shy of eight o'clock, to find Cesar in dismay at the state of dinner, and worried for Fleming's welfare. "I am sorry, sah, but dinner is . . ."

Fleming held out the jacket. "Sir William is missing. I found this. I fear we will have to mount a search for him."

Cesar stared at the jacket. "Dear me," he said. "That cut is most distressing."

"No doubt," Fleming agreed. "Do what you can to salvage dinner for later, then you and Joshua join me. Sorry, but there's nothing for it. Bring lanterns and help me make another search."

"Do you think Sir William . . . met with foul play?" Cesar seemed mesmerized by the slash in the jacket.

"I think something has happened to him. I don't know what yet, and I am trying not to leap to conclusions." Fleming set his lantern down and blew it out, taking care to turn the wick lower. "This is almost out of fuel. If you'll refill it when we return?"

"Of course, sah," said Cesar.

"Excellent," said Fleming. "We'd better be about our work." With that, he went into the entry-hall to take another lantern, which he again lit with his cigarette lighter. He hung the ruined jacket on one of the pegs on the wall, and called out to Cesar. "Hurry."

"I will," said Cesar, his tone forlorn at the ruin of dinner. As soon as he had most of the dinner secure and the fire in the stove banked, he took off his apron and went to get his nephew.

Chapter 4

JOSHUA HEARD Fleming out with no alteration in his stance or expression. "You found this jacket on the rocks at the west end of the cove?" He was just entering the beginning of manhood, a gangly, loose-jointed boy whose cheeks were starting to show promise of a beard.

"Yes," said Fleming.

"Nothing else?" The boy had a keen mind, as Fleming had discovered when he had started playing chess with the youngster a year ago at the urging of Bathsheba.

"That is why we're making another search," said Fleming.

"Before the tide turns," said Joshua. "We had better hurry."

"My point precisely," said Fleming, handing him a lit lantern. "You and your uncle can take the beach, where the trees come up to the sand."

"You think he might be in the trees?" Joshua asked.

"I think we must try to find him," said Fleming, and gave another lantern to Cesar. "If you find anything, no matter how trivial, summon me at once."

"Very well," said Cesar, his face somber in the soft glow of the lanterns that turned his skin to a glossy shade of mahogany.

They went out the main door and around the verandah to the path down to the beach. No one said anything, but all three swung their lanterns, watching the shadows retreat and swell, swell and retreat in an eerie dance. The smell of kerosene mixed with the odor of flowers and decay. As they reached the sand, Fleming pointed off to the left. "He went that way."

"Then I will stay at the edge of the forest, and you will follow the path he took," said Joshua in his composed way.

"Make sure you do not lose sight of us," Fleming warned.

"I'll try not," said Joshua, and took his first step along the edge of the trees.

Satisfied that he had made acceptable arrangements, Fleming began to climb through the shifting sands, looking for the indentations he and Sir William had left there already. The lantern-light showed the sand in high relief, deep shadows and soft glowing light, making it unfamiliar. The dry sand gave way to damp, and the footprints were more easily read. Walking was easier, too, and Fleming made better time now, and Cesar lengthened his stride to keep up.

"He was moving fast," Cesar observed as he stopped to examine one of Sir William's footprints.

"The deep toe impression?" Fleming said. "I agree. I noticed it when I was searching for him." He wished he had some devise that was a more reliable tracker than just the three of them and the light from their lanterns.

"That, and the bit of sand cast up by the toe. It would appear, sah, that he knew where he was going and was in a hurry to get there. If there were other footprints, I might suppose someone were chasing him." Cesar hurried along behind Fleming, taking care to disturb Sir William's footprints as little as possible.

Fleming looked at Cesar. "You may be right," he allowed, and resumed walking. "But those are my footprints you see going along beside his. When I followed him, there was only the one set—Sir William's. No one was behind him, or in front of him, unless he walked in the other's footprints so perfectly that they could not be seen. In soft sand, that is nearly impossible, even when the pursuer is careful, which seems unlikely. In which case, I doubt he would be running, as it appears he was." He glanced toward the edge of the trees, and saw Joshua's lantern swinging, like a large firefly, against the deep shadows cast by the trees.

"And if the leading man was running, what then?" Cesar asked.

"Then we would have a real conundrum on our hands," said Fleming.

"What a strange thing, sah, however Sir William happened to come here," said Cesar as they strove to walk in the footprints Fleming had left. "You say he had never been here before? He was unfamiliar with your estate? He had not seen your house until this afternoon?"

"No, he had not. He said he had visited a friend on the island before he came to see me, but I don't know who that was: he didn't mention a name." Fleming paused to listen and heard only the sough of the wind and the rocking of the surf. "I only met the man today, his telegram came yesterday, informing me of his impending visit. If he has other friends in the area, beyond the one, he did not mention them to me. You might learn more from the village gossip."

"And yet he came this way on an unfamiliar beach," said Cesar, ignoring Fleming's last remark. "It does not appear he walked without purpose."

"It is strange," Fleming agreed, beginning to worry about what it might mean. He wished now that he knew more about Sir William, who, until this afternoon, was nothing more to Fleming than a name in Whitehall. Since his arrival, Sir William had been willing only to discuss this covert project of his, revealing nothing of himself. "Perhaps he is the sort of man who is purposeful even when he is wandering."

"Do you think he was looking for something, sah?" Cesar asked. "That might account for it."

"If he was, it would appear he knew where he might find it," said Fleming, his perplexity increasing. What on earth was he going to tell Lord Broxton in the morning?

"Do you think he went to meet someone?" Cesar asked. "Was he summoned here?"

"I have no idea," Fleming snapped. "Still, it may be. But I doubt he intended to vanish. He would have taken his things if he planned on leaving."

"Could he have gone into the sea, sah?"

"I don't know," was Fleming's acerbic answer. "All I know is he is gone and his suit-coat gives one to wonder. That slash doesn't suggest a friendly meeting."

"No, sah," said Cesar.

They had almost reached the place where Fleming had found the jacket, and the stones under their feet were brackish and wet. Their lanterns made fretted patterns on the spent waves, both beautiful and eerie. Fleming began to search the rocks for anything he might have missed when he found the jacket, aware that the lantern was something of a hindrance, but he did not discover anything new, and after ten minutes, he abandoned his search.

Suddenly Joshua shouted from the tree-line, now a quarter mile distant from where Fleming and Cesar stood. He raised his lantern high in the air. "I've found something, sah!"

"What is it?" Fleming yelled back.

"It's . . . a revolver!" He swung his lantern back and forth at shoulder level to show where he stood.

"A revolver?" Fleming repeated, baffled.

"Yes. With two bullets fired," Joshua called.

"The coat was cut. With a blade of some kind," said Cesar. "There was no sign of a bullet."

"So it was—cut, not shot," said Fleming, his thoughts puzzled. He kicked at the rock and shrugged. "Perhaps it means nothing, and someone has lost a revolver that is in no way associated with Sir William." He looked up into the night sky with its festooned stars. At another time, he might have found it a pretty sight, but now it was only a distraction. "Well, we haven't found damn-all out here. We might as well have a look at this revolver."

"If you advise it, sah," said Cesar, clearly keeping his opinion to himself.

Fleming said nothing but started along the beach toward the line of trees. As the sand grew silky and dry underfoot it became harder to keep going, and he had to struggle to keep up his pace. Fleming could hear Cesar panting behind him and knew he sounded much the same, and that his shoes were quite ruined.

Joshua raised his lantern in greeting as Fleming and his uncle approached. "Here it is, sah," he said, pointing down to a Police Special .38, made by Smith & Wesson. "American."

"So it is," said Fleming, squatting down but not touching the gun. "And recently dropped, by the look of it. The barrel still has a sheen of oil on it, and there is only a little dirt on it, on the one side." He felt around for a stick and used it to pick up the revolver by the trigger-guard. "I doubt there is anything to learn from this, and it may have nothing to do with Sir William's disappearance."

"Very true," Joshua said. "But it is a strange thing to find such a weapon lying at the edge of the forest. One might think that there was a guard posted, who has now left his post. Perhaps unwillingly."

"Guarding what, or whom?" Fleming asked, keeping his own thoughts to himself.

"Sir William," said Joshua. "Or his abductors."

"Assuming he has been abducted," Fleming put in.

"Assuming that," Joshua allowed with the fine arrogance of youth.

"But abandoned his weapon," said Fleming. "That's the perplexing part."

"Perhaps it was Sir William's guard, and he met with the same fate Sir William did." Joshua let the suggestion hang in the air. "Whatever that fate might be."

Fleming shook his head. "I don't like the sound of that, Joshua."

"Nor do I, sah," said Joshua.

"But is it possible?" Cesar asked, looking about with an air of apprehension.

"I suppose it may be," Fleming mused. "And if it is, it means that someone other than Sir William and I knows of his mission, someone on this island. Perhaps the man he visited earlier. Furthermore, it suggests that whoever was watching supposes I am involved in this—this whatever-it-is." Fleming rose, bringing the pistol with him. "I'll wrap this in a towel, for the authorities. They may be able to determine its owner, and how recently it's been fired."

"It's too dark to look much further, sah," said Joshua, a bit reluctantly. "We can start again tomorrow."

"Tomorrow I must go make my report. I'll need you to keep

on here, Cesar. I don't want to leave the house empty if there is going to be trouble. Keep an eye out for anything out of the common, and report it to me. If you're willing, Joshua, I'd appreciate your coming back to this spot and seeing what else you might turn up." Fleming held up his hand. "See you don't miss school on this account."

"I won't, sah," said Joshua.

Fleming made a last perusal of the beach, then, dissatisfied, he said, "Well, let us go back to the house. There doesn't seem to be anything more to do here."

Cesar did his best to smile approval, but his expression was uneasy. "Do you think we should post guards at the house?"

"I don't think so, not yet, in any case," said Fleming, starting back on the flattened grasses that marked the edge of the beach. This was firmer footing than the sand provided, and he lengthened his stride, making Cesar and Joshua hurry to keep up with him. "If you'd feel better with a guard, then have a nip round to town while I'm making my report and hire a couple of your mates for tomorrow night. You may offer them a pound apiece for the job, with a half-crown more if they discover anyone lurking about the place. In the meantime, fetch Dominique's two mongrels for tonight. She'll let you have them for one night. They'll bark at anything, and they're not afraid to bite. Give her ten shillings for their use." The pay was low, though not unreasonable, particularly since Fleming doubted there was any need for such precautions. However Sir William had vanished, those who had caused it were long gone, he was certain of it.

Cesar did not speak at once. "I shall think about it, sah, and tell you what I have decided when dinner is over."

"Oh, God," said Fleming. "I do apologize for any damage our traipsing about may have done dinner."

"It is all right, sah," said Cesar, adding impishly, "you will have to eat it."

Chapter 5

By TEN that evening, Fleming had gone through most of the papers in Sir William's briefcase and had started on the contents of the portfolio in his valise. With the papers spread out on the guest bed in loosely arranged stacks, Fleming had managed to piece together the basics of the case that Sir William had brought to him, and it troubled him: British atomic secrets had ended up in Soviet hands, and the source had to be an inside one, going back to the British members of the Manhattan Project, or those working closely with them. Three spy-catching cryptographers known as Moan, Groan, and Sigh had been in charge of the investigation, Moan doing the brunt of the work, given the tenor of the reports. In any event, thanks to the dogged efforts of those three men, the reckless disregard for world safety was very apparent in the files, and Fleming began to consider the ramifications of this security breach, becoming more troubled as he read on. According to Moan's analysis, there was also a suggestion that these secrets had been sold to other powers, not nearly so well-identified as the Soviets: this was more disturbing than the first instance of betrayal, for it implied that there was a power somewhere in the world wealthy enough to afford such weapons and still remain virtually unknown. Moan was of the opinion that the culprits were closely associated with British Intelligence, if not actually part of it; Groan and Sigh didn't concur, Groan going so far as to say that the accusation was ludicrous and potentially subversive, turning men assigned to intelligence work against one another, thus destroying their effectiveness under the pretense of insuring security.

"Will you want a nightcap, sah?" Cesar asked from the doorway.

Fleming looked up. "What? A nightcap? Oh, yes, please," he said. "And ask Joshua to have the car ready first thing in the morning. I have to go in and report this incident. Lord Broxton will want to know that Sir William has gone missing." He was not looking forward to providing this unwelcome information to so bellicose a man as Lord Broxton.

"As you wish, sah. He will have it ready by six-thirty. Will the Napoleon do?" Cesar inquired.

"What?" Fleming answered his own question. "Yes. Fine. In a snifter, if you would, Cesar." Absentmindedly Fleming lit up a Players.

"Yes, sah," said Cesar, and went off to fetch the brandy.

There was no doubt that there had been damage done: the files made that plain. But by the look of it, the culprit or culprits were not yet identified. One or two minor functionaries had been caught—Theodore Robertson and his American colleague, James Hendley, for example—but they were insignificant figures in the scheme outlined in the briefs and reports that filled Sir William's files. That they were to be kept utterly secret was beyond question. Fleming took the largest stack—Moan's reports—and began to read through it more closely, looking for information that might offer a clue to the principal players. Nothing came out at him. He slogged on, trying to find the illusive tidbits of information he sought.

Cesar returned with the brandy. "Joshua has tied up Dominique's dogs at either end of the house. She vouches for them, saying that if anything moves, they'll bay loudly enough to wake the dead, and if any stranger tries to enter the house, they will attack."

"Just as well," said Fleming. "Still, I hope it's a quiet night. I need some shut-eye. Tomorrow's going to be a busy day." Just the thought of dealing with Lord Broxton made him uneasy. In previous encounters, he had found the fellow bombastic and pig-headed, not a man to trust with a secret, but he was the appropriate man to receive the report of Sir William's disappearance, little as Fleming liked the notion. That realization grated, and he decided he would have to ration what he provided to Lord Broxton, for the man was notoriously garrulous in company and could not be counted upon to check his tongue. He would tell Lord Broxton no more than he had to. "Wake me at six, if you would. Two baked eggs and a broiled tomato for breakfast, I think. Coffee, not tea." He smiled briefly.

"Yes, sah," said Cesar. "I will wake you at six." Not quite bowing, he withdrew, leaving Fleming to his reading.

"Is he going to be all right?" Joshua asked his uncle as they met in the kitchen under the hanging kerosene lamps.

"I hope so," said Cesar.

"Why do you say that, Uncle?" Joshua asked, his head angled in such a way that the light caught the side of his face and made the rest of it its own shadow.

"He is a good employer. So long as he is here, I have nothing to worry about," said Cesar.

Joshua laughed with the cynicism of youth. "You are used to his money."

"Of course," Cesar agreed. "He is easy to work for. I would not like to have to change employers at this time of my life.

Mister Fleming pays promptly and always the full sum. He doesn't carp about the kitchen, and he lets me have time to myself every day."

Joshua said nothing.

"Don't hate the English because of what they are," said Cesar. "There are others who are much worse."

"Nazis and Communists, you mean?" Joshua scoffed. "It's possible, if you believe all you hear."

"But you don't believe it," said Cesar. "You have followed the trials in Germany, and you know what those men did. The British held out against them. We should be grateful to them. The Nazis would have done to us what they did to the Jews."

"That's Fleming talking," said Joshua.

"And I agree with him," said Cesar.

"I admire their courage under fire," said Joshua, looking a decade older than his fourteen years. "But I dislike how they see us, how they treat us. They regard us as they regard clever children, or dogs."

"You play chess with Mister Fleming," Cesar pointed out. "You have the run of his library."

"And I win some of the time, at chess," Joshua added.

"You don't think he has done well by you?" Cesar asked.

Joshua snorted. "I am a convenience, as you are. I provide him with entertainment that is reliable and inexpensive. So long as I don't interfere with him, that I make myself useful, he will indulge me. But if I fail to do as he wants, then it will change in an instant."

Cesar was worried. "Joshua. I thought you liked Mister Fleming."

"Oh, I do—much the same way as he likes me," said Joshua. He stood still in the yellow lamplight.

"You are full of youth, Joshua," said Cesar. "Remember your father was proud to be a British soldier."

"And what good did it do him? He got killed, Uncle." He glared at the lamp. "I'll have Mister Fleming's car ready in the morning, don't worry. And I'll take the dogs back to Dominique."

"Thank you for that. Tell her Mister Fleming is grateful," said Cesar, regarding his nephew with troubled eyes. "What makes you think this way? Surely not Father Dermott?"

"He's worse than Fleming! Fleming isn't a fool, exactly, and he thinks a little about the world. But Father Dermott?" Joshua burst out. "No, I do not listen to the priest." He straightened up. "No. Monsieur Soleilsur—he is a friend of Dominique's. Sometimes he visits her, and when he does, he talks to me, and to a few of my friends. He tells us about how the world is changing, and how we must be ready to make the most of it."

Cesar shook his head. "You should not be talking to Dominique's . . . companions."

"Why? Because she runs a woman's house?" Joshua challenged. "It is all right to use her dogs, but not to speak to those who visit her, is that what you are saying to me, Uncle?"

"No, Joshua, I do not say that to you. I tell you that such men as come to her in secret, and that whatever else they may do, it is well to know nothing about it." He tossed a mango to his nephew. "The police are bribed, but if they should have to act, the less you know, the better." Cesar wagged a finger at Joshua. "If you object to accommodating the English, why should you risk anything for the men like that Monsieur—"

"Soleilsur," Joshua provided.

"French," Cesar said firmly. "They have nothing to boast

about, you know. They have their colonies, as the British have.
And one hears stories about them that show the French very
badly."

"I know," said Joshua. "And he is not French, not entirely.
He is Moroccan on his mother's side. He knows how it is for
people like us. He says we must learn to turn the might of our
oppressors against them, that we must erode them from within,
through their own failings. We must halt their greed without
hesitation or mercy."

"That's appalling," said Cesar.

"It is the only way, according to Monsieur Soleilsur," Joshua
maintained.

"Be sure that Monsieur Soleilsur is not telling you this to
make you his pawn." Cesar held up his hand. "You are ardent:
you are young. As much as he says he will turn the English
against themselves, remember he may well be doing the same
to you."

"You can't see it," Joshua said, shaking his head slowly. "You
have allied yourself with them."

"It may seem that way to you." Cesar shook his head. "Well,
keep to yourself when you take the dogs back in the morning."

"I will, Uncle. Besides, Monsieur Soleilsur is not there any
longer. He left yesterday, I think. I will not see him again for
some time, he said. I may never see him again—who knows?
I hold him in high regard, no matter what." He was about to
leave the kitchen when he added, "Do you think something
bad has happened to Sir William?"

"I fear it may have," said Cesar, very serious now. "It is
never a good thing when a man vanishes."

"Especially an English official," Joshua added with a kind
of determined satisfaction.

"As you say," Cesar conceded, not wanting to argue with his nephew anymore.

Joshua reached the door. "I think someone killed him and put his body in the sea."

"It may be so, though I pray not," said Cesar, aware of how closely his nephew's view coincided with his own. "Go rest. We must be up and about early tomorrow."

"Very well," said Joshua, pausing in the door. "But, Uncle, don't you ever want more than we have here?"

"What has wanting more ever brought but trouble? We have a good place to live, we have a little money saved, we have bicycles, we never go hungry, and a reasonable man employs us. I have saved enough to keep us for two years without difficulty. You have a school to attend. My wife has a sewing machine and an icebox. How many can say as much? That is enough for me."

Joshua shook his head. "Monsieur Soleilsur says that if you do not want more you will never have more."

"Or you may lose everything. If you are not the one to reap the reward, what good is the sacrifice," said Cesar, an admonitory finger raised. "Off with you, boy. It's time you were asleep." He watched his nephew go with worry in his eyes, and set about the last of his evening chores.

Cesar was putting the compost out on the steaming heap near the rear door when the excited barking of two dogs reminded him that Dominique's pair were on guard for the night. He spoke soothingly to the animals, using their private names, saying, "Be calm, Legba, I am a friend, Ghede, your friend," which only served to aggravate them. Ghede sprang to the end of his chain, snarling at Cesar. As he was preparing to retreat into the house, he saw Fleming appear on the balcony above him. "Sorry to disturb you, sah."

Fleming chuckled. "I wondered what could have set them off." He lifted his hand, showing he held a pistol. "Don't fret. I won't shoot, either you or the dogs. I'm glad they're so . . . enthusiastic."

"They'll be quiet when I come inside," Cesar said with more hope than certainty.

"Unless someone or something disturbs them, I hope," said Fleming, retreating into his bedroom and pulling the door closed behind him.

Cesar stood still for a moment, wondering if he should say anything to Fleming about what Joshua had told him. He decided against it, reminding himself that his nephew was young, just coming into the age when he would have to test himself to show what kind of man he might become. Most youngsters went through many phases in the years between their first beard and the time they were counted as men, and Joshua was no different than many others. Time enough to speak to Fleming if the boy still clung to those resentments and theories— and the mysterious Monsieur Soleilsur—in a year or two. In the meantime, Sir William's disappearance was a more pressing problem, and one with a greater chance of resolution than the frustrations of youth.

Chapter 6

MORNING WAS heralded by a vast number of cocks crowing, a duet of thunderous barks, and the rumble of the motor on Fleming's 1935 Lagonda Rapier. The classic sports car was the envy of all Fleming's neighbors, for he kept it in perfect running condition and its blue-green finish polished to a high shine.

Joshua met Fleming at the side of the house, standing by the automobile with deep pride in the machine. "She's all ready, sah. Petrol at three-quarters full, the oil changed last week."

"I'll bring back a set of spark plugs, Joshua," Fleming said as he stepped into the vehicle, putting down one of Sir William's two bags on the seat beside him. "I should return by evening. Please ask Cesar to have his guards here no later than three."

"As you wish, sah," said Joshua, stepping back to allow the splendid auto to roll past him, leaving a curling wake of dust in the glowing morning.

The road into Kingston was crowded, and there was only one opportunity for Fleming to put on a burst of speed: the section of road leading to the airfield that had been paved seven years before, to ensure that troops could be transported between airplane and Kingston in any weather. He took full advantage of it, roaring along the stretch of blacktop with the exuberance of a boy. In his capable hands the Rapier responded as if it wanted to race, dodging around the occasional saloon car and lorry with panache. Then they reached the outskirts of town and had to slow down once again to accommodate the carts, bicycles, autos, donkeys, children, and other occupants of the road. Fleming headed for the Government House, with its white-washed Georgian facade and imposing wrought-iron gates. He parked his car in one of the stalls set aside for visitors, took Sir William's bag from the seat, dropped his ruined coat over his arm, pulled the canvas hood over the seats and steering wheel, then loped up the stone stairs into the impressive lobby of the building.

Two guards were on duty, and a secretary sat behind a broad mahogany desk, dressed more for Pall Mall than the Caribbean. He sized up Fleming in his well-pressed linen suit and asked, "How may I help you, Mister Fleming?"

"Hello, Stowe. I'm here to see Lord Broxton, if he can spare me a minute," said Fleming, doing his best to sound at ease.

"Lord Broxton is out just now. I expect him to return in an hour. Would you like to wait?" Stowe maintained a neutrality of tone that Fleming might have admired under other circumstances.

"Not unless he will be back within ten minutes," said Fleming.

"It is unlikely," said Stowe.

"Well, in that case, will you be good enough to tell him I must talk with him? It is urgent," he said, putting the bag down and folding the slashed coat on top of it. "And if you will hang onto this for me? Keep it safe, if you will. It isn't something I want to haul through the streets. I'll just take care of a chore or two while I have the chance."

Stowe was puzzled. "If you want to leave your bag, you may

prefer to put it in the cloakroom with the attendant. I am sure it would be more appropriately left there."

"Ah, but it isn't my bag," said Fleming, tapping his nose. "That's part of what I must speak to him about."

More perplexed than before, Stowe nodded. "All right. I will keep them here behind my desk. Shall I give them to him when he returns?"

"If I'm not back yet, I should be grateful if you would hold them for me. Ta," he added and started for the door.

"Mister Fleming," Stowe called after him.

Fleming turned. "Yes? What is it?"

"Lord Broxton has a meeting at ten."

"Thank you, Stowe. I'll keep that in mind. I shouldn't need more than thirty minutes with his lordship."

"Very well. But return promptly. No later than half nine, if you would," said Stowe.

"I'll be here," Fleming promised, then went out into the splendid sun and down the steps. He decided against taking the Rapier. It was only a half-mile to the shops he sought and he would make as good time on foot as in the auto. His long legs carried him swiftly to the bustle of the marketplace, and to the shop of Henry Long, where every kind of automotive and nautical equipment and supplies could be found. The chandlery was vast and dark, the shelves filled with items that shone brass and steel in the muted light.

Henry Long himself was seated behind the front counter, a vast man with a dark face and a voice that rumbled out of his cavernous body, low and resonant, just the way a mountain might speak. He paused in the act of cleaning his glasses—absurdly small, round spectacles that perched on his broad nose like an attenuated species of insect—and waved vaguely.

"Welcome to my chandlery. Come in, come in." He offered a dark-brown cigarillo to Fleming, who accepted it, and a light.

"You'd welcome the devil himself, wouldn't you." Fleming laughed as he conducted a quick perusal of the aisles, satisfying himself that no other customers were in the chandlery. "Put your specs on, Henry. You're hopeless without them," he said, coming up to the counter and grinning.

"Ah, Mister Fleming," said Henry as he fixed the temples behind his ears. "It is good to see you, sah."

"It is good to see anything with eyes like yours," said Fleming good-naturedly; they had joked about his poor sight for more than a year.

"The bane of my life, sah," Henry agreed. "How are Cesar and Bathsheba Holiday?"

"They are well, thank you," said Fleming, not bothered by this inquiry after his houseman and his wife, for islanders were notoriously casual about such things.

"Tell them I would be glad to see them one day soon." He ducked his head. "But here I am, so what am I going to do for you?"

"I need spark plugs for the Rapier," Fleming began, "and a two-gallon tin of kerosene for the house; I'll pick that up on the way out of town. And I was hoping you might know something about a man disappearing from my cove last night." He said the last as easily as he spoke the rest, but there was an urgency in the inquiry that caught Henry's attention.

"A man disappearing?" Henry repeated, a questioning lift at the end. "Now why should I know that, man?"

"Because you know everything that happens on Jamaica," said Fleming easily, a hard smile adding to his endorsement.

"Perhaps," said Henry. "Tell me more about this disappearing man."

"From England. Came in by plane." Fleming had lowered his voice, in spite of his certainty that they were alone.

"A public servant, that sort of man from England?" Henry inquired.

"Yes," said Fleming, certain now that Henry Long knew something. "What have you heard?"

Henry shrugged. "I don't know, man, but I was told that a fast boat was rushing around your cove last evening. I think it might have taken someone aboard. It was a strange meeting, if it happened."

Fleming sighed, knowing this was apt to be an inconclusive and protracted exercise. "Who told you about this?"

"The spark plugs you want are on aisle four, third shelf down." Henry reached for a churchwarden's pipe and tamped tobacco into the bowl. "Bring them here, man, so I can write them up."

"About the man and the fast boat?" Fleming asked as he went to fetch the spark plugs.

"I am trying to recall," Henry announced, lighting his pipe with a wooden match and sucking on it to draw the smoke.

"Continue your efforts, by all means," said Fleming, spotting the spark plugs and taking the whole box, carrying it back to the counter and setting it down. "There. I'll have the lot."

"It will cost you, man," said Henry, and neither of them thought he meant the spark plugs.

"So I supposed. Write them up." Fleming reached for his wallet inside his linen jacket while Henry pulled out a tattered receipt book.

"The fast boat might have been a cigarette boat, according to Micah, the fisherman who was setting out to sea last evening. He heard it, but he admits he didn't see it. He went out an hour early, to get ahead of Samuel, his brother, who is a poacher," Henry said as he wrote an incomprehensible scrawl on the receipt book with the stub of a pencil. "He came in this morning for a new wrench and told me of the boat."

"Is he sure about the boat? Does he know anything about its owner?" Fleming asked, pulling two ten-pound notes from his wallet.

"I cannot say, but Micah is a truthful man, except when he is drunk," said Henry, taking the money and slipping it into his pocket. "Seven pounds, two, and six," he went on, handing the receipt to Fleming, and a small paper bag for the spark plugs. There was no change offered.

"Thanks," said Fleming, scooping the spark plugs into the bag. "If you should hear anything more, will you send word to me, please?"

"If I am able to," said Henry.

"Yes." Fleming understood what he meant. "I will be glad to pay for any reliable information you may have, of course."

"Very good of you, Mister Fleming. I will have the kerosene ready for you in an hour. Two gallons you wanted, sah?" Henry held his pipe between his big white teeth and chuckled. "You are a most curious man, sah. You do not think of your own safety, but of the safety of your guest."

Fleming stopped still. "Is that some kind of a warning, Henry?"

"You may take it however you wish, sah," said Henry with a beaming smile. "So long as you pick up the kerosene."

"I won't forget," said Fleming, and stepped out of the chandlery into the full glare of the morning sun. He dropped the cigarillo in the street and stepped on it to put it out, using this commonplace activity to take a quick look around the street. He squinted and shaded his eyes with his hand, then when he was sure he could see, he loped off up the street toward the Government House, arriving a few minutes later to find Stowe frowning in displeasure.

"Lord Broxton has arrived," Stowe announced. "He is in his office. He says he can give you ten minutes."

"Good enough. May I have the bag and suit-coat I gave you?" Fleming said as if this slight meant nothing to him.

"Of course," said Stowe, and brought it out from behind his desk. "A fine piece, if I may say so, sir."

"I suppose it is; it isn't mine, you know," said Fleming, enjoying the chance to tweak the supercilious Stowe. He took the bag, adding, "You needn't tell me the way. I know where Lord Broxton's office is. End of the hall, with the double doors, do I have it right?" he asked, knowing he had.

"Just so, sir," said Stowe woodenly, and retreated behind his desk while Fleming went down the main corridor toward Lord Broxton's inner sanctum.

The walls were deeply wainscoted in mahogany, with dark-green above, a color more suited to Lord Broxton's Cottswold home than to Jamaica. The furniture was mostly Restoration vintage, heavy, carved oak intended to impress. The draperies flanking the tall windows were a dull-gold velvet. This all served to remind Fleming why he preferred to live in this place than at home, and nothing contributed more to his conviction than General Lord Peter Broxton himself.

Standing by the first of two tall bookcases, Lord Broxton was a tall man, top-heavy with broad shoulders and barrel chest over long, spindly legs that seemed to have come from another man. His face was square and florid, made more startling by a mane of greying hair that framed his features in a silvery halo. His habitual expression was indignant, rather like an owl. He was wearing full diplomatic kit, and had the look of a man who has become out-moded without knowing it. He glowered at Fleming, ducking his head to take advantage of his thicket of eyebrows. "Well, Fleming, what have you got to say for yourself?"

"I hope I see you well, Lord Broxton," he replied, aware that the General was a stickler for formality.

"As well as this poisonous climate will allow," he said. "What brings you to me in this harum-scarum manner?"

The old-fashioned expression almost made Fleming laugh, but he managed to keep his countenance. "I am afraid I have a possible abduction to report to you," he said gravely.

"That is hardly my concern," said Lord Broxton importantly.

"In other circumstances, I would agree. But the man in question is Sir William Potter of MI5. He arrived at my house yesterday on urgent and highly sensitive business—"

"With you?" Lord Broxton demanded incredulously.

"Yes, m'lord. With me," said Fleming.

Lord Broxton made a sound indicating his doubts, but said, "And what had this man to say to you?"

"It is not what he said, but the fact that he went for a walk on the beach at my place and never returned that concerns me," said Fleming bluntly. "Two of my staff and I searched for him, and the only thing we found was this." He bent down, grabbed the coat, and held it up dramatically, hoping to gain Lord Broxton's full attention. "And a revolver," he added under his breath.

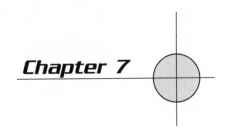

Chapter 7

Lord Broxton stared, blinking. "And what is this?"

"Sir William's coat. You will see it has been cut and there appears to be blood on it," Fleming said, vaguely disappointed that he had not startled Lord Broxton with his announcement.

"Ah, yes," said Lord Broxton. "Bring it here, Fleming. I want to have a closer look at it."

Fleming bit back the impulse to suggest he don his specs if he wanted to see the garment properly. "Here it is, m'lord."

Lord Broxton took the coat and held it up. "Dear me," he said as he inspected the long rent in the front. "Dear me."

"My staff and I could find no trace of him," said Fleming. "We searched thoroughly, well past dark. Since Sir William comes from Whitehall, I felt it would be best to bring his bag to you. I'm sorry if it is an inconvenience, but I could think of no one else whose position is so appropriate to this duty as yours." He did not mention the second case still back at his house, secure in the safe between his dressing room and the guest-room closet. "Someone has to notify his superiors, and it would be better coming from you than from me." This unaccustomed humility seemed vaguely amusing to Fleming but he kept it up in order to get through this discussion as unscathed as possible.

"Are you reporting him dead?" Lord Broxton asked, the color in his cheeks getting higher. "Are you saying someone has killed him? What am I to tell Whitehall, sir? How am

I to—What do you assume has happened?" The question snapped out as if Lord Broxton still commanded troops.

"I assume nothing, m'lord. I only know the man has disappeared, and his suit-coat is slashed," Fleming repeated. "I am sorry it happened, I wish I knew who did it, or, indeed, anything more, that might make finding him easier."

"There is blood on this coat," Lord Broxton said accusingly. "It has dried, but I know that color for what it is."

"So there is," Fleming agreed. "I wish I could tell you why it is there."

"No doubt," said Lord Broxton, implying the opposite. "You say that the man is missing. How does it happen that you have this coat and not the man, or indeed, anything more?"

Fleming took umbrage at this. "M'lord," he said stiffly, "if I had done anything to harm or endanger Sir William, I could have kept his visit to myself. I could claim he never arrived. But I have done my duty and brought his disappearance to your attention in a timely manner."

"Get off your high ropes, Fleming," said Lord Broxton in his most condescending tone. "You have no reason to leap to such conclusions as you have done. There might be any number of explanations as to how this coat came to be in this condition, and why Sir William is missing, that does not mean he has met with any misfortune. Why, he may have fallen, or his coat may have been cut in some other accident." He began to pace the room. "Do you know the reason Sir William sought you out?"

Now Fleming took the tack he had decided on late last night. "No. I suppose it had something to do with my brother, as it seemed to have nothing to do with my work as a journalist. I didn't have the chance to inquire; I was surprised to have him visit me, and I was looking forward to finding out why he had done so. He did mention he had visited someone else before me, but did not provide a name, or a reason for his call. Perhaps he might have revealed more, but when Sir William arrived, he was tired, and proposed to take a walk to restore himself. The last I saw of him he was headed down to the beach."

"Very strange," said Lord Broxton. "Coming here unannounced to me."

"So it is. It seemed to me that as he went to such efforts to keep his presence here private, it behooved me to try to maintain his confidence by bringing the whole matter to your attention instead of reporting directly to my editor, or the police."

At the mention of the police, Lord Broxton quailed. "No, I should think not. We don't want the police mucking about. You know what they are—local lads and planters' sons. They can't be trusted to hold the line. Nor the press. Ferrets, the lot of them. Might as well announce it to the world."

"And you wouldn't want that, would you?" Fleming said. "Since the purpose of Sir William's visit may have been clandestine. It would explain why he told me nothing of his other call."

"So it might. Men of his stripe run all manner of errands, don't they? Losing one could look awkward all around. MI5 doesn't like showing its hand, if you take my meaning. Good thing you decided to come directly to me. No reason to start the rumor mills turning." Lord Broxton straightened formidably. "You said something about a revolver?"

"Yes, sir. A thirty-eight, very recently discarded," said Fleming.

"What has that to do with Sir William's disappearance?" Lord Broxton demanded.

"I can't tell, sir," said Fleming. "I can only report that it was found near the place where Sir William vanished."

Lord Broxton rocked back on his heels. "Look here, Fleming. I don't mean to tell you your business, but I don't want to read any kind of balderdash about this in the newspapers. It would be worse than calling the police."

"Of course you won't," said Fleming. "This may effect my brother, m'lord, and I have no desire to compromise him."

"Oh. Yes. Right-o," said Broxton, as close to chagrined as he was capable of being. "Didn't think."

"That is one of the reasons I want to discover what happened to Sir William, what his mission was. I know it would be improper to pursue the matter myself, so I have brought the matter to you." Fleming managed his glib account without a single qualm of conscience.

"Why not last night?" Lord Broxton demanded. "You said he was carried off yesterday."

"Yes, he was, quite late in the afternoon. I did not stop my efforts to find him until late. I thought it would be best to wait until morning, just in case he should return; I thought he might have arranged to meet someone—perhaps the person on whom he called before coming to me. Or it could be something much simpler, if you don't mind my saying so." Fleming warmed to the story he had created on his drive into Kingston. "You see, m'lord, there is a women's house in the town near my estate, and occasionally men will nip round there for a kiss-and-tickle before getting down to business. The suit-coat made me think that mischief had happened, but if it was not the case, I didn't want to . . . cry wolf."

"Are you saying this coat caused you no alarm?" Lord Broxton was turning a fine shade of plum.

"It caused me a great deal of alarm. But it also occurred to me that it is possible that it was *intended* to be alarming. Surely you recall the unfortunate dust-up that took place when the Duke of Argyle sought to have a . . . private weekend in Barbados? I didn't want to create another such embarrassment."

Lord Broxton, who had been in the middle of that unfortunate event, nodded ponderously. "I take your point, Fleming. Very prudent, I'm sure. Just the sort of misadventure that would start people talking." And no one more than Lord Broxton himself.

"As I have said, I don't know what Sir William wanted with me, or what it might have to do with my brother, so I have decided to err on the side of caution." He gave Lord Broxton a vulpine smile.

"You're a canny one, Fleming," Lord Broxton approved grudgingly.

"I try to anticipate trouble when I can," Fleming responded, still smiling.

"You were right to bring this to my attention, of course. I'll put out a few discreet inquiries and I'll let you know what I learn, if it isn't against orders. I'll try to find out whom he came to visit. And," he added magnanimously, "I'll inquire after your brother. He's in Denmark, isn't he?"

"Norway," Fleming corrected.

"Same thing, same thing," Lord Broxton said with a dismissing wave of his hand. "Good man, doing this the right way," he added stiffly. "I'll delve into this matter at once. In the meantime, mum's the word."

"I'll keep that in mind," said Fleming. "And I have detained you long enough, m'lord. You have a meeting shortly. I'll leave you to prepare for it."

Lord Broxton glared at the window. "Just so. Come back in four days, Fleming. I may have something to tell you." He waved in the direction of the door.

"Thank you for seeing me, m'lord," said Fleming, heading out of the room.

"And Fleming," Lord Broxton called after him, "say nothing of this event to anyone. Is that understood?"

"Perfectly, m'lord," said Fleming, and let himself out. He strode down the corridor, fighting off a sense of dismay, for he was certain that Lord Broxton would make a complete cock-up of any inquiry. He had already half-decided to do something on his own, now he was convinced that if he did not act, nothing would be done. He was glad he had withheld information from Broxton, for it would have tied his hands utterly if he had surrendered all of Sir William's things. He paused at Stowe's desk. "I will need an appointment with Lord Broxton in four days' time."

"Four days," said Stowe as if the possibility had never occurred to him.

"Not too late in the day. I don't want to be caught here for the afternoon siesta." He leaned forward, using his height to impress Stowe. "Something before ten would suit very well."

Stowe consulted his agenda. "I can't accommodate you in four days. Would five do as well?"

Realistically, Fleming supposed it would make little difference. "Five will do."

"Then half nine in five days. I have it down, Mister Fleming." He held up his pen as if it were a weapon. "You see?"

"Thank you, Stowe," he said, and stepped back from the

desk. "Give my regards to your sister, if you would." Satisfied with the look of stern distress on the secretary's face, Fleming ambled out-of-doors and down the stone steps toward his Rapier. He removed the canvas cover and was about to climb in when he noticed a scrap of yellow paper on the driver's seat.

Curious, Fleming bent down and picked it up, turning it over in his hands. There was writing on the other side of it, made with a grease pencil, written in capital letters with considerable force: LET WELL ENOUGH ALONE, it read.

Fleming was perplexed. He looked around but saw nothing unusual on the street, nor did he notice anyone paying him undo attention. He held the paper and, after a brief period of consideration, thrust it into his breast pocket. He would peruse it later, when he had the opportunity. Slowly he climbed into the auto, stowing the cover behind his seat instead of the boot. As he maneuvered out of the car park, he kept alert for anything that would hint how the paper had got onto the seat of this auto, for surely it had not been there by chance.

He turned left and drove toward Henry Long's chandlery; there was kerosene to pick up. As he thought of it, it no longer seemed such a good idea. If anything should happen, he would be carrying a potential bomb with him. The petrol tank was problematic enough. He pulled in on the side of the chandlery and called out, "Henry, it's Fleming. Send it out to my place. I'll pay the cartage."

From inside, Henry's deep voice came back. "It won't be until tomorrow, man. Possibly late, when I've closed up here."

"That's fine," said Fleming.

"I might bring it out myself, if I have anything to tell you," he added, sounding supremely lazy, which Fleming knew was a ruse.

"I'd be pleased to see you, Henry," he said with feeling, and slipped the Rapier into gear, sliding along the alley to the next street, dodging a flock of ducks that had wandered, noisily, out of the ill-fenced yard. Fleming slowed to keep from running over the loquacious birds, and as he watched them, Henry Long noticed a man, tallish, dark-skinned, but not Caribbean, leaning in a doorway observing him intently. He went to the rear of his store and sat down at his ham radio, announcing his identifying call and summoning someone he referred to as Inform Trust that Ian Fleming appeared to have at least one surveillance agent watching him, and possibly more. Inform Trust instructed him to monitor the situation but do nothing yet. Not entirely satisfied, Henry Long returned to his front counter, wondering what all this could mean.

A couple miles down the road the ducks quacked and flapped out of Fleming's way, and he was able to increase his speed, thinking as he did that it was disquieting to be so narrowly scrutinized by a stranger. He reminded himself that in some parts of Kingston, white faces were a rarity, but he could not shake off the feeling it was more than that. He turned onto the graded, graveled street and started off toward the stretch of blacktop leading out of the city, all the while checking his rear-view mirror for any sign of pursuit. That he saw nothing did not calm him, for he had been unable to keep the hairs on the back of his neck from rising. It would have been wonderful to have some kind of device that could identify pursuers and track them; perhaps one day there would be such a machine. He chided himself inwardly for allowing Sir William's disappearance to fuddle him so, but he could not dismiss the notion that he was being watched—not entirely.

He drove faster than he had intended to, almost colliding

with a lumbering omnibus bringing in villagers to the city for work. He leaned on his hooter and dragged on the wheel, and thanks to the agile design of the Rapier, he avoided a smash. He also reduced his speed as he swung onto the rougher road, but kept up a respectable pace for the next few miles, pondering as he did the note that seemed electric in his breast pocket.

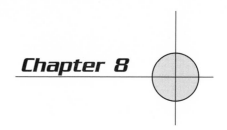

Chapter 8

CESAR WAS waiting for Fleming as he pulled into his own driveway at the head of a self-generated dust-storm. "Good to have you back, sah."

"Thank you, Cesar," said Fleming as he shut off the motor. "Anything happen while I was gone?"

"As a matter of fact, sah, I found a pair of scorpions in your study. I disposed of them, although I do find it strange that they should be there. Also, Dominique came by. She would like you to call at her house this afternoon. She says she has something to tell you." From the perfectly level tone of Cesar's voice, Fleming suspected that he disapproved.

"About her dogs, I suppose. Very good. As soon as I've had a bite to eat, I'll nip round there." He put the cover over his treasured auto and made his way into the house, moving as lightly as possible, as if he thought someone might be listening. The thought of scorpions in the house made him uneasy, as well.

"I'll have lunch ready in an hour," said Cesar. "I didn't want to begin it until you returned."

"That was considerate. Very well. An hour." He entered the house through the kitchen, and noticed that Cesar had a new-killed chicken thrust into a bucket of scalding water to ease in plucking. "Is that dinner?"

"Well, it couldn't be luncheon, sah," said Cesar playfully. "Yes. I'll stuff it with mango and shrimp."

"Sounds lovely," said Fleming, not stopping for more gustatorial discussion, but continuing on into the front of the house, going to the north side of the house where he had his study-cum-library. He closed the door, pulled back the draperies, and sat down at his antique desk, then took the note from his pocket, smoothing it carefully so as not to smudge the grease pencil letters, and set himself to study it, hoping to learn something from it.

The wording was very English, but anyone on Jamaica with more than a rudimentary education would know how to give such a note an English flavor. The writing, in block capitals, revealed very little about the writer, and the paper was cheap, such as anyone could purchase in any stationers, or might use in school. The only thing he was certain of was that the writer presupposed he would know to what the note referred, and could identify Fleming by his Lagonda Rapier.

That thought brought him up short. Suppose he had been mistaken for someone else? But he was sure the warning was intended for him. Unsatisfied, he rose from his desk, leaving the note tucked in a small drawer above the writing surface, and wandered into his dressing room, making for his safe. He paused to remove his jacket and hang it up and to change from shoes to sandals, then got down to business. The five-number combination was the date of his first completed sexual encounter, when he was fifteen. To make sure it was not likely to be happened upon, he had the numbers arranged in reverse order. Inside was Sir William's valise with all its files tucked neatly into it. He took out the bag and opened it wide, retrieving all the contents, then carried them back to his study, putting all but three in the lowest drawer—the one that locked. The remaining files he opened and began to read them again, concentrating on the holes in the information rather than the information itself.

In forty minutes he had made a small list of things that troubled him in the reports he had read; he had also smoked two cigarettes and was beginning to feel the yen for another. Something had happened in New Mexico, that much was certain, and it had made it possible for atomic secrets to be carried out of America and England. While it was certain that some had gone to the Soviets, there were odd gaps in the information that suggested that another buyer had participated. He sighed. He reckoned he would have to travel, and just when he wanted to spend more time working on his house.

"Sah. Your luncheon's ready," Cesar called out.

"Very good," said Fleming, taking care to lock the three files he had been studying, along with his notes, in the lowest drawer before leaving the study and going along to the dining room where Cesar had set his place and put out a crab omelette and a wonderful small salad of greens and fruit in a dressing that was sweet and tangy at once.

"I've opened a Mosel white, the one your brother sent in August. It should have rested enough," said Cesar.

"That cache of his—German wines. Mustn't be too curious about how he came by them, of course," said Fleming, nodding his approval for Cesar to pour. "If the prices on the French weren't so ruinous, I suppose I should scorn German wines."

"The grapes did not wage war, sah," Cesar pointed out. "And I will use the balance of the bottle in tonight's soup."

"Very good. It won't keep in this heat," said Fleming. He ate, enjoying the meal in spite of the various disquieting thoughts that vied for his attention. The whole of the puzzle began at Los Alamos, that much was certain, and although it wasn't war-time, atomic research continued there. He had never been to New Mexico. If it weren't for the Manhattan Project, he doubted he would know exactly where it was; the arrangement of the United States was so confusing. But the War had taught him a great many things about America and Americans. He pondered his options as he finished the crab omelette and the second glass of Mosel wine: he could go to Florida or New Orleans and then fly to somewhere in Texas, and from there he should be able to reach Los Alamos. He would have to talk to his editor to have a proper cover for his activities—to say nothing of a story to file, justifying his travel—but something could be arranged. He would need an assignment that was appropriate, not too innocuous, but not too controversial, so that he would be able to gain the support of those who worked there. Satisfied that he had the beginning of a plan, he rose from the table, determined to go to Dominique's to receive whatever message she had for him.

Cesar heard him leave and called out, "How long will you be gone, sah?"

"I have no idea," Fleming answered. "An hour or two, I should guess. If I'm not back by sundown, send out the hounds."

"Very good, sah," said Cesar, going back to the kitchen and his freshly plucked chicken.

Fleming walked down the road in an easy stride, his long legs eating up the distance with ease. It was not too hot to enjoy the early afternoon, but he could feel sweat on his face and neck, not an unpleasant sensation. He rolled up his sleeves as he walked, noticing how tan his arms were—no boiled-lobster Englishman he! Beginning to whistle, he covered the last half mile in good time, arriving at Dominique's pink-and-white house shortly before two.

The doorman was a hulking fellow with a cast in one eye and shoulders of imposing mass. He admitted Fleming and indicated the side-parlor. "Dominique is waiting for you."

"Thank you," said Fleming, and went through the hanging beads into a room that was hung with painted velvet curtains and decorated with small statues of voodoo saints.

Dominique herself sat on an enormous hassock of wine-red velvet, her dress of layers of gauzy shades of red silk spread out around her, almost as fantastical as the other ornaments of the parlor. Her dark-chestnut hair was twined with gold ribbons and dressed elaborately on top of her head in a style more in keeping with the seventeenth century than 1949. She was a fine figure of a woman, all luxurious curves and rich, milk-chocolate skin, with long, shapely legs; her features were a magnificent mix of European and African, with the special manner that went with her Haitian upbringing, and a smile that was incendiary to the point of being dangerous. Fleming doubted he had ever heard her last name; Dominique needed only her Christian name to be recognized from one end of Jamaica to the other. She extended her beautiful hand to him. "It's been too long, Ian," she purred.

"No doubt it has, Dominique." He took her hand, bowed over it, and kissed it, noticing she had changed her perfume from sandalwood to Chanel. "I wanted to thank you for the loan of your dogs."

"Ajax and Hector are fine animals," she said, using their public names and smiling her approval; her mouth was generous and painted an intense dark red that made Fleming think of ripe fruit. "I am glad they were of use to you." She paused. "Would you like a drink? I can offer you all manner of rum. Bonsard is a wizard with his concoctions."

"If you are drinking, I will join you. If not, there is no reason to go to such trouble on my account." Fleming remained standing, as if he didn't intend to remain long.

"Such a well-bred answer," Dominique approved. "I am going to have one of Bonsard's creations. I shall ask him to make one for you, as well."

"Thank you," said Fleming, and finally sank into the maharajah's chair across from Dominique's hassock.

She rang a small bell and called out her orders to Bonsard in Haitian French, then gave her full attention to Fleming. "I understand you had a visitor yesterday. One straight from England."

"Briefly," said Fleming, letting her set the pace of their conversation.

"He departed most inauspiciously," she went on, still favoring him with her spectacular smile. "Everyone in the village is talking about it."

"I was alarmed," Fleming allowed.

"Oh, Ian," she cajoled. "So proper and cool, and with the fires of hell seething inside you." She held up her long, lovely hands. "Do not dispute this. I know men very well, and I know what I see. I know also to trust what I see more than what I am told." Leaning back on her hassock she looked up at him through her long, black eyelashes. "So. You tell me you are a self-disciplined fellow, that you have your passions well in hand, while, in truth, I can see you are a volcano with snow on its crest."

Fleming took out a cigarette from the case in his trousers pocket, tamped the cigarette, then lit it with his gold lighter.

"If you say so, Dominique. I would be churl to disagree with a woman in her own house."

She laughed. "I have offended you. I apologize." She looked up as the lumpish Bonsard brought their drinks on a wide lacquer tray. "How very good of you." She was about to take one of the two tall glasses when she changed her mind and motioned to Fleming. "You are my guest. You choose whichever suits you, Ian."

"I should think there is no difference between them," said Fleming, his head up, exhaling smoke through his nostrils.

"How very gallant," she said, emphasis on the second syllable of *gallant*. "Very well. I will take the nearer glass, and you may take the farther, if that suits you." She nodded to Bonsard. "Offer the tray to Mister Fleming. And, Ian, you may change your mind, if it pleases you."

Since Fleming had been considering just that, he said, "No, thank you. Your arrangement suits me very well."

"Excellent," Dominique approved, nodding as he claimed his glass. "I know you are a careful man, and who can blame you? Strangers disappearing from your cove. Scorpions in your house." She tisked as if these were social gaffes. "You had your work cut out for you in the War, hadn't you?" She took her glass from the tray and lifted it in an ironic toast. "Now, tell me what you have come here seeking."

"Anything I can find out about my guest," he said, and tasted the persimmon-colored drink: Dominique was right—it was delicious.

"He arrived in a government auto, but you knew that," she said, one brow arched to show she was curious.

"So he did," Fleming murmured.

"He stayed with you for almost three hours, then went for

a walk on the beach at the cove. He reached the western rocks and then he vanished. That is what everyone in town is saying. You and Cesar and Joshua looked for the man for two hours, then gave up the search." She studied his face. "Is that truly what happened, Ian?"

"*I* am asking *you*, Dominique," Fleming reminded her. "You are supposed to provide information to me, not the other way around."

Her laughter was a lovely ripple of sound. "Of course. You cannot blame me for being curious, can you?"

"No," he said. "Women are all curious as cats."

"And who can blame us, in such a world as men have made?" She took a second, longer sip of her drink. "Well, I can only tell you what the rumors are, and I will spare you the most far-fetched," she said.

"Thank you," Fleming told her with feeling.

"Although there are those who say he was a sacrifice to Agwe, the sea loa, but that isn't very likely," said Dominique. "He would be a poor selection, for he was not a sailor himself."

"I thought you said you would spare me," Fleming reminded her. "It never crossed my mind that this was about voodoo."

"Of course," she said, and changed her posture subtly so that she was no longer invitingly languid, but businesslike and attentive. "I have spoken with Aunt Charlotte—Charlotte Penniman—you know the widow who makes clothing?"

"I know her. She has three children, doesn't she?"

"Four," Dominique corrected him. "She brought some material here this morning and told me that her neighbor, Bartholomew, the net-maker, was saying that he saw a very fine cigarette boat of polished teak rushing just offshore yesterday afternoon. He had not seen the boat before. It was new and very fast. He boasted that he had watched it for almost half an hour, as it raced back and forth between Hook Point and the fishermen's pier in Whitecross. There were three men aboard it, two white, one mixed." She cocked her head in direction of the next town over. "Ambrose the butcher also said he saw such a boat, but he didn't watch it for long. It had SS on its bow."

"All right," said Fleming. "Then what do you make of this in regard to my visitor?"

Dominique shrugged. "I don't know. But they happened on the same afternoon, and in such a place as this, coincidences are quite rare."

Fleming considered her observation carefully. "Coincidences are rarely what they seem."

"My point exactly, Ian," said Dominique. "Now, Samson the barber says that the cigarette boat was some kind of signal, but he cannot say of what or to whom."

"Is that one of the theories you mentioned?" Fleming inquired, and had a bit more of his delicious drink.

"It is one of the more sensible ones, yes," said Dominique. "I was struck by what Rafael—you know him, the one who repairs boats?—well, he said he thought the people in the boat were looking for something. He also thinks that your guest was absconding with vast amounts of money, so that is a bit beyond the pale."

"So it is," said Fleming, recalling everything he had read in Sir William's files.

"But it may be that he is right about the people in the boat," said Dominique.

"Any notion of whom it belongs to?" Fleming could not

keep from watching her keenly, though he feared she would notice his interest and use it to her advantage.

"No," she answered bluntly. "It may be that the owners have only come for a short stay, or they may be new to the island."

"Very possible," said Fleming, thinking this provided some room for further investigation.

"If you like, I will ask my women to pay attention to what they hear," Dominique offered. "Women hear all manner of things, Ian."

"Pillow talk," Fleming dismissed.

"Some of it," Dominique conceded. "But not all. You should have learned that in the War."

Fleming thought, and then allowed, "Occasionally they provided good intelligence."

"Then you will not mind if my women do a little sleuthing." She smiled. "It makes a change for them, you know."

"I don't imagine they lack for variety," Fleming said lightly.

"Oh, Ian, so like a man!" Dominique shook her head emphatically. "When one has done this a number of times, there is little novelty left. Some men are kind, some are generous, some are weak, some are cruel, but, when all is done, there are only so many places and so many ways to accomplish the thing, and then all is repetition." She blinked, an expression of utter innocence on her sensuous face. "I have wounded you," she exclaimed. "Of course. All men want to be different. And so you are, but still very much the same."

Fleming decided the drink was a great deal stronger than it tasted or Dominique would not say such things to him. He sampled a bit more of it and then set it aside. "I bow to your superior experience."

"Now you are huffy. Well, never mind," she said. "I don't suppose it is important, but Geoffrey Krandall—the man who owns Swan's Way, beyond Whitecross?"

"I know him slightly," said Fleming.

"Well, he was found beaten to death two days since. The authorities have done their best to keep the killing under wraps," said Dominique. "The police have two young men in custody, young men who worked for him, and who had been dissatisfied with their conditions for some time." Dominique managed another seductive smile. "The police are keeping it quiet, because they have heard rumors that there is a band of young men—young *white* men—in the region who might become dangerous."

"Is that why I have heard nothing about it? You would think there would be rumors floating everywhere, wouldn't you?" Fleming asked, distressed that a man much like himself could be killed and he not learn of it; Cesar usually told him all the gossip and rumors. Why should he fail to report such a real crime, and one that might give Fleming pause.

"The whites are ashamed and the others are afraid. The only reason nothing is bruited about is because the Chief Constable is keeping the young men locked up and has ordered that no word of the killing get out; it is very embarrassing, as they are white boys, so it is not likely they will remain in gaol for long. They were employed by Krandall to set up his generator and put the wires in his house for lights and such. Their parents will give a bond, and their sons will be out, and no one the wiser unless there is court action, which there may be, since Krandall was white, too," said Dominique. "The Chief Constable often comes to see me, and he talks when he has finished his other business."

"Good Lord! How lax of him," Fleming cried out. "And his men obey him? Usually the police are the most determined rumor-mongers on the island."

"They are afraid," said Dominique by way of explanation. "Anything that might cause trouble can be dangerous to them. Two white boys in gaol can mean trouble for all of them."

"As well they might be," said Fleming severely. "What does Kingston have to say about this?"

"They haven't been informed yet," said Dominique. "The Chief Constable wants to contain the matter as best he can."

Fleming took a rather larger sip of his drink than he had intended. "Astonishing," he said. "And you are certain it is true?"

"Oh, yes," said Dominique in a tone of voice that banished all doubt from Fleming's mind. "My source is impeccable. There are things one may be certain of, and this is one of them."

"I see," said Fleming. He mulled the series of coincidences over in his mind. "What do you think—are these three things connected?"

"I do not know how, but I suppose they must be," said Dominique quietly. "If you examine each on its own, they are not connected, but their proximity in time and place makes me believe that there must be more than happenstance at work here."

"You say Geoffrey Krandall was beaten to death?" Fleming asked to be sure he had heard right.

"That is what I was told." She shook her head. "A terrible end for a man who did so much to help win the War."

"Yes, indeed," said Fleming, who had forgotten until then that Geoffrey Krandall had been a Cambridge don who had gone to work for the government in '38, doing something hush-hush. Fleming had always assumed it was translation or code-breaking, one of those academic things, but he reckoned now he had better find out what Krandall had done in the War. That would take a little time, and he suspected he didn't have much to spare. He would have to find a source of information, and quickly, who could tell him everything about Krandall's efforts in the War. He realized that Dominique was watching him, a faint smile lingering in the corners of her exquisite mouth. "You've given me a great deal to think about, Dominique. I thank you for it."

"I can tell by your tone that you are planning on leaving," she said regretfully. "I suppose I should be grateful you found time for this short visit."

"I'm afraid I am leaving, reluctantly, of course," said Fleming, "unless you have anything more to tell me?"

"Only this: it is possible that when your guest was set upon, those attacking him supposed they were attacking you," she said.

Fleming chuckled. "Sir William was in worsted pin-stripes. How could anyone mistake him for me?"

"You are English and he was walking on the beach by your house. If those attacking did not know you on sight, they might have been confused. You know that some of your countrymen maintain their English habits here, in the face of all reason."

" 'Mad Dogs and Englishmen'? " Fleming suggested, knowing there was a great deal of truth in Coward's satiric little ditty.

She lifted one shoulder, her eyes alight with an emotion he could not identify. "I am not saying I am convinced it is true, only that you may want to consider it."

"Very well, I shall," he said, and put his unfinished drink aside before he rose to his feet, aware as he did that the alcohol had made its presence known. "Thank you for your hospitality, and your information. I appreciate both." He nodded his head as a sign of acknowledgment.

"You are welcome at any time, Ian. My door is always welcome to you." Dominique didn't rise, but she made a magnificent gesture of farewell.

Chapter 9

By the time he reached his house, Fleming had a headache burgeoning behind his eyes, and a blister on the side of his foot where a pebble had lodged under the strap of his sandal. He was generally dissatisfied with how the meeting with Dominique had gone, for she had learned as much from him as he had from her; it was one of her skills that he couldn't help but resent. He knew that she often traded in information as well as flesh—he would have paid her no mind if that hadn't been the case—but now he wondered if he were the only buyer, and if so, to whom she would peddle what she learned from him. He trod up the steps to his front door and twisted the bell, waiting for Cesar to come to answer the summons.

It took Cesar a long time to come, and when he did, Fleming could see there was a bruise two shades darker than his skin forming under a lump on his forehead.

"Pardon, sah," he said somewhat breathlessly as he tugged the door open.

"Good Lord, Cesar, what happened?" Fleming demanded as he stepped through into the foyer. "Let me have a look at that." His intention to question Cesar about Krandall quite fled his thoughts.

"It's nothing, sah," said Cesar faintly.

"I doubt that; that's a nasty bump and you cannot tell me you aren't in pain," said Fleming, taking Cesar by the upper arm and all but dragging him toward the kitchen. "I want to have a proper look at that, and I want you to tell me how you come to have it. Bathsheba would never let me hear the end of it if I don't do this."

Cesar was becoming embarrassed. "It was nothing, sah," he repeated emphatically. "Young hooligans, trying to kick up a little trouble. There were four of them, all under twenty. I will speak to their parents tonight, if you will give me an hour or two to attend to it. I warned them off with the shotgun—"

"You mean you fired on them?" Fleming asked, less shocked than he would have been an hour ago. "And you knew them?"

"No, sah. I did not fire. They were white. I could see the skin around their eyes through their masks."

"Did you recognize them?" Fleming asked. "Were their voices familiar?"

"I think I might have heard one of them before. He had a Scottish burr, not very strong, but definite. Another was from the north of England. You know what family that must be, as you know who the Scot is. There are only two choices among the Scots, and one of the families only has daughters." He set his jaw. "White or not, if they had tried to get in, I would have shot them. I'd aim for their legs," he added, knowing how the law would frown on even that degree of resistance.

"Good Lord!" Fleming expostulated. "It must have been a prank. What else could it be?" They had reached the kitchen, and Fleming all but shoved Cesar onto a stool so that he could examine the bump on his forehead. "What did they hit you with?"

"A rock, sah," said Cesar, wincing as Fleming gently touched the injury. "They had a pistol with them, but I didn't pay any attention to it. They never so much as raised it."

"You should have assumed the worst. Not all whites are

honorable, sad to say. I wouldn't want you getting shot on my account." He smiled tightly, thinking that Cesar had put himself in a precarious position no matter how the encounter turned out. "I don't pay you enough for that."

"I wouldn't have let them in, sah. I give you my word." Cesar pulled away from Fleming's careful inspection. "I should watch after your house, and keep it safe. Besides," he added more sternly, "I wondered if they had something to do with Sir William's disappearance."

"Why should you think that?" Fleming was mildly upset. "One need have nothing to do with the other."

"They happened so close together, and these young men were . . . I cannot describe it."

"Just so," said Fleming, going to the drawer with the first-aid supplies and bringing out a sticking plaster, unconcerned about Sir William at present. "I'll attend to that later. For now, I want to put some antiseptic on that bump of yours, in case you have—"

Cesar took the sticking plaster and the tube of ointment Fleming had taken out of the drawer. "I'll tend to it, sah. But I have a hard head. It will heal."

"I should hope so," said Fleming. "Still, it makes sense to help it along."

"I'll take care, sah," said Cesar. He started in the direction of the half-bath just beyond the pantry. "I've arranged for Jacinth and Alphonse to keep guard tonight. They'll be here at six." The two brothers were the biggest men in the village, both Army veterans, now carpenters with strong backs and broad shoulders, men who would not hesitate to return force with force.

"Very good," said Fleming, relieved to hear this. "I think

we may have need of them." He hated to admit so much, but there had been too many incidents for him to dismiss with a shrug, as he often dismissed Cesar's concerns.

"So do I, sah." He was about to go into the bathroom when he stopped. "The young men said they wanted the Englishman. I don't know if they meant you, sah, or Sir William. I didn't ask."

"Good for you. You don't want to incite such rowdies, it only gives them an excuse to be more violent. You're a sensible fellow, Cesar," Fleming approved. "Did they venture anything else?" The headache he had been nursing had changed now, an element of anger in it as well as rum.

"Not as such," said Cesar. "They wanted to get their way, and that's the whole of it." He slipped inside the bathroom, leaving the door ajar. "I didn't ask for particulars."

Fleming paced about the confines of the kitchen, making himself rein in his ire so that he would not take any of it out on Cesar, who had already suffered enough, and might soon be driven to panic if any more unpleasantness occurred. He went to the door and stared out into the afternoon, as puzzled as he was furious about the men who had hurt Cesar in his absence. He wanted to find them at once, to demand an explanation for what they had done, even though he was keenly aware that this would be foolhardy, particularly if he had truly been their intended target. He stopped to stare out the window by the sink, as if suspecting they might be lingering in the vicinity. Nothing, of course; he knew it was what he ought to expect.

There was the sound of the front door opening, and Fleming swung around to face the hallway. He was startled to see Merlin Powell, his assignment editor, lumbering along as if he was expected and sure of his welcome. Fleming stared, trying to think why Powell might be here, but could not find an explanation for the man's presence. Powell's corpulent body and sedentary habits did not often bring him out of his office, let alone so far from Kingston.

"Powell," Fleming called out, leaving the kitchen behind and striding forward. "I didn't hear you ring."

"The door was open," Powell said, about to go into the lounge. "I need a word with you, Fleming."

Fleming covered his confusion with a simple nod. "Whatever you like."

In the lounge, Powell sank into the settee as if he intended to take root and grow there. "It's a very unpleasant business." He had taken off his straw fedora and was using it to fan his face.

Alarmed, Fleming disguised his concern with a lightly sardonic tone. "What have you heard?" he asked, in order to find out what was troubling Powell.

"Only that the poor devil was found with every bone broken. The police are keeping their mouths shut, but they are worried about this one, take my word for it." Powell looked up. "When were you planning on telling me about it?"

"If you mean when was I going to break the story about Geoffrey Krandall, I was hoping to have something solid to report about the police before I called you." He almost sighed with relief at this save, but worried that he would be premature in his respite. Taking a Players and lighting it, he thanked Dominique in his thoughts; her casual remark had saved him from being completely foolish in Powell's eyes. "How does it happen that you've come in search of the story?"

Powell lowered his voice. "I wanted to see if I could speak to the parents of the young men in custody before the next edition is put to bed. No luck so far." He coughed. "You should have undertaken the task yourself, Fleming. A murder like that shouldn't wait for police endorsement to report. I should think you would be scouring the towns and villages for anything you can glean." Powell looked annoyed, his large, square body showing disapproval in every line.

"The trouble is," Fleming improvised, "I think there is more to this story than anyone is letting on. I haven't learned much, but what I have done gives me to wonder if there isn't another level to the story." He saw Powell was interested. "I believe that Krandall did something covert and important in the War, and I can't shake the notion that his death was associated with his War-time activities. His actual duties are still protected by the National Securities Acts, and I don't know what I'll have to do to get through *that* mine-field, but I do think I should pursue it."

"What is it you think Krandall did?" Powell said, all but quivering with interest.

"I think he was a spy-catcher. At the very least I think he was given encoded messages for decryption and translation." He thought about what he had read in Sir William's files, and began to realize that the figure known as Moan might well be Krandall. Nothing had been said about the three except that they had all retired. It was a plausible enough notion. "We can't print that, of course, but we can say he was part of the War effort in London before moving out here."

"As you did?" Powell suggested archly. "How well did you know the man?"

"Hardly at all," Fleming admitted. "He was very reclusive.

I don't think we exchanged more than twenty words in the last year. He lived a very secluded life, and I respected that." He looked about. "I can offer you something to drink. Tell me what you'd like."

"Anything wet, cool, and alcoholic," said Powell. "Not too strong. I have a busy evening ahead."

"Let me see what I can concoct." He went to the bar and looked at what was stored there. He began with the cooler, and noticed that there was a fresh pitcher of orange juice in it, sitting on top of the block of ice. "How about orange juice with a touch of gin?" He put out his cigarette.

"Add a little tonic, and it will suit me down to the ground," said Powell. He put his hat on the coffee table. "Thanks, Fleming. The afternoon is a bit close."

"I could almost wish for a proper storm, to clear the air." He went about making the drink for Powell, giving the lion's share of the glass to the orange juice.

"So, Fleming. Get on with it. You think there is more to this Krandall killing than simply a burglary gone wrong? That's what the police are bruiting about—robbery botched and a tragic result. The parents aren't talking to anyone but solicitors and barristers." Powell waited for a long moment, his manner expectant. "Well?"

"Yes, Powell, I do; I think his death is only a small part of the puzzle," said Fleming, handing his editor the drink he had made. "Sorry it isn't colder, but . . ." He shrugged.

"You could get a generator," said Powell.

"And spend my entire salary on petrol, as well as keep half the village up at night? No, thank you. I bought this place for privacy as much as beauty. When I have finished my renovations, perhaps I'll be able to have it wired, but I can see no use in a generator, much as electricity would be handy. What would be the point in having a machine so loud that it trumpeted my presence? Eventually we'll have electricity, never fear, and telephone lines, and all the rest of it. For now, I am content with things as they are. At least there is running water. That much is a help." He poured himself a glass of orange juice, thinking he had mixed enough drink for one afternoon.

"You have a point, though I would find it inconvenient," said Powell, and sipped. "Tell me more about Krandall."

Fleming had been thinking furiously, trying to tie Krandall's murder to Sir William's disappearance without having to reveal anything more than absolutely necessary, and now he said, "I may have to travel to get all the information I need. This story has more to it than it appears to have, I assure you, Powell. That's probably why the parents are incommunicado. I am certain I am on the trail of something very big. I need you to back me up."

"I don't know," said Powell. "They're cracking down on expenses, you know. What kind of travel were you considering?" He was wary, remembering how eager Fleming was to run up his expense account in all manner of ways. "I don't need to remind you that we'll have to be careful about this."

Fleming put it as bluntly as he could. "I think it would be wise of me to go to the States, to Los Alamos."

"God in heaven!" Powell sputtered. "Why?"

"Because that's where a lot of those code-cracking johnnies were used, and I will get more information there than I will from MI5 in London. And Robertson was there." Fleming held up his hand. "I may have come across some information that isn't generally known, and it points directly to Los Alamos and the Atomic Bomb."

"Robertson." Powell went a lighter shade of pink. "That's . . . damned serious stuff, Fleming," he managed to say. "If it is true, we still might not be allowed to print it."

"Very true. But think of the coup if we may," said Fleming, knowing he had Powell hooked.

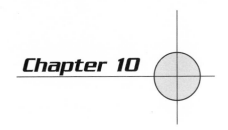

Chapter 10

W<small>HEN</small> P<small>OWELL</small> left it was about an hour before sunset and the sky was obscured by massing clouds. Fleming had secured a promise of a travel voucher for New Orleans, and money for a stay of four days maximum, a concession that Powell had given reluctantly, though he could not argue with Fleming's assessment of the distances he would have to travel; he had required daily reports to which Fleming had agreed, secure in the knowledge that he could be able to extend his stay if he filed stories that satisfied Powell's demands. It would also return him to Jamaica in time for his appointment with Lord Broxton. He sought Cesar out in the kitchen, where the houseman was busy with preparing dinner.

"It ought to rain by tomorrow, sah," said Cesar. "That will make everything more pleasant."

Fleming regarded Cesar narrowly. "So tell me, Cesar, when were you planning to inform me of Geoffrey Krandall's murder? In all the excitement, I forgot to ask."

Cesar shrugged and went on chopping squash. "I didn't want to pass on all the rumors. I supposed your people would tell you about it, while you were in Kingston. It must be in their hands by now."

"Or did you hesitate because the young men detained are white?" Fleming asked softly. "Do you think I am unaware of the shortcomings of my people?"

This time Cesar hunched his shoulders. "I didn't want to

make matters more difficult, sah. You had Sir William to worry about."

"And it never occurred to you that the two events might be connected, that I might need to know of his death?" Fleming said, his tone dangerously cool. "Or that there might be something in common with what has happened here? Those boys breaking in on you? Did you think there could be a link from the death to your intrusion?"

"No, sah. Not until the youngsters left. It was not the same problem, these boys were not the suspects, for those boys are in gaol, and you were gone. I did think it was an easy matter to see the two events as linked, although they might not be so." He stared down at the chopping block. "Then I thought it was my apprehension, not the events, that troubled me."

"Did it occur to you because you were struck with the rock?" Fleming could see that Cesar was miserable. He relented. "I'm sorry, Cesar. You did your best, I'm sure. This whole farrago has me going round in circles, I'm afraid."

"Small wonder, sah," said Cesar, putting his knife aside and turning to Fleming. "Jacinth and Alphonse should be here shortly. That should make the evening easier."

"I hope so; I don't look forward to sleeping with one eye open and a pistol under my pillow for a second night, thank you," said Fleming, another thought crossing his mind. "Has Henry Long been here today? He's supposed to deliver kerosene."

"No, sah. He has not," said Cesar.

"Strange," said Fleming.

"Henry has many things to do, and it is a long way from Kingston," Cesar pointed out. "He will probably come later, when his shop is closed."

"Well, you had better warn Alphonse and Jacinth that he's coming, in any case. I don't want them challenging him at the head of the drive." He did his best to appear at ease about the coming delivery.

"Of course," said Cesar, and took a more formal tone. "Dinner will be ready in an hour, sah."

Fleming nodded absently. "Where's Joshua?" he asked, realizing he had not seen the lad that afternoon.

"He is with his aunt this evening. You remember her: Lolanda? She gives him a dinner from time to time," said Cesar. "She misses her sister, and it does her good to see her nephew."

"Ah, yes," said Fleming. "Is she doing better?"

"As to that, who can say? She complains little, and she asks for nothing more than to keep her house and enough money to live on," Cesar answered, and Fleming knew the woman was not improving.

"That's unfortunate," he said, and turned to leave the kitchen.

"So it is. Bathsheba spends afternoons with her, when she can," Cesar added, pleased that his wife was so attentive.

"That's good of her," said Fleming, and went on more crisply, "I am going up to shower and change. I'll take sherry in the lounge in half an hour."

"Very good, sah," said Cesar, glad to be back on such familiar ground. "There is a nice bit of swordfish and a stuffed chicken." He waved his employer away, and picked up his knife again, busying himself with executing his menu, his mind on his routine as a way not to be worried about the events of the last twenty-four hours. A little while later the rush of water in the pipes added a soothing purr to the kitchen that Cesar welcomed as he took a chicken from the icebox and began to cut it into thin slices. When this was done, he took a tub of fresh-churned butter out of the icebox to soften. He was beginning to feel a bit more comfortable and was glad of his routine, for it helped him to set aside the events of the day and he relaxed into it.

A sharp rap on the kitchen door pulled him out of his reverie. Cesar put his knife aside next to the heap of chopped squash, celery, and cardunes. He wiped his hands and went to answer the summons, pausing to call out, "Who is it?" before lifting the latch. It was a foolish precaution, but his disruption earlier in the day had made him jumpy and more suspicious than he liked.

"It's Jacinth and Alphonse," called the voice from outside. "Who else might it be?"

Cesar opened the door at once, admitting the two carpenters eagerly. "Come in, and welcome. Be comfortable. I will tell you what you must do, and I have your money ready."

"Give it to us at midnight, when our watch is half-over," said Jacinth. "We'll like it better then."

"As you wish. Midnight it will be. It is a good thing you are doing," Cesar said as he motioned them to stools on the far side of the kitchen. "Accept Mister Fleming's hospitality while I make coffee and sandwiches for you. He's a little high in the instep, but he won't begrudge you something to eat. I'll give you some sandwiches now, and then you can take up your posts for the night. There will be more at midnight, and I'll make sure there's plenty of coffee for you."

"That's good," said Alphonse, the taller of the two. "If we have to be up all night, we'll need coffee."

"Of course," Cesar agreed. "And I'll leave fruit out, in case you want something between sandwiches."

"So long as they aren't bland. The English like everything bland," Jacinth complained.

"Mister Fleming is not so strict," said Cesar, "and he doesn't mind some pepper in his food."

"That's good, then," said Jacinth. "Where are the lanterns?"

"In the entry hall, near the front door. I've refilled them, so two should get you through the night." Cesar had taken a loaf of bread and was cutting it into generous slices. "This was baked this morning."

"Then it is fresh," Alphonse approved. "Very good, Cesar. If the food is good, it doesn't matter if the pay isn't."

"He's not cheating you," Cesar said abruptly, his voice sharpened by anxiety. "Your pay is not too low, and there is food. That's not cheating."

"No, it's not," Alphonse said at once. Then he cocked his head. "How does it happen that you have a sticking plaster on your forehead? You hadn't one yesterday."

"There was an incident, here, this afternoon," said Cesar. "That's one of the reasons it is good to have you here tonight. Not that I anticipate more trouble, but you never know."

The sound of water in the pipes stopped, making the next remark sound louder than it was.

"Is there more than one reason for having a guard tonight?" Jacinth asked.

"There was one last evening, and it is reason enough for guarding the house. Now there are two or three reasons," Cesar answered.

"Is any of it about Mister Krandall's murder?" Jacinth didn't seem bothered by his question.

"We don't know," said Cesar. "It is possible."

Alphonse tossed his head. "How do you come to be hurt? What about Mister Fleming?"

"He wasn't here. I don't know if the . . . young men who came were looking for him, or just bent on trouble." He reached for the tub of butter, tested it with a small spatula, and began to smear it on the sliced bread.

Jacinth pursed his lips. "This may be a tricky night."

"It may," Cesar agreed, putting the butter back in the icebox. "You will need to be very alert. Henry Long is supposed to bring out a tin of kerosene this evening. You ought to expect him."

"Very good," said Jacinth. "We won't shoot him."

"Excellent," said Cesar, taking the tops of the cardunes and chopping them for sandwich greens; they were tough but their flavor was excellent. "If anyone other than Henry or my nephew Joshua tries to come here, stop them, find out what they want, and send word to Mister Fleming before you decide anything."

"Of course," said Jacinth, familiar with guard procedure. "He may not like being wakened in the late night."

"He would prefer it to being killed," said Cesar, carefully disposing the greens on the buttered bread. He could smell the chicken in the oven, and he knew he would shortly have to get to work on the swordfish.

"That he would," Alphonse said with a chuckle.

"Keep that in mind while you watch," said Cesar. He began to pile the sliced chicken breast onto the bread and greenery.

"That is a good sandwich you're making," said Jacinth as if he had just noticed Cesar's efforts.

"I am not finished yet," said Cesar, smiling in spite of himself.

The two brothers exchanged glances. "This and coffee is very good."

Cesar took a string of onions from their hook on the wall and cut away two large ones, then hung the string back in place. "Do you want one or two slices?"

"Two," said Alphonse.

"One," said Jacinth.

"Very good," Cesar said, stripping the papery outer layers off the onions and plying his knife expertly. When he had finished adding the onion to the sandwiches, he sliced the rest of the onion and the second one, then reached for a black, cast-iron sauté pan.

"Mister Fleming eats well," said Alphonse.

"So he should," said Cesar. He was about to say something more when a loud explosion thundered through the night air.

The three men were frozen in place for two eternal seconds, and then they all rushed for the door even as Fleming, half-dressed, came down the front stairs barefoot shouting, "What the devil?"

Cesar was the first through the door. He pointed to a column of black smoke beyond the trees rising into the lurid light of sunset, coming from under the clouds and turning them smoldering red. "That's near the main road through the village." The thought of fire in that gathering of mostly wooden houses was a frightening one, and all of them recognized it.

"Or on it," said Fleming. "Good Lord! What next?" He made a clicking sound with his tongue. "You three, go see what's happened, and help out if it's needed."

"Are you certain?" Cesar asked nervously.

"Yes, indeed. Go now. I'll come along as soon as I put on some shoes. Have Dominique phone for help." He turned away and sprang up the stairs.

Jacinth stepped out on the porch, frowning portentously. "It is a bad fire, I think."

"It may be. We won't find out standing here," said Cesar, already starting down the drive. "Hurry up. Alphonse, you go to Dominique's. Jacinth and I will see what has happened. You might ask Dominique to pay attention to everything she hears."

"Very good," said Alphonse, trotting off at a good clip.

"Come, Jacinth," said Cesar. "We have work to do."

Chapter 11

By the time Fleming reached the scene of the explosion, at the edge of the village fishing dock, there were half a dozen men in an improvised bucket brigade throwing water on the fire that had reduced a shed to rubble and ashes; the villagers were making the main effort to save the pier and the boats beyond. He set down his lantern and took up a place in line, his dress-shirt rolled up at the sleeves and his hiking boots at odds with the rest of his clothing.

Cesar, who was working the pump, called out, "The fuel-storage tank exploded, sah!"

"I can see that." Fleming swung a full bucket to Jacinth, who was next in line, and reached for an empty one coming back from the front of the brigade. "Does anyone know why?"

"Haven't had the chance, sah," said Jacinth. "Got to keep the fire under control." He took the next bucket and passed it along.

Fleming continued to work while the buckets were filled, water tossed on the fire, and the buckets returned. For more than an hour, he labored with the rest, falling into the rhythm of the task. Gradually the water beat back the fire. After the first twenty minutes, he noticed that the flames were losing ground, and soon the clouds rising had white steam mixed with the oily black smoke. In another forty minutes, the last of the fire was out, and the men working the bucket line stopped their efforts. All of them had smuts on their clothes, arms, and faces. They showed up most plainly on Fleming's pale face and formerly white shirt where the lantern-light struck him; yet every man in the bucket brigade was speckled with ash and cinders, visibly or not, so they didn't tease Fleming.

Jared Smith, whose boat was now safe, was the first to break away from their line. "I'll go get rum," he volunteered, and was encouraged by a ragged cheer. His brother Timothy stretched and yawned as if just awakening rather than ending two hours' labor.

Thomas Hatcher, the town butcher, began to stack the empty buckets. "Time enough to view the damage tomorrow, I think," he declared.

Dominique's houseman Bonsard came to the head of the line just as it broke apart. "My employer offered twenty-five pounds toward rebuilding."

It was a substantial amount for this village, and Thomas Hatcher, who was one of the village leaders, nodded. "She is a very generous woman, your employer. Tell her we are grateful."

"That I will," said Bonsard, and turned away, preparing to go back to Dominique's house.

"Tell her that I hope her gift is an example to us all," Hatcher called after him, glancing at the men still gathered between the dock and the pump.

Fleming sighed, knowing what was expected of him, but worried about spending so much. "I'll give twenty pounds," he called out, and was rewarded with a smattering of approving hoots.

Cesar came up to him. "That is money from your building fund, isn't it?"

"I'm afraid so," said Fleming with a philosophical nod and a smile that didn't quite work. "It's expected of me, and at least it will go to build something."

"But it delays the work on the north side of the house," Cesar reminded him, as if it might have slipped Fleming's mind.

"Don't trouble yourself," Fleming recommended. "There's almost two hundred pounds in the safe. In six months, I'll have enough, with or without this twenty for the pier." He noticed that Alphonse and Jacinth were coming toward him, their eyes shining with excitement. "Are you ready to go back to your guarding?"

"If there's lots of coffee," said Jacinth. "This was a hectic evening."

"Let us hope it is the last episode of the sort for the rest of the evening," said Fleming. He went to pick up the lantern he had carried into town, checked its flame, and took up Cesar's as well.

A general whoop announced Jared Smith's return with a half-gallon jug of dark rum. There was a surge in his direction, but Fleming remained where he was.

"It is a good reward," said Alphonse a bit wistfully, going to retrieve the other two lanterns.

"Not before guard duty," said Jacinth. "We would fall asleep before midnight." He looked directly at Fleming. "We will take our reward in the morning, sah."

"And you shall have it," Fleming promised, starting to walk back toward the road that passed his drive.

Cesar clapped his free hand to the sticking plaster on his forehead. "The chicken will be ruined," he lamented.

"There's still the swordfish," said Fleming. "Sauté it with the squash and things, it will suffice so long as there's a tasty soup."

"A beef stock with onions, barley, and diced ham," said Cesar, glad now that he hadn't put the soup on to heat before the explosion rocked the town. "New bread. There should be sufficient for all."

"A lucky thing this didn't happen three nights ago," said Jacinth, lengthening his stride to keep up with Fleming.

"Why is that?" Fleming asked. He could remember no event that would have kept the villagers from working on the dock.

"Monsieur Soleilsur's yacht was still at the pier, and it would probably have burned," Jacinth said as if this must be obvious. "It is a fine old ship, kept in magnificent shape, a ketch, sleeping eight plus crew."

"And who is Monsieur Soleilsur?" Fleming inquired.

"He is a good friend of Dominique's," said Alphonse. "He was with her for five days."

No wonder Dominique had been so gracious about paying for repairs, thought Fleming, who recalled he had heard some rumor about Dominique's wealthy patron, who it was likely would in future want to tie up his fine ketch again at the dock. "It would have been a shame if any boats were damaged."

"So it would. And a wealthy man like Monsieur Soleilsur could make his loss a misfortune for the village," said Jacinth.

"How could he do that?" Fleming could think of a few ways, but he was curious to know how Jacinth saw the problem.

"He could do many things. He could blame the villagers for the fire, and demand recompense from the courts. It has happened in other towns, sah, and you know it." Jacinth did his best to show a ferocious grin.

"This is hardly the same," said Fleming, feeling suddenly awkward, for he knew it was an easy thing to blame misfortune on ignorant natives; even when they were responsible, the burdens imposed upon them were heavier than for whites.

"You have more trust in Monsieur Soleilsur than I do," said Jacinth without apology. "It is a good thing he left before the fire."

"As you say," Fleming agreed. They were almost to his drive and the darkness of full night was enormous, the lanterns insignificant as matches against it. He raised his lantern to take stock of what lay ahead. There were indentations in the dust, small three-quarter circles indicating a donkey had passed this way recently.

Cesar grinned and bent over the hoofprints. "This is Jonquil," he exclaimed, smiling broadly. "See? There is a notch missing from the off-side rear hoof."

"Oh, Lord," said Fleming.

"That means Bathsheba is at the house," he added for the benefit of Alphonse and Jacinth. "Why else would Jonquil walk down this road?"

"Not a reason in the world," said Fleming, and chuckled. "It will serve you right if that pestilent donkey of yours has eaten up the kitchen garden."

"Bathsheba would not permit it," said Cesar. "No," he went on, "you may rest assured, sah, that my wife will take care of your house and grounds as carefully as she looks after your clothing and shoes." He walked faster, entering Fleming's drive ahead of the rest.

There was a long slow curve around to the left that finally brought the house into view. Lamps were lit in four of the rooms and there was a lovely aroma coming from the open kitchen door. At the side of the house, a dun donkey was tied to a fencepost on a short lead. Looking at it, Fleming was almost overwhelmed by a rush of assuagement, and he realized he had been afraid that the explosion and fire might have served as a distraction for other acts, acts that might have been disastrous for him and his house. He told himself that occasionally coincidences were only coincidences, and he could not persuade himself it was true.

Cesar was up the steps and into the house four strides in advance of the rest. He blew out his lantern and carried it toward the kitchen, calling out, "Bathsheba!"

"There's no need to shout, Cesar," came her deep, comfortable voice. "Come in. Come in."

By now Fleming was inside, Alphonse and Jacinth immediately behind him. Fleming went along to the kitchen, anticipating a scolding from Bathsheba. "Well, I suppose I have you to thank for saving the food? It was good of you, Bathsheba."

She flung up her hand as she caught sight of Fleming. "You! You are a trial, Mister Fleming, that you are. Keeping all manner of hours. And your garments! Shoes and trousers last night, a shirt and trousers tonight. There's no dealing with you, sah. Indeed there's not." Her strong, dark face and robust body always commanded Fleming's respect, and he showed it now.

"You are too good for any of us, Bathsheba," he said.

"As well you know it," she responded sharply. "When I saw everyone running to the center of the village, I decided you would be with the rest, and I doubted that Cesar would take the time to bank the stove or put the dinner in the warming ovens." She shot him a look of victory. "You are a good man, Cesar, but you are too impulsive."

"The dock was burning," said Fleming before Cesar tried to defend himself. "Would you have let it burn?"

She snorted derision. "I have coffee ready, and the sandwiches are in the icebox," she told the men. "You, Mister Fleming, had better get out of your clothes and into something you cannot ruin. Put your clothes at the foot of the stairs and I will take them on my way out."

"As you wish," said Fleming, making his concession too quickly for Bathsheba to enjoy it. "How long until—?"

"You have slightly more than half an hour," said Bathsheba, dismissing him. "Now," she went on to the other three, "you must wash up at once. There is work for all of us. Jacinth, you go first, and then take up your post. Then Alphonse. And last of all, you, my sweet." She bustled about the kitchen, readying the last two dishes. "No loitering."

Jacinth left the kitchen at once and ducked into the half-bathroom near the pantry. In a moment, water was whispering through the pipes.

"How long have you been here?" Cesar asked his wife.

"Somewhat more than an hour," she answered. "I knew you would leave everything in disarray. Men always do when there is an emergency. I decided I had better come along. Still, it took time to arrange things at our house, with Joshua being with Lolanda. He wanted to fight the fire with the rest, but I said he must not, that there were men enough to deal with it, and that Lolanda needed his help more than the men at the dock did."

"That was good of you," said Cesar, ignoring Alphonse, who was listening with undisguised interest. "Lolanda would be troubled if there was such danger and she was alone."

"Given her situation, who can blame her?" Bathsheba asked, almost accusingly. "She needs to be helped, and she cannot rush at anything."

Husband and wife exchanged an uneasy glance that held messages only the two of them could read. It was into the silence that Jacinth walked as he left the half-bath, a towel in his hand, his hair wet.

"Now you, Alphonse," said Bathsheba as if there had been no moment of quiet.

"Of course," said Alphonse quickly. He made a signal to Jacinth. "You get on duty. I'll be ready shortly." With that, he closed the door behind him and almost at once the sound of water in the sink revealed his efforts.

"Here's coffee," said Bathsheba, almost filling a large mug. "Bring it back when you're done and I will give you more."

"Very good," said Jacinth, trying to smile. "How soon will Mister Fleming be down?"

Cesar peered at the kitchen clock. "Five minutes at most," he said. "He'll go right to the lounge for sherry."

"Do I need to speak to him again?" Jacinth wondered aloud, accepting his sandwich wrapped up in waxed paper.

"Probably not," said Cesar. "You might as well go up the drive toward the curve and find a place to watch. You'll still be able to see the house and you'll have a view of anything coming toward the house from the road. Alphonse can patrol the path to the beach."

"Very good," said Jacinth. "I'll be about it, then."

"Plan to come back at midnight. You'll get your wages, another sandwich, all the coffee you can drink, and you can give a report." Cesar turned as he heard Fleming coming down-stairs. "Hurry along now."

Jacinth made for the kitchen door. "That I will." As he stepped outside, the donkey Jonquil brayed fulsomely.

Bathsheba gave Cesar a thoughtful look. "I know you, Cesar. You are troubled, and it isn't only because of that knot on your forehead."

Cesar touched the sticking plaster as if he could not imagine how it came to be there. "I have nothing to tell you, yet. In time, I may."

She waggled a finger at him in admonition. "A fine thing, when a man keeps secrets from his wife."

"It may be," he said, and started toward the corridor. "I must speak with Mister Fleming. Shall I tell him his dinner will be ready in—?"

"Fifteen minutes," Bathsheba declared. "He had best drink his sherry quickly."

"Very good," said Cesar, hastening away from the kitchen. The hall clock chimed the half hour as he passed it, its muted voice seeming to come from a great distance. He thought that nine-thirty was an acceptable hour for an evening meal. As he stepped into the lounge, he became aware that water was no longer running in the house, and he assumed that Alphonse had left the half-bath and would shortly take up his watch on the beach path.

Fleming had donned soft flannel trousers and a smoking jacket—no shirt beneath. His hair was damp and showed the furrows left by his comb. There was a half-empty sherry glass in his hand, and a lit cigarette on the lip of the ashtray. He smiled at Cesar. "Much better. How are things in the kitchen?"

"Dinner will be on the table in a quarter of an hour, my wife says. She is about to sauté the vegetables." Cesar knew the sound of the sautéing, and now that the water was off, he recognized it.

"I'll be glad of it. I'm hungry." He was about to tip back his head and toss off the rest of his drink when the roar of an engine came from the drive, answered at once by a stentorian bray from Jonquil. Fleming shook his head. "Bloody hell! What now?"

Chapter 12

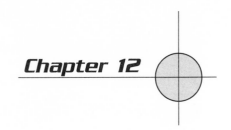

"It MUST be Henry Long," said Cesar, his calm returning as quickly as it had failed him. "There was no outcry from Jacinth."

"Not that we would have heard it, had there been, with all this racket." Fleming got up from the settee and went out through the open French doors onto the verandah in time to see Henry Long's battered 1933 Aston Martin tourer heave around the corner of the house and pull up in a billow of dust.

The big man extricated himself from his auto with habitual difficulty that made no impact on his huge grin. "Fleming!" he bellowed. "I have your kerosene!" If he thought Fleming's clothes were an odd choice for receiving guests, he gave no indication of it.

"Thank God for small favors," said Fleming. "Come in, Henry, and tell me the news. Cesar will take care of the kerosene."

"You have better news than I have, man, from what I could see on the road," Henry said. "The tin is in the boot. It's open. Have one of your guards remove it for Cesar, and offer me a drink to wash the road out of my mouth." He was already trudging up the steps, his massive body moving like a force of nature. "A fire at the dock. Do you know anything about it?"

"Only that it took over an hour to put out and it started with an explosion," said Fleming, resigning himself to inviting Henry to dine with him, and hoping there was enough food in the house to do the job. He stood aside to let Henry enter the lounge. "What may I get for you?"

"I see you're having sherry. How English. I'd like something more vigorous, if you have it." Henry smiled. "You've painted in here since I saw it last."

"Yes," said Fleming, and took up a bottle. "Grand Marnier is your tipple, isn't it? and what?"

"Cognac, if you don't mind," said Henry. "What an infernal racket! I hope that's not your animal."

"You mean Jonquil?" said Fleming as he poured out a generous libation for Henry. "No, that's Bathsheba's."

"Hum." Henry took the glass Fleming handed to him. "Well, she must have her uses."

"I devoutly hope so," said Fleming. He held up his sherry. "Chin-chin." He had an eerie moment as he realized he had made just such a toast to Sir William. "I thank you for bringing the kerosene. Given what this day has been like, I don't think I could have come to get it for another day or two."

"I said I would bring it to you. Do you have enough to last? Without what I have brought? You generally wait until you're very low to replenish your supply." Henry chose the most substantial chair in the room, a blocky, squat relic of the last century. He sank into it. "That fire certainly stirred up excitement. When I drove through the village, almost everyone wanted to talk about it. So, as you might suppose, there is all manner of gossip making the rounds." This was an opening, one that invited response.

Fleming did his part. "Oh, and what does it say?"

Henry beamed. "There is no end of trouble in this part of the island. There is talk of Krandall's murder, each retelling more lurid than the last, and there are many who say that Krandall was executed, but no one can say who has done it. Some say the Americans are behind it, others claim you British discovered he had sold secrets and was silenced, some say the Germans did it, some blame the Russians. By tomorrow the tales will be more fantastic still." He chuckled. "Someone even said you were behind it."

"I?" Fleming was genuinely shocked. "I was on the bucket line for well over an hour."

"That only shows you're a subtle one. And by tomorrow more people will repeat it," said Henry, enjoying himself.

"Dear God," Fleming said. "You don't suppose anyone will believe such rot? Why on earth would I do such a thing?"

"Well, motives are not really an issue for such rumors," said Henry. "And you're more plausible than the mysterious Monsieur Soleilsur, who is another subject of rumor."

Fleming shook his head. "You aren't serious, are you? He had already left when the explosion took place. He'd been gone a couple of days, I'm told."

"Yes, I have heard that, as well, and to the extent that these are the rumors, I have discounted it. But you know the popular mind. Truth is not the first thing it seeks. I cannot tell—nor can anyone else—which of the current crop of hearsay will attain the greatest currency." He leaned as far back as the chair would allow. "Don't worry, Fleming. I ate before I came. You may sit down to dine without offering me a place at your table."

Somewhat nonplussed, Fleming said, "You're more than welcome, of course."

"Don't be silly. You've postponed the meal for the fire, and by the smell of it, it's ready to serve." Henry displayed another grin. "If you don't mind giving me a dish of soup, I'll continue our conversation."

As if by plan, Cesar appeared in the door. "The tureen has been brought to the table," he announced.

Fleming signaled his readiness. "Henry would like some soup. I trust we can spare him some?"

"Oh, yes, sah," said Cesar, carefully avoiding Henry's broad wink. "I'll set a place for him at once."

"Thank you, Cesar. Henry, if you'll join me?" Fleming indicated the way to the dining room just across the hall.

"You're good to me, Fleming, no doubt about it. I am grateful." Henry rose out of his chair and followed his host. Cesar was putting down a cork-backed place mat on the right side of the table's head. Henry stood back while Cesar attended to the work, aware that many of the English living on Jamaica would not receive a black man as a guest. He appreciated Fleming in a way that he doubted Fleming would understand.

"There you are, sah," said Cesar as he finished putting the soup plate on the place mat and reached to remove the lid of the tureen. "Shall I serve?"

"No need," said Fleming. "Bring in another two rolls, and butter, if you would, and wine."

"The 'thirty-six claret?" Cesar asked. "You are having chicken."

"Red with fowl?" Fleming asked. "Well, why not? We have more of it than my brother's German whites."

"Very good, sah," said Cesar, leaving Fleming alone with Henry.

As he sat down, Henry reached for the ladle, and measured

out two of them into his broad shallow bowl. "I hope you do not mind."

"Certainly not; you're my guest," said Fleming, helping himself. "I'm hungry myself."

"I shouldn't be, not after my dinner, but there is a deal of me to keep up, as you know." Henry patted his girth with pride.

Fleming made a sound of approval, then said, "So what more have you heard, Henry? I don't doubt that tales aplenty have been pouring into your ears." He picked up his soup-spoon as a signal to Henry but did not actually taste the liquid himself.

"More than about the fire, that's sure," said Henry, looking up as Cesar came back with a bread-basket and a ramekin of butter.

"Thank you, Cesar," said Fleming. "Have you decanted the wine?"

"That's next, sah," said Cesar. "I've taken the liberty of preparing a bowl of broth for Jacinth and Alphonse."

"Very good," Fleming approved. "Is Bathsheba doing well?"

"She's making a creme brûlée for your dessert," said Cesar. "I told her you wouldn't mind if all you had was pudding."

"Bathsheba is a treasure, Cesar," said Fleming with feeling. "Tell her I thank her. And perhaps she will have enough for Henry?"

Cesar winked at Henry. "I wouldn't be surprised." He turned and left.

"You have a good man there, and he has a good woman. That is a rare thing, Fleming; I hope you know it," said Henry. "He is loyal and dedicated. Taking in his nephew was a kindly act."

"You need not fear that I don't know Cesar is a treasure. I am the envy of half my friends. And as to taking in his nephew—no one else was going to, and Joshua is a very promising lad," said Fleming. "I know Cesar has high hopes for him." He at last tasted the soup. "Now, what do you have to tell me?"

"You won't be pleased. It seems that the boys accused of killing Geoffrey Krandall were released from gaol this morning, very quietly. They're supposed to be sent to England as soon as a school can be found to take them. They're not going to be tried for the killing." He coughed gently. "There is something going on there, you may make book on it."

"I would think so," said Fleming. "Good Lord! What do you mean, there isn't going to be a trial? Have things gone so far as that?"

"There seems more to it than an attack." Henry paused to rip apart a roll and dip it in his soup. "It isn't simply a question of young men becoming violent, or that they attacked the man they did. Their reason is important." He took the bread and began to chew it vigorously.

"Do you think that's the truth? Or is it only an excuse?" Fleming was more disturbed than he wanted to admit. "Whatever their motives might be, they would have to be significant for this kind of maneuvering to take place."

"As to that, who can say?" Henry dunked another section of bread.

"I think you can," said Fleming knowingly. "I don't underestimate you, Henry Long. You have more information at your fingertips than half the government officials."

"True," Henry conceded. "But that doesn't mean that I have all the information, particularly in a case as strange as this one." He paused in his energetic eating. "If you want me to tell you what I think, I will. But you must keep in mind it is only my opinion and nothing more. I do not offer you fact."

"I understand all that." Fleming took another bit of soup, much more interested in what Henry had to say than in his dinner. He was becoming convinced that Sir William had come to him as much because he lived near Geoffrey Krandall than because he had been involved in spying during the war. Once again he began to consider the possibility that Sir William's disappearance and Krandall's death might be connected in some way. Too coincidental by half, he thought.

"Well," Henry told him, his voice lowered, "I think that there *is* more to the story than they are letting on. Krandall kept to himself more than any other man I can think of, and I have supposed for some time he had good reason to do it. I don't know what he was hiding from, or whom, but I have no doubt that he was trying to be as invisible as he could be." He stopped talking while Cesar returned with the wine and went through the ritual of tasting and pouring with Fleming. Only when Cesar was gone did he continue. "I have heard from a very reliable person that the boys who killed him were told that Krandall had been working for the Russians all through the war."

"They were our allies," Fleming pointed out. There had been plenty in Sir William's files about the Russians.

"The Russian people, yes. Comrade Stalin was not, any more than he is now," said Henry. "He made a pragmatic arrangement to save his country while he went about killing as many as Hitler did—very likely more."

"Well, yes," Fleming said. "I must agree with you on that point." He sipped his wine and listened intently.

"Anyway, the boys were told that Krandall had betrayed England, and that there was no way he would be brought to justice. That being the case, they were persuaded to support their country by killing him." Henry drank half a glass of wine eagerly. "Very good."

"How much of that do you believe?" Fleming asked.

"Most of it. I think the boys were convinced they were being patriotic, that killing Krandall was doing England a service," said Henry. "How much of the rest is true, who knows? But there was a cloud over Krandall, and it was associated with what he had done in the War." He finished the wine in his glass and smiled as Fleming filled it again.

"Do you think those boys might have been told the same thing about other men on the island?" Fleming thought back to the events of the afternoon. What might those boys have been told about Fleming himself—if they were the same boys who had killed Krandall?

"Something bothering you?" Henry asked, pausing in devouring the last part of the roll.

"I was just thinking," said Fleming as he reached for his wine, "that I had better get off this island before anything more appalling transpires."

"You mean before someone else gets killed," Henry said, coming as close to endorsing Fleming's decision as he could without revealing too much.

"Yes," said Fleming. "That is what I mean."

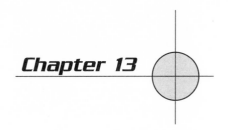

Chapter 13

MERLIN POWELL looked up from his cluttered desk as Ian Fleming came through his door shortly after nine the following morning. He took in the tweed jacket and woolen slacks and the jaunty hat. "Going somewhere?" he joked.

"America. New Orleans to start, and then points west. As you've arranged. I need my travel voucher and visa at once. I've booked my departure for eleven forty-five." Fleming smiled his determination as he glanced at his watch. "That's less than three hours from now, and I must present myself at the airport forty minutes before departure. My bag's in the Rapier. All I need is money and authorizations."

"Well, you *are* keen on this. I didn't think you were yesterday, not the way you were sounding then," said Powell.

"I've done a little digging in the nonce, and I think I'm on to something," said Fleming. "You were right that there's more to that killing than there seemed to be."

"Not buggery, I hope," said Powell. "The parents won't say anything to anyone if that's the case."

"I wouldn't have to go to America to find out about that," Fleming scoffed. "It may be a rumor, that he tried nastiness with the boys, but I think there is more to it, less venal and more corrupt."

"Trying to have his way with the lads would account for the behavior of the police. Letting the boys out of gaol. No mention of a trial. Sounds like buggery to me." Powell sighed.

Fleming didn't give in. "Too easy an explanation," he said. "Not that there might not be an element of truth in it, but it is not the whole of it, I'll wager my Rapier on it."

"You're damned serious, then," said Powell, his senses alerted. "You don't risk your auto on anything but a sure bet."

"That's true, and you may take it as indicative," said Fleming. "So let's get this done so that I can be on my way to America. I need a letter from you, saying I am traveling on business for you, to augment the visa and press credentials. I don't want to have to explain everything to the Americans."

"God, no," said Powell, and handed a slip to Fleming. "Take this down to Eccles in Accounting and tell him to step on it. I'll have your letter ready as soon as you're done."

"Thanks. If you'll just call ahead, so I won't have to try to persuade him to call up here?" Fleming took the slip and read the amount written in. "A reasonable amount for a change. Thank you, Merlin."

"Just go tend to it," said Powell briskly, shooing Fleming out of his office with a fussy gesture.

Fleming went along the hallway at a good clip, down the stairs at a quick pace, and along the lower corridor at a speed approaching a trot. The Accounting Department sign stuck out over the door and Fleming slipped inside, coming up to a high counter beyond which a row of desks were filled with paper and adding machines; the sound of punched keys and pulled cranks filled the room with their clatter rather like the noise a passing train would make. "I need to see Mister Eccles. On Powell's order," Fleming said to the clerk at the counter.

"You may have to wait a bit," said the clerk, exercising what little power he had to the full.

"If you ask him, Mister Eccles will tell you he is waiting for me," said Fleming.

"That's as may be," said the clerk, and was about to say more when a voice behind him rapped out his name.

"Crumpin," Eccles said. "Let Mister Fleming through. He's in a bit of a rush."

The clerk frowned but lifted the section of counter to give Fleming passage into the part of the room where the desks were.

"He takes his work seriously," said Eccles, guiding Fleming back to his own desk behind a tall partition. "I'm giving you the greater part of your funds in American dollars. You won't have to change pounds at a bank; it'll save all manner of questions. There's four hundred fifty in tens, twenties, and fifties. And a hundred pounds in twenties," said Eccles as he reached for a packet on his desk. "There is an auto arranged for you at Dallas, so you will drive to New Mexico. You'll leave less of a trail that way, in case anyone is following you." He patted Fleming on the shoulder. "Are you taking your pistol?"

"Of course," said Fleming. "And ammunition." He had also taken the deadly force authorization from Sir William's files, just in case he should need to take action against any foe he might come across.

"Be careful. Americans have a great many guns, you know." Eccles handed him the packet. "There's a record sheet included, and I recommend you keep track of everything you spend, otherwise you may have to make up the difference when you return."

"I understand," said Fleming, tucking the packet into the concealed pocket on the inside of the rear waist of his coat. "I'll do my utmost."

"Good," Eccles approved. "There's also a number for emergencies which you can use if you find yourself in difficulties. There is a great deal of unease in America these days, and you may have to deal with it. Newsmen can be suspect, in spite of what the American First Amendment may guarantee. If you need legal representation, call Mason Caldwell. He will know what to do." He held out a small, folded sheet. "Your visa, arranged through us."

"Very good," said Fleming. "I should be back in three or four days."

"If you are going to be gone longer, you will have to let Powell know as soon as possible, so arrangements can be made." Eccles gave him a sign, indicating he should leave.

"Thanks," said Fleming as he headed out of the Accounting Office and made his way back to Powell's desk.

"Here you are. I typed it myself," said Powell, holding out a letter on his own stationery. "I trust you won't need it, not with your press credentials in your wallet. They *are* in your wallet, aren't they?"

"Naturally," Fleming said, glad he had them as well as the deadly force authorization. "Well, I'll try to call you tomorrow, but if I can't for some reason, don't worry. I understand Texas and New Mexico are still fairly wild places."

"No doubt," said Powell, and gave him a casual salute. "Off you go, then."

"Thanks," said Fleming once again, and left Powell's office, hurrying down to the street to get into his Lagonda Rapier and begin his drive to the airport.

There were ten other passengers waiting for the airplane to carry them to New Orleans: two of them were women, and they sat together somewhat apart from the rest—men, mostly, like Fleming, dressed for business, but one in much more casual attire. The two women were put-away in ensembles that showed they had money as well as taste.

A cabin steward arrived in the waiting area to send them out onto the runway to climb aboard the smallish airplane—a twin-engine sixteen-seater—while baggage handlers stowed suitcases and valises in the lower hold. Fleming had a briefcase that he carried into the cabin and held on his lap while the cabin attendants readied them all for departure, announcing that they would serve cocktails as well as tea and coffee on the flight, and a light meal of fruit and scones.

Fleming found himself seated next to one of the two women, and he decided to make the most of their limited time together. "I'm Ian Fleming. I'm a journalist," he said, holding out his hand.

"I'm Alysa Sissons," she said, not quite shaking hands. She was slightly more than average height, slim, with carefully groomed brown hair set off with a fetching, wide-brimmed hat worn at a rakish angle; her ankles were trim. Her suit was a Dior New Look of deep-green wool crepe, an outfit that certainly was not to be had on coupons. Her shoes had fashionable Louis XIV heels and slender ankle straps. She carried a small, dark-brown handbag of fine leather that hung from a short, narrow strap around her wrist. The pearls at her throat were undoubtedly genuine, as was the square-cut golden topaz in her lapel brooch. "Missus Walter Sissons," she added, in case Fleming should jump to the wrong conclusion. "My husband is meeting me in New Orleans."

"How nice for you both," said Fleming at his most mannerly. "Will this be your first time in America?"

"Good gracious, no," she exclaimed as the first of the two

engines began to turn. "But it will be my first time in New Orleans."

"I hope you'll enjoy it," said Fleming. "I certainly have, when I have gone there in the past."

The second engine sprang into life, and the two of them roared in duet.

"I intend to," said Alysa Sissons.

The plane began to taxi, making steady progress down the runway, picking up speed as it went, its nose lifting into the air.

Beside him, Missus Sissons closed her eyes. "I hate taking off and landing. But I love to be in the air. It doesn't make sense, I know."

"I can understand your feelings," said Fleming, holding on to the arms of his seat and trusting his seat belt was tight enough.

The plane rose, the engines changing pitch as they climbed. A few minutes later the landing gear was retracted and the pilot announced on the cabin speakers that they would be climbing for the next ten minutes, and that he recommended swallowing frequently or yawning to adjust to the pressure. "Nothing wrong with your ears popping," he added jovially. "It's quite the usual thing."

This announcement did not reassure Alysa Sissons, who swallowed hard twice, as if to test the pilot's remarks. She looked at Fleming from the tail of her eye. "How do you stand it?"

"I tell myself it won't last long," said Fleming, smiling a little to show he was joking. "You get used to it, in time."

"Well, I haven't," she said. Her pout showed her pretty, encarmined mouth to advantage.

By the time the plane leveled off, Jamaica was behind them, and the expanse of the Caribbean stretched out ahead, a shiny version of the sky, with Cuba lying along the horizon.

"It's quite lovely from up here," said Alysa, turning to face Fleming so he could see her smile.

"Very much so," he agreed. He enjoyed this elegant kind of flirting, and it would while away the hours to New Orleans. He took his cigarettes from his pocket and offered one to Alysa and, when she declined, lit one for himself. "Flying can be exciting, can't it?"

"We're quite above everything," she said.

"That we are," Fleming told her.

A cabin steward came along the aisle of the airplane to offer tea or coffee to the passengers, or a cocktail.

"I'd like a Brass Monkey," said Alysa. "I assume you can make one?"

"Indeed I can, Ma'am," said the steward. "And you, sir?"

"A Martini, I think. It's so American." He nodded. "Very dry, if you would."

"Very good, sir." The steward passed on to the next seats.

"I do feel rather wicked, drinking so early in the day, but what else is there to do, way up here?" She flicked the tip of her tongue over her lips.

"Nothing very much," said Fleming. "More's the pity."

She made a pretend-slap at his hand on the arm of the seat between them. "You're a very audacious chap, Mister Fleming."

"Pays to be, when you're a journalist," he said in mock-contrition. "You never know what a little push will get you."

Her smile softened. "No, you don't, do you?"

They exchanged glances again, this time longer and more

questioning. "What a lucky man your husband is," said Fleming.

"He thinks so, and so do I, for he is the best of all men," she replied in a belated display of loyalty. "He's fortunate in many ways. He's good-looking, he's wealthy, he's a decorated hero, and he's about to enter politics."

"In Jamaica?" Fleming said, startled, for he thought he knew all the politicos and up-and-coming politicos on the island.

"Gracious, no," she said with a quick laugh. "In England, of course. At home. Jamaica is our retreat, a place where he can set aside the demands of his work and enjoy himself."

"But he is in New Orleans?" Fleming asked her questions automatically, wanting to sort out who Mister Walter Sissons might be. He remembered reading an account of the firm currently improving the airport and bidding to do a project at one of the harbors. "SS Industries—am I right?"

"Yes. SS Industries, for Sissons and Soleilsur. My husband is in America on business again," she said, "with his tiresome partner, Monsieur Soleilsur. Perhaps you've met him?"

"I haven't had that pleasure. I have heard of him, of course," he said, beginning to think he should find out more about Soleilsur, for the name had come up often enough to tweak his curiosity, and to be put in juxtaposition with a major engineering firm like SS Industries suggested an involvement that could have serious repercussions for the island. "He was on Jamaica himself, not too many days ago."

"Yes. He was arranging something on the island while my husband made things ready in America. Walter doesn't tell me much in regard to particulars, but he does tell me that he has much to do, and that it is necessary to our future. He and

Monsieur Soleilsur have important plans, or so I'm told." She managed a hint of a smile that was at once smug and sad.

The cabin steward appeared with their drinks, in the appropriate glasses. "Here you are," he said, serving Alysa first. "A Brass Monkey. And your Martini, sir."

Fleming handed him two-and-six, a generous tip, all things considered, and lifted his glass to his seat partner. "Chin-chin," he said, and sipped at his drink. It was appropriately cold but a bit too puckery. Still, he thought, not too bad for a bar in mid-air.

Alysa tasted her drink and smiled. "I do like these."

"Just as well then that the steward could make it for you." He watched her as she drank again. His cigarette was burned down most of its length, so he put it out in the arm-rest ashtray.

"I suppose it will help steady my nerves," she said as she put the glass down on the arm of her seat, smiling apprehensively.

"Nothing to worry about," said Fleming. "The report was for fair weather all the way to Louisiana. Probably nothing more than a bump or two." He wanted her to keep talking, and not simply because he was enjoying her company.

"A bump," she repeated as if she were talking about bombs. "They say in future, everyone will fly."

"Only if they have wings," said Fleming, and was rewarded with a giggle.

"You know what I mean," she said.

"Yes," he responded, a bit more seriously. "And I suppose it is inevitable. The War made us rely on airplanes, and now we don't know how to get along without them."

"That's what my husband says," she said, boasting a little.

"Does he fly a great deal, in his business?" Fleming asked

solicitously, for it was apparent that his wife did not.

"Yes, he does," she said, annoyance under her genial answer. "His business is very demanding, and once he enters politics, I suppose it will only get worse. He has commitments all over Europe, and may soon have some across the Pacific."

"It sounds very difficult for you," said Fleming, hoping to get her to volunteer more information.

Her laughter was edgy. "Goodness, no. Nothing of the sort. It is what I must expect—Walter Sissons must travel."

"And you, will you travel with him?" He wanted to sound sympathetic.

"I don't know," she said, looking away from Fleming and staring into a distance that existed only in her thoughts.

"It sounds as if there are many demands on you, as well," said Fleming.

"Nothing a good wife would not hope for her husband," she said as if repeating a painfully learned lesson.

Fleming backed off at once. "I didn't mean to imply anything else, Missus Sissons. I only thought you must find such calls on your husband a bit trying—as many another woman would."

She glanced toward the window. "I suppose it could seem that way. If Monsieur Gadi Soleilsur did not have so many plans, it might be different, but as it stands—" She stopped herself. From that moment until they landed in New Orleans, she said very little, all of it pleasant, but offering nothing more in the way of information.

Chapter 14

NEW ORLEANS was warm under an elaborate display of gathering clouds, all pink and white as if cherubs were expected momentarily. The stillness of the air hinted at possible rain later that night. The city itself, low-lying and green, smelling of the sea and vegetation, showed equal parts of style and decadence, a combination that Fleming found heady, seductive, and enticing. He was sorry he would have only four-and-a-half hours here, but he had to be in Dallas in the morning, and that meant taking the ten-thirty flight for Hensley National Airport, and spending the next four hours in the air. He handed over his declaration statement to the uniformed agent and answered half a dozen routine questions before having his passport stamped; he remembered to declare his revolver that lay in a special holster along the small of his back. Leaving the Customs area at Moisant International Airport, he bade Alysa Sissons good-bye as they walked toward the exit; he could see a tall, good-looking man in an expensive suit waving a bouquet of roses at her. Fleming cast a last, appreciative glance in her direction, and intercepted a quick flicker in her eyes.

She paid only the slightest attention to Fleming, as if glad to see the last of him; her hand was raised and all her attention on the handsome man at the rail. She might as well have never said a word to Fleming, let alone flirted with him over drinks.

Fleming picked up his luggage, consigned it to a rental-locker, pocketed the key, and decided to take a brief turn into the city; he wanted a quick meal and was aware that New Orleans was famous for food and jazz, and decided to try to find both. The cabbie asked him where to, and he said, "Somewhere I can get a good dinner at a reasonable price, hear a little music, and still get back here by eight-fifteen."

"Something in the French Quarter?" the cabbie asked, already turning into the traffic that buzzed around the air terminal. "Most people from out-of-town want to go there."

"Why not, if it will fit the bill?" Fleming looked about at the other autos and noticed a Lincoln pulling ahead of them, driven by a hawk-faced man in light-colored clothing. "A grand auto, that."

"If you want to lay out more than three thousand bucks for a car, I guess so," said the cabbie with ill-concealed envy.

"That's a lot of money. A Rolls-Royce would cost you more," said Fleming.

"More money than sense," said the cabbie, and steered onto the street that led toward the heart of the old city—a concept that seemed ludicrous to Fleming, who could not imagine anything in America being old.

They pulled up at a white-fronted restaurant on Bourbon Street, and the cabbie accepted his fare and his tip readily enough. As Fleming got out of the cab, he asked, "Will you call back for me in an hour and a half? I'll double your fare to the airport if you'll agree?"

The cabbie considered the offer. "All right. I'm due for a dinner break." He took the five-dollar bill, smiling. "Right nice of you, sir. I'll be here in ninety minutes." He touched the brim of his leather cap.

"Thank you," said Fleming, and went into the restaurant, noticing its vaguely Roman, vaguely Georgian interior. The aroma of the place was eloquent testimony to the quality of the food they served. He told the maître d' that he was a party of one, and asked to be seated away from the door, a request the maître d' honored, finding Fleming a table in an alcove at the far end of the room. "Excellent," Fleming approved.

"The crayfish stew is very good tonight, sir," said the maître d' as he handed Fleming the leather-bound menu, before he returned to the reservation desk.

On the far side of the dining room a piano and double bass were pouring out easy, rhythmic music. Fleming tapped his toe as he opened the menu. The selection was extensive and varied, favoring seafood and regional dishes. While Fleming perused the menu, he kept a sharp watch on the room beyond, taking note of everyone who arrived and where they were seated. He could not bring himself to believe that he was under such close observation, but he was also aware that he might be watched. He gave his order—alligator soup, oysters *Bonne Femme*, spinach soufflé, and cheeses to finish—and sat back to sample a first taste of his split of a white Burgundy while he waited for his meal.

Taking stock of the other patrons, he noticed that of the nine tables occupied, one seemed to be filled with businessmen from out-of-town. There were eight of them, dining boisterously. Another table held a couple of advanced years, both dressed in high fashion for 1933. A third table accommodated a family of five, the oldest youth in a military uniform. At a fourth table a couple, very likely honeymooning, judging by their behavior. The fifth table held two women of middle years, well-dressed and determined. One—the more attractive of the two—wore a black twist around her wedding band, indicating widowhood. Over at the sixth table two men and a woman pored over some item the older man held out in a small case. At the seventh table a harried-looking man in his thirties dined alone, his whole attention on his meal. The eighth table was the site of a birthday party for a lovely young woman, visibly pregnant, with a doting husband and an older couple, parents or in-laws. Table nine was occupied by four young men, all in conservative suits and with the manners of attorneys; they were into a second bottle of champagne, noisily congratulating one another on getting a favorable decision. Nothing too disquieting about any of them, he thought. But still. Only three of the other patrons noticed Fleming that he was aware of.

The soup was interesting, tangy with peppers. Fleming enjoyed it, but wasn't so impressed that he wanted to get the recipe for Cesar. The next course—the oysters—were delicious, and Fleming was glad he had ordered them. As he ate, he was aware that the woman with the widow's wedding band was watching him, her expression all but blank. Fleming nodded to her, and did his best to look flattered by her attention. He poured out more wine and waited for the spinach soufflé. When it arrived, it was accompanied by rice with slivered almonds. The soufflé was light, risen magnificently, and Fleming ate it appreciatively; he left all but a couple forkfuls, anticipating the cheese.

The rollicking attorneys paid and left, the men jostling one another as they made for the door.

When the cheese tray was delivered, Fleming ordered coffee, thinking that at home in England, he would have had port instead. But he would be in the air again soon, and that required staying awake and remaining alert. He lit a cigarette to accompany his coffee.

Just before his coffee was brought, another party arrived at the restaurant, an angular man, not quite six feet tall, of middle years, with a lean face that showed a mixed heritage, an unusual guest in such a place as this restaurant, although the French Quarter was more eclectic than much of the city, to say nothing of the American South. His hair was tight-waved, turning from mahogany to white, grey-green eyes, and a thin, straight mouth. He wore a tan tropical jacket over a white silk shirt, and cream-colored linen slacks. Simple his garments were, but they were also of top-quality cloth and expensive tailoring, which may have explained why the man was so welcomed by the maître d', who apparently knew this patron of old; he was given a table near the front, and seemed to spend an inordinate amount of time looking over the other patrons, or so it seemed to Fleming. He ordered an appetizer but nothing more.

Watching him, Fleming had the uneasy feeling that the man was surveilling the diners, for he took the time to look over the dining room with more than passing interest. For an instant their eyes met, and then the man's passed on, leaving Fleming thinking he had looked into the eyes of a reptile. He drank his coffee and scalded his mouth. The cheese had little savor for him, and he knew his burnt lips were not the reason for the tastelessness.

He paid the bill as soon as it was presented, adding a ten percent tip as Americans expected. Then he rose from his table and made for the door, aware that he was being covertly scrutinized by the lean man in the tropical jacket. As he reached the curb, he saw the cabbie waiting for him, leaning in his rolled-down window, on the other side of the street. Fleming lifted his hand and strode across to the cab, pausing for a horse-drawn carriage filled with men and women. One of them was singing the "Pineapple Rag" to the applause of the others.

Reaching the taxi, Fleming saw the cabbie had slumped, his hand limp on the door handle. "Wake up, fellow," he said as he pulled open the rear door.

The cabbie remained inert.

Fleming paused and stared at the man, leaning down to smell him to determine if he was drunk. Only then did he see the blood leaking from under his cap, and realized the man had been shot in the back of the head. His breath stopped in his throat and he swallowed hard against the sudden nausea that roiled in the back of his throat. He was at once aware of how exposed he was, and what questions and delays might come out of this. He could not remain here, though leaving seemed to be disloyal to the cabbie, who had been willing to call back for him, and now was dead—perhaps because he had gone to this trouble. After a long moment, Fleming stepped back from the cab and slammed the door, shouting, "You're in no fit state to drive!" and then walked away, going down the street, half-expecting to feel a bullet tear into his back as he went.

Two blocks later he flagged another cab and asked to be taken to the airport. "I'm in a bit of a hurry," he said. "I've an eight o'clock flight." He doubted the man would ever be questioned about him, but he wanted to make sure any information he provided was erroneous.

"So you're going to St. Louis," said the cabbie, showing off how well he knew the airline schedules. "You got it." With that, he swung his cab down the next narrow street and headed out of the French Quarter, back to the town of Kenner where the Moisant International Airport was located.

At the airport, Fleming retrieved his luggage from the locker and looked about for an inconspicuous place to wait, finding it at the back of a bay of seats near the gate from which he would leave. He bought a paper and opened it wide, hardly caring what he read, but wanting the protection it provided. The death of the cabbie troubled him. How did it happen? More important, why did it happen? Had he anything to do with it, or was his presence of no significance? That last question ate at him as he ran his unreading eyes over the columns of type.

The plane to Dallas left fifteen minutes late, and for Fleming, those minutes dragged unbearably. He got aboard the airplane with relief, saying to the stewardess, when she asked what he wanted to drink, that he would like a brandy. She brought it to him as soon as they were airborne, and he took a deep swig of it as he fished a cigarette from his pack.

"Nervous flyer?" she asked sympathetically.

"Something like that," he said.

"Better keep your seat belt fastened, then. We may have, perhaps, a bit of a storm," said the stewardess with a broad smile. "There could be head winds, as well. You might as well expect to land a little late."

"Thanks. I'll keep that in mind," said Fleming and took another sip of brandy, liking the way it warmed him all the way down. He checked his seat belt, although he knew it was secure. Then he lit his cigarette, enjoying the mingling of brandy and tobacco fumes.

The flight went on into the night, becoming bouncy as the night deepened. The stewardess no longer patrolled the aisle, staying in the front of the cabin with the steward, buckled in against the weather.

Fleming tried to sleep, reminding himself that he had endured worse during the war, but found it impossible to quiet his mind. He found himself mentally circling over the events of the last two days, beginning with the disappearance of Sir William. Perhaps, he thought, Sir William's arrival was as important as his vanishing. He had assumed that Sir William had only the one purpose—to see him—but what if that weren't the case? What if Sir William had had other fish to fry? Then there was the death of Geoffrey Krandall, which might or might not be connected with Sir William. The two young men who had attacked Cesar—what was their part in this, or was it only happenstance? If that event was connected, *how* was it connected, and *why*? Had Cesar been the intended target? Had his house? Had he been the one the youths sought? What of the scorpions Cesar had found? Were they an accident, or was someone trying to eliminate him? If so, why? Was he, himself, presently in danger, or had he imagined the association? Was he becoming paranoid, looking for connections in a series of events that had nothing in common but time and locale? Had he allowed himself to be rattled enough not to be able to observe clearly? He was very much afraid the answer to that last question was yes. The whole thing was so tangled, and perhaps the tangle was only in his thoughts. But Krandall was dead, Sir William was missing, Cesar had been attacked, and the cabbie had been shot. Taken separately there was only a parade of misfortunes, but seen together, they suggested a pattern. He felt like a cat chasing its own tail.

The airplane bucked, shaking him out of his unhappy reverie. He sat up straight in his seat, wishing he could get another brandy before they reached Dallas. He looked over the empty seat beside him toward the window, but could see nothing more than the misty texture of clouds.

When the airplane finally began its descent, he was thoroughly rattled and jangled, longing for sleep and knowing he could not find it.

Chapter 15

As THE airplane landed nearly an hour late, Hensley National Airport was wet, and a slow drizzle kept the tarmac shining. Walking into the air terminal Fleming felt the chill of the early, early morning magnified by the damp, and wished he had brought a proper overcoat. Dawn was nearly three hours away. He made his way to the front of the terminal, toward the information booth, presently manned by a young man who was drowsing over a calculus text. Most of the terminal was minimally staffed, with only one or two clerks on duty, and a few janitors busy cleaning the linoleum and ashtrays in anticipation of another busy day. Fleming came up to the information booth, saying just loudly enough to demand the clerk's attention, "Excuse me, but I need to find an auto rental."

The young man almost jumped, but he recovered himself enough to say by rote, "What can I do to help you, sir?"

"I need to rent an auto," said Fleming.

"Commercial or pleasure?" asked the young man, gathering his wits.

"I am a journalist—I suppose that counts as commercial," said Fleming. "I am here on business."

"Commercial, then," said the young man. "That'll be 66 Commercial Travelers' Car Rental. It's open at six. You'll have time for breakfast at the Night Owl Café. Any cabdriver can take you there. There should be a couple left on duty at this hour."

"Thanks," said Fleming, and went to claim his luggage, then hurried to the front of the terminal to hail a cab. "66 Commercial Travelers' Car Rental," he said as he climbed into the second taxi in line, his bags laid on the wide expanse of floor in front of the passenger seat.

"You're supposed to take the first in line," said the cabbie in a broad Texas drawl. "I'm about to go off duty."

"I'll make it worth your while," said Fleming. "You're driving a Checker."

The cabbie shrugged. "Whatever you say, pardner." With a jolt of his gears he swung into traffic. "Where're you from?" the cabbie asked a quarter of a mile on.

"England," said Fleming. "I'm British."

"Yep," said the cabbie. "You sure enough talk that way."

Going through the nearly empty streets in the pre-dawn darkness, Fleming was careful to keep an eye on the rear-view mirror, just in case they were being followed. As they reached the offices of the 66 Commercial Travelers' Car Rental, he was relieved to see a dozen late-model automobiles drawn up in the fenced lot beside the office. Across the street, a neon sign in the vague shape of a bird announced the Night Owl Café, open twenty-four hours.

"That'll be two seventy-five," said the cabbie.

"Fine," said Fleming, and handed him three dollars with fifty cents for a tip; it was an extravagance, but Fleming had offered the cabbie a reward, and it was the least he could do.

"Hey, thanks, pardner," said the cabbie as Fleming got out of the car with his luggage. "Good luck," he added before he sped off.

Fleming crossed the street to the café, his bags feeling as if they contained anvils. He ordered coffee and flapjacks, the closest he could come to breakfast pastry in that establishment. Rubbing his chin, he decided he needed a shave, and asked the waitress where the men's room might be.

"All the way back, on the left," she said. "Rough night?"

"Bad weather in an airplane," said Fleming, and took his luggage with him to the men's room, where he took out his toiletry kit and retrieved his razor, shaving soap and mug.

When he emerged from the men's room ten minutes later he looked a bit more spruce than before. His hair was brushed, his face clear of stubble, and he had neatened his tie. As he sat down, the waitress returned with his breakfast. "I heated up your coffee."

"Thanks," he said, and settled in for his meal.

Twenty minutes later he was back at the 66 Commercial Travelers' Car Rental just as the door was opened. He explained to the yawning clerk in the silverbelly Stetson who he was and where he wanted to go, adding, "I have proof of all this, if you need it."

"I gotta see your passport, you being a Limey and all," said the clerk, adding, "I spent some time in England during the War. Flew out of an airfield in Sussex. Quite a place."

"Thanks." Fleming took out his wallet from his inner breast pocket and removed his passport.

"Ian Fleming," said the clerk, pronouncing the first name Eye-ahn. Fleming didn't bother to correct him. "Newpaperman, eh?"

"Journalist," Fleming said testily.

"I got to ask you to fill out this form," the clerk said, shoving a clip-board toward Fleming, and a pencil. "You gotta press hard. There's a carbon."

Fleming began to fill in the blanks on the sheet, reading

each line carefully. When he was done he handed the clip-board back to the clerk. "There you are."

"Going to New Mexico." He considered. "It's quite a drive, you know. Not like driving from Bath to London."

"I've seen the map," said Fleming, keenly aware that he was tired and that was making him brusque.

"I'll need a fifty-dollar deposit and ten more for insurance," said the clerk. "When you leave the state we have to get a fifty-dollar deposit."

"Sounds reasonable," said Fleming, taking the appropriate bills from his wallet. "Do I have to bring the auto back here, or is there an office in New Mexico where I can turn it in, if my business concludes there?"

"66 Commercial Travelers' has offices all along Route 66, from California to St. Louis. We've got an office in Albuquerque, on Central," said the clerk proudly. "Course, Dallas is south of 66. You go north to Gainesville and then take 82 over to Amarillo and pick up 66 there. If you have any trouble, you stop off at the 66 Commercial Travelers' in Amarillo. The company's got an office in Denver, too, north of 66." He beamed. "From Amarillo, it's a straight shot to Albuquerque. You'll have to call here and tell us that's what you're planning to do about the car, that is if you decide to leave it in Albuquerque. There'll be a surcharge for dropping it off. Twelve bucks." He pulled the carbon copy off the form and handed it to Fleming, who folded it and put it into his wallet. "You pay it at that end."

"All right," said Fleming, wondering what Eccles would make of these charges.

"Anything else you want to know?"

"How long a drive is it?" Fleming asked, making a mental note of the names and numbers the clerk had reeled off.

"Well, now, it's sixty plus miles to Gainesville, then about three fifty to Amarillo, and another three hundred or so to Albuquerque. If you don't want to go that way, you can take 180 out of Dallas, go west to Hobbs, then turn north at Carlsbad and head up through Roswell on 285. It goes up to Santa Fe, but there's an easy turnoff for Albuquerque. The Amarillo drive is easier, not so away from things. You being a stranger here, I'd go Gainesville-Amarillo." The clerk was enjoying his display of knowledge, wanting to impress Fleming.

"Do you have a map I could buy?" Fleming asked, feeling a trifle pulled.

"Yessiree. I got Rand McNally's latest. You can't go wrong with Rand McNally." He reached into a drawer and pulled out a multi-folded map: *Road Map: Southwestern United States*, it read. "Fifty cents," he announced. "A bit high, but worth every penny."

"I'll take it," said Fleming, finding the appropriate coin in his pocket and handing it to the clerk. He secured the map and vowed to study it once he was in the car.

"Now, we got Packards, deSotos, Dodges, and Hudsons. I kind of like the Hudson, myself." The clerk tipped his Stetson back on his head, a gesture Fleming had only seen in Western films.

Fleming considered. "Which is the smallest?"

"Smallest?" the clerk repeated incredulously. "Well, I guess the Packard coupe."

"I'm not used to autos of the size you make them in America," said Fleming, doing his best to sound apologetic.

"Well, then, the Packard. Think about it, though. It's a long drive. You'd be more comfortable in something a bit bigger. Rides easier."

"I'll take the Packard, if you don't mind," said Fleming, smiling. "Thanks for the recommendation, though."

"Sure thing," said the clerk, reaching around to a display of pigeon-holes and fished out a key-ring with three keys on it. "Square top is the trunk, the round one the ignition, and the diamond one is the door. You'll figure it out in time. It's the coupe, the only one on the lot, in the corner, maroon with tan upholstery. The license plate number's on the key-ring. You got your self-sealing Goodyears on that car. That's a plus. Be careful how you use the choke." He handed the keys to Fleming. "We recommend you getting your gas at Texaco stations."

Fleming realized the man meant petrol, and so he said, "I'll keep that in mind."

"Our cars get a ten percent discount at Texaco stations, and it adds up. Twenty-two cents a gallon instead of twenty-four makes a difference on a long drive like you're going to make," the clerk said by way of explanation. "All you have to do is tell the kid who pumps the gas. Mind you tell him to check the oil and water, too."

"Good to know. I will." He picked up his bags. "Well, thanks for all the information. I'll be off now." He started toward the side door leading to the fenced car park.

"Hold on there, pardner," said the clerk. "I got to unlock the gate. Give me a couple of minutes."

"I'll load up the auto," said Fleming, continuing toward the door.

"Okay," called the clerk, waiting until the door was firmly closed before he picked up the telephone on his desk and dialed the operator and asked for a number in Baton Rouge. When the ring was answered, he said, "This is McKinnon in Dallas. I think I got your man, just like we were told. Fella named Fleming, right? Newspaperman. English. Going to Albuquerque."

"Albuquerque," said the French-accented voice in Baton Rouge, rising in disbelief. "New Mexico? Are you sure?"

"That's what he said. Do you want me to call deSilva, warn him to keep an eye out?" the clerk asked.

"No. I'll do it. You call our other men in your area and tell them what you've told me. Tell them what he's driving."

"A Packard coupe," said McKinnon. "I told him to use Texaco stations, for the discount."

"Good. Good. They'll keep track of him for us," said the man in Baton Rouge. "Make sure you follow him. We have to know where he's really going, and keep tabs on him while he's getting there. Gas stations are useful, but don't forget about planes and cars. We don't want him to get away from us."

"Whatever you say," the clerk said, and prepared to hang up.

"And we don't want him finding out about Robertson's connection to Preussin and Cathcart," the voice in Baton Rouge warned.

"Do you think there's any chance of that? We don't know for sure that's what he's looking for, do we?" McKinnon asked. "They're pretty well shielded, aren't they? Robertson won't say anything about them."

"Let us hope so," said the other man, a threat in his tone. "He has been warned not to reveal too much to the authorities."

"That's my point. Preussin and Cathcart are safe. So we

don't want to raise any more of this Fleming's skepticism We're going to have to be careful with this." McKinnon put his hand to his forehead. "I got to get out there and open the gate for him, before he gets suspicious."

"Off you go, then," said the man in Baton Rouge, and hung up.

McKinnon took the padlock key and bustled out of the office, holding the key aloft as he saw the Packard coupe pull out of its place and maneuver toward the gate. He struggled with the lock, and then fumbled with the chain, but was finally able to get the gate open. Standing aside, he watched Fleming drive off, belatedly swinging into the right-hand lane. He shook his head and smiled, thinking that for the life of him, he couldn't figure out what it was about Fleming that Soleilsur was afraid of. Reporters could be a pain, but the way you got rid of them was ignoring them; Fleming was no different than the rest.

Chapter 16

ON IMPULSE, Fleming decided on going west on 180, taking the route the clerk hadn't recommended. He told himself that this was caprice, but he couldn't shake the conviction that he was still under observation, and he felt that he would be able to catch any followers if he took the less traveled highway to New Mexico. He discovered he could maintain a decent speed in the Packard, and cover the long distance quite handily. The country was mostly flat and, after thirty miles at a good clip, boring. It would probably be as boring the other way, he thought; there was no sign that the land to the north was more varied. Besides, coming into New Mexico this way, he thought, Highway 285 would take him directly to Santa Fe, and from there he could reach Los Alamos without fuss. He was glad he wasn't making this journey in high summer, for the late September heat was imposing enough. About ten in the morning, he pulled off the road, found his dark glasses in his suitcase, and put them on against the ferocious west Texas glare as he made his way through Albany to Snyder, where he stopped to fill his tank with petrol at the Texaco station, as the clerk suggested, to get a cup of coffee, and to try to make a call to Merlin Powell before continuing westward. It was time to check in.

The overseas operator demanded four dollars and eighty cents in coins before she made the connection, and explained in a treacly drawl that this was for two minutes only.

"I understand," said Fleming, beginning to count out all the dimes and quarters he had accumulated since arriving in New Orleans, and feeding them into the appropriate coin slots, listening to them ring, clang, and bong. "Cut me off when the two minutes are up."

"A'right, if that's what y'all want," said the operator, and put the call through.

Powell's secretary answered. "I'm sorry, Mister Fleming, but Mister Powell is out of the building just at present."

That annoyed Fleming, but he said, "Tell him I called, will you?"

"Of course, sir," said the secretary, and rang off before Fleming could say anything more.

The coins clattered into the innards of the phone, and the overseas operator said, "D' y'all want me to try again? It'll be another four-eighty."

Breathing a curse at Miss Butterly's efficiency, Fleming said, "No. Never mind," and hung up, leaving the phone booth abruptly. It bothered him that Powell would not know where he was, as he had insisted. At least he had made an effort to comply, he told himself. Miss Butterly had intervened. He strode out of the bar-cum-restaurant, leaving its smoky interior for the hot afternoon. Much as it frustrated him, he knew he would not reach Los Alamos today. He would have to break his journey somewhere—perhaps, he thought, consulting his map, he would get a room at Roswell.

The sun, which had hung behind him, then overhead, was now dropping lower in the sky ahead of him as he stopped again in Lamesa, had a meal, topped off the petrol in his tank, then headed westward again, taking 137 north-west to the aptly named Brownfield, then picked up 380 to Roswell, shaving, he hoped, an hour or two off his journey by avoiding the southward swing to Carlsbad. Between Plains and Tatum he crossed into New Mexico. The emptiness of the land through which he was driving amazed him, for although he knew from maps that the Southwest was filled with open spaces, the extent of those open spaces, and the comparative insignificance of the occasional towns, gave him a sense of vastness that before now he had only felt on the ocean. The land was not as flat as Texas had been, and the gullys and rises created everchanging vistas as grassland gave way to upland scrub and piñon trees.

Roswell, when Fleming got there, turned out to be a small town made possible by the military presence of Walker Air Force Base, some little distance away. It was a dusty, dry collection of buildings, most of them not more than thirty years old; the last blaze of sunset over the mountains to the west gilded the town, imparting a kind of beauty to it that Fleming suspected would not be there in the full light of day. Men in jeans and chaps mixed with youths in uniform on the streets, a slightly uncomfortable ambience resulting from the combination. There were bars and diners and two hotels, one wood, one brick, offering rooms at a discount for men in uniform. Fleming drew up in front of the wooden hotel, a three-story affair that must have seen the Wild West in its full flower, judging by the quasi-Victorian architecture and the etchedglass windows. The sign over the main door proudly proclaimed this the Pecos Vista.

The reception clerk was a man of advanced years, whitehaired and whip-thin, with skin like an old saddle. "What can I do for you, young fella?" he asked as Fleming approached across the pillared lobby.

"Room for one, if you please," said Fleming, hating to admit how tired he had become.

"That'll be twenty-nine dollars. First night payable in advance." He turned around the old-fashioned registry.

"Kind of high, isn't it?" Fleming said, pulling out his wallet.

"You think there's better to be had for less, no one's keeping you here," said the clerk.

"Twenty-nine it is," said Fleming.

The clerk nodded his satisfaction. "Sign here, and put in all the information. Gotta have it, this being a missile base, for National Security," he added, hitching his thumb in the general direction of the Air Force Base. "The FBI checks up on me from time to time."

Fleming signed his name, put his occupation as journalist and his home address as London, England. "Is that sufficient?"

"If I can have a gander at your passport, it is," said the clerk. "How long're you staying?"

"Just tonight." Fleming handed the man three tens.

"Can't say I blame you. Nothing much to do around here, unless you're in the military, or an Indian. Even then, there's nothing much to do." He chuckled at his own familiar joke. "Okay, then. You'll want to park your car around back. Gotta do that for insurance. Breakfast's served from six to nine-thirty, lunch at noon until three. You can still get dinner if you don't dawdle. The kitchen closes at eight-thirty. No room service but coffee. The bar's open until eleven." He reached for a key to hand to Fleming. "Number 14C, at the end of the hall, top of the stairs. It faces the back of the building. It's quieter than the street side tends to be." He winked. "You know what I mean?"

Fleming made a noise of agreement. "Around back you say? The auto?"

"That's right. You'll see. Just follow the signs," said the clerk, smiling to himself.

It didn't take long to move the car; the rear entrance to the hotel was clearly marked and brought Fleming to the lobby of the Pecos Vista's saloon, a dark, noisy room smelling of cigarettes and beer, with cowboy music on the jukebox in the corner and men huddled on stools along the brass rail of the bar. He paused, his luggage weighing heavily in his hands, then shrugged and continued on to the front, going up the stairs and along the hall to the room he had been assigned. It was smallish, having a tall chest-of-drawers with an old mirror mounted atop it on one wall, a double bed in a brass frame with a handmade quilt spread over it against the other, a small night-stand beside it, a doily laid over it. A bed-side lamp on the stand and a floor-lamp promised night-time illumination. The door to the tiny bathroom stood half-open, and Fleming slipped into it long enough to relieve himself and have a look at his general appearance.

His eyes were reddish with strain and fatigue, he needed a shave, and his clothes were impossible. He combed his hair and did his best to smooth the front of his jacket, trying to make himself look more respectable even as he wondered if anyone would notice. "Just a light meal," he told his reflection, knowing he had to eat, or he would be useless in the morning. He took out his shaving kit and his small travel alarm, putting the folding clock on the night-stand and his kit in the bathroom, which was the extent of his unpacking. Leaving everything else in his luggage, he set his bags in the bottom drawers of the chest before taking the key, carefully locking the door, and going down to the restaurant, where he had a steak, a bowl of chili, and a shot of tequila before climbing the stairs again, the rigors of the long day catching up with him. He got his jacket, shirt, and shoes off before falling into bed, his holster still buckled on, his pistol lying at the small of his back; he felt as if he were still in the War, and those recollections accompanied his fall into the arms of Morpheus.

It was sometime later when a sound awakened him abruptly. He remained still, not wanting to reveal he was no longer asleep. He was lying on his side, his right arm under him, the left crooked around the pillow, making it difficult to move surreptitiously. With all the concentration he could summon, he listened intently to discover what had brought him so suddenly out of his much-needed sleep. The room was dark, and what little light came in from the window was distorted by the curtains hung there. Out of the corner of his eye, he could see the shadows slither with the slight breath of air that must have come from the hall, since the window was closed. He put all his attention on listening, and was rewarded with the soft fall of a footstep, nearly silent compared to the beating of his heart. He wished he could reach his jacket, or even to dare to make a move for the revolver in the holster at the small of his back.

A quiet, sharp click sounded as loud as a gunshot, and it focused all Fleming's attention on the movement in his room. He had to exercise all his self-control to keep from trying a desperate move; let the trespasser assume that he was still asleep. He resisted the urge to hold his breath, certain that his intruder was listening closely, too.

There was the sound of a drawer being pulled open, and Fleming knew this was his one chance. Easing his hand around for his revolver, he flung back the covers and quilt, sat up in bed, and drew his weapon all in one move. "Stay right where you are."

The figure bent over the middle drawer of the chest-of-drawers froze. "You don't want to do anything foolish," he said.

"I'd take my own advice, if I were you," said Fleming, swinging his legs out of bed, his air never wavering.

"I'm Hotchkiss, Lemmuel Hotchkiss, FBI. You know what that is, don't you?" The man had not moved from his crouch.

"Federal Bureau of Investigation. Hoover's Hounds," said Fleming, deliberately using their uncomplimentary nick-name.

"And proud of it." The man waited a moment while Fleming stood up. "D'you mind if I straighten up? My back's beginning to hurt."

"Do it very slowly, Mister Hotchkiss," Fleming recommended, keeping enough distance between him and the other man to make wresting his gun from his hand problematic.

Hotchkiss complied. "Here I go," he said, and rose to his full height—perhaps two inches above Fleming's. He kept his hands somewhat extended, away from his body. "Mind if I turn on a light?"

"You were the one who chose to come in in the dark," said Fleming. "There's a floor lamp behind you. Step back and turn it on without turning around, using your left hand."

"Right you are." He did as Fleming ordered, very slowly. "Don't do anything stupid," he recommended as he fumbled for the switch.

"I won't if you don't," said Fleming, raising his hand to shield his eyes a half a second before the light came on. "Don't try it," he said as he saw Hotchkiss start to move in the sudden brilliance.

Hotchkiss froze in position. He was revealed as an open-faced man with dark-blond hair close-cut and beginning to grey, bluish eyes under straight brows, with the kind of features that seemed very American to Fleming; the man resembled Randolph Scott, rugged and pleasant at once. He wore black slacks and a black-and-tan checked shirt. His shoes had pointed toes and Fleming guessed Hotchkiss was wearing cowboy boots. He had no visible weapon on him, but Fleming knew better than to assume he was unarmed. "Can't blame a guy for trying," he said, shaking his head. "You know a thing or two about these situations."

"I was in the War," said Fleming at his most blighting.

"Sorry," said Hotchkiss with what seemed genuine contrition. "I should have guessed."

Fleming took a step back. "I want you to sit down, on the floor. Do it now."

With a sigh, Hotchkiss did as he was ordered. "You aren't helping yourself, Fleming."

"If you are who you say you are, you may be right. But given your method of introduction, you'll have to make allowances for what I'm doing." He took a deep breath. "Use your left hand. Take out your identification with your thumb and forefinger. Toss it onto the bed."

"So you don't have to bend over." Hotchkiss did as he was ordered. "I can give you a contact number to call, if you like."

"That can be arranged," said Fleming. "Besides, I doubt the switchboard is open at this hour."

"You got a point," said Hotchkiss as he watched Fleming flip the wallet open and scrutinize his ID and badge.

"So, Special Agent Lemmuel Hotchkiss," said Fleming,

holding out the identification. "I thought you chaps only wore charcoal-grey suits?"

"I'm supposed to fit in out here," said Hotchkiss. "If I wore the uniform, I might as well stamp FBI on my forehead and be done with it. Not that Hoover doesn't prefer the conservative suit-and-tie look. He insists that away from this assignment, I toe the line like everyone else."

"Nothing remarkable in knowing that," said Fleming, gesturing to Hotchkiss. "You might as well get up. This is pretty convincing; if it is false, it is a most convincing forgery."

"You gonna put that gun away?" Hotchkiss asked, not yet moving.

"Not quite yet, I think," said Fleming. "I still don't know why you came into my room."

Hotchkiss sighed. "Look, Fleming, we got a whole raft of expensive missiles over at Walker, and some pretty valuable planes. When foreigners show up, the brass gets antsy, and you can't blame them, considering." He got to his feet slowly. "They wanted me to check you out."

"You chose an odd way to do it," said Fleming.

"Hey, look," Hotchkiss protested, brushing off his palms on his slacks. "I was told to do it this way." He cocked his head. "If you have something to hide, would you tell me about it if I asked?"

"No," Fleming allowed, thinking of the authorization to use lethal force in his wallet. Hotchkiss would find that highly suspicious, he knew, and with good cause.

"That's what I mean," said Hotchkiss. "So I'll tell you something that might make you ease up a bit."

"What's that?" Fleming asked, unconvinced.

Hotchkiss grinned. "I'm left-handed."

Chapter 17

"I was on assignment here when I got a call from Bert. He's the owner of this hotel, does all kinds of work around the place." Hotchkiss was relaxing now, becoming suspiciously loquacious; Fleming listened to him, curious to know why this FBI agent would be so willing to confide in him. "He said he had checked in an Englishman to room 14C, claiming to be a journalist—"

"I *am* a journalist," said Fleming. "I have papers to prove it. My editor gave me a *To Whom It May Concern* before I came to the States." He was standing, his back against the chest-of-drawers, watching Hotchkiss, who was sitting on the end of the bed. He had lit a cigarette and was smoking it desultorily; he hadn't bothered to offer one to Hotchkiss.

"—and he thought I should check you out. A call to Washington confirmed that you had entered the U.S. at New Orleans, so I came along to make sure you were what you said you were." Hotchkiss studied Fleming. "I don't know what to do now."

"You might let your bosses know that I'm no danger to them," Fleming suggested.

"I don't know if they'd believe me," said Hotchkiss. "They're certain that any foreigner coming to this part of the country must be up to no good. This isn't high on the list of tourist places. Carlsbad maybe, for the caverns, but not Roswell." He looked down at his hands. "Sorry. That's the way it is."

"You don't have anything to be sorry for," said Fleming, slipping his revolver back into his waist-band holster. "But keep in mind, I'm not a tourist."

Hotchkiss caught his lower lip in his teeth. "Fleming," he said at last, "I know I haven't the right to ask, but what brought you here? Something about the POW camps? The Germans are really interested in those."

"No, nothing like that. My editor assigned a case to me, having to do with the English who were in America during the War," said Fleming readily, and plausibly enough. "I suppose he thought the work I'd done with Americans during the War made the job easier for me than for many others."

"What kind of work did you do?" Hotchkiss asked. "We'll have it in our files, but you might as well save us the effort."

"The boring-but-necessary kind," said Fleming, who knew what was in his cover material, and that no matter what Hotchkiss said, it would be checked out. "I coordinated reports and intelligence from the various Allied forces, preparing briefs for our various commanders, so that there would be less confusion—if that's possible in a war."

"Did you see any action?" Hotchkiss asked.

"In the beginning I did. Then I was given this other work to do. And, of course, there was the Blitz." Fleming took a deep breath. He stubbed out the cigarette on the saucer on the night-stand.

"Of course," said Hotchkiss, faintly embarrassed. "I gotta ask, you know that."

"Yes, I know," said Fleming, thinking about his mendacious military records, the ones Sir William did not have with him, and he was relieved he had left them back at his house in Jamaica, secure in his safe. It was not the kind of information

Fleming wanted floating about in the intelligence community. He glanced toward the window. "What time is it? It's late, that much is obvious. My watch stopped some time ago. I forgot to wind it."

"It's two thirty-eight," said Hotchkiss, checking his own watch. "What difference does it make?"

"I want to know how much sleep I can get before I have to be on the road again," said Fleming. "Not that I don't find your presence intriguing, Hotchkiss, but I have work to do, and a long way to go before I do it."

"Why here?" There was just enough suspicion to put Fleming on guard.

"I'm going to Albuquerque, and I took what I thought was a shorter route from Dallas." He smiled with what passed for self-deprecating amusement. "Your distances are a trifle daunting, you know."

Hotchkiss laughed. "Yeah. And England didn't turn out to be as big as I thought it would be. I spent a couple months there in 'forty-six."

Fleming decided to ignore that conversational gambit. "So in the name of expeditious travel, I ended up here instead of—"He paused, trying to think of the names he had seen on the map.

"Tucumcari or Santa Rosa, if you'd taken 66," said Hotchkiss.

"Yes, although I wouldn't have pronounced Tucumcari as you do," Fleming told Hotchkiss with a slight chuckle.

Hotchkiss stood up. "Sorry about the skulking, Fleming. I didn't mean to—" He stopped. "Oh, hell. Yes, I did mean to spy on you. That's what I'm expected to do. I'm sorry it didn't have to happen this time."

"Have you had many foreigners to investigate here? I wouldn't have thought so," said Fleming.

Realizing he might have said too much, Hotchkiss demurred. "No, no. Occasionally there's foreign officers at Walker—I have to keep an eye on them—you know the kind of thing, from your War work—and twice we had Germans in town, one trying to find out about the POW camps, the other one coming back, after having been in a camp. He liked the desert so much, he decided to move here, and start over. He bought a place just outside Truth or Consequences—that's a town, by the way—and set up a spa there." He held out his hand. "Well. Glad to have met you, Fleming."

"You, too, Hotchkiss," said Fleming, taking the Special Agent's hand. "I hope you'll tell your comrades that I'm not dangerous."

"Oh, I wouldn't go that far," said Hotchkiss. "But I will tell them you're on our side." He hesitated. "If anything more happens, you give me a call. Just have the operator get you Bert: he'll know how to find me. I'll get back to you as fast as I can."

"Much appreciated," said Fleming, hoping that he would not end up in such a predicament as Hotchkiss imagined, and went to let the FBI agent out of his room.

"Don't blame Bert for calling me. He was only doing what he's been told to do," Hotchkiss said as he slipped out of the room.

"I'll keep that in mind," said Fleming. "Perhaps I should tell you that I'm going to place a call to Jamaica in the morning, to my editor's secretary, a Miss Louisa Butterly. Just so you're aware of it."

"Your editor's secretary is in Jamaica?" Hotchkiss was instantly suspicious.

"So is my editor, Merlin Powell. I have a house there where I take holidays, and when I do, my paper puts me under Mister Powell's supervision." He smiled. "My permanent home is in London."

"So you came in from Kingston," said Hotchkiss, his eyes narrowing.

"Yes. I might have done so, arriving from London. There is a flight that goes to Kingston en route to New Orleans," he pointed out. "That wasn't the flight I took, but I might have." He did his best genial expression. "Just thought I should mention this."

"You're right," said Hotchkiss, his manner reverting to cordial. "Merlin Powell, you say?"

"Yes. His secretary is Louisa Butterly. I can provide the number, if you—"

"No," said Hotchkiss, eager now to be gone. "I'll tell Bert to put you through."

"Thanks awfully," said Fleming, eager to go back to bed and hoping he would be able to fall asleep quickly. He had had the knack in the War but was a bit out of practice.

"Have a good trip, Mister Fleming," Hotchkiss said by way of farewell.

"I'll do my poor best," said Fleming, and closed the door. He remained where he was until he heard Hotchkiss's steps retreat down the corridor, and then he went back to bed, trying to will himself to sleep. He thought it would be impossible, but as he put his revolver back in its holster, he yawned hugely. His shoulders were stiff and he had the beginning of a head-

ache. As he lay back on the bed he strove to put the events
of the last half hour from his mind. Just when he decided it
couldn't be done, he lapsed into slumber.

The alarm jangled him awake at seven forty-five. He looked
about him, taking stock of the room, disoriented, then he sat
up, everything of the last three days coming back to him, finally bringing him fully awake in room 14C of the Pecos Vista
Hotel, of Roswell, New Mexico. He sighed. Rising, he made
his way to the bathroom and turned on the shower, then got
in, starting with the water hot, then steadily turning it down
to chilly, so that by the time he emerged, ten minutes later,
he was fully alert. He shaved and toweled himself dry, then
went out into the bedroom to dress.

Knowing it would be warm again today, he chose cotton twill
trousers of pebble-grey, a light-weight white cotton shirt, and
a navy-blue linen jacket. He wouldn't exactly blend in, but he
wouldn't be too out of place, either. Taking care to lock his
luggage, he then carried his bags down to the lobby, where he
found Bert behind the reservation desk, aside from a different
shirt looking precisely the same as he had the evening before.

"Morning there, young fella," he greeted Fleming. "Hope
you had a good night."

"Good morning to you," Fleming said as he reached the
desk, saying nothing to the second part of his question. "I need
to arrange to make an overseas call. How shall I do it?"

"You can use the desk phone; just make sure Marta keeps
track of the time so I can add it to your bill," said Bert pleas-
antly as he shoved the telephone toward Fleming. "Just tell
Marta what you want when you pick up the receiver."

"All right," said Fleming, aware that he would not have any
privacy for the call: what Bert could not overhear, Marta could,

and he was certain that Special Agent Lemmuel Hotchkiss would have a complete report within ten minutes of his placing it.

Marta assured him that she would keep track of charges for him, and then put him through to the overseas operator, who took four minutes to put him through to Powell's office.

"Fleming, where the bloody hell are you? And you better have a bloody good reason for not keeping me informed," Powell exclaimed as soon as Miss Butterly had apologized for cutting him off yesterday, and put him through.

"I am where you sent me. In New Mexico. That's between Texas and Arizona," he added helpfully.

"Don't be cheeky," Powell warned. "Tell me how it's coming?"

"I haven't reached Albuquerque yet. I should be there this afternoon." He paused. "Any news from your end?"

"You mean Krandall? No, nothing worth mentioning. The authorities are still being chary with comments." Powell was being as careful as Fleming.

"Is there anything more I should know about before I leave here?" Fleming asked.

"Just where is here? Beyond being in New Mexico?" Powell asked, so solicitously that Fleming knew his editor was running out of patience.

"Roswell. It's a little town with an air-base," Fleming replied.

"Cowboys and Indians?" Powell asked indulgently.

"With the occasional military-types," Fleming confirmed.

Powell chuckled, his good humor apparently restored. "Call me this evening, if you would. Carry on."

"You, too," said Fleming, and rang off. A moment later the

telephone rang and Marta announced that the charge would be eight dollars and forty cents, which Fleming duly reported to Bert.

"Okay," Bert said. "Make it ten, and that'll cover your breakfast, too. Steak and eggs, if you like."

"Sounds substantial," said Fleming, handing him a ten-dollar bill, then went off to lock his bags in the trunk of the Packard before he headed for the café for a real meal. He looked about for a proper newspaper but found only three-day-old copies of the Chicago *Sun*, which was hardly to his liking. He didn't linger over breakfast and was on the road at nine-fifteen, the Packard humming along the narrow road that led north-north-west. There wasn't a lot of traffic out, and Fleming was able to keep up a good pace as the morning advanced.

Chapter 18

ON A lonely stretch between the Highway 20 fork toward Fort Sumner and East Vaughn, Fleming became aware of a drone of airplane engines near-by. Nothing too imposing, not a military airplane, he felt, but loud enough to command his attention. A twin-engine sound, and traveling at perhaps as much as two hundred miles per hour, he guessed, since the airplane wasn't directly overhead, allowing him to do a more accurate assessment. He looked about to find the shadow of the airplane, trying to guess where it might be going, but he couldn't make it out in the dry scrub that covered the rising slopes. Never mind, he told himself. It'll pass soon enough.

The sound of the airplane faded, and Fleming continued his drive. In the distance he made out a herd of pronghorn antelopes and, somewhat farther on, a pair of men on horseback. When they waved in his direction, he waved back, continuing on, carried on a surge of good-will. He drove up over a rise and felt the Packard jerk in his hands, and the steering suddenly became stiff and difficult. He pulled to the side of the road, remembering that the 66 Commercial Travelers' Car Rental had said that the Packard had self-sealing tires—surely he couldn't have a flat, not out here.

Leaving the engine on idle, Fleming climbed out of the coupe and had a look at the tires. He discovered that the fender on the left front was bent, a deep pucker in it, the chrome chipped. Bending over, he inspected the damage and could not

shake the conviction that it had been done by a bullet, something heavy, intended to inflict impairment, or worse.

Fleming stared at the dent, wondering what he would tell
the rental company. It was one thing to have a fender dent
because of careless driving, but quite another to have one because he was shot at. He tested the bumper, trying to determine if the impact had loosened it; luckily, the bumper felt
sturdy enough, if misaligned. He could continue on without
mishap. Getting back into the auto, he looked about uneasily,
the remote beauty of this place suddenly ominous, the fine
out-croppings of stone now sinister. He put the Packard in gear
and resumed his travels, keeping his speed down to around
sixty, anticipating other, unpleasant possibilities up ahead. At
least, he told himself, the tires are all right. He did not have
to worry about having to change one out here in the middle
of nowhere, an expression that now had a reality to it that
Fleming had not comprehended before.

Pulling into East Vaughn, Fleming chose the first service
station with an open bay and asked the attendant to have a
look at the damage to the bumper. "And make sure the tires
haven't lost any air pressure, if you would."

The mechanic on duty grinned. "Goodyears. You're lucky.
Those self-sealers are a real godsend out here. Okay. Come
back in a couple of hours, I should have everything checked
out." He patted the bonnet of the Packard. "Good car, this
one, and gets pretty good mileage."

"If you could do it sooner—" Fleming began, not wanting
to waste time discussing the virtues of the auto.

"I could, but it would be a half-assed job, and you wouldn't
like that, now would you? If you got something to do in town,

you might as well do it now. If you don't, then take it easy for a bit." He smiled ferociously. "Try Rosaria's Cantina, just down the street on the right-hand side, next to the stationers. The food's good and they've got great Mexican beer."

Fleming bowed to the inevitable. "I realize you're not a Texaco station I'm supposed to patronize, and I imagine you don't give discounts to this rental agency, so I'd appreciate it if you'd keep the price within reasonable limits."

"Tell you what: if I go over, say, eighty bucks, I'll send someone down to Rosaria's to tell you, and you can make up your mind about what you want to do about it."

"That's satisfactory," said Fleming, wishing he had brought something to read. He had a suspicion that the local paper wouldn't hold his interest, but he doubted there was much of anything else he could find on short notice. He ambled out into the mid-day sun and squinted at the street in front of him. His eyes stung, even with his dark glasses to mitigate the light. He started down the street toward Rosaria's, hoping his luggage would be safe in the boot of the Packard. He decided it was best not to make a fuss about them, and figured that there was no reason for the mechanic to look inside them. He reminded himself that the most important files were in the concealed compartment on the bottom of the larger bag, all but invisible to moderate inspection. His authorization to use lethal force was still in his wallet, right above his heart, and concealed in the pocket in the lining where it could not easily be found.

ROSARIA'S CANTINA WAS a stucco building painted a fulvous pink with hand-lettered signs in Spanish and English saying the place served good food, was open every day until 10 P.M., and had air-conditioning. This last made it more irresistible than the other advantages combined. Fleming crossed the street and made for the screen door, pulling it open on wailing hinges. He blinked and removed his dark glasses, trying to adjust to the darkish interior of the cantina.

To one side of the cantina was a small, bright room with ten stools pulled up to a counter. Just now a rope barred the way with a sign hanging from it reading THIS SECTION CLOSED. To the other side was a cavernous room, shuttered against the daylight. A dozen of the twenty-four tables were occupied, mostly by big men in dusty work-clothes—clearly locals. Two tables had families, men and women with children, and one had three women with the closed faces of women alone.

Fleming hesitated, wondering where he should sit, and while he did, a handsome woman, about thirty, fine-figured, dark-haired and dark-eyed, came up to him. "Take a seat, stranger," she said in an accent Fleming assumed was Mexican Spanish on top of American English.

"What about something where I can keep an eye on the door? The mechanic may need to talk to me," said Fleming.

"Jed? Sure. Okay," she said, thrusting a menu at him and waving her hand in the direction of the center of the dining room.

Fleming selected one of the tables, ignoring the stares he attracted. He sat down and read the menu as if it were a masterpiece of literature. When he set his menu aside, the attractive woman bustled up to him, rubbing her hands on her apron and pulling an order pad from her pocket.

"What can I get for you?" she asked.

"Pork and chicken enchiladas—did I say that right?" He did

his very best affable expression. "And an order of poached eggs on tortillas."

"We say *tor-TEE-yas*," the woman corrected him.

He repeated the word. "Thanks. And coffee, if you would."

"Coming right up." She hurried back toward the kitchen, calling out, "Hey, Rosaria!" followed by a rapid burst of Spanish that Fleming assumed was his order. Then she came back with a mug of coffee. "Cream and sugar?"

"Milk, if you would," said Fleming. He pulled another cigarette from the Players pack and lit it with a match from the packet set out on the table.

"It's half-and-half," she said, putting a little jug on the table. "Should take about ten minutes. Hope that's okay." Then she was gone to wait on another table.

As she went away, Fleming heard the drone of airplane engines over the town, and thought back to the airplane earlier that day. There had to be all manner of airplanes in this part of America, he told himself, many of them with two engines, but could not shake the sensation that he was being pursued, a notion he insisted to himself was absurd.

Fleming was half-way through his meal when the mechanic came through the door. He spotted Fleming and came over to him. "Rosaria's taking good care of you?"

"The food is excellent," said Fleming in mild surprise. "Thanks for recommending this place." He took a last drag on the cigarette and put it out in the ashtray.

"Only café in town worth eating at," said the mechanic, and put his elbows on the table. "The thing of it is, I can get my hands on a new bumper for you, from the salvage yard in Vaughn. They can have it here forty minutes, and I can put it on in an hour or two. But it's a rental car, and I shouldn't do

anything without the company's permission. You'll have to pay
them for the damage when you return the car unless you can
get authorization to let me do the work."

"I know," said Fleming. "But they'll charge me a deal more
than you will if I bring it back with that dent." He motioned
to the waitress. "Bring some coffee for—" He gestured to the
mechanic.

"Hi, Jed," said the waitress, a mug in hand already.

"Hi yourself, Inez." He winked at her. "Your aunt keeping
you busy?"

"I don't mind," said Inez, and put down the mug in front
of him before going to take another order from a newly filled
table.

"Hard-working girl," said Jed approvingly. "Don't let no-
body tell you Mexicans are lazy. Rosaria and Inez are the bus-
iest people in the town." He tasted his coffee and made a face.
"Too hot."

"About the Packard," Fleming prompted.

"Oh. Yeah. I know what you mean about the company. So
if you want me to fix it, unofficial-like, I will. I'll charge you
a little extra for losing the paperwork, but I think it should be
okay for you. I can make a receipt for you if you have to account for the money to someone, but it won't be for replacing
the bumper. It'll run about a hundred, hundred ten bucks."

"That's reasonable," said Fleming, hoping it was. Although
he knew this plan was of questionable legality, Fleming said,
"If you don't mind doing it that way, I don't mind."

"Okay, then." He drank half the contents of his mug. "Bullet damage is hard to account for, isn't it?"

"If that's what it is," said Fleming carefully.

"Oh, it sure is, all right," said Jed. "Probably some Apache kid out there trying to bag a pronghorn for himself. Crazy Indians. Always shooting as if the bullets never went anywhere except where they aimed." He finished the coffee and got up from the table. "I'll get to work. You figure another couple of hours and you'll be under way again."

"Very good." He watched Jed go, and went back to his meal.

Finishing his meal, he left a seventy-five-cent tip on a three-twenty meal for Inez, then went next door to the stationers, where he bought four newspapers—one from Albuquerque, one from El Paso, one from Phoenix, and one from Denver—intending to fill his waiting hours with gleaning as much information as he could about the general region. He found the town oddly devoid of places to sit, so he wandered back to the service station and asked Jed if he might have a chair he could occupy while the bumper was being changed.

"Sure thing. There's an old glider around back, in front of my house. You can have a nap on it, if you like. Make yourself comfortable." Jed noticed the armload of newspapers Fleming carried and he blew out a whistle. "That's a lot of reading, ain't it?"

"I thought I'd find out about this part of the world. I'm new here," he replied. "It'll make my story better."

"That you are—new here," said Jed, and went back into the bay of his service station.

Fleming walked down the path to the rear of the building and saw a small clapboard house behind it, an old-fashioned porch facing to the south-east, so that the worst of the afternoon sun couldn't touch it. The glider had yellow cushions on it and creaked only a little when Fleming sat down. The slight motion took a little getting used to, but in a short while Fleming was comfortably settled, reading the papers he had brought with him.

On the third page of the Albuquerque paper he found an article that caught his attention: *Former Los Alamos Physicists Held on Spying Charges*. Fleming looked closely at what followed. *James Hendley continues in custody while the evidence against him mounts. His trial is set to begin in three weeks. Hendley and his British colleague, Theodore Robertson, were arrested on charges of selling atomic secrets to the Russians. Robertson is being held in England, on charges of espionage, and the search continues both here and in England for other associates of Hendley and Robertson who may also have been involved in this treasonous activity. Both Hendley and Robertson worked at Los Alamos on the Manhattan Project . . .* There followed a summary of the nature of the work they had done—at least as much as the public could know. *Prosecutors indicate that the charges may be extended to include the sale of nuclear secrets to powers other than the Soviet Union. The FBI and CIG have not confirmed or denied this most recent allegation, but they have said that the search for other conspirators has been on-going for the last year.*

Fleming nodded, remembering the furor around Robertson's arrest. And, he reminded himself, Krandall was supposed to have been at Los Alamos during the War. Was there any connection to Robertson, or Hendley? What about these so-called associates mentioned in the article? Could Krandall be one of those? He stared up into the vast expanse of blue, wondering distantly if he was as informed as he needed to be. He decided to find out more about Robertson and Hendley, and their relationship—if any—to Krandall. He folded the paper, intending to take it with him, and was about to open the Phoenix

Sun when he saw Jed coming toward him, something cupped in his hands.

"Hey, Mister Fleming," he called as he approached. "You got anyone out there tailing you?"

"I don't know," said Fleming, deliberately hiding his concern behind a friendly smile. "People do follow journalists, from time to time. Why?"

"Well," said Jed, opening his hands to reveal a metal box about the size of a cuff link box, with a spray of wires coming out one end of it. "I found this hooked up to the underside of your car. Either the rental company keeps close track of their cars, or someone's trying to keep tabs on you. They can track this thing for a couple of miles away, car or plane, and you'd never even know they're there. I seen a lot of these things in the War—Signal Corps—and I didn't like 'em then, when they made sense. But this? It's a crappy thing to do." He waited a moment. "What do you want me to do with this? I hate these bastards!"

Fleming could not tell if Jed meant the electronic box or the men who used them. "I don't know what to say," he told Jed.

"I don't blame you." Jed scowled. "Tell you what. You came in here for bumper trouble, didn't you? Well, who's to say this didn't fall off? You can't think of some way this could have got dislodged, can you? Come on. A lot of things get knocked off cars. Your bumper got damaged, didn't it, so it figures something like this could be dislodged. I can send it with the old bumper to the salvage yard." He grinned at his own plan.

"That could work," Fleming allowed.

"Of course it could," said Jed. "If anyone asks—not that I think they'd have the balls to, mind you—I can say it wasn't part of the standard equipment, so I didn't bother to reinstall it."

"Do you think you'll have to do that?" Fleming didn't want to cause Jed any trouble—he was already bending the rules.

"No. I think it'll only throw off the schnooks following you. If it's anyone other than the car rental company. It seems a bit over-kill for a car rental place to do this, so I'll figure it's more than that, and deal with it accordingly." Jed gave a kind of salute. "Just you wait and see. I'll handle everything. I'll have them running around in circles."

"Why would you do that?" Fleming asked, not wanting to be too much in this man's debt.

"Because I don't like snoops," said Jed bluntly. "The whole country's looking over its shoulder, and everything is monitored. You think none of the bastards in Washington never read the Constitution, they way they're carrying on, accusing people of doing things they got a perfect right to do. They're getting as crazy as the Communists they're supposed to be getting rid of, using innuendo and suspicion instead of evidence to convict the guys they don't like. That's not what America's supposed to be all about, and I'm not going to help it be that way."

Listening to this, Fleming felt a moment of humility followed almost at once by his conviction that Americans could be endearingly naive. "Okay," he said, deliberately using that most American expression. "I hope it won't get you into trouble."

"Who cares if it does?" Jed responded, a martial light in his eyes. "Let 'em try to make something of it." With that, he turned, pocketed the electronic device, and strode off in the direction of his service station as if to defend it like a castle.

Chapter 19

FLEMING PULLED into Santa Fe shortly before five that afternoon. He was feeling a bit sleepy and light-headed, responses he attributed to the altitude, for he was more than a mile high. He took stock of the main plaza, reminding himself that this sleepy hill town was a state capital. He was hoping to find a hotel, and after a brief reconnaissance, noticed a sign down a side-street that declared itself in two languages to be the best hotel in New Mexico. He wandered down to it, inquired about a room, and asked where he could park his car.

"Anywhere, señor, anywhere," said the clerk.

Not at all satisfied with the answer, Fleming went to fetch his bags, promising himself to read Sir William's files again, seeing what information they might contain on Robertson and Krandall that could throw light on this case. He ate in his room and kept the files secreted in their hiding place except when he actually read them. Bracing a chair under the doorknob, he slept soundly that night and was awake again at six-thirty, ready to complete his travel to Los Alamos as soon as he notified Merlin Powell of his whereabouts.

"Still in New Mexico?" the editor blustered when Fleming was finally connected to him.

"I had some trouble with the auto yesterday, and it delayed me," said Fleming, deliberately vague in his description.

"That's unfortunate," said Powell. "Well, you can't help that, I'd guess."

"Very likely not; the distances here are a force to be reckoned with, and that contributed to my delay," Fleming agreed, certain their conversation was not private. He tried to sit on the small wedge of a stool in the booth and discovered it was too small and too low for him, so he leaned against the corner. "I'll probably fly out of Albuquerque tomorrow, assuming there is a suitable schedule. I'll let you know more as soon as I've made arrangements."

"See that you do." Powell was sounding annoyed. "About the story."

"I don't know if I can establish the link between Robertson and Krandall after all," he said, and hoped that Powell wouldn't say anything too compromising. "I haven't turned up what we'd thought might be there."

"Oh?" Powell responded.

"Yes. I haven't come upon a connection so far. I don't know that there is one, beyond the fact that they worked in Los Alamos during the War. That may be the whole of it. I suppose I might do a sidebar on the troubles with War-time security." He coughed slightly. "You might want to tell Broxton that his information was faulty."

Powell hardly missed a beat. "I'll do that."

"It may be that the connection we're looking for happened through the POW camp here in New Mexico. That seems a long shot, but I could check it out if you like." Fleming hoped that whomever was listening would jump to a number of wrong conclusions.

"Hardly seems worth it, unless you find hard information."

"Do you want me to dig?" Fleming asked. "It would mean having to stay on a day or more."

"If you don't turn up anything promising, no." He paused. "Well?"

"I'll make a cursory check. So long as I'm here, I might as well take the time to make sure we're on the wrong track, as on the right one. Don't you think?"

"So long as you're there," Powell echoed. "Shall I call Broxton, or do you want to do that yourself."

"I have an appointment with him—tomorrow, I think. If you'll arrange for it to be moved to a later hour, I'll make my report to him, and then give a full account to you." Fleming did his best to sound bored. "All this excitement over Robertson has really got out of hand, don't you think?"

"People are scared, Fleming," said Powell. "You can't blame them, when something like the atom bomb is at stake."

"True," said Fleming. "But in this case, I very much doubt there's anything to find." He paused again. "Still, just in case—"

"Miss Butterly will call Lord Broxton for you," Powell offered. "Is there anything else?"

"Yes. If you would, send someone 'round to Henry Long, to find out what he knows about Krandall's killers." He heard Powell choke back an expletive. "That should cover it. I'll let you know when I'm arriving." He was ready to hang up when Powell managed one more question.

"Anything new about Robert Swathmore?" This name was a code indicating that there were complications and potential trouble; in this case, it was a warning from Powell.

"Could be. I'll be on the look-out, if you like," Fleming answered, keeping his tone of mild imposition.

"If you would," said Powell with a nonchalance that implied volumes. "Well, ta," and rang off.

Fleming left the phone booth and headed for his Packard, his bags in his hands. When he reached the auto, he saw something under the windscreen-wiper blade, and he muttered at having got a ticket. After stowing his luggage in the boot, he plucked the folded sheet from the windscreen and was about to roll it into a ball when he noticed a note written on it: LET WELL ENOUGH ALONE.

For a good two minutes, he stared at the words, his thoughts shocked to immobility. The same words as he had seen in Kingston, and in the same hand. How on earth had they come to be on an automobile in New Mexico, unless it was also intended as a warning that he was under surveillance? But who would be watching him, and why? Belatedly he looked about the street, trying to determine who had left it there. No one caught his eye, and he was left to climb into the Packard and resume his travels to Los Alamos, accompanied by the nerve-wracking conviction that his every move was being observed by unfriendly eyes.

The turn to Los Alamos led off into the hills, a road framed by piñon trees and red rocks. He finally approached a gate with a guard-booth under the sign incongruously identifying this as the University of California Los Alamos Laboratory. A polite U.S. Army corporal came out of the booth to inspect Fleming's identification, then got on the telephone. After a brief discussion, the corporal said to Fleming, "Take the first right and pull into the second lot on your left."

"All right." He held out his hand for his passport and letter from Powell.

"I'll hold these, sir, until you leave," said the corporal, deferentially but with firm purpose. "You have your press credentials. That's all you'll need."

"If that's the way of it." Fleming quelled the apprehension rising in his gut. "Right, second lot on the left?"

"That's it, sir. Take any place marked PRESS."

"Thanks," said Fleming, and put the Packard in gear as the bar rose to admit him. He made his way down the dusty road between buildings that looked like an army base rather than a research installation. He made the turn and found the car park easily enough. He pulled in beside an Oldsmobile and a Jeep, noticing that the Jeep was in a military space, the Oldsmobile in a press slot. He made sure the Packard was fully locked, then headed for the clapboard building with PRESS over the entrance. He was keenly aware that this building was away from the main part of the facility, isolated by its location as much as by its purpose. As he trod up the stairs, he heard laughter from the other side of the door.

A private sat at a desk facing the door, and beside him stood a hale, stout man, about fifty, perhaps five foot three or four, with friendly, rough features, a pleasing manner, and a splendid voice—at least six foot two and rangy as John Wayne—heard on radios all over Europe and the Pacific, the very spoken soul of all that was American. Fleming didn't need anyone to tell him that this was Dennis Goodbrother, whose reports had followed the action from 1944 to the aftermath of Hiroshima and Nagasaki.

"Excuse me," said Fleming, interrupting the shared chuckles of the two men. "The guard at the gate told me that I should come here." He stepped up to the desk, pulling out his credentials. "My name's Fleming."

The private took the proffered documents. "English. The gate just called about you."

"Yes. The guard at the gate has my passport and other—" Fleming began.

"They like to hang onto paper," said Goodbrother, holding out his hand to Fleming. "Dennis Goodbrother. Pleased to meet you."

"And I to meet you," said Fleming, liking the hearty handshake. "I know your work, of course."

The private handed back the identification. "What can I do for you, Mister Fleming?"

A bit nonplussed, Fleming answered, "I'm here looking for information on Theodore Robertson"—he saw the private wince—"and Geoffrey Krandall, who worked here during the War. Krandall did something with encryption and code-breaking, as I understand it."

"Is this about Robertson?" Goodbrother asked.

"Not precisely, no," said Fleming. "We're looking for a connection—if there is one. Krandall was murdered and there appears to be some question as to why it happened."

"Krandall," said the private as he thumbed through a large binder. "That's with a C or a K?"

"K," Fleming answered. "And Geoffrey spelled the English way—G-E-O, not J-E-F."

"Thanks," said the private sincerely.

"My pleasure," said Fleming, determined to be polite. He glanced at Goodbrother.

"I'm afraid this could take some time," said the private as he thumbed through the pages in the binder.

"I'm prepared to wait," said Fleming and, out of habit, turned to Goodbrother and asked, "What brings you to Los Alamos. It seems an unusual place for you, if you'll forgive me for saying it."

"Oh, I agree." He chuckled, a rich, plummy sound that made Goodbrother sound like the perfect confidant. "I'm doing a program about the work they do here, trying to reassure our fighting men that we know how to control The Bomb. After all, we invented it. You know how that reassures the public."

"Best of luck," said Fleming, his sarcasm not sufficient to offend the other two men.

"Exactly," said Goodbrother, reaching out and snagging Fleming's elbow. "The private's right: this could take some time. Why not come into the hospitality room? There's coffee and doughnuts, and booze, if you're not adverse to a nip in the morning." He indicated a door about ten feet away. "Benton, we'll be in there when you have a report for Mister Fleming."

"Thanks," said Fleming, at once flattered and wary.

The hospitality room was a large, draughty hall, kept a bit cool by open windows on the east wall. There were a number of couches covered in worn Naugahyde, and a collection of chairs, most of them wooden with wheels under them, but a few in ancient upholstery. At the far end was an array of tables with food set out on them, along with two coffee urns, smelling just now of fairly fresh-made American blend, and an oaken bar. No one was in sight.

Chapter 20

GOODBROTHER STEPPED up to the bar with the ease of one long accustomed to military installations. "What's your pleasure, Fleming? I'm having a wee bit of Scotch. We've got Bourbon, Gin, Brandy, in fact everything but Vodka." He chuckled again. "Can't have suspect drinks about at a secured research lab, now can we?" He reached for a glass and poured out two fingers of a single malt whiskey. "Join me."

Fleming hesitated only a moment. "Very well. I'll have what you're having, only one finger, not two."

"As you like," said Goodbrother with a shrug, and poured a drink for Fleming.

"Thanks," he said as Goodbrother handed him his Scotch. "Chin-chin."

"Bottoms up," Goodbrother agreed, and drank. "How'd you get here?"

"How do you mean?" Fleming asked.

"Did you come in from Albuquerque? And how did you get there? It's not the sort of place you wander into by accident, I wouldn't have thought." He favored Fleming with a pleasant smile as he took out a Camel and lit up with a gold lighter. "I'm always curious how newspeople get around."

"Much the same way you do, I suspect," said Fleming. "I flew to New Orleans, then to Texas and drove the rest of the way." He deliberately kept some of the details to himself.

"Quite a drive," said Goodbrother.

"That it was. I don't look forward to making it again." He took another sip of Scotch and thought it might be prudent to eat something. He ambled over to the tables where the food was, picked up a salad-sized plate, and proceeded to select three sweet rolls and a cake doughnut.

Goodbrother followed along, selecting crullers and cheese puffs. "Quite a combination."

"Scotch and pastry?" Fleming nodded. "But eggs and sausage wouldn't be any stranger."

Goodbrother was beaming with amusement. "So how long do you figure to be here? The accommodations are a bit Spartan, but I've had worse."

"I'll be on my way as soon as I get the report on Krandall. I'll look for anything that might tie him to Robertson." Fleming chose a Victorian chair, and sat down, paying no attention to the lumpy seat. "This could be a wild goose chase, but it's the assignment, so—"

"I know the feeling," said Goodbrother, sinking onto the nearest sofa. "Tell me about Krandall."

"I don't know very much about him. He worked here during the War, doing something with codes and maths. Then he retired to Jamaica where he was found murdered." He knew Goodbrother could find this much out in a matter of an hour or so, and decided there was no reason not to provide the basic information. "There's so much worry about Robertson that it's an angle we have to check out." He smiled. "I got a twelve-hour head-start on the rest of the press."

"Sounds like your editor's a clever bastard," Goodbrother observed through a mouthful of cheese puff.

"That he is," said Fleming.

"Kind of a mixed blessing, I should think," said Goodbrother. "I mean, there's no telling what he might set you up for."

Fleming cringed at this typically American mangling of the language, but he answered, "At least a clever editor has a reason for what he asks—a foolish one simply makes demands."

"You got that right," said Goodbrother, and finished off his Scotch. "So is there a Missus Krandall?"

"No family in Jamaica, and none that we've traced so far," said Fleming, aware that he was being pumped for information. "It could be he lost family in the War; so many did."

"That's so," Goodbrother agreed solemnly as he dropped the Camel butt onto the floor and ground it with his heel. "And a phone call should get you answers about that, shouldn't it?"

"If the information isn't classified in some way, very likely." Fleming got up and went to draw a cup of coffee from the urn, adding sugar and a touch of what was surely cream and not the milk he preferred. He went back to his chair. "Not very busy around here, are they?"

"No, at least the press isn't. The scientists are working pretty much round the clock." Goodbrother sighed. "Just after the War, this place hummed like a dynamo. But in the last year or so, with the security clamp-down, there's been a lot less press." He yawned suddenly. "Sorry."

Fleming caught the yawn. "Hendley and Robertson, you mean." He took a Players from his diminishing supply and lit up without offering one to Goodbrother; he was beginning to run low.

"Yep, and a real scare about Communists," said Goodbrother, apparently unconcerned about the unintentional slight. "No one trusts the Russians, and the brass is making sure all the leaks are plugged. A little late, but isn't that always the way?"

"You're right," said Fleming. "Like it or not, we're stuck with the aftermath."

"Hard on the press," said Goodbrother, and had another cheese puff.

While he sipped his coffee, Fleming began to wonder about how he would get back to Jamaica from here. His plan to go through Albuquerque seemed risky, since anyone pursuing him was likely to wait for him there. But if not Albuquerque, where should he go? Denver was a possibility. He could return to Texas, but that made him uneasy. He wished he could consult his map, but that would be too obvious.

"Say, Fleming," Goodbrother cut into his thoughts, "d'you have time for any sight-seeing? Taos is pretty interesting. I bet you've never seen an Indian pueblo before."

"No, I haven't," said Fleming. "Except in films, of course."

"Not the same thing. Go up to Taos. Get a good look at the mountains. You'll see what I mean," Goodbrother assured him.

"It *is* an interesting notion," said Fleming, trying to figure out what Goodbrother was telling him.

"Well, don't say I didn't mention it, okay?" He went to the bar and refreshed his drink. "Want any more?"

"Not just at present, thanks," said Fleming, nibbling on the pastry he had selected. "This is very good."

"Better than the usual army grub," Goodbrother agreed. "They take good care of us."

"But so much," Fleming said. "With just the two of us to eat it."

"The brass ordered the spread, and that's what they put out

every morning, rain or shine, no one here or fifty."

"That seems a thought wasteful," said Fleming, thinking of the on-going shortages in England.

"If this is the worst the army does, we should be grateful," said Goodbrother. "I don't think this is gonna put a dent in the budget." He strolled about the room. "There's nothing much to do but sit around and wait for bulletins, or, if you get an interview, to go into one of the side-offices and try to get information."

"Is that what you've been doing?" Fleming asked, putting out his Players.

"Something like that, yeah," said Goodbrother. He glanced toward the door. "That Krandall guy you want to find out about—is there any reason they might want to stall you?"

"I don't know," said Fleming, alert now. "I suppose if there is a connection to Robertson, they might want to avoid embarrassment."

"That's a civilized word for it: embarrassment," said Goodbrother with a sour chuckle that not even his rich voice could disguise. "No one here wants any questions asked about anything."

"Who can blame them, considering," said Fleming, wanting to sound reasonable in case they were being overheard.

"I think it's pretty obvious that they'll do their best to keep things under wraps as long as they can."

"Are you saying I might not get anything out of this visit?" Fleming asked.

"I'm saying it wouldn't surprise me if you didn't," Goodbrother answered. He peered at his wristwatch. "I'm going to make a call, to see what's holding things up." He turned and headed for a corridor leading back into the building.

Fleming watched him go, and pondered their conversation, looking for clues in Goodbrother's remarks. He might have been less sanguine had he been able to listen to what Goodbrother had to say once his call was placed to a number in Baton Rouge.

"I tell you, he's here," Goodbrother insisted. "I've been talking to him." He listened to the blistering burst of French and English invectives, then said, "I don't care what you were told. He's here." He listened to another outburst. "Look. He got here. I don't know how, and I can't very well ask why his bug dropped off the map, can I?" He snapped his mouth closed as another outburst began. "I wouldn't be talking to him if he hadn't, would I?" This time he listened a little longer. "He's checking up on a guy named Krandall. Apparently he was murdered. He worked here during the War, and Fleming's supposed to get information on him." He listened. "He didn't mention any other connection." He listened again. "Yeah. Fleming's been assigned to get the goods on Krandall's work here: that's what he said." He listened to the man on the other end. "I don't know what he suspects. He hasn't said anything much about it. Why should he, if he's suspicious about—" Another pause, and he said, "He didn't say anything about being followed, or—" He shut his mouth. "And how am I supposed to do that without revealing more than I should know about him?" He frowned. "I tried to nudge him toward Taos, so we can get back on his track, but I don't think it'll do much good." He listened briefly. "I'll do what I can, but I'm warning you he might cotton onto what I'm up to. He *is* a reporter, remember, and no dummy." He listened. "All right, all right: I'll do what I can, but I don't know how much—" He stopped, stifling his indignation. "I said I'd do my best.

But I don't want to put him on his guard. You don't want me to do that, do you? I didn't think so." There was a longer silence. "Okay. I'll call back after he leaves."

He returned to the main room to find Fleming on his second cup of coffee. "How's it going?"

"Nothing yet," said Fleming.

"Par for the course," said Goodbrother. "I couldn't find out anything much. Sorry."

"As you say—par for the course." Fleming took his plate back to the table and set it down.

"Have you set up to get away from here?" Goodbrother smiled awkwardly.

"I drove in, I'll probably drive out," said Fleming lightly. He did his best not to show the discomfort he felt being asked this question.

"Well, of course," said Goodbrother.

Fleming studied the other man. "Do you mean there could be trouble getting a reservation?"

"That's a possibility," said Goodbrother. "And you may end up staying here late into the afternoon."

"Why? Because they don't want to give me the information I want?" Fleming kept his voice level while his thoughts whirled. What was going on here? He didn't like the turn of events but couldn't think how to change it. "Why don't they just say no and tell me to go away."

"Because they don't work that way," said Goodbrother.

"Trying to show me who's boss?" Fleming said, doing his best to do an American gangster's accent.

"That's part of it. They're also making sure their asses are covered." Goodbrother laughed aloud. "And this way, it looks like they're doing something more than passing the buck."

"According to President Truman, buck passing isn't acceptable," said Fleming.

"And if you asked for information from the President, he just might order it given to you, but you can bet your socks that the brass would take their sweet time getting around to giving it to you." Goodbrother stared at the far door as if he expected someone to arrive.

"Then you recommend I drop the matter?" Fleming asked.

"No, nothing like that," said Goodbrother. "Just be prepared for frustration and delay. These people are masters at dragging their feet. That's their way, so you'll be satisfied with as little information as they can get away with giving you."

"My, how cynical," said Fleming.

"Realistic," said Goodbrother.

"Well, you've dealt with them more than I. I'll take your word for it. Hendley and Robertson have already done their damage; withholding information now won't change that, will it," said Fleming, hating the notion of remaining in New Mexico for another night. He filled his coffee-cup a third time, using more cream than before. "Is there anything I might do around here while I wait?"

Goodbrother shrugged. "Most of Los Alamos is restricted to visitors, especially foreign visitors. If you leave and come back, you might have to wait twice as long."

"That's encouraging," Fleming said sarcastically.

"Hey, you asked. I'm just answering." He held up one hand as if to deflect Fleming's attack.

"Sorry," said Fleming, not wanting to alienate Goodbrother.

"No problem," said Goodbrother, who suddenly brightened. "I just remembered. There's a basic press book on Los Alamos, very complete and handsomely presented. It gives all kinds of background. And it's all unclassified." He rushed out of the room and came back with a large, slick magazine-like publication. "Here."

Fleming took the book he was handed: *Los Alamos: The Race for the Atomic Bomb* was blazoned across the photographic dust jacket showing a distant, brilliant mushroom cloud. The work was published by the University of California Press, and was privately distributed by Los Alamos Laboratories.

"It means the army hands out the copies," said Goodbrother, noticing what had held Fleming's attention.

"I'll have a look at it," said Fleming, nodding his thanks and sitting down once again in the aged Victorian chair, propping the oversized book on his crossed knees and beginning to read while Goodbrother poured himself another two fingers of Scotch.

Chapter 21

IT WAS almost three hours later, and Fleming was about halfway through the book, when the private came in from the front desk, a greenish file in his hands.

"Mister Fleming?"

Fleming closed the book and rose. "Yes?"

"This is as much as we can give you about Krandall. My commanding officer suggests that you ask your MI5 about Krandall. They should have more material than we do." He held out the file. "These are copies. You may take them with you."

Fleming flipped open the file and saw six sheets, obviously much-reduced, four standard American 8½ × 11s to the page, photostatic copies of reports on Geoffrey Krandall. "Is this all?" he asked, thumbing through them.

"It's all we can release," said the private in a tone that suggested he had said that many times before.

"I see," said Fleming. "Well, if that's the way of it—" He closed the file. "I suppose my editor will have to be content."

"Sorry, sir," said the private, and turned to leave.

"Is there anyone I could speak to about this? Can someone tell me anything about whose reports these are? I see the names are blacked out; is there someone who could tell me why?" Fleming called after him; he ignored Goodbrother's snort of laughter.

"Not at this time, sir. If you'll come back in two days, you can talk to the security director. Maybe he'll be able to give you a little more."

"Told you," Goodbrother muttered from where he reclined on a couch.

"No, never mind," said Fleming, waving the private away. "Yes, you did warn me. I have to admit, I hoped you were wrong."

Goodbrother offered a mirthless grin. "If you stick around, you might get a little more, but it probably won't be worth the hassle. The more you push, the less they give."

Fleming nodded. "I shall have to do my poor best with this." He tapped the file with his free hand.

"Oh, by the way," Goodbrother said, dropping his voice to a stage-whisper. "I'd lose that file-cover as soon as possible. Stash the pages somewhere safe and inconspicuous. You don't want the MPs busting in and saying you've taken official government files."

"I was given them," Fleming pointed out.

"Hell, that doesn't mean squat to a paranoid MP—and, by the way, around here, that *doesn't* mean Member of Parliament, it means Military Police," said Goodbrother. "You have to be careful with any kind of official material. Take my word for it. Carry those pages anywhere but in a Los Alamos file jacket."

"All right," said Fleming. "I'll keep that in mind." He started for the door. "Thanks for all your help, Goodbrother. It was a pleasure meeting you." This was very nearly sincere.

Goodbrother waved negligently from the couch. "Go file your story, Fleming. I hope you don't run into any trouble with it."

"So do I, Goodbrother," said Fleming, leaving the hall behind and passing the desk where the private sat. Just before he left the press building, he noticed a large-scale wall map hanging by the door. He paused to look at it, hoping to appear casual, but taking close stock of what he saw. "Amazing country, this," he remarked to the private.

"Yes, sir," said the private, no longer interested in Fleming. He went back to reading a magazine about automobiles.

Knowing now where he was going, Fleming went to the Packard and drove out of the Los Alamos Laboratory, stopping at the guard station to pick up his passport and other identification. "About how long does it take to get to Albuquerque from here?"

"Albuquerque? About two, three hours, depending," said the corporal.

"Thanks," said Fleming, and headed for Highway 84, going north toward Colorado instead of south toward Santa Fe. It was already later in the day than he had hoped, the long wait at Los Alamos had thrown him off his intended schedule, and as he stopped in Ojo Caliente for petrol, heeding the sign that read NEXT GAS 70 MILES he took stock of his situation, aware that he would have to be careful not to draw undue attention to himself, or risk having more auto trouble. Finding no Texaco station, he drove into a Hancock, and filled up on petrol, wishing he had a reserve tin, just in case: this was the part of America where someone—such as himself—could get lost, through misadventure or active malice; he didn't want to court either. He paid for his fuel, made sure the oil and water levels were adequate, the tires at the proper pressure, then headed off north, up narrow, twisty, impressive Highway 285, toward the Colorado border and Alamosa Municipal Airfield.

Between Ojo Caliente and Los Piños the land was empty,

the road a two-lane ribbon winding along a range of mountains rising spectacularly around him. Fleming drove with care, keeping watch of his surroundings. From time to time he would pass small villages, some of them what Americans called wide spots in the road. He saw distant ranch houses down dirt roads, and occasionally Indians making their way along the road, some on horseback but most on foot. Twice he heard the drone of airplane engines, and had to quell a sense of foreboding, remembering the tracking device that Jed had found. The isolation of this road made him feel momentary vulnerability, a response he did his best to put aside. The device had been removed, he told himself. Territory on the expansive scale as this needed to be crossed with airplanes; he had nothing to worry about.

In the late afternoon, when the mountains cast long purple shadows along the high valleys of the Rockies, he pulled into Los Piños, driving into another Hancock service station for more gasoline and the opportunity to use the telephone. There was a booth at the side of the station, and Fleming went inside it, closing the door firmly before he dialed the operator and asked for the auto rental agency office in Dallas. He paid out the three dollars in dimes and quarters, then waited to be connected. When the telephone was answered on the other end by a honied female voice, Fleming wasn't sure she was as familiar with his situation as the clerk he had spoken to the day before yesterday, so he quickly read the pertinent information off the rental agreement, then said, "Here's the rub: my plans have changed and I'll have to fly out of Colorado, Alamosa, to be precise. I know it isn't a large air-field, and the town is fairly small, but I need to arrange to leave off the Packard, if there is some way I can arrange it. I know there's a drop-off fee, so—"

"Well, yes," said the young woman. "Basically, we have reciprocals with other car rental companies. You gotta have that out here. You can leave the car you've rented with any licensed agency, and for twenty-two fifty surcharge, they'll get it back to us. It doesn't have to be a commercial rental—a vacation company will do; there should be one near the airport. Don't you worry about a thing, Mister Fleemie. It happens all the time."

Fleming didn't bother to correct her mispronunciation, saying only, "Thank you very much. I appreciate your help."

"Oh, you're welcome." Then, in a gush she added, "And they can say what they like about Yankees—you Boston boys sure are polite." With that she hung up, leaving Fleming speechless, a condition that quickly gave way to mirth. He would have been less sanguine if he had heard her superior's outburst an hour later.

"You what?" McKinnon demanded.

"Well, it is standard procedure, isn't it?" The young woman gave him an irritated frown. "You make arrangements like this every day."

"Not for . . . for foreigners. That's a different situation," McKinnon blustered. "Damn it, Mandy, now I've got to phone Baton Rouge." His voice dropped and he glanced furtively at the telephone as if he expected it to strike at him.

"So?" Mandy was prettily petulant, her large blue eyes open, her lips pouting.

McKinnon shook his head. "You wouldn't understand," he said, and retreated to his office to make the dreaded call.

There was a small auto-rental desk at Alamosa Municipal Airport. Fleming paid the surcharge, turned over the rental agreement and the keys, got a receipt, then went to find a flight out. He thought about calling Powell, then realized he hadn't enough change, and didn't want to take the time to get some. He hurried off to the ticket counter to have a look at the possibilities, telling himself he would leave a message with Powell's night man when he finally landed.

The first east-bound flight he could take was headed at eight-ten for Wichita, and Memphis, and after a moment's hesitation, he bought a ticket through to Memphis, reminding himself he could get off in Wichita if he had to. On this flight the seating was catch-as-catch-can, so he chose an aisle seat near the door, where he could see everyone coming aboard, and leave as soon as the door was open, should that prove necessary. He carried his smaller bag aboard, pulled out Sir William's and the Los Alamos files from the hidden compartment, and took advantage of the flying time to read, comparing what he saw in one set of papers with the other set, making the best of the crowded seating and poor lighting.

Most of the passengers were sturdy western types, the sorts that Fleming had assumed existed only in films. Yet here was a pair of men in jeans and checked flannel shirts, their boots still dusty from work. After them was a businessman in a chocolate-colored suit, wearing a Stetson and silver jewelry. Behind him, a tired-looking priest chose a seat near the front, huddling down in his seat as far as it would allow him. Three nondescript men, middle-aged, very likely salesmen, judging by their outgoing behavior, sat together, one across the aisle from the other two. Then a man in an Army uniform, corporal's stripes on his sleeve. He was followed by a white-haired woman in a somber black dress and a hat with a veil. Next came a man about twenty-two or -three in a very new dark-blue blazer over a white shirt and striped tie, his face shining—off to a new position or back to university, Fleming supposed. A woman in her thirties in slacks and a suede jacket took a seat a row ahead of Fleming; she had been pretty, but her skin was turning leathery and there was an air of hard work about her that shocked him. Last came a family—father, mother, and three children, all under the age of ten, which Fleming viewed askance; the last thing he wanted on an airplane was fussing children.

Fleming drank coffee, knowing he had to stay awake and attentive while he reviewed the reports, making notes in pencil in the margins of the pages. About forty minutes into the flight, the stewardess offered him a sandwich, but he turned it down, not wanting to interrupt his work, or risk spilling anything onto the pages.

At Wichita—where the cowboys and the white-haired woman got off—he decided to stay aboard to Memphis, and to go on reading, sure he was on to something. The airplane departed on time, and Fleming continued to go over the reports. He found what he wanted on the fifth photostatic copy of the Los Alamos papers, a scribbled note in the margin, so small in the reduction that he had missed it before. Peering at it now, he realized the tangle of lines said, *Ref: Groan. W. Potter.* He held the sheet up, scrutinizing the notation, trying to determine if he had read it correctly. Yes, that was what it said. Potter had been investigating Moan, Groan, and Sigh, according to his files. And here was a notation on the Los Alamos papers with Sir William's own notation on it. The document was signed by a J. Cathcart, a name Fleming didn't recognize, although he felt that rush of excitement that meant he had found something of importance at last. Sir William, Geoffrey Krandall, and J. Cathcart were somehow linked. He began to read the photostatic copy more closely, wishing he had a magnifying glass to help decypher the reduced print. He struggled to read the page, and gave it up, knowing he would need brighter light than what the airplane cabin provided. He put the files back in their folders, and once again slipped them into the concealed compartment in the bottom of his bag.

"Can I get you anything to drink, sir?" The stewardess appeared at his arm again. "Coffee? Something stronger?"

"Actually, a little of your Bourbon would be nice. The best you have aboard." He gave her his most engaging smile.

"Yes, sir. Anything with it?" She beamed back at him.

"Good God, no. But thanks for asking," he said.

"Bourbon, straight. Ice?"

"No, thank you," he said, his mind already turning back to the photostatic reproductions. If only they weren't so hard to read, he thought. He would see if he could purchase a magnifying glass at the Memphis airport.

About forty minutes outside of Memphis, the weather turned stormy, winds buffeting the airplane, and rain spitting at the windows. Night made it worse, for the darkness was disorienting. Fleming was glad of the Bourbon, for it helped him keep his composure while the other passengers became increasingly worried and upset. After fifteen interminable minutes of this roistering, the pilot came on the cabin speaker.

"Sorry to announce that due to severe weather conditions, we are being diverted to Jackson, Mississippi. The airline will provide a bus to a contracting hotel, where there will be rooms set aside for your use. The night's dinner and lodging are at our expense, along with our apologies for this inconvenience, and along with our assurance that we will get you to Memphis just as soon as possible. We'll also pay for two telephone calls for each of you. Again, sorry for the inconvenience, folks. Mother Nature isn't in a very good mood tonight."

Fleming did his best to visualize a map of the United States, trying to recall where Jackson, Mississippi, was. He seemed to recall it was south of Memphis, about half-way between Memphis and New Orleans. Or was that Little Rock? Was Mississippi farther east? In an hour or so, he would know, and he wanted to console himself with that.

"Weather permitting," the captain's voice sounded again suddenly, "we will fly to Memphis at nine tomorrow morning. Please be at the airport by eight-thirty. We will have a bus from the hotel available."

Fleming signaled to the stewardess. "Is there some reason we must return to the airplane tomorrow?"

"Well, sir, you paid for your ticket and we're obligated to take you to your destination."

"But what if I don't want to wait all night to get there? Perhaps I could rent an auto, and—" Fleming suggested.

"You would have to sign a waiver, and frankly, I think anyone out on the roads in weather like this is going to run into trouble," she said, strict as a schoolteacher. "You think it over, sir. If the weather is bad enough to keep planes out of the sky, then it's probably a good idea not to travel in it."

"I'll think it over," said Fleming, wondering how he could find out about road conditions south of Jackson. He realized he would also need to look at a map; he had plans to change.

Chapter 22

IT WAS a miserable night in Jackson: persistent, wind-driven rain thrashed the roads, tossing tree limbs about and drenching everything. Water splashed up over the running-boards of the few vehicles on the road, and left wakes behind them. The bus that carried Fleming and the other passengers into town had leaky windows and a bus driver who was nursing a ferocious cold. Everyone on the bus was annoyed and inconvenienced, so there was little conversation until they pulled up in front of the Magnolia Hotel, an old, colonnaded wooden structure of a style now a century out of fashion, where Negro bellboys hurried out to unload the luggage from the bays under the passenger cabin.

Arriving at the registration desk a bit after half-nine, Fleming asked about auto rentals and was told that the rental desk off the lobby wouldn't open until morning. The clerk then repeated all the admonitions the stewardess had delivered, and recommended Fleming take the night to think about it.

"May I make a telephone call?" Fleming asked.

"Sorry. The phone lines are down." The accent was strong but comprehensible. "We probably won't have service until some time tomorrow, if the storm lets up. We could lose the lights." The registration clerk shrugged. "It's no different all the way to the Gulf."

"That seems pretty wide-spread. Is the storm really so severe?" Fleming had been through a few Caribbean storms and

knew how devastating they could be, but he had not considered what a bad blow could do to southern America. "How
wide-spread can it be?"

"Seems like it goes from the Gulf to Missouri, or so the
news said before they stopped broadcasting," said the clerk.
"I put you in room 313. That's on the third floor, to the left
of the elevator."

"Thank you," said Fleming, abandoning his questions and
taking the proffered key. He carried his own luggage, and
earned a covert frown from the bell-boys.

The elevator was operated by a middle-aged Negro in a
hotel uniform. He asked the room number and started the
cabin moving upward so creakily that Fleming wasn't convinced they would arrive at their destination before morning.

Leaving the elevator, Fleming felt a distinct sense of relief.
Looking both ways along the corridor, he saw illuminated signs
for stairs at both ends, and told himself that he would have to
be careful, since anyone could come up the stairs virtually unnoticed; he would block his door if he could. He was making
his way along the corridor and had just reached his room when
the lights flickered and went out. Fleming swore, and heard
other outbursts from behind closed doors. The darkness in the
hallway was the more intense for its suddenness, looming and
engulfing. Fleming told himself he was tired and letting his
imagination run wild. He longed for a torch to light his way as
he felt for the lock and managed to let himself into his dark
room. One hand extended in front of him, the other holding
his bags, he touched the wall and used it to guide him into
the room. He knocked against the luggage rack, and continued
on, finding a dresser, a closet door, three curtained windows,
and, finally, a bed. He put his luggage on the bed and sat down

next to it, feeling discouraged for the first time since he began his journey.

Some while later, there was a knock at the door. "House staff, sir," said a well-modulated voice. "I have a branch of candles for you."

Fleming was delighted to hear this. He got up and went to open the door, hesitating at the last moment. "House staff?"

"Yes, sir. We're bringing candles to all the rooms, sir." The voice was calm and sensible.

Chiding himself for being a fool, Fleming opened the door, and faced a Negro with a rolling cart filled with five-branch candelabra, all of them lit. "Very good," he approved.

"Thank you, sir," said the Negro. "I'll be back shortly with a few more candles, in case yours burn down." He handed Fleming a candelabrum and accepted a fifty-cent tip with good grace. "Very nice of you, sir." Then he moved on to the next room.

Fleming took the candelabrum and set it on the broad head-board, letting its pleasant illumination shine down on him as he opened his luggage. He decided to have another look through Sir William's files, for in candlelight, he could not make out the reduced pages in the Los Alamos report. As he set to work, he had a quick, disturbing thought: no one knows where I am. This seemed troublesome and exciting at once, for it could mean he was no longer being followed. When the bell-boy returned, he took the extra candles and went back to work. He banished his worries and set to reading, Sir William's files spread out on the bed around him. As he struggled to read in the soft candle-glow, the rigors of the long day caught up with him, and he gradually drifted off to sleep.

His own coughing awakened him sometime later. There was

smoke in the room, though none of Fleming's candles—two of which had guttered—was the cause of it. Quickly he gathered up the papers, shoved them into the files, stuffed them into his luggage, grabbed it up, and rushed for the door. He could hear shouts of disorder in the corridor, and somewhere far below, a steady clang was sounding. Throwing his door open, Fleming rushed into the hallway, and blinked against the billows of smoke. The only light in the hallway was supplied by candles, and just a few of them, so that it was all but impossible to see any distance along the corridor in the steadily increasing smoke.

Someone in a bathrobe shoved past him, shouting, "It's on the floor below. We gotta get out of here!"

A woman shrieked, and Fleming could hear her sobbing. He paused. "Are you in need of help, ma'am?"

"I'm scared of fire," the woman's voice wailed.

"Everyone is," said Fleming, trying not to cough and knowing he had very little time left. "If you come out, I'll lead you down the stairs. They're at the end of the hall."

"Okay," the voice said, and a moment later a figure moved out of the dark toward him, a woman in her late twenties, with pale hair and tense features that might be pretty under other circumstances. She was dressed in a roll-top pull-over and slacks, with boots rather than shoes on her feet. "I was trying to get up the nerve to leave," she said.

"Take my arm," Fleming told her. "We're going to the end of the corridor and down the stairs."

"Not the elevator?" Her voice rose half an octave.

"The power's out," he reminded her. "It's the stairs or nothing." He did his best to walk steadily, but it was becoming difficult. "Lower your head," he recommended, doing the same, remembering his air-raid training.

"Okay," she said, trying not to cough.

"Keep hold of my arm," Fleming ordered, then continued on toward the end of the corridor, pounding on every door he passed until he reached the exit. He laid his hand on the wood to be sure it wasn't hot, then carefully opened it. He encountered smoke, but nothing so thick as he had found in the corridor behind him. By now his eyes were streaming and his nose hurt, but he began to hope that he would be able to get out relatively unscathed. He felt the woman's hand on his arm tighten, and that reassured him. "Just a bit longer, ma'am," he said, his voice breathless and scratchy.

"Okay," she repeated, wheezing.

"The stairs are just off to your right. I'm going to step down. Put one hand on the rail and keep the other on my shoulder," he said, struggling to speak.

"I will," she said, and set action to her words at once.

There was the sound of people below them, and in the distance, a siren was wailing. All of it became unreal as the two of them made their way down through the smoke, which grew thicker as they descended. At the next floor, the smoke was so dense that both Fleming and the woman with him could hardly breathe, and moving was becoming difficult. Fleming realized they would have to get out of the smoke quickly or risk collapsing and succumbing; he almost laughed, but it came out a gagging sound: that he, after all the strange events of the last four days, should end up dying of smoke inhalation in Jackson, Mississippi! He made himself keep moving in spite of the discomfort and giddiness he was feeling.

The sirens were much louder now, either closer to the hotel or he was more acutely aware of them. He could hear stumbling steps behind them as others tried to make their way down the stairs. There were shouts and coughing and shrieks and prayers coming from the hall beyond them, and those sounds spurred Fleming on.

They reached ground level to find firemen preparing to climb the stairs, most of them in protective gear, one in a flapping rubber-clad garment that Fleming had heard called a poncho. Suddenly he was forcefully reminded of the Blitz and all the other bombings in England, and he had to submerge the recollection as he continued toward the door. There were helping hands around them now and less confusion.

"Hey! You two! Over here!" A white-coated attendant was standing just beyond the outer door, next to an ambulance drawn up among the four fire engines.

The activity was purposeful, determined, and disciplined as the firemen deployed hoses and other equipment in the rain. Fleming allowed himself to be directed toward the ambulance. He was breathing in gasps, and the woman behind him was sobbing.

"Com'ere! Com'ere!" the attendant was shouting, gesturing broadly.

Fleming headed toward him, lungs and eyes stinging. He stopped suddenly, coughed, bent over at the waist, and nearly fell to his knees. The woman behind him almost fell with him, but somehow managed to keep them both erect.

The firemen were running, lugging their hoses, pointing up at the flames on the second floor. There was the sound of breaking glass and a general cry of dismay, cut short by a pulpy thud.

"Oh, my God!" the attendant exclaimed. "He *jumped*!" Then he began running toward the hotel, leaving the ambulance unattended.

Fleming staggered toward it, dropped his luggage, and reached for the sheet on the stretcher. He rubbed it over his face and handed it to the woman behind him. "I'll see what I can find," he said, and climbed into the ambulance. He took a bottle of saline solution, opened it, and gave it to the woman. "Wash out your mouth with this."

"Okay," she said, and did as he ordered.

Fleming took a second saline bottle and opened it, pouring it into his mouth so quickly that he sputtered and spat. Then he sluiced out his mouth and began to breathe less stridently. He was taking down a bottle of eye-wash when the attendant and two firemen came hurrying up, a man slung between them, his wet nightshirt spotted with blood.

"Hey!" The attendant pointed at Fleming. "You ain't supposed to be in there."

Fleming turned and saw the three men, and slowly got out of the ambulance. "Sorry. I didn't know how long you'd be and I thought—"

"Where're you from, anyway?" one of the firemen interrupted. "You're sure as hell not from around here, so don't say you are."

"England," said Fleming. "My airplane was diverted here," he said as he climbed out of the ambulance.

"Some diversion," the fireman remarked, eyeing Fleming truculently. "The police"—he put emphasis on the first syllable—"said we should be on the lookout for unfamiliar people."

"Most guests in a hotel are just that," Fleming said a bit testily; he didn't want to explain, but he was resigned to making the attempt when he was spared the necessity.

"Hey, you," the woman spoke up, her voice still raspy. "You lay off him. He just saved my life."

There was a pause as the firemen took stock of the situation.

"Perhaps you'd best get that man to the hospital," Fleming suggested, standing back from the ambulance. "He doesn't seem to be in good condition."

"You're right about that," said the attendant, and reached for the stretcher. "Get him aboard and loaded in."

The firemen put the man on the stretcher; he was moaning and he clearly had a broken shoulder. The attendant buckled him onto the stretcher, taking care to brace his shoulder with a rolled towel. The firemen loaded the stretcher and the attendant went to the front of the ambulance, climbed in, and started the motor.

One of the firemen headed back toward the hotel, but the other stayed with Fleming and the woman, his attention now veering to suspicion. "So you're not married, the two of you?"

"Married?" The woman laughed. "We just met up there"—she gestured toward the hotel now billowing flames—"and he brought me out. I don't even know his name."

The fireman gave a very pointed stare at her left hand. "You were there alone?"

"Yes. I was alone. I checked in at six last evening. If you can find the desk clerk, he'll tell you." The woman sighed. "Look. My husband's in a veterans' hospital. I got a living to make. I'm on my way to Monroe for the Southern Quarter Horse Show. I have a horse farm outside of Tullahoma in Tennessee. My horses are being stabled at McShane's farm on the north side." Her face was smeared with mucus and soot but she had the manner of an authoritative matron. "You ask Linus McShane. He'll vouch for me."

"The phones are out," the fireman reminded her.

"Well, ask the clerk at the front desk, then; he's got to be around here somewhere," she said. Then she looked at Fleming. "My name's Myra Rinaldo, by the way." Suddenly shy, she held out her hand to him. "Born Adler, by the way, in Wyoming." This last reminded him of the American nurses he had met in the War, who always included where they were from in their introductions.

"Ian Fleming, born Fleming, from England," he said, taking it. "Pleasure, Missus Rinaldo." He was aware that her accent was flatter and more clipped than those he heard around them.

"You don't know the half of it," said Myra Rinaldo. "I was sure I was going to die." She looked at the fireman. "So get your mind out of the gutter and go help put out that fire."

The fireman hesitated, but then a bellow from the hotel caught his attention and he hurried away, leaving Fleming and Myra Rinaldo standing together in the rain.

"What are you doing in Jackson?" Myra Rinaldo asked after an awkward pause while they saw another five people run from the hotel. "They aren't all going to make it out, are they?"

"Probably not," said Fleming, answering her second question first.

"Wonder what caused it?" Myra asked.

Fleming did his best to keep his answer calm and rational. "It may take a while to find out, unless someone set it. The power failure might have something to do with it. A short, perhaps, or unprotected candles."

"On the second floor," said Myra dubiously.

"It would seem so," said Fleming.

"It's going to be bad, isn't it?" She turned away from the fire.

"Yes." He doubted the firemen could bring the fire under control before most of the building was damaged beyond repair.

"I guess I do owe you my life," she said frankly.

Fleming shrugged.

"So what happens now?" Myra said as another ambulance wailed up to the fire engines.

"They put the fire out and take care of the victims," said Fleming.

"But that's going to take hours, and who knows where they'll send us? What about a place for the rest of tonight?" She cocked her head. "We can't stay here."

"No," said Fleming, almost laughing. "I think not."

"Then come along with me, Ian Fleming. I'll take us back to McShane's. He'll put us up." She turned on her heel and walked away.

Puzzled, Fleming hesitated. "If that's the case—"

"Why didn't I stay there?" Myra guessed, stopping. "There's a very good reason. McShane is a widower."

"Yes?" Fleming picked up his luggage and started toward her.

"I'm a married woman. My husband's in a hospital with his mind gone. People would talk, particularly around here. Gossip is the biggest industry in the South, and it could wreck everything I've worked for." She folded her arms, looking unexpectedly vulnerable.

"Is it any different now?" Fleming asked.

"After a fire like this? You bet. And you, being a third person, turn it into something other than two people in a house alone."

"I should think it could be seen as something worse," Fleming said, catching up with her.

She resumed walking. "Maybe, but I doubt it. Come on, if you like. Or stay here and talk to the firemen and cops until noon. I'll try to work out a way to deal with the talk. Maybe I'll sleep in one of the stalls."

"I take your point," said Fleming, and hastened after her, his steps splashing in the flame-ruddy puddles, his luggage slapping against his leg.

Chapter 23

Myra Rinaldo's vehicle proved to be a new, dark-colored, one-ton pickup truck made by Chevrolet. It was parked a block away next to a service station—not, he noticed, a Texaco. She unlocked the door and let Fleming in. "Throw your bags behind the seat." She climbed into the driver's seat and put her key in the ignition.

Fleming did as she said, and pulled the door closed as she gunned the motor. "What now?"

"Now we hope the roads are open. Linus's place is ten miles outside of town." She turned on the headlights and put the truck into reverse, released the brake and backed up, then pulled out of the parking space. "Hang on, and watch out for headlights."

"Anything you say," Fleming assured her. He folded his arms, feeling cold for the first time, and realized that between the smoke and rain, his clothes were ruined. He would have to make the most of the change of clothes in his bags.

"I'll turn on the heater as soon as the engine warms up. That'll help dry us off a bit." She swung onto a wide street, going north. "It won't take us too long to get there. Fifteen minutes, maybe." She handled the big truck with the ease of habit, proceeding carefully in the darkened city. "Keep your eye out for the Highway 51 sign. It's a little way up on the right." The windows were beginning to steam up. "Wipe off the windshield for me, will you?" She handed him a wash-flannel.

Fleming nodded. "I'll do it." For an instant he missed his Rapier, and then, surprisingly, the Packard he left back in Colorado, but the impulses passed as soon as they arose.

"Thanks," said Myra, reaching to turn on the heater.

A 1931 Cadillac passed them, splashing them in its haste.

"Damn fool," said Myra. "Driving like that in a power outage. It'll serve him right if someone runs into him."

Fleming finished wiping the inside of the windscreen and put the wash-flannel aside. "Maybe he's in a hurry."

"Hurry or not, he's stupid," said Myra, and settled in to driving.

"I think there's a sign for the highway up ahead," said Fleming, squinting out into the rain that shimmered in the headlights.

"Sounds good," said Myra, preparing to turn.

"Look out!" Fleming warned as the headlights picked up branches and leaves.

A large tree had fallen and blocked the road ahead. Myra swore, double-clutched down and braked, pulling on the steering wheel. The pick-up leaned, tires squealing, but kept going as Myra swerved around the oak.

"Very good," Fleming approved. "They should have let you drive the ambulance."

"Too top-heavy," said Myra, gunning the engine over railroad tracks.

"And this isn't?" Fleming asked.

"Not as much sway," said Myra, slowing for a dark intersection. "Okay. If there're more downed trees, you let me know. You ride shotgun pretty good."

Fleming had seen enough westerns to know what she

meant, but he was mildly startled to hear her use such language. "Riding shotgun," he said, and chuckled, beginning to put the shock of the fire behind him.

Myra smiled. "My granddad did," she said. "For Wells-Fargo. He claimed to have been held up by Black Bart once, but I don't think he was."

"Why would you doubt him?" Fleming asked, fascinated by this connection to the Old West.

"Because Black Bart always worked alone, and in California." She smiled faintly, the light from the dashboard showing the curve of her mouth. "He said Black Bart had a gang."

"Perhaps it was someone *claiming* to be Black Bart," Fleming suggested.

"In Wyoming?" she scoffed. "It made a great story."

"And you enjoyed it," said Fleming, sensing her satisfaction. They were picking up speed, but not moving so fast that Myra could not maneuver if they should encounter more trouble on the road. "You said you raise horses?"

"Quarter Horses, yes. Good, solid, dependable animals. Not high-steppers like Tennessee Walkers or Missouri Foxtrotters, but strong, good-natured stock horses." She grinned. "I've got fourteen mares and two studs back on my farm. I'm selling three geldings and a two-year-old mare. If I get them to the horse show, I've got a good chance to make a sale."

Fleming smiled. "Some polo players ride Quarter Horses," he told her.

"Sure. They're sprinters," said Myra, then changed the subject. "Where are you going? And what are you doing in Mississippi?"

"I was on an airplane bound for Memphis. The storm forced

us to land in Jackson, and they're supposed to get us back to Memphis when it's safe." He shrugged. "I need an airport to get a plane to Jamaica."

"I don't know about Jamaica, but there's an airport in Monroe. If you want to ride along with me, I'll take you there on my way to the horse show." Myra's voice was tentative, but it was apparent that her offer was sincere.

Fleming considered for a moment. "Why not?" he said at last. "I don't think the airline could get me to Memphis any sooner. So long as I can get out to an international airport, it's all one to me."

"Good," she said. "I owe you and this will make it a bit easier for me."

"I appreciate this," said Fleming. "But you don't owe me anything."

"That's not for you to say," Myra said firmly. "I know what you did, and I'm grateful to be alive." She turned the headlights onto high beams: a larger wedge of light cut through the dark rain. "I'll probably get the whim-whams later tonight. I'm running on nerves right now."

They passed a church with a fallen branch staving in the roof, and a telephone pole canted against the steeple at a precarious angle.

"Nasty storm," said Fleming, glad to have something safe to talk about.

"That it is," said Myra, her attention on the road ahead. "You didn't say what you do."

"I'm a journalist on a story," he said glibly. He had a momentary yen for a cigarette but it faded almost as quickly as it had risen; the fire and smoke were still with him, and spoiled the desire.

"And you got a deadline to meet, I bet," she said. "My brother-in-law works for the Chicago *Sun*. He's always on a deadline."

"Yes; I have a deadline," said Fleming, glad she made the assumption.

"I guess you can't tell me very much about it until it's printed," she said knowingly.

"Your brother-in-law has taught you well," said Fleming, smiling a bit in spite of himself. "Who is he?"

"Elihu Einhorn; my kid sister's husband. He covers business and commerce," she said.

"I've heard the name," said Fleming, relieved that he had. "I don't cover that kind of story."

She managed a partial smile. "I didn't think you did."

They passed a cluster of small houses with lantern-light in the windows. Then that beckoning light faded behind them and they were on an empty road hurtling north as the storm flailed around them.

"How much farther?" Fleming asked a short while later.

"Almost to the turn-off," said Myra, beginning to slow down.

A wash of water around the tires warned of flooding ahead.

"Hang on. This may be rough; there're ruts in the road," warned Myra as she pulled on the steering wheel and double-clutched down into second gear. The truck swayed as it turned onto the side-road, lurching at the uneven grading that was a mix of mud and gravel.

Fleming swore and hung on to the dashboard as the truck lumbered down the road. It was a bone-rattling ride that left a messy swath on the road behind. Fleming bit back a sharp observation, knowing this was neither the time nor the place for such comments. "How long is it like this?"

"Another two miles—not long," said Myra. "There's a rise up ahead. That should help some."

"Any chance of trees in the road?" Fleming asked, noticing the bushes along the road. His clothes were clammy on him, and his head felt stuffy, the after-effects of the smoke he had inhaled. He was chilled, too, as the surge of energy that had carried him since he left his hotel room finally faded.

"No. Linus keeps them cut back. He knows what these storms can do," said Myra, holding on to the wheel with the tenacity of a badger. "He wants the road to stay clear."

Although unconvinced, Fleming said, "A prudent idea." He stared ahead, wanting enough light to read his watch, and sorry now that he hadn't looked while he had the chance.

"What's the matter?" Myra asked, noticing his restlessness.

"Just wondering what time it is," he said. "I was in New Mexico yesterday morning—I do trust it is after midnight?— and my sense of time is thoroughly distorted."

"Why didn't you say something. There's a dashboard clock," she said, and glanced at it. "Two-forty, plus or minus."

"What will this Linus McShane think of us arriving at this hour?" Now that they had almost reached their destination, he was apprehensive.

"He'll understand. He's good folk." She followed a broad curve in the road that bore around to the left. The headlights reached into the darkness, showing the rain beginning to slacken. Up ahead there was a large, red-and-white barn with a high loft, and then a second one behind it on the same pattern but somewhat smaller, paddocks between them. Beyond that was the outline of a two-story house. Myra kept the truck headed for the house, slowing down steadily, and tapping the horn twice as she pulled up in the circular drive at the foot of the broad steps. "Wait a sec, Fleming. I'll explain things to Linus."

Fleming wondered what they would do if this Linus Mc-Shane said no to them: sleep in the truck, perhaps, or look for a barn to bed down in. God knew he had had worse bivouacs than the truck or a stall, but he was hoping for a bit more comfort than the truck provided. Lantern-light spilled from the open door of the house, and as Fleming watched, Myra stepped inside. It took a while, and Fleming busied himself wiping off the fogged windows with the wash-flannel and tried not to make out the movements of the hands of the dashboard clock.

It was almost ten minutes later when Myra came out of the house, an umbrella over her head, a kerosene lantern in her hand. She rapped on the passenger-side window before tugging open the door. "Come on in," she called almost merrily.

Fleming got out of the truck and reached behind the seat for his two bags. "You sure this is all right?"

"It's fine," said Myra. "Linus is good folk, I told you." She reached into the well behind the seat and pulled out a large duffel bag, then took his elbow and tugged hard. "Come on. He's making a toddy for us. Well, actually, Avery is making the toddies."

"Avery?" Fleming asked.

"Linus's houseman. Colored, of course. Been with Linus for thirty years and more. His sister Muriel is the cook." She all but dragged him up the steps to the door.

"A toddy will be welcome," said Fleming, his thoughts going to Cesar and Bathsheba.

"Then hurry up," said Myra, hauling him into the house and closing the door behind them.

Chapter 24

LINUS MCSHANE proved to be an amiable host, a tall, straight-backed, white-haired gentleman gracefully approaching sixty, and behaving as if sooty guests arriving shortly before three A.M. was a standard event. He received his visitors in a plaid robe over dark slacks and a crew-neck pullover of dark-blue-green; the only indication that he had been in bed until a few minutes ago was the slippers on his feet. Unperturbed by the lateness or the occasion, he ordered the water-heater fired up and promised hot showers in half an hour. "Avery'll see to it. There's plenty of wood for the fire-box. It won't take long to get it ready. Looks like both of you could use a little soap and hot water." He then ambled into the front parlor, as if unconcerned about his carpets or furniture. "Take it easy, Mister Fleming," he said when Fleming hesitated taking any seat. "Charcoal ain't the worst thing these couches ever had on 'em." He indicated the lanterns providing the light. "Sorry the power lines are down."

Fleming remained standing, his luggage still in his hands. "It would still be a shabby thing to do, ruining your upholstery."

McShane shrugged. "Suit yourself." He motioned to Myra. "You're not so persnickety, are you?"

"Hell, no," said Myra, and dropped onto a hunter-green couch. "You're being a good friend, Linus."

"Nothing of the sort," he said. "Neighbors got to help

neighbors or the whole thing goes to bits." He heard the door open in the rear of the house. "That'll be Avery with toddies."

A few seconds later a broad-shouldered Negro approximately the same age as McShane came into the parlor, a tray in his hands. He had on a dressing gown but comported himself as if he were in full kit. "Your drinks, sir," he announced as he put the tray on the coffee table.

"Thank you, Avery. You can go back to bed now." He smiled after his servant. "Don't know what I'd do without him."

"I know how that can be," said Fleming.

"You English have whole generations of servants, don't you?" said McShane, and without waiting for an answer, handed one of the oversized china cups to Myra. "You taste this. It's Avery's specialty."

Myra brought the cup to her lips, then set it down. "Too hot, Linus." She sniffed. "But I'll be glad of it."

"Whatever you want," said McShane. He gave his attention to Fleming. "So you're a journalist, Myra says."

"Yes, I am. Just now I'm working out of Jamaica, but I am based in London." He smiled, aware that it was what Americans expected.

"Nice town, London. I was there in the Great War. I supposed it's changed since the last one."

"Yes, it has. The Blitz did a lot of damage," said Fleming.

"That's what they showed in the newsreels." He picked up the second cup and handed it to Fleming. "It might be cool enough to drink now."

"Thank you," said Fleming, dropping his luggage at last and taking the cup and its saucer. He was beginning to think he had better sit down. There was a straight-backed wooden chair by the unused hearth, and he chose this. "It's been a busy day."

"Myra tells me she's giving you a ride into Monroe tomorrow—well, later today." McShane regarded him with curiosity. He finally chose the second couch to sit upon, and Fleming realized that McShane would have remained standing as long as he did.

"I need an airport. She tells me Monroe has an airport." He tasted the toddy, and found it excellent—spicy and potent with a citrus tang. At another time he would have wanted to get the recipe for Cesar.

"That it does," said McShane. "Well, sounds all right, then." He smiled at Fleming. "Always nice to have a guest from overseas to stay. Gives me all kinds of bragging rights."

"You remember what I told you about gossip?" Myra said, picking up her cup again and blowing on its contents.

"I didn't doubt you," said Fleming, taking another sip of his toddy and feeling its warmth spread through him.

"I bet you didn't," said Myra, giggling a bit. She tasted her drink. "That's real good, Linus."

McShane inclined his head. "I'll tell Avery." He looked around as the mantel clock struck three, its high, delicate chimes sounding strangely loud. "Water should be hot in another ten minutes. I'll tell you where your room is, Fleming, so you can go there as soon as you've showered."

"Thanks," said Fleming, and took a more generous mouthful of the toddy.

"Top of the stairs on your left, second door. The first door's a linen closet, so you'll know if you go wrong. I put a lamp in there for you. Just make sure you blow it out before you go to sleep."

"I know about kerosene lanterns, Mister McShane," said Fleming.

"O'course you do," said McShane. "Anyone who's been through a war knows about 'em." He got to his feet and strode the length of the parlor. "What time do you want to be up in the morning? I'll have Clem feed your horses at six. What about you?"

"Get us up at nine," said Myra. "We need sleep, and five hours is just barely enough." She glanced at Fleming. "That okay with you? We'll be out of here by ten-thirty, a good breakfast to carry us. And it'll be about four hours to Monroe, with the trailer and all, putting us there at mid-afternoon."

"Fine with me," said Fleming, wishing he knew more about this part of America than he did.

"The weather should be better," said McShane. "The rain's slacking off—has been for an hour or more." He rubbed his hands together. "Okay. Nine it is. Breakfast at nine-thirty. I'll tell Muriel when I get up."

"That's very kind of you," said Fleming, trying not to be skeptical about McShane's generosity.

"You'd do the same for me if the shoe were on the other foot, wouldn't you?" McShane said, and caught Myra's endorsing nod. "Well, then."

Myra finished her toddy and put the cup down. "If you don't mind, gentlemen, I'm getting first dibs on the shower. You can come along in about fifteen minutes, Ian." She grinned and winked as she left the parlor.

"Fine lady, Myra Rinaldo," said McShane when Myra was safely at the top of the stairs.

"That she is," said Fleming. "I only just met her, but it's clear that she's an admirable woman." He drank most of his toddy. "Is it true that her husband's in a veterans' hospital?"

McShane nodded. "Yep. He came back from Germany with a real case of the whim-whams and it's only got worse over time. Sits in his room in a corner, staring at nothing." He gave Fleming a speculative stare. "That bother you?"

"Only to the extent that I had a comrade in the War who suffered a similar fate. Do they hold out any hope for recovery?" Fleming asked as gently as he could.

"Not really. Oh, they say something could happen, that he might turn around, but you can tell they don't really expect it to." McShane took a long breath. "Myra's made a go of the business—that's something."

"I'd think it's a great deal," said Fleming, preparing to rise and take his luggage up to his assigned room. "I can't thank you enough for this. If you're ever in London, or Jamaica, you must give me the opportunity to return the favor. I'll leave my cards with you."

"That's real nice of you, Mister Fleming," said McShane. "Now, you get a good night's rest. We'll talk more in the morning."

"I'm looking forward to it," said Fleming, fatigue spreading over him like a blanket. He made his way up the stairs, his bags feeling like loads of bricks in his hands. He could hear the shower running, and determined which room it came from. That would be where he would go after he put his bags down. Thank goodness he would not have a tub to recline in, or he might well pass the night there.

The room he entered was of generous proportions, facing the south-east, with a neat bay-window that was now speckled with rain. The bed was double, with an intricately embroidered coverlet over the hand-made quilt. Fleming pulled the coverlet back and folded it carefully, hoping as he did that he would be warm enough to sleep comfortably. His damp clothes had reached the clammy stage and he was well and truly chilled. He undressed down to his underwear quickly, putting his holster and revolver under his clothes before taking his nightclothes in his arm and stepping out into the gallery that overlooked the entry and the doors to the parlor and the dining room. He hurried around to the door where he had heard water running—it was quiet now—and tapped on it. When no one answered, he went in, and found himself in a room of white tile, a lantern set on a shelf next to folded towels providing illumination. The mirror over the sink was clouded by steam, and a wet face-flannel hung over the side of the sink. The shower was a stall affair, with a curtain to draw across the door. Fleming stepped in and was soon basking in steaming water.

When he emerged, some ten minutes later, he felt ready to fall asleep. He toweled himself briskly, wrapped the towel around his waist, gathered up his underwear, and went back to his room. Digging his pajamas out of his bag, he made sure his files were safely in the concealed compartment before he blew out the lantern and got into bed.

It seemed hardly more than a moment had passed when Fleming was awakened by a knock on his door. He opened his eyes, trying to orient himself, then remembered where he was and how he got there. "Just a moment!"

"It's me, Ian," called Myra. "Wake up. It's ten past nine. Muriel will have breakfast on the table in twenty minutes."

"Very good," said Fleming, scrambling out of bed and reaching for his bags. He took out his light-weight grey-flannel slacks and his tweed jacket as well as a pale-blue linen shirt. He had intended to wear this for more business-like occasions, but with his other clothes ruined, this would have to do. He dressed quickly, then went into the bathroom to shave, thinking as he did that he could do with another two hours' sleep.

Myra met him at the foot of the stairs. "Come on. We're in the breakfast room." She was actually quite good-looking with the soot out of her hair and her skin clean; she had donned a pale-peach cotton shirt and long jodhpurs of Prussian blue, and the worst of the strain was gone from her, leaving all her grace for Fleming to admire. "Don't you love these old-fashioned houses?"

"Nineteenth century is hardly old-fashioned," Fleming said before he could stop himself.

Myra grinned. "I'm not going to let you insult me, Ian Fleming. This house was built in 1827, and around here, that qualifies as old." She slipped her hand through his arm, half-leading him to the breakfast room.

Fleming went along with her, feeling suddenly very conspicuous with his holster and revolver lying across the small of his back under his jacket. "That was before your Civil War, wasn't it?"

She nodded. "That's right. The War Between the States hadn't happened when this house was first built. That makes it medium aged for the area. Some of the plantation houses went up in the early 1700s." She gently shoved him through a swinging door into a north-east-facing room that had a large bay extending the room outward on three sides. A table was laid and a wood stove in the corner provided enough heat to make the room more than comfortable. "You sit down at the foot of the table," she said. "Muriel will bring in the food." Ringing a small glass bell, Myra sat down on Fleming's right.

A massive Negress in her early fifties came through the door, two covered trays in her hands. "Mornin', Miz Rinaldo," she said. "I got coffee for you and tea for the gentleman." She nodded to Fleming. "Eggs two ways, bacon, sausage, griddle-cakes, biscuits and gravy, syrup, butter and honey; preserves and cream coming, with cream cheese pastry."

"Good Lord," Fleming exclaimed. "Do you eat this way every morning?"

"Most times, yes," said Muriel smugly. "Mister McShane, he keeps a good board, if you know what I mean." She put down the covered platters and headed back to the kitchen for the second round.

"That's an astonishing amount of food," said Fleming.

"Linus's hands work hard. He feeds them like he means them to work," said Myra, reaching to put sausage and bacon on her plate, and then poached eggs. "Linus'll be offended if you don't make a hearty meal."

"If I do, I'll fall asleep in the truck," Fleming warned as he helped himself to eggs and preserves.

"Fine with me; I'm driving," said Myra.

"I'll keep that in mind," said Fleming, and took a couple of thin golden griddle cakes onto his plate, then added butter and syrup. "This is sumptuous."

"Linus eats and then goes out to work with his horses all morning. By noon he's hungry as a bear." She cut up the sausages into inch-long bits, and impaled two on her fork. "I thought you English liked big breakfasts."

"Some do, some don't," said Fleming, thinking back to the shortages of the War that were still not at an end.

"Well, make the most of this, Ian Fleming. It's going to be a long drive, and I don't want to stop until we're in Monroe.

Except for gas, of course." This last addendum was a concession that she made reluctantly.

"I'll keep that in mind," said Fleming, looking up as Muriel came back in with more food and two silver pots, one of coffee, one of tea.

"By the way," said Myra as she poured coffee into her cup, "you know, you clean up real good, Ian Fleming."

He smiled. "So do you, Myra Rinaldo."

Chapter 25

THEY CROSSED the Mississippi at Vicksburg under clearing skies, and Fleming found himself trying to remember something about the role that city played in the Civil War. All he could recall was it was prolonged, and he decided that wasn't enough to mention it. He stared at the huge river, making note of the amount of traffic he saw on it, and paying attention to the damage left behind by the storm.

As they neared Monroe, Fleming was aware that Myra was growing more and more quiet. He wondered if he should ask her what was on her mind, but was spared the trouble when Myra said, "I'm gonna miss you, Ian. You saved my life and you treated me like a proper gentleman. Not many would. My husband couldn't ask for more—if he had it in him to ask anything." She pointed to a road sign that said MONROE 22. "We'll be there in little over half an hour. I'm sorry it's gonna be over so soon. A woman in my position doesn't have many chances to spend time alone with a real gentleman."

"I'm sorry, too," said Fleming, mildly surprised that he meant it.

"I don't mean to sound like a broken record, but I'm really grateful. I'd be dead without you." She held on to the steering wheel more tightly. The truck was moving more heavily than the previous night, for now the horse trailer with its four occupants gave weight and complexity to the load.

"I might say the same for you. I might not have kept going,

had I been alone." He had said much the same to her earlier, but now she seemed to comprehend him.

"That doesn't change what you did," she insisted. "You're a prince of a guy, Ian Fleming, and I'll never forget you, or what you did." There was a wistful note in her voice now, but she remained unshaken.

"I won't forget you either, Myra," he said, a bit too automatically.

"You got my number and my address. You damn well better write to me," she said, trying to maintain a bantering tone and almost succeeding.

"I'll do that, Myra," he promised her. "I'll let you know as soon as I get back to London, but that might not be for a week or two." He hoped he would remember, and not consider it an imposition to send her a letter or two. Women could be such pesky creatures.

"Your bags are behind the seats," she said, controlling her emotions.

"Yes. I know." He noticed the houses were closer together and the streets were better-tended. They must be coming into Monroe.

"We'll go by the airport first, and then I'm off to the fair grounds. If anything happens, you give me a call there and I'll come get you," she said, a hopeful note creeping into her voice.

"I will," he said.

"It's in the phone book—the fair grounds office," she went on, slowing for the first traffic light suspended above the center of the intersection. It was actually working, which gave Fleming hope for catching a flight out shortly.

"I'll look it up if I have to," said Fleming, uncomfortable

with his level of misrepresentation. He changed the subject. "Please thank Mister McShane for me again, if you will."

"I'll do that, not that you didn't thank him enough already," said Myra. "He doesn't need thanks. He'll have it all over the South that he had an English guest during the storm. By the time he gets through telling it, you'll be royalty on the run from the Commies. That man talks worse'n a coop full of hens."

"Will anyone believe him?" Fleming was horrified and fascinated.

"Some will. Most'll just chalk it up to Linus's love of a good story," said Myra, signaling for a left turn and easing out into the intersection.

"That's reassuring," said Fleming, adding, "I don't want the competition to get on my trail. So far, I'm ahead on the story."

"Okay," said Myra, heading down the four-lane road. "The airport's about five miles along this way."

"Fine," said Fleming.

"Thanks for buying the gas back there in Tallula. You didn't have to do that," Myra said, sounding as conscientious as a schoolgirl.

"I'd have had to pay for one kind of transportation or another," said Fleming lightly, although the nearly four dollars to fill the tank surprised him a little.

"True," she allowed. "Still, I didn't expect it, and I thank you for it."

"As you Americans say, you're welcome," Fleming answered, hoping he could get some more change at the airport. He had telephone calls to make before he left Monroe.

A low-flying airplane alerted Fleming and Myra to the nearness of the airport, and Myra blinked twice as she strove to contain her emotions. "I'll drop you off at the curb, if you don't mind. Finding a parking place for this rig isn't easy, and I don't like to leave the horses unguarded."

"You needn't apologize. This will be just fine," said Fleming, who preferred to be on his own again. "I hope your horses fetch a good price."

"So do I," said Myra with feeling. "Look," she went on more tentatively, "I don't know if you'll ever be back this way, but if you are, you be sure to come see me, okay, Ian?" She turned onto the road that led to the airport. Even at this distance they could see expansion was under way.

"Okay," he said deliberately, shifting around to grab his bags. "And let me know if you're going to be in London, or Jamaica."

"I will," she promised him as they approached the single-story building that was topped by a tall, bulbous tower. "This is where we say good-bye for now." She pulled to the curb in front of the terminal building and stopped. "It's been too short a time."

"But we both have things to do," said Fleming, opening the door.

"Oh, what the hell," she said, and reached over, grabbed him by the shoulders, and kissed him with more enthusiasm than expertise. When she let go of him, she was breathless. "I've been wanting to do that since halfway to Linus's place last night."

Fleming shook his head, startled. "Myra—"

She touched his mouth. "Don't say anything. You'll ruin it." She moved back into the driving position. "Have a safe trip, wherever you're going."

Still somewhat nonplussed Fleming got out of the truck and

closed the door, waiting until Myra pulled away from the terminal. Then he turned and entered the building and looked about for the schedule board and the reservations desk. He studied the various flights coming and going, and at last settled on getting a reservation to Houston on a flight leaving at four-forty, almost two hours from now.

"Passport?" the clerk asked when he had finished making out the ticket. "Gotta make a record of the number for aliens."

Fleming handed his over. "All current and correct," he said lightly.

"We don't joke about things like that in this country," the clerk said stiffly. "You never know who's gonna be sneaking into America to do mischief." He handed the passport back with a snap.

Fleming wanted to ask what mischief he could do in Monroe, Louisiana, but thought better of it and asked for five dollars' worth of quarters. "I have to make a couple telephone calls."

The clerk was instantly suspicious, though he handed over two paper rolls. "You'll need a couple dollars' worth of dimes, too," he said. "Lucky you weren't traveling tomorrow. We shut down for most of Sunday."

"Then I *am* lucky," said Fleming, adding two dollars for the dimes, then went in search of a telephone booth. He found a line of them outside the men's loo, and chose the middle one. His first call was to the Pecos Vista Hotel, and to FBI Agent Lemmuel Hotchkiss. "Tell him it's Ian Fleming calling," he added.

The registration clerk—and hotel owner—said, "I know who this is. Just you hold on a minute. I'll see if I can find him." Without waiting for an answer, he stepped away from

the PBX—Fleming could hear his footsteps retreating and, a
minute or two later, approaching again, a second, heavier tread
accompanying his.

"Hotchkiss here," he said as he picked up the receiver.
"That you, Fleming?"

"Yes," said Fleming. "I was wondering if you could check
out a name for me—a Cathcart, initial J. He may have something to do with James Hendley and Theodore Robertson, if
what I have discovered is in any way significant."

"Spell the last name," said Hotchkiss, all business.

"C-a-t-h-c-a-r-t," Fleming obliged. "Anything you can tell
me about him."

"Will do. Where can I reach you?" He waited for an answer.

"I don't know," said Fleming. "I'll tell you what: I'll call
you again when I get to Houston this evening."

"Houston?" Hotchkiss sounded startled.

"It's complicated," said Fleming. "Anything you have on
Cathcart, and any associates of his—especially one called Geof-
frey Krandall—G and K—I should be aware of, let me know."
He paused. "If there is any connection of any of them with
Sir William Potter, I'd like to know that, too. If that isn't too
much of a favor."

"The material may be classified," Hotchkiss warned.

"If you need to check my security clearance, do. MI5 can
supply the particulars. I got this from information given me by
the press liaison at Los Alamos, so it can't be completely under
wraps." Fleming wanted to show Hotchkiss the photostatic
prints he had been given; it was frustrating not to be able to.
"If you doubt me, check with the press office at Los Alamos.
Ask them what they supplied me."

"I'll do that," said Hotchkiss. "About what time do you think you'll be calling back?"

"Probably about nine. I'll have to find a place to stay for the night. I'll call you from there." He considered. "Is that eight in New Mexico?"

"That it is. I'll be here, and I'll tell Bert to expect your call," said Hotchkiss. "Anything else?"

"I don't think so." He was about to ring off when something else did occur to him. "You wouldn't have happened to attach a tracking device to my auto, would you?" He was taking a chance asking.

"Me? Hell, no. Why would I?" Hotchkiss sounded more puzzled than indignant.

"Would you tell me if you did?" Fleming pursued.

Hotchkiss gave a single chuckle. "Probably not," he allowed. "But in this instance, it would be the truth. If there was a tracking bug on your car, I didn't have it put there."

"I suppose I have to take your word for it," said Fleming, not at all satisfied with this response.

" 'Fraid so," said Hotchkiss. "If anyone did something like that, it wasn't the FBI. You might want to keep an eye out, if you've got someone on your tail."

"Right you are," said Fleming.

"I'll be here in the lobby around eight tonight," Hotchkiss said. "I hope I have something to tell you."

"So do I," Fleming said, adding "Ta," before he hung up. He was about to try to reach the overseas operator when a headline on the paper in the newsrack across the corridor caught his eye: *Fourteen Dead in Jackson Hotel Fire*.

Chapter 26

"Where the bloody hell *are* you?" Merlin Powell bellowed as soon as he answered the telephone.

"Where's Miss Butterfly?" Fleming asked lightly.

"It's Saturday, in case you had forgot it," Powell said sarcastically. "And that ploy won't fadge, Mister Fleming. I won't be fobbed off. Where are you? Lord Broxton's secretary has been calling. I hardly knew what to tell him. His lordship is displeased. *I* am displeased. I trust you have an adequate explanation for your absence?"

"I have," said Fleming stiffly.

Powell snorted. "Err on the side of plausibility." He paused. "So tell me where you are and when you will be returning to us?"

"I should be back tomorrow, or Monday at the latest. I may have to lay over one extra day, because of reduced travel on Sunday." He sighed. "I am presently in Monroe, Louisiana, and I'm bound for Houston, Texas, in ninety minutes or so. I have been in Los Alamos in New Mexico, in Colorado, and in Jackson, Mississippi, when the airplane in which I was flying was diverted from Memphis, Tennessee, due to bad weather. I will call and leave the information of my plans with the night desk."

Somewhat mollified, Powell said, "Well, it sounds as if you've been moving, at least."

"That I have," said Fleming. "And it isn't over yet."

"Not if you're in Louisiana. You have been junketing around, haven't you?" Powell took a deep breath. "I'll call Lord Broxton and try to explain. I hope he isn't too offended. You know how touchy he can be."

"None better," said Fleming.

"And you should be prepared to get the rough edge of his tongue for failing to keep your appointment, no matter where you were when it was scheduled, or why you failed to appear." Powell struggled to calm himself. "You're putting yourself in a most difficult position, Fleming; I don't have to remind you that you're out on a limb on this one."

"I was delayed by a storm," said Fleming calmly, deciding not to mention the fire; he would tell Powell about it later. "I was off-course and there was nothing I could do about it. Had there been no storm, I should have returned in time to keep my appointment—I had no choice, and no other means of reaching Kingston in the storm. If that is enough to earn me such condemnation, then so be it." He was in no mood to fight, but he was prepared to defend himself if necessary—as it now seemed to be. "If you would explain that: that had there been no storm, I should have been able to keep my appointment, as well as hand over a story to you." His repetition was emphatic, as if repeating it made it more persuasive.

"A story? You mean you found something?" Powell's whole manner changed. He was now eager and ready to hear more.

"I may have," said Fleming carefully. "I'm hoping to get confirmation this evening. I won't file without confirmation."

"Quite right, of course; it would be irresponsible to do otherwise," said Powell promptly, but with a note of disappointment creeping into his tone.

"Naturally," said Fleming, and knew he would have to tell

Powell some of what he had found no matter what Hotchkiss had for him. He waited a second or two, then said, "I'll let you know when I'll arrive."

"Do, please. Merriwell will be here tomorrow and he'll relay any messages to me at once." Powell cleared his throat. "I don't doubt that you've been diligent, Fleming, I only hope that your diligence has produced results."

"And I," said Fleming with feeling.

"I should jolly well think so." Powell faltered a moment, then said, "Well, until tomorrow then, old chap. So this won't cost you a fortune."

"Until tomorrow," said Fleming, and hung up, waiting for the operator to tell him how much more he had to deposit for the call. He counted out the remaining quarters and dimes, knowing he would have to give up a number of them. The ringing jarred him so that he nearly dropped the dimes. When the operator asked for another three dollars and sixty cents, Fleming deposited the money as quickly as possible, then got out of the phone booth, took up the bag he hadn't checked, and went to the departure area and read the paper he bought as soon as he reached the newsstand.

The account of the fire was somewhat confused, but the gist of it said that arson was suspected, and pending a formal investigation, there would be nothing done to clear away the rubble, although some complained that this might cause a public nuisance. The report revealed that preliminary accounts indicated that the fire had broken out on the second floor near the elevator shaft. It also stated that thirty-nine persons had been taken to hospital to be treated for injuries and smoke inhalation. Two firemen had been injured, one of them severely, when a stairwell collapsed. Among the dead was the co-pilot and steward of Central South Airlines. Survivors had been sent to a number of Jackson hotels.

Fleming scowled at the paper, trying to decide what to make of it. If the fire had been set, what had been its purpose? If it had not been set, what was its cause? It was easy to think that the fire had somehow been his fault, but that was impossible, and he was well-aware of it. Sternly he reminded himself that no one knew he was on that airplane, or that it would not reach Memphis. That didn't entirely quiet the distress he felt, but it gave him a moment of wry amusement. "Not everything is your fault, old boy," he murmured to himself.

A half-dozen men were among those waiting, most reading magazines or newspapers. An airline employee stood at the desk, doing paperwork. The afternoon seemed suspended, lassitude overwhelming all other sensations. Fleming browsed through the rest of the paper, wishing he had something more entertaining or substantial to occupy his thoughts. Finally, as he was about to doze off, the steady drone of propellers announced that the airplane was pulling up and the employee at the gate announced that boarding would begin in ten minutes. More passengers came into the waiting area, and the air of stultification vanished. Fleming joined those forming a line at the gate, handed over his ticket, and was given a stamped receipt with a seat number on it: 10C. He took his bag and made his way across the tarmac to the stairs, climbing quickly up and into the airplane.

"Do you need any help finding your seat, sir?" asked the smiling stewardess.

"No, thank you," said Fleming, making his way to the tenth row and shoving his bag under the seat in front of him. He wondered who would occupy the window seat, and was not entirely displeased when no one claimed it. The airplane took off on time, and Fleming decided to nap. Much as he disliked admitting it, he was growing tired. It had been a long couple of days, he realized, and it was catching up with him. He tilted his seat back the half-dozen inches it would go, tried to find a comfortable position without unfastening his seat belt, and closed his eyes.

He opened them again an hour later, a fragment of a dream fading from his mind. It had something to do with Sir William, Fleming could recall that much. He could not retrieve the images more clearly than that, though he had the disquieting feeling that there was something important in the dream. He told himself that this was nothing new: dreams often felt most significant when they were their most incoherent.

"You're awake," the perky stewardess said as she came down the aisle, a pot of coffee in one hand, a stack of paper cups in the other. "Would you like some coffee?"

It smelled dreadful, but Fleming said, "Yes, if you would. And milk and sugar." He was certain he would have to do something to disguise the burnt taste.

"I'll be right back," she said, handing him a cup and filling it two-thirds full. On the way up the aisle she stopped at three other rows and handed out cups.

Watching her, Fleming thought her dark-grey uniform didn't become her; she would look far better in a flared skirt and shirtwaist blouse. He was still enjoying imagining her in a variety of costumes when she brought him two little packets of sugar and a small tin container of cream. "Thank you," he said to her, amused by his thoughts. If only women weren't so demanding, he thought, they would be so much more enjoyable.

"If you want any more, just press the call button." She pointed to the knob on the arm of his seat.

"I will," he said, and set about making his coffee marginally more drinkable.

The rest of the flight was uneventful. They landed shortly before eight that evening, and Fleming went to pick up his second bag, and then made his way to the ticket desk for international flights.

"Where to?" the clerk asked.

"Kingston, Jamaica," said Fleming.

Hearing the accent the clerk smiled faintly. "Limey. Well, well."

Fleming knew it would serve no purpose to object to this. "Yes. English. I arrived from Jamaica at New Orleans," he said, handing over his passport and visa. "The smallpox certificate is in the back."

"It's smart of you Limeys to have that in the passport instead of separate, the way we do." He checked his schedules. "The first flight out is on Monday morning at six-thirty. If that isn't too early for you?"

"I can be here," said Fleming, a bit grimly.

"We need you here an hour in advance. It's required for all international flights." He looked a bit mischievous. "That means getting here at five-thirty. You might want to get a room at a hotel near here."

"Can you recommend one?" Fleming asked.

"Sorry. You might ask at the Information desk." He waited a moment. "So, do you want the reservation?"

"Yes. Of course." He was becoming impatient with the clerk. "Ian Fleming. Do I need to spell it?"

"I can read it off your passport," the clerk said, writing the particulars down.

Fleming held out his hand for his passport. "Which gate is the departure gate?"

"It's in the east wing. It's marked INTERNATIONAL FLIGHTS. There's a Customs shed right next to it. You can't miss it." He began to type up the ticket, his eyes on the keys. "Remember, you have to be here an hour before departure."

"I will." Fleming waited for the clerk to hand him his ticket. "Thank you."

"You're welcome," said the clerk as if by rote. "That'll be two hundred thirty-four dollars and sixty-nine cents."

Fleming thought his cash reserves were growing low, but he paid the amount without flinching. He had enough to last him another day, and that was reassuring. He took his bags and went out to the Information desk to explain his plight. As he walked, something about the clerk came to his mind: the man had not had a Southern or Texas accent—his inflections were the flat-vowel sounds of the Midwest. Fleming told himself that the man might have had any number of reasons for working in Texas, and that his accent meant little. He shrugged it off and asked about hotels in the area, deciding on the Lone Star, which was nearer to the airport than any other. He might have been less sanguine had he heard the telephone call the clerk placed to Baton Rouge twenty minutes later.

"You're the one looking for a Limey named Fleming? The one who sent all the mimeo sheets?" the clerk asked when the telephone was answered on the far end.

"Yes," said the French-accented voice.

"Ian Fleming, going to Jamaica?" the clerk persisted.

"That's right," said the man in Baton Rouge.

"Well, he's booked on the six-thirty Monday morning flight out of here—Houston, that is." The clerk glanced over his shoulder. "He'll be around here tomorrow. Probably near the airport, since he has to be here early on Monday. That means six or seven hotels."

"Did you recommend one to him?" the man in Baton Rouge asked.

"It's not allowed. I told him to check with the Information desk. It shouldn't be too hard to figure out where he is."

"All right," came the response.

The clerk hesitated. "So what about the money? Your man said you'd pay a thousand bucks for delivering this guy to you."

"And I will, when I know where he is," said the man in Baton Rouge.

"He's here, in Houston," said the clerk testily.

"Yes," said the man, his voice becoming silky. "And when I know *where* in Houston, you'll be paid. Not an instant before then."

"But you will pay," said the clerk, far less confidently than he had before.

"Oh, yes. I will pay. Make no doubt about it," said the man. "The money will be given to you in person. My man will deliver it to you—the same one you spoke with before. You remember him, don't you?"

"Yes," said the clerk, picturing the quiet stranger with the air of menace about him.

"Then we're settled, aren't we? You'll be paid." The man didn't wait for a response to break the connection.

"Fine," said the clerk, suddenly frightened. "Fine," he repeated, and hung up as if to put distance between himself and the sinister voice in Baton Rouge.

Chapter 27

THE LONE STAR was the product of World War II, a two-story building of strictly utilitarian design. Though hardly more than five years old, it already had a look of dejection about it, from the austere front to its rooms that were duplicates of one another, furnished the same way: a double bed, a chest of drawers, two night-stands, a small table with two chairs, two night-stand lamps, and a floor lamp. Everything was beige or toast color, from carpet and draperies to bedspread and lampshades. Fleming had seen similar buildings during the war and it provided him with the same dreariness of spirit those buildings had inspired. At ten minutes before nine, he left one bag in the room, but carried the one with the secret compartment and files back to the lobby. He found the telephone booths and went into the nearest one, and dialed the long-distance operator, giving the number of the Pecos Vista. He deposited two dollars and ten cents, and waited while the phone rang on the other end of the line.

"Pecos Vista," said an unfamiliar voice.

Somewhat taken aback, Fleming gathered his thoughts. "I am looking for Lemmuel Hotchkiss and was told I could reach him here. I thought he was expecting my call."

The man at the other end chuckled. "Just a minute," and called out, "Hey, Grampa, it's that English guy you told me about. Looking for Hotchkiss."

There was a scramble and then Bert came on the line. "Ev-

enin', Mister Fleming. Lemmuel asked me to get your number—said he'd call you back in an hour."

Fleming looked at the dial on the pay phone, then said,
"I'm at the Lone Star hotel in Houston. The number in this
booth is"—he read it off to Bert, repeating it carefully. "I'll be
here in an hour, if that's what Agent Hotchkiss wants."

"Yep." Bert read the number. "I'll tell him you'll be waiting."

"Thanks," said Fleming, and hung up, listening to the clang
of coins. He sat still for a few minutes, trying to decide what
to make of Hotchkiss's absence. It seemed ominous to him
that the FBI agent wasn't where he had agreed to be, but at
the same time, he was aware that this could be his anxiety
speaking: Hotchkiss might have any number of good reasons
to be away from the hotel that in no way was tied to his inquiry.
But the anxiety lingered as he rose from the telephone booth
and made his way into the café—calling itself a coffee shop—
just off the small lobby.

There were a dozen men alone and one family of four oc-
cupying the booths and counters, taking up about half of the
seating; the color-scheme was dark-red and maple-stained
wood, making the room darker than necessary. Fleming chose
a booth toward the rear of the room where he could watch
everyone else without being conspicuous himself. He put his
bag on the Naugahyde seat next to him and picked up a menu
from the holder behind the juke-box selection unit. He read
the various possibilities slowly, thinking that the quantities of
beef being served as single portions here would suffice for a
family of four in London. He noticed the lack of wines available and wondered what he could order from the bar.

A waitress came up to this table, a woman in her late twenties with a boyish build and a fixed smile, almost pretty, in a leggy sort of way. "What can I get you?"

"Can I order a drink?" Fleming asked, knowing there were still some odd laws in America, left over from the days of Prohibition.

"Sure. Bar closes at midnight." She held up a notepad.

"I won't be that long," Fleming quipped.

"What can I get you?" she repeated as automatically as she smiled. "We got Bourbon, Scotch, Gin, Brandy, ladies' drinks, beer. Take your pick."

"Your best Scotch," said Fleming. "No ice."

"One finger or two?" The waitress scribbled on her pad.

"Two," said Fleming.

"Be right back," said the waitress.

Fleming put his elbows on the table, and braced his chin in his hands. He had to admit he was tired. Eager for a smoke, he dug out his Players and lit up, taking a long drag and exhaling slowly. The nap on the airplane hadn't done much to restore him; if anything it had made him a bit groggy. Like it or not, he was certain that he would have to get a decent night's sleep or be way off his game tomorrow, when he suspected he might need to be particularly alert. The Scotch should help the rest, he said, and waited for the waitress to return.

"Made up your mind yet?" she asked as she set a squat glass down in front of him.

"I'll have the Porterhouse steak, rare, with sautéed mushrooms, a salad with French dressing, and an order of potato wedges. Coffee at the end of dinner, if you would." He had decided that was the most reasonable meal he could get from what was offered.

"Porterhouse, rare, 'shrooms, salad with French, and wedges. Coffee afterward," she repeated, to be sure she had it right. "Should be about fifteen minutes."

"That's fine," said Fleming.

"Good. Some guys, y'know, can't wait for a meal. They eat'n'run, eat'n'run." She kept her meaningless smile in place as she went off to place his order, leaving Fleming to sip his Scotch and mull over the events of the last few days. Sitting alone in the corner of the room, he wanted to review all his material but didn't feel safe taking out such papers in so public a place as this coffee shop. He even hesitated to make notes, for fear they might be seen by the wrong people.

The waitress appeared again. "Want a refill?" She pointed to the empty Scotch glass.

Fleming looked at it. "If you would, please," he said after a brief consideration.

She took the glass and hurried away, returning with another two fingers of Scotch in a squat, wide-mouthed glass.

A man sitting at the bar glanced Fleming's way once, but other than that, he appeared to be attracting very little attention. He took another look around the room, satisfied himself that he was ignored, and went back to pondering as he finished his cigarette.

Once again Fleming was lost in thought, and was startled out of it by the waitress bringing his meal. He thanked her and set to eating, missing Cesar's cooking more than he wanted to admit, though the steak was excellent. He ate steadily, keeping an eye on his watch in anticipation of his call from Hotchkiss. He finished with twenty minutes to spare, so he ordered coffee and asked for the check.

"Everything okay?" the waitress asked. "I seen you looking at your watch."

"Fine. Just trying to adjust to the time change," said Fleming less than truthfully.

"Oh, yeah. Lots of people have trouble with that," she said, and went to get the bill.

Fleming paid and left a generous fifteen per-cent tip—more than good service required, but not enough to be conspicuous. Taking his bag, he went out into the lobby and back to the telephone booths, and was relieved to see that the one he sought was empty, although one of the others was occupied. He slid into it and closed the door and occupied himself with looking through the telephone book chained underneath the little writing shelf.

At the sound of the ring, he nearly dropped the telephone book, and reached for the telephone as if to silence it instead of answering it. "Fleming here."

"It's Hotchkiss," said the FBI agent.

"I thought it might be," said Fleming, his voice betraying nothing of his alarm.

"Is there any way for you to get a secure line?" Hotchkiss asked.

"No," said Fleming, wary and excited by this request. "Not without a great deal of inconvenience, and taking a risk of making myself noticeable. I'm not sure I'd be given one, in any case."

"Damn," Hotchkiss said.

"I'm afraid so," said Fleming, keeping his voice level.

"Well, I'll do the best I can, and hope no one's listening. If the operator is eavesdropping, she better get off now, or risk having her name in FBI files." There was a faint click on the line. "Much better," Hotchkiss approved, then continued more seriously, "this is touchy stuff, Fleming. I could get into real trouble doing this. So could you, for that matter." He paused. "It looks like you might have found something hot, Fleming."

"Hot?" Fleming repeated.

"*Real* hot. The names you asked me to check out?" He coughed delicately.

"Yes," said Fleming. "JC and GK, and anyone associated with them. SWP and anyone else I should consider important."

"Yeah. Well, I can't find out very much about the last guy. All I know is he did some vetting on some of the English and English-like at the lab, and watch-dogged most of them. You follow me?"

"Certainly," said Fleming brusquely. "You're not the least obscure."

"Good," said Hotchkiss, seeming not to mind Fleming's tone. "Anyway, JC and GK worked for a time with a third man, a Canadian called Maxwell Preussin. So far as I can find out, he's taken off for the north woods since the War ended. At least that's what the RCMP told me. They have nothing current on him. So far as I can tell, no one has."

"Can you spell the name for me?" Fleming asked, and wrote it on a page in the telephone book when Hotchkiss did. "A mathematician? Breaking codes?"

"Nope. A geophysicist, top-notch, according to the Canadians. Working on assessing the potential damage of atomic bombs. Apparently he monitored a lot of the early tests, and kept at it until two years ago, then he suddenly pulled out. Some of the Mounties think he's trying to find someplace safe from the Bomb," said Hotchkiss. "WP did some kind of coordination for them, more than the rest he was looking after, at least for about six months. Your government insisted that they have one of yours keep an eye on them, so WP was the guy given the job. Seems Churchill didn't trust Hoover, or Donovan, or any of them."

"I see," said Fleming, more perplexed than before.

"I'm glad you do," said Hotchkiss. "I wish I did."

"Anything more?" Fleming held his pencil, prepared to make more notes.

"Well, JC has left his old work and is apparently employed by some kind of important French industrialist. The man's a mystery."

"Who is that?" Fleming asked. "And in what capacity is C employed—do you know?"

"A guy named Soleilsur. French father, African mother, or so they say. Rich as all get out, with fingers in a lot of pies. He's got everything from power plants and oil wells to calculating machines." He paused. "I don't know what C does for him."

The name all but screamed in Fleming's mind. "Soleilsur?"

"Means sun-south, or so my boss tells me, if that's important," said Hotchkiss. "I don't know what more I can give you on him, except that he has a couple of houses in this country, a place in Paris, another in Nice, and something in Morocco, but his official residence is on a private island. Our files are pretty skimpy. But he's foreign, which makes him CIG territory."

Fleming knew the animosity between the CIG and FBI was intense, so he didn't pursue the matter. "I'll see what MI5 have on him."

"I bet you won't find much. Men that rich are good at covering their tracks."

"Only if they have something to hide," said Fleming. "As the Nazis found out when Churchill sent his men after them." He coughed once. "Not that that has anything to do with the present situation."

"You hope," said Hotchkiss.

"Bet on it," said Fleming, gathering his thoughts once again. "Is that it, or have you something more?"

"Not just now," said Hotchkiss. "I might get additional material for you before you leave. When are you taking off?"

"Early on Monday," said Fleming.

"Then a word of advice," said Hotchkiss.

"What is it?" Fleming asked, hearing something sharp in Hotchkiss's tone. "Is something wrong?"

"I don't know. But you don't want to take the chance. Change hotels tomorrow morning, and spend the day at the airport. If someone *is* on your trail, make it hard for him." He paused. "When you call me again before you leave, call from the airport. You can call at any hour. Bert'll wake me up."

"I will," said Fleming, aware how prudent these precautions were. "Thank you, Hotchkiss."

"You're welcome." He made a sound between a laugh and a cough. "So long as I can call on you sometime."

"Of course. Anytime you like," said Fleming, and prepared to ring off. "Is that it?"

"For the moment," Hotchkiss said. "Watch your back, Fleming." With that, he broke the connection, leaving Fleming alone with the telephone book open to Heating Supplies with notes scrawled in the margins. He carefully tore the page from the book, folded it up, and stuffed it in his pocket.

As he got out of the telephone booth, he saw that the one on the right of it was still occupied. For a second he felt a twinge of concern, and wondered if he should check on the man, but changed his mind, not wanting to give anyone reason to notice him. Bag in hand, he went back into the lobby, and considered having a nightcap at the bar, but changed his mind and went off to his room; he had a great deal to do, and he needed his mind keen for the work ahead.

Chapter 28

THREE HOURS of poring over the photostats and Sir William's notes had produced four theories, and Fleming had fallen asleep with them contending in his thoughts after long work with the information he had gathered and had spent the evening analyzing. Tempting as it was to choose his favorite theory and then look for material to support it, he realized this would do a disservice to his mission and to the danger that was still all around him. He continued to review and evaluate the theories, at last taking them to bed with him, his thoughts circling like a flame-enchanted moth around the role Gadi Soleilsur played in this destructive drama; the more he thought, the less he liked the images his imagination conjured for him of a man of vast wealth without the checks of law or custom upon him, answerable only to his own ambitions. Sleep came over him in a muffling cloud, putting all thoughts of Soleilsur to rest along with his tired bones. This time, if he had dreams, they faded before he woke just after sunrise; he jolted out of sleep as if to answer a summons, wakened by a sudden loud noise in the corridor. He rose, showered and shaved, then dressed in the same garments he had worn the day before, thinking as he did that he ought to modify his appearance somehow, for if anyone were pursuing him, he would recognize Fleming by his tweed jacket more easily than by his face. He knew whatever he chose, it would have to conceal his holster and revolver on his belt at the small of his back. He needed something less conspicuous to wear, something his followers wouldn't expect.

When he checked out of the hotel an hour later, he took a cab into the city, not to the airport as had been recommended, but to downtown Houston. Luggage in hand, he chose a sporting goods store, and looked for a roll-top pull-over, selecting one in navy-blue, and then a hunting jacket of a similar shade. Last, he chose a dark fedora, and went in search of a men's room, where he changed clothes in a stall, and put his shirt and jacket into his luggage. Satisfied with his appearance glimpsed in the mirror, he went out into the street and hailed a cab, and asked for the recommendation of a good hotel, and went there. He took his bags into the lobby and found a chair off to one side, and spent the morning watching people come and go, taking relief from his anonymity. He decided not to return to the airport until late that night, in case the airport were under surveillance.

Shortly thereafter, the man who had occupied the telephone booth next to Fleming the previous evening used it again. "Sorry, boss," he said when the man with the French accent answered the ring, "I lost him."

"How could you?" The man in Baton Rouge asked the question silkily, which made it worse.

"He didn't go to the airport. He went downtown." The man could feel panic rising beneath his breastbone.

"Is he meeting someone?"

"I have no idea," the man in the telephone booth said. "He didn't call anyone other than that FBI fella in New Mexico." He coughed. "Some of the information was about you."

"So you told me," Soleilsur said in a dangerously bored voice.

"What should I do?"

Soleilsur considered his answer. "Go to the airport and wait for him. He'll have to end up there eventually. I rely on you to keep watch over him once he arrives. I only hope no mischief has been done: Mister Fleming has proven to be most elusive quarry."

"Yes," said the man in the telephone booth with ill-disguised relief. "He has."

"According to my sources, he was a spy during the War. He must have kept his hand in." There was a brief silence. "It's a pity that he got away from you."

The man in the telephone booth cringed. "I'm sorry," he said again with feeling.

"No doubt." Soleilsur paused. "Are you booked on the flight with him?"

"Just like you told me," the man said eagerly, wanting to show his competence in some way.

"Very good," Soleilsur approved coolly. "See you don't manage to lose him on the airplane."

If the sarcasm stung, the man didn't protest. "I'll be careful," he promised. "Is there anything you want to happen to him?"

"Yes. But not yet." Soleilsur cleared his throat for punctuation. "See he gets back safely, and keep watch on him. Telephone me once you know where he has gone, and I will tell you what you are to do. You will follow my orders expressly."

"I'll do it," said the man in Houston and hung up before Soleilsur could say anything more to him.

At noon, Fleming changed hotels, finding another lobby where he could sit and study the people. Apparently there was a convention in town, for men with name-tags and red vests gathered in noisy groups near the bar. For a short while Fleming wondered if he ought to try to join them, but he knew he could not fit in, and that would make him more obvious than he was. He kept to his chair.

By four-thirty in the afternoon he was heartily bored, and he was becoming restless. He didn't think it was time to go to the airport yet, nor did he have any other destination in mind. Finally he took his bags and went out into the street to walk the fidgets out of his legs. Making no particular note of where he was going, in forty minutes, he was thoroughly lost, as the streets seemed to sink under looming buildings; the sky was beginning to darken as the sun dropped low in the west, setting the high clouds ablaze with orange, magenta, and purple.

"¡Ehi! ¡Hombre! ¿Tienes cualqui' dinero?" The youth at his elbow was no more than sixteen. He went on in awkward English. "Money. You got any money? Hey! I'm talking to you."

Fleming glanced at the lad, sizing him up. "Only English money," he said. "It won't do you much good, I'm afraid." He had put his pounds in his wallet and his dollars in his inner pocket in anticipation of his arrival in Jamaica, and to resist the temptation to spend any more than necessary of the ninety-two dollars left to him.

"Give it to me," said the young man, reaching into his capacious trouser pockets and pulling out a knife.

Fleming thought of his revolver lying along his back in its holster, and made himself remain calm. "I think not," he said, taking stock of his situation in a swift survey of his locale. He had gone down a side-street and was now surrounded by small, shabby houses, most of them with tiny, fenced, dry gardens in the front. A few people were on the street, but none of them paid any attention to what was going on, and Fleming doubted anything less than an explosion would command their attention.

"I want your money," the young man insisted.

"You may want it all you like. You will not get it," said Fleming, finding a sudden rush of welcome excitement running through him. He had wanted a fight for the last three days, and finally he was to have one! His only concern was for his luggage, and that made him hesitate.

The youth mistook this for fear, and grinned, assuming he had seized the advantage. "You scared? Huh? ¿Hace temer, gringo?" He mocked Fleming, thinking he had gained the advantage with the knife. He made a dramatic slash at the air, and yelled in outrage and pain as the side of Fleming's hand chopped at his upper arm, rendering his hand and fingers numb. The knife clattered onto the street, the noise startlingly loud.

"No, not a jot," said Fleming, an eager light in his eyes. "I'm not afraid. But you should be." With that, he swung around, his leg rising, and slammed his foot into the young man's back.

With a shout, the young man tried to lunge, grabbing the knife awkwardly in his left hand and holding it low, ready to slice at Fleming's guts.

Fleming moved quickly, side-stepped the youth and kicked out, catching his attacker in the side of the knee.

The boy howled and fell forward as Fleming bent down and picked up the lad's fallen knife.

"Don't mess with the English, my boy. The Spanish learned that lesson with the Armada. See you keep it in mind." He picked up the knife and put it in his trouser pocket. He felt invigorated and energetic in a way he hadn't in days. He could almost find it in himself to be sorry for the youngster who had tried to rob him. All but whistling, his pulse elevated with excitement and triumph, he took his bags and went back the way he came, ready for supper and anything his unknown opponents might throw at him. By the time he reached a brightly lit business street, he was feeling hungry and confident, and he made for a restaurant that boasted the "Best Italian Food in Texas."

By the time he had finished his tolerable meal, he decided he was ready to go to the airport. He called a cab from the Bella Napoli, and asked to be taken to the airport. When he arrived, he decided not to go into the customs inspection line and the International Wing immediately, where he might be expected to go, but to the central waiting area. He noticed the last international flight out left at ten forty-five, bound for Buenos Aires; he would go through with those passengers, he decided.

He found a sofa in the smoking lounge next to the restaurant café and sat down to enjoy a cigarette or two. Reviewing all he had learned, he hoped that Hotchkiss would be able to provide him some additional information in the morning, for he was certain that he needed more in order to help him decide which of his theories would be the one to pursue. For the next two hours he went through six cigarettes, then decided he needed a cup of coffee—even lackluster American coffee—to clear his throat.

When he had had two cups of coffee, he went into the newsstand next to the café and bought two newspapers and a notebook. He knew it was dangerous to write down his thoughts, in case his musings should fall into the wrong hands, but he needed to grapple with the situation as he understood it more concretely, which meant writing it all down. If only he had some kind of device that would obliterate writing for all but the writer, he thought, how useful it would be. He watched as the crowds began to thin, until, after nine, the air terminal was growing empty. Two of the airlines shut down their counters for the night, and three uniformed janitors began to clean and buff the floor.

At nine o'clock he took his luggage and went through the terminal into the International Wing, and handed his passport and ticket to the Immigration officer, who read both and remarked, "You're not leaving until tomorrow, according to this." He held up the ticket.

"At a heathenish hour," Fleming agreed. "I thought it wiser to stay here than hope to find a cab at five A.M."

"You got a point," said the officer. "Just don't pass through this gate again, or you'll have to get stamped again, and it'll be a real hassle."

"I'll stay on this side of the gate," Fleming promised, and went on to the lounge where he discovered three men already sitting, luggage at their feet, prepared to nap the night away.

Fleming chose a modern sofa by the window where he could set up his bags as a pillow and a hassock, made himself as comfortable as possible, and began to scribble notes to himself, summing up all the elements of the last few days. He wasn't sure he should take Hotchkiss up on his offer for an early morning call, but decided to hold that option open. He continued to make notes, generally columns of initials of the men who appeared to be involved in this perplexing situation. Cathcart seemed to be a crucial part of the puzzle. What was Soleilsur's role in all this? And who *was* Soleilsur? That question niggled at him as he continued to write initials and draw arrows. He added two pairs of question marks for whomever had been following him. He marked Krandall with a cross as a reminder he was dead, and Sir William with a minus, indicating his missing status. He put a question mark by MP, and added *Canada?* after.

It was almost midnight when Fleming rose to stretch his legs, and have the luxury of another cigarette. He noticed it was the next-to-the-last in the Players pack, and he decided that he would save the last one for the morning. He would buy another pack when he got back to Jamaica.

"Anything I can get for you?" asked one of the Immigration clerks patrolling the waiting area.

"A bunk and a pillow," Fleming quipped, then added more seriously, "nothing, thanks. I need to walk about."

"Very good," said the clerk. "Just remember not to leave the area."

Fleming took a turn around the gated portion of the International Wing, using this opportunity to look at the other travelers spending the night in the waiting room: one was a man in his fifties, with greying hair and an expensive suit; another was clearly a student—young, faintly scruffy, with an old jacket over a roll-top pull-over and dark slacks; a third was a nondescript man in a tropical-weight khaki suit; a fourth was a Latin American businessman with patent-leather black hair and a pencil mustache in a pin-striped suit and a wide silk tie; the fifth was a man in a leather jacket so hunched in his chair that his face was concealed; and the sixth was in the Colored section of the waiting lounge, a middle-aged Jamaican in an elegant suit, and with a carnation in his buttonhole. No one moved as Fleming walked by. A second circuit of the room didn't enlarge much on his primary impressions. He went back to where he had been sitting and made himself as comfortable as possible and tried to get a couple hours' sleep.

Chapter 29

More than an hour before sunrise Fleming was up and stretching, trying to get himself prepared for the flight back to Jamaica. He scrubbed his fingers through his hair and strove to muster his energy.

There were more than twenty people in the lounge now, most of them looking half-awake. The Immigration desk had three clerks at work, and two guards flanked the gate into the lounge. One man, a large fellow with massive shoulders and a strong Texas drawl, was trying to talk the guards into letting him go back into the airport for a newspaper.

A thin black man in a janitor's uniform rolled in a table with a large coffee urn on it which he proceeded to set up on the far side of the lounge. There was a hand-lettered sign hung on the urn: COFFEE 25 CENTS, with a glass put out for the coins. "It'll be ready in ten minutes," the janitor announced.

Fleming took advantage of the intervening time to take his bags and go to the men's room to freshen up. He dug his brushes and toiletry case out of his bag and brought his hair into a semblance of order, managed to shave and brush his teeth and generally make himself presentable. Two other men came in—a new arrival, and the Latin American fellow—to make similar efforts; none of them spoke. By the time Fleming left the men's room, the coffee urn was exuding a satisfactory odor, and Fleming fished in his pocket for a quarter to pay for a cup of what he knew would be terribly weak coffee. Still, he told himself, it was hot and with sugar and milk would be tolerable enough.

Four other men were standing near the table with the coffee urn. One of them, a pudgy man with a thick neck and large ears, said to no one in particular, "Twenty-five cents for coffee! What's the world coming to?"

"It was the War," said the man in the leather coat. He proved to be an innocuous sort, about thirty-four or -five, with the manner that suggested he had seen his share of action—perhaps more than his share. "The rationing drove prices up."

"When you could get it at all," said the one who had spoken first. He had got himself a full cup and was now attempting to drink the scalding liquid.

"True," said another, and did his best not to yawn.

A speaker squawked to life and said that the flight to Jamaica would begin boarding in ten minutes. "Please have all necessary travel documents in hand and be ready to present them at the boarding gate."

"Guess that means us," said the portly man with the big ears.

Fleming looked around for a telephone booth, wanting to make his call to Hotchkiss. He found one, dialed the long-distance operator, paid in his coins, and was connected with the Pecos Vista.

Hotchkiss himself was on the switchboard, and greeted Fleming tersely. "I had word from the RCMP around midnight. They found Preussin. He'd been butchered—their word—and his cabin destroyed."

"Butchered," Fleming repeated, disliking the implications. "He didn't get on the wrong side of a bear or anything like that?"

"Gutted and skinned. Tongue cut out and hands hacked off. Bears don't do that. Left in a neat pile, according to the RCMP. Very deliberate. Sending a message, of course. And intended to frighten anyone left alive that might be connected to whatever is going on into keeping their mouths shut."

"Are you certain of that?" Fleming asked, already convinced.

"As certain as I can be without a signed confession. I don't know what you've got yourself into, Fleming, but I'd be real careful, if I were you. Whoever's behind this doesn't like being studied, that's for damn sure." Hotchkiss sounded upset.

"Seems like it," said Fleming. "I'll keep this in mind."

"You better," said Hotchkiss. "The RCMP told me that Preussin had been out of touch with everything, then he came into town—some remote place near Hudson's Bay—to mail a package. They figure someone was watching for him, and followed him back to his place."

"How did the Mounties find him?" Fleming asked.

"It is now three minutes," the operator cut in. "Please deposit two dollars to continue the conversation."

Fleming fed eight quarters into the telephone.

When the operator had gone, Hotchkiss resumed his report. "They received a telegram saying that there was a dead man at a private lodge. The telegram gave specific directions to the lodge. They decided to check it out, and they found Preussin."

"So it wasn't necessarily Preussin's cabin, or lodge, but it might have been," said Fleming, thinking aloud. "It could be a place where he was held. Are they sure he was killed there?"

"They say so—blood everywhere," Hotchkiss allowed. "Anyway, these bastards play for keeps. You keep your eyes peeled."

"I will," said Fleming. "Anything else?" This was quite enough, he told himself.

"I have a hunch that you've picked up a tail again," said Hotchkiss. "Nothing I can prove, but the back of my neck says so, if you know what I mean."

"None better," said Fleming, realizing he had a similar sensation.

"Well, then." Hotchkiss cleared his throat. "If your editor'll let you, give me a call tomorrow, just to tie up any loose ends. I'll pass on what I know, and you can do the same."

"I'll find a way to use a secure line." He thought he ought to persuade Lord Broxton to let him use a secure line at Government House. "Or I'll tell you if I can't get one."

"Okay. Tell Bert when you call to connect you to line fifty-one." He paused. "Take care of yourself, Fleming."

"I will," said Fleming, glad now he had the knife as well as his revolver.

"Tomorrow. Make sure you call. If you don't, I'm putting in a call to your embassy in Washington."

"You think this is that serious?" Fleming said, surprised in spite of his own misgivings.

"Yes. And frankly, I don't want to stir up an international hornet's nest. I'll find myself assigned to Fargo or Sitka if I pull a stunt like that and can't turn it to the Bureau's credit." He chuckled cynically. "Hoover's got expectations. He doesn't take disappointment well."

"So I've heard," said Fleming, and prepared to hang up. "I'll call you, one way or another. They're boarding my flight."

"Okay. Get going. But be careful." Hotchkiss lowered his voice. "Watch—"

"—my back. I will. Thanks," he said, and broke the connection, waiting for the operator to request the extra money. He paid in another dollar sixty, then left the telephone booth, bags in hand, documents in his jacket pocket, and made for the boarding gate where he was given his boarding pass and a Customs declaration statement for Jamaica.

"Please fill this out before landing in Kingston," said the gate attendant, sounding like an automaton.

As he made his way to his seat—J4—Fleming couldn't help but wonder who among these passengers had been set to follow him, if, indeed, any of them had. He put one of his bags on the shelf overhead, and the other under the seat ahead of him, and buckled in for the ride; his revolver was an uncomfortable presence against the small of his back, and the knife in his pocket felt unusually heavy. His window seat wouldn't afford much of a view for another hour, so he slid the shade up and prepared for a cat-nap.

"Do you want a pillow, sir?" the stewardess asked, making her first sally down the aisle.

"That would be very welcome," said Fleming, noticing how attractive she was, and how infuriatingly awake. Such a beautiful woman, and so useful, he thought.

"Very good. I'll bring it directly," she said, and went on down the aisle.

A man of middle years with a pronounced limp came along to take the aisle seat next to Fleming. He achieved an uneasy half-smile and sat down, giving Fleming a hint of a greeting. "Almost didn't make it," he said. His accent was British, but two class strata below Fleming.

"Um," said Fleming.

"David Dunstan," he said, holding out his hand with the air of one used to being friendly as part of his business. "Dunstan

Marine Engineers. Family business, as you might guess. My uncle's the boss right now. We do all sorts of marine installations—piers, platforms, bunkers, the lot."

Fleming gave his hand a perfunctory shake. "Ian Fleming. Journalist."

"Sounds exciting," said Dunstan, then rattled on, "Been consulting with the Yanks about building locks against those terrible hurricanes that cause so much damage along the coast here in Texas. Don't know if they'll give us a contract, though. They like to keep their projects among their own."

"Can't blame them for that," said Fleming, conspicuously yawning.

"I suppose not," said Dunstan good-naturedly. "But a man has to try when opportunity presents itself, to make the most of it. Which is why I'm off to Jamaica, to put in a harbor expansion plan bid." He frowned. "That French firm is putting in a bid, too, but I, for one, wouldn't trust a French engineer to make a sandbox. Still, it's their affair. The Texans are leaning our way, and that's the bigger project. Jamaica is attractive but nowhere near as lucrative. Let them choose whom they like. I'll make my presentation this coming weekend, along with the others, and we'll have a decision in thirty days, or so we've been promised." He finally noticed that Fleming wasn't interested. "Sorry for nattering. I've spent the last four days in meetings, and I suppose it's stuck to me."

"Happens to us all," said Fleming, relenting a bit.

"But that French firm has really got my back up," said Dunstan apologetically. "They did work for the Nips before the War. Hardly seems right to give them contracts when they did that."

"They didn't know there would be a war, or so they claim,"

said Fleming, looking up as the stewardess arrived with a pillow. He accepted it gratefully, put it between the seat-back and the window, and prepared for a nap. "I've been up most of the night," he said so he would not be too rude.

"Oh. Yes. Sorry," said Dunstan, and fell silent but twitchy. About twenty minutes later he said, "You see some bloody odd things along the shore these days."

Fleming, finding it difficult to sleep, cocked his head. "Bloody odd in what way?"

"Well," he said in his most confiding tone, as if he needed to tell someone—anyone—about what was troubling him, "I've seen a couple big harbors with underwater storage bunkers filled with explosives. This isn't unexploded bombs, or surplus mines—I've seen my share of those, and I know the difference between them and these other devices. I don't like the look of that, even if it is left over from the War. Things like that can be dangerous. Some of them are radioactive; they've got the mark on them. I've mentioned them where I've come across them, but no one seems to know anything about them. Or to care, for that matter, though I don't like the look of them."

"Are you sure that's what they are?" Fleming asked.

"As sure as I can be. I was walking on the bottom of the mouth of—well, that isn't important. But I found three cement bunkers. I told the Harbormaster and the Navy about them, but no one believed me, or they assumed I was mistaken, that I'd seen a sunken ship, or a portion of an old submarine net. Scared me right out of my wits, I can tell you. They say radioactivity can make you sterile." He gulped and stared straight ahead.

"Couldn't the bunkers have been something left over from

the War? Is that so impossible? The records are still sealed on some of those projects." Fleming could see that David Dunstan was frightened.

"Could be. But the damn things looked new. Seawater takes a heavy toll, and anything submerged for any length of time shows the effects. The things I've seen couldn't have been down there much more than six or seven months." He gave an abashed half-smile. "Sorry. Didn't mean to carry on. Don't let me disturb you."

The airplane had taken off on time, into a cloudy sky, and headed out toward Cuba and Jamaica beyond. Fleming had finally got to sleep when the stewardess roused him to offer him coffee or tea. He decided to take his chances with tea this time, and was brought a metal pot of moderately hot water and a tea-bag. There was a small breakfast pasty included with the rest, and Fleming ate it while he prepared a most unsatisfactory cup of tea. He moved his pillow over and put the shade down, seeing the apricot-and-peach streamers of dawn stretching up into the clouds.

The flight remained largely uneventful except for occasional episodes of rough air that bounced them around and rattled nerves. Dunstan made occasional attempts at conversation that Fleming avoided by taking out his notebook and making an entry about Preussin, wondering where his murder fit into this. There was entirely too much murder going on, he thought, and felt a shudder go through him like a wind through a tree.

"Something more?" the stewardess asked a short time later.

"Not for me, thank you," said Fleming, his appetite quite gone.

Dunstan asked for another pasty, "If you've got one to spare. And a sherry, dry."

"With pleasure," said the stewardess, addressing Dunstan but smiling at Fleming.

"I don't look forward to this coming presentation, I can tell you," he said to Fleming out of nowhere. "Too private, too much like a party. That makes it difficult for anyone who isn't on the inside, if you know what I mean. They hinted I should let well enough alone, but I have an invitation, so I'll attend. You know how it is out there."

"None better," Fleming said as he smiled back at the stewardess, glad to have something cheery in the midst of hazards and danger; that phrase *let well enough alone* sounded an alarm within him, which he told himself was only coincidence, that the phrase was not obscure, that anyone might use it. He saw that the stewardess was smirking, but upon a moment's reflection, he decided this was nothing more than a tired professional smile. He dismissed the idea that she was his pursuer, for a woman in her occupation had her time accounted for, and could not easily deal with him beyond serving him drinks and coffee. He went back to his notebook and began to put together something he could hand to Merlin Powell.

"Working?" Dunstan asked a bit later.

"Nature of the job," said Fleming.

Dunstan did his best to look sympathetic. "You're a dedicated fellow."

"I'm a journalist with a dead-line and an editor who gets his knickers in a twist when things are late." Fleming continued to write, doing his best to keep in mind how much he had told Powell.

"You seem to take the pressure well," Dunstan observed. "Better than I do, that's for sure."

"Nature of the job," Fleming repeated. This mild exchange

restored his equilibrium and lightened his mood enough that when Dunstan spoke to him again, he was able to answer with a semblance of interest that lasted until the pilot announced they were beginning their descent to Kingston.

Chapter 30

FLEMING MADE it through Customs without a hitch, then took off toward the car park to retrieve his Rapier. He paused to light up his last cigarette, then flung his bags into the boot, got into the auto, and started it up, taking satisfaction in the reliable sound of the motor. Until that moment, he hadn't realized how uncertain he had been about the Rapier, for other, more pressing concerns had occupied his thoughts. The note he had found in the Rapier that matched the one in the Packard had been relegated to minor irritations, but he was now keenly aware that he had feared for his auto as he had feared for the Packard. He knew he had been concerned about the auto, his house, and Cesar, for all of them were his responsibility. He swung onto the road and headed toward Kingston, planning to call upon Merlin Powell to hand in his accounting and turn back his remaining funds—minus ten pounds on general principles.

The road was crowded and progress was slow, which troubled Fleming, who still felt he was being followed, and could not shake the apprehension no matter how much logical argument he offered himself. Uncomfortable thoughts traveled with him, unwelcome companions, and he had to fight off the impulse to give into the funk they engendered in him. For a couple of miles a taxi followed him, and this made him uneasy until the vehicle turned off and made for a cluster of hotels near the shore. With a sigh, Fleming finished his Players and tossed the butt into the road as he headed toward the building that housed the editorial offices. He wondered if there had been any word on Sir William, and tried to formulate a way to ask it without revealing that he had withheld information from Merlin Powell.

He found a parking place a half-block away from his goal. He pulled the canvas over the cabin and secured it, then decided to take his luggage with him, for on the street this way, it struck him as very exposed. If only he had some kind of alarm that would frighten off anyone getting near his auto! Or, better yet, something that could identify and mark anyone attempting to damage the auto or rifle through its contents, or an auto that would recognize him and give access to no one else. He was still thinking of the various possibilities when he stepped into the little tobacconist's shop across the street from Powell's office where he purchased two packs of Players and a paper, which he tucked under his arm before he crossed the street, bags in hand, and went up to Powell's office.

Miss Butterly gave Fleming a wide smile. "So good to see you back again," she told him.

"Good to be back," Fleming answered. "His nibs about?"

"In his office. I'll buzz you through. Just let me let him know you're coming." She fiddled with the interoffice communicator on her desk. "Mister Powell, Mister Fleming has just returned. Shall I send him in?"

A growl came from the machine.

"Go on in. You know the way." She gestured grandly, and Fleming bowed slightly as he went past her desk.

Merlin Powell was ruddy and exasperated today. He puffed and slapped his thick hands on the desk. "So. What have you to say for yourself?"

"I'm back," said Fleming at his most genial. "And I think there is something very rum going on."

Powell's glower softened to a scowl. "How do you mean?"

Without any extensive preamble, Fleming began, "I have the basic information here, and I found out that another of Krandall's colleagues was murdered a short while ago. That strikes me as more than a nasty coincidence." He put down the notes he had made during the last hour of the flight, notes that attempted to create order out of his thoughts and experiences. "Someone's definitely trying to hide something; we're being thrown off the track, deliberately so, which means that who-ever is doing this is aware that he is being sought. I'll say this for him: he's infernally clever, and wants to put me off the scent, or confuse me so that I cannot recognize it amid the general chaos, like a fox running through a stream to elude the hounds. And so far, he's doing an excellent job of it."

"Do you have sources to prove this?" Powell was sitting forward in his chair. "Anything we can use?"

Fleming offered the file from Los Alamos. "There's enough to ask questions. I can show a connection between Krandall and Preussin—both deceased recently and unnaturally. And there is a third man, a J. Cathcart, present location or condition unknown. The first two men were comrades of Cathcart's, part of the same work during the War. I can't point to a specific culprit or motive, but off-hand, I'd say someone is hunting them down; I'm not alone in that conviction, incidentally—there's an FBI agent who concurs. Assuming this is an accurate assessment of circumstances, I wouldn't want to be J. Cathcart right now."

Powell had picked up a magnifying glass to read the pho-tostatic copies. "How did you get this?"

"I asked for it at the press office at the Los Alamos Laboratories and military base," said Fleming cheekily. "I spent the better part of a morning waiting for it. This is what I was given."

As he continued to read, Powell said, "We can publish some of this, but not all of it, of course. And we can cover the deaths of Krandall and Preussin from the perspective of men working on the same project who came to violent ends. It doesn't say anything about Preussin's death in this report."

"It doesn't say anything about Krandall's, either." Fleming cleared his throat. "Sorry. I didn't mean to make light of this. I only just had the information from an FBI agent, who was reporting on what he had from the RCMP. I doubt whether it has drawn much attention in Canada."

"I can have the teletypist send an inquiry to Canada. Do you know which province the murder occurred in?"

"Only that it was near Hudson's Bay," said Fleming, feeling slightly less harried than when he had come into the office. "I gather the location was fairly remote, but that's not remarkable in that part of Canada."

"All right," Powell sighed. "That will have to do. There can't be too many horrible murders reported in that region, can there? What is the connection to Krandall again?—Los Alamos and the Manhattan Project? Is there anything more? With Krandall and this other chap killed within a short time, all commonality can be significant."

"Los Alamos, for a starting point," said Fleming, thinking about what he had read in Sir William's files. He could not use that material, of course, but he could try to find ways to confirm what he knew. "Anything more on the Krandall case?"

"The lads are in England, and now they say they didn't do

it, that they only witnessed the killing, by accident, and that they wanted to get away, for fear of reprisals against them. They said they confessed to be safely in the hands of the police. It's just the sort of desperate move a youngster in trouble might make." He slapped his hands on the desk again. "Not a bad story, in its way, but under the circumstances, hardly convincing. Too pat. As if they cooked it up between them on the flight to London."

Fleming wasn't so sure. "Who do they say killed him?"

"A man they didn't know—well-dressed, soft-spoken, good manners—until he took to cutting Krandall up. They say the man was known to Krandall, who welcomed him, albeit reluctantly, to Swan's Way. Apparently he had business with Krandall, or so the young men insist, because Krandall was upset when the fellow arrived, saying he had nothing the man might want. They said he looked like an important person. He spoke some kind of French part of the time, but they couldn't—or wouldn't—remember what he said." Powell shook his head portentously. "It's an interesting tale."

"So it is," said Fleming, growing more uneasy as he listened.

"Tell me what you make of it," said Powell sharply.

"I don't know," said Fleming, frowning as he tried to sort out the increasing puzzles. "I'll mull it over this afternoon, and tell you tonight, if you'll come out to my place. I'll try to give you an installation on my coverage by tomorrow morning."

"That will be satisfactory," said Powell. "And we'll discuss the whole of the story when I arrive. Have Cesar make some of that wonderful chowder of his. This could be a long evening."

"I'll tell him you asked for it," said Fleming, smiling slightly. "You'll want a whole meal, I suppose. I'll tell Cesar to be ready for you." He paused in the act of turning toward the door. "Oh. I'm going to stop to have a word or two with Lord Broxton. I'm late with my report to him, and it may take me a while to soothe his ruffled feathers, as they say."

"I don't envy you that mission." He chuckled and tapped his big fingers on the desk. "Still, soonest done, soonest over."

"My thoughts exactly." He didn't think he should mention Agent Hotchkiss, not yet. "If I get home at a reasonable time, I'll do a rough draught for you. If I don't, we'll discuss what it's to have in it."

"Acceptable, provided I have your first installation by noon tomorrow." Powell held out his hand. "You have something for Eccles?"

Fleming pulled out his wallet and handed over the unspent money. "Count it and give me the receipt. Sorry this was such an expensive trip. I'll give you a full listing on all my expenses, and you can give it to Eccles at your leisure."

"You didn't indulge your taste for high living, did you?" Powell asked sharply as his hand closed around the money.

"I was only in New Orleans for a couple of hours. I don't know that there *is* high living in Roswell, New Mexico, or any of the other places I went. Certainly no gambling, other than poker, and only one woman showed any real interest, and that was because the building was on fire." He thought of Myra for a moment and said, "She was hardly seduceable: married, not young, not the sort you'd look at, usually, but she was attractive in her own way."

"Doesn't sound like your usual flirt," said Powell.

"She wasn't," Fleming agreed.

"How much did you spend on her?" Powell asked wearily as he counted out the few remaining dollars and the pounds.

"I bought her a meal in a diner and a tankful of petrol," said Fleming. "It was all she wanted."

Powell laughed his incredulity. "If you're brazen enough to say so, I'm gullible enough to believe you." He took a sheet from his memo pad and wrote out a receipt. "There. I see you didn't use any of the real money." He tapped the roll of pounds. "All here."

"Almost all. I'll tell you about it all tonight." Suddenly he yawned. "Sorry. It's catching up with me. I slept in the airport lounge last night."

"That must have been unpleasant," said Powell.

"You can't imagine," said Fleming. "I want to sleep the clock around." He said it lightly enough, but he knew it was the truth.

"What about tonight, then? I need your story tomorrow, but if you're going to fall asleep—" He let the matter hang between them.

"I won't fall asleep," said Fleming, a bit curtly. "But I may not rise at dawn, either." He put his hand on the doorknob. "Shall I expect you at five? Tea and sherry?"

"Five it is," said Powell, and waved Fleming away. "And give me your expense records then."

"I will. I have them in my luggage." Fleming cocked his head.

"Your luggage is with you," Powell reminded him.

"Oh, very well," said Fleming, and got his bags, opened up the outer compartment and took out his notebook, flipped it to the back and tore out a sheet of paper. Then he handed over a number of crumpled receipts paper-clipped together. "This is what I kept. There's a bit more in my notes, but not for significant amounts." He closed his bag. "Anything more?"

"If you would, explain why you needed a jacket and shirt and trousers?" Powell said, glancing over the page.

"I took one full change of clothing. It was damaged by smoke and soot. I'll tell you the whole of it later." He started toward the door. "May I ask Miss Butterly to pave the way for me with Lord Broxton?"

"Certainly, if you want him to build up a full head of steam before you get there." Powell winked.

"Ordinarily I wouldn't, but I'll have to ask to use a secure line to talk with the FBI, and for that I'll need some soothing done in advance. She's adept at soothing, isn't she?" Fleming waited for the agreeing nod, then pulled the door open and stepped out of the office.

Miss Butterly smiled at Fleming, a bright, professional smile that even an American could envy. "Now that wasn't too bad, was it?"

"Not at all," said Fleming. "And you could make it better by calling Lord Broxton and informing him I have some confidential intelligence to deliver to him. I'll also need a secure line to place a call to an American FBI agent in New Mexico. I'd appreciate it if you could explain that to him, or to his assistant Stowe, and make the appropriate arrangements."

There was a long silence from Miss Butterly as if she were trying to determine whether or not he were serious. Then she said, "If you have the gall to ask this of me, I have the nerve to make the call."

This didn't seem too encouraging to Fleming, but he nodded to show he accepted her offer. "Thanks," he said, taking his bags and going toward the stairs, all but running down them, already feeling he was lagging behind.

Chapter 31

STOWE TOLD Fleming that Lord Broxton was expecting him. "Lord Broxton has a distinguished visitor with him; you will have to wait to speak with him. By the way, your office rang up and requested a secure line for your use."

"I'll be glad to wait," said Fleming, then added, "perhaps you could provide me with that secure line while I'm waiting? That way I'll have an up-to-the-minute report to give his lordship."

"Second office on your left. We'll see that you get your call through." Stowe had not changed his expression by so much as a hair, but Fleming had the clear impression that he was enjoying this.

"Very good; I'll appreciate it," said Fleming, wondering how secure the secure line would be. He decided to proceed on the assumption he was being overheard, no matter what he said, and was uneasy about the larger implications of that conviction. It distressed him to know that even within this center of government, he could not be entirely safe. He went into the office—it was anonymous enough: a desk, three file cabinets, two chairs, two lamps, and a hunting print on the wall—and sat down behind the desk, then reached for the receiver. He noticed there were no ashtrays on the desk, and so kept his cigarettes in his pocket.

The Government House operator responded at once. "You are requesting a secure line. Overseas or Jamaican?"

"Overseas. United States. New Mexico." He took his note-book out and gave her the number at the Pecos Vista. "I'll speak to extension fifty-one there." He waited while the op-erator placed the call, heard the American operator connect the call, and heard Bert answer. Finally, he listened for the coffee-grinder noise of a secure line being activated, and a moment later, Lemmuel Hotchkiss picked up the telephone and the noise stopped.

"It's Ian Fleming," he said.

"I thought so. It was you or Captain MacGregor of the RCMP, and I talked to him twenty minutes ago. Not to say that I won't hear from him again." Hotchkiss cleared his throat. "Good for you, calling back this way. I have a little more to tell you. You got something to write on?"

"That I do," said Fleming, slapping his notebook open and reaching for his pencil. "Go on. I'm ready."

"Okay. Here goes." He coughed. "This is as much as we've been able to verify, between our sources, the RCMP, and MI5. At the end of the War, three men were approached by a French industrialist called—"

"Soleilsur," Fleming said.

"Yes. How did you know about that?"

"His name has come up in connection to this case," said Fleming, deliberately unspecific.

"I can just imagine," Hotchkiss said, and went on, "The three men were a J. Julian J. Cathcart, who apparently accepted his offer; a Geoffrey David Angus Krandall, who did not; and Preussin, who you know about already. He turned down So-leilsur and left for the backwoods of Canada for reasons that still aren't entirely clear, but from what the RCMP told me, Preussin thought Soleilsur was up to no good—what that no good might be is anyone's guess. There were notebooks, all burned but for a few scraps, one of which seems to be about methods of mining harbors with atomic mines, and using them to control shipping all over the world. That's partly a guess, based on three charred bits of paper, and it is a bit of a stretch to come to that conclusion on so very little evidence, although it does fit. However, since we've no notion what was lost in the fire, we cannot assume that we have the whole of it. It could be real, it could be the kind of writing some madmen do. Hell, it could be part of a novel, or God knows what."

"Nothing else?" Fleming said as he looked over his sparse notes, hoping he would be able to make sense of them later. He poised his pencil and gave Hotchkiss his full attention.

"Maybe. The Mounties have a file on Soleilsur, and I'm supposed to be getting a copy of it." He paused. "I'll send you the salient points, if you like; I'll use the address of your publisher, if that's satisfactory."

"It will be. I'll let Powell know to expect it. That should please him now that he has my expense record to deal with." Fleming chuckled slightly. "He could have had to pay a great deal more."

"Kept you on a short leash, did he?" Hotchkiss asked and, without waiting for an answer, continued, "Soleilsur does marine salvage, and other kinds of undersea engineering; he's been working around the Mediterranean for twenty years, and has been expanding his business since the War—lots of work for him to do, and he's made a fortune at it. There are other business enterprises, but exactly what they may be we haven't found out yet. That's what makes Preussin's work troubling."

"No fear," said Fleming in agreement.

"Actually, I'm becoming quite afraid. Everyone worries

about the Russkies getting the Bomb, but we keep pretty good tabs on them. What worries me is if someone we *don't* know about develops atomic capabilities: what then? All this shit about Communist infiltration of the CIG won't mean anything if the real trouble has nothing to do with Marx and Stalin. If we're up against a greedy man with enough money and the materiel—" He stopped suddenly, as if aware that he was speaking against current FBI efforts. "Just thought I should mention it."

"And I thank you for doing it. My government has many of the same assumptions, and as you say, it leaves them badly exposed if they aren't correct in their suppositions." He had a moment of feeling queasy, a recognition of just how dangerous an unknown power with atomic weapons could be.

"Well. Keep your eyes—"

"—peeled," Fleming finished for him, glad for the tweak of amusement the expression provided.

"Just what I was going to say." He coughed again. "Look, Fleming, I don't want to discourage you, but you're in pretty damn deep, and you might want to get out while you can. This isn't a job for newspaper reporters, if you take my meaning."

"I haven't always been a newspaper reporter, you know," Fleming reminded him gently.

"So MI5 told me," Hotchkiss responded. "But that was during the War with your government behind you. Right now, all you have is an editor, and I wouldn't count on him to back you up if this turns bad on you."

Privately Fleming shared Hotchkiss's doubts, but he kept up a game front. "I don't think the government would hang me out to dry, not if this is as big an issue as you imply it is."

"Okay, but don't say I didn't warn you," Hotchkiss told him.

"Give me a call tomorrow. We can trade information."

"I'll try. I don't know if I'll be able to," Fleming said. "If I do call, it'll be from my editor's office on an unsecured line."

"I'll keep that in mind," said Hotchkiss. "In the meantime, good luck. I think you're going to need it."

"Thanks. You, too," Fleming said, and rung off, unhappy thoughts clumping in his mind like public school oatmeal. He slapped his notebook closed, put his pencil back in his inner pocket, and stepped out into the corridor.

From his desk, Stowe regarded him narrowly. "It will be a while before you can go in. Would you like a cup of tea while you're waiting."

"Yes, if you would. White, please," he said as he dropped into one of the uncomfortable chairs along the wall.

Stowe lifted his receiver and gave a terse order to the operator who answered, then went back to reviewing the stack of newspapers that had been brought to him. "Don't see your name on many of these articles, Mister Fleming," he observed.

"I do features work," Fleming said, only partially listening. He was preoccupied with what he had just heard from Hotchkiss and paid little attention to Stowe's dig.

"A luxury for you," said Stowe, and went back to reading.

Fleming shrugged off the comment, putting it down to the jealousy of petty bureaucrats. Much as he wanted a cigarette, he waited, not wanting to give Lord Broxton any excuse for complaint. When a steward brought a pot of tea with a cup-and-saucer and a jug of milk on a tray, Fleming accepted it, and realized he was famished. He poured the tea, noticing it was strong and fragrant, quite unlike the cat-lap he had had to endure in America. Adding the milk, he had a sudden thought of how easily he could be poisoned: something in the milk, something in the tea, or something in the cup, and he would keel over for no apparent reason, and that would be the end of the investigation. He told himself he was being foolish, that here in Government House he was as safe as he would be at Whitehall. This reassurance did not have the effect he sought, for he was still aware that he could be done away with there as readily as anywhere else. As he picked up his cup, he made himself swallow, ignoring his own trepidation. What was the matter with him? He was acting as if he were in the enemy camp. Finishing the tea, he considered leaving and returning at a later time, but knew he had offended Lord Broxton already, and didn't want to compound the error.

A single ring to Stowe's telephone brought a prompt response from the fussy secretary, who snatched the receiver from the cradle and spoke in an obsequious hush. "Very well, my lord. I will do as you request." He hung up the receiver and looked directly at Fleming. "Lord Broxton's guest is about to leave, but you are asked to go down to the office now. You know the way, do you not? Down the hall to the end?"

"Yes, I do. Thank you, Stowe. I appreciate the tea. If I may leave my bags with you?" Accepting Stowe's nod for agreement, Fleming slipped his notebook into his jacket pocket and strode down the corridor, keenly aware of the revolver lying against the small of his back and the knife in his pocket. What would Lord Broxton think if he knew Fleming was armed? He dismissed the matter from his mind and headed toward the door.

The door to Lord Broxton's office stood open and Fleming could see the choleric peer standing beside his desk talking to a tall, imposing man in a finely tailored business suit; there was something vaguely familiar about him, but Fleming couldn't place him. The visitor wore an expression of slight condescension that startled Fleming, who didn't suppose that Lord Broxton was often treated to that mild contempt.

". . . and we will expect you and Lady Broxton on Thursday night," the visitor was saying. "Don't disappoint us."

"I wouldn't think of it, Mister Sissons. This is a pleasure indeed. I can't tell you how pleased I am to receive your invitation. Now that you've returned to Jamaica, I hope we might become better acquainted." Lord Broxton sounded almost giddy with excitement. "We shall be there at three."

"We dine at five, sherry at four. The concert is at eight. You will stay until Sunday, of course. Monsieur Soleilsur and I will not hear of anything less. We count on your expert opinion in regard to our project." Mister Sissons's smile was a bit reptilian; Fleming almost expected to see a thin, forked tongue flick over his lips.

"We will look forward to it, Lady Broxton and I. Thank you and Monsieur Soleilsur again for your gracious—" His effusions were cut off.

"Yes. Our pleasure. I'm sure this will be a most profitable venture for us all. Your endorsement will be a valuable service to us." He picked up his hat from the seat of the upholstered chair facing the desk. "I won't keep you. No doubt you have many demands on your time, Lord Broxton."

Lord Broxton glowed with importance. "Indeed I do."

"Then I am doubly grateful for the time you have given me," said Mister Sissons in growing haste to be gone.

Lord Broxton wasn't quite finished emptying the butter-boat over his visitor. "But I can always make time for you, Mister Sissons, and for Monsieur Soleilsur. I anticipate our dealings will be satisfactory to all of us. Your SS Industries will be a boon to everyone in Jamaica. I am encouraged by what you have shown me of the new harbor installation plans; I am confident that this will prove a great asset to the island." His obsequious smile surprised Fleming as much as it disgusted Mister Sissons.

Mister Sissons said, "Until Thursday, then," and left before Lord Broxton could think of a way to detain him. Passing Fleming in the corridor, he gave a glance such as one might show to an insect impeding his path.

So that was Alysa Sissons's husband, Fleming thought as he went on to Lord Broxton's door, the man who had met her in New Orleans, the man with political ambitions and a personal fortune. Fleming regarded his departing figure with wary interest, trying to convince himself that seeing the man here was just another coincidence.

Chapter 32

"THERE YOU are, Fleming," Lord Broxton almost shouted, his subservience replaced with his customary self-important bluster. "About time you got back here."

Fleming resisted the urge to speak brusquely to Lord Broxton, for that would accomplish nothing more than renewed animosity between them. "I'm sorry, Lord Broxton. My work turned out to be more complicated than I had first thought it would be."

"So your office informed me," said Lord Broxton abruptly.

"For which I am grateful; my travels proved more extensive than I had first anticipated," said Fleming. "It has been a demanding time."

"With Sir William still missing, I should think so," said Lord Broxton. "You've gone about things in a most perplexing manner, if you don't mind my saying so."

"In regard to Sir William, I guess you have seen or heard nothing of him? He hasn't been found by anyone? No one has asked for ransom, or made any threats concerning his welfare?" Fleming was doing his best to keep his manner cordial, but it was an effort.

"Were you expecting something of the sort?" Lord Broxton demanded.

"No, but I thought it was possible that there might have been some word, or—" He left it hanging. Why were such bombastic fools as Broxton allowed to hold diplomatic posts, he wondered.

"I have heard nothing one way or the other, except for the confirmation of your report vouchsafed me by MI5. No one has reported anything to me." Lord Broxton began to pace, his countenance set in petulant lines. "Well? What have your inquiries told you?"

"There are two deaths that appear to be connected to Sir William's disappearance, for they were men who have been his colleagues," Fleming said bluntly in the hope of getting Lord Broxton's full attention.

"Two you say," Lord Broxton challenged. "Geoffrey Krandall and what other?"

"There was a Canadian scientist who was found in the wilderness near Hudson's Bay. He was part of the Manhattan Project, as Sir William and Geoffrey Krandall were." He decided not to say much of anything about Cathcart; if Lord Broxton were going to be spending a long week-end with Soleilsur, the less he knew about the situation the better, for he could easily let something slip that could ruin this investigation. "There may be a third party, but I haven't been able to confirm either his existence or his present location."

"He may not be part of this?" Lord Broxton asked, a shade too quickly.

"He may not exist, as I've said, but I am going on the assumption that he does. There were three men called Moan, Groan, and Sigh. If Sigh isn't Sir William, then he must be another man, but I cannot discover whom he may be." He wasn't entirely comfortable with his lies, but he didn't dare trust Lord Broxton with the truth. He hurried to bring his thoughts into order.

"What has this to do with your investigation?" Lord Broxton asked. "Does it mean that you suspect yet *another* culprit?"

Fleming didn't allow himself to be distracted. "I can't say for sure, not yet. I don't want to make unfounded assumptions, or accusations. I'll have to try to find out more about Sir William's activities, but you do understand that it may be difficult to get all the information I may require."

Lord Broxton rounded on Fleming, "See here: you can't go poking about in military secrets on the off-chance that you may discover a tid-bit of information that might help you to find Sir William. If the case is that difficult, best leave it to the professionals."

"I *was* a professional," Fleming reminded him.

"Was," Lord Broxton repeated.

"Some of those secrets are my secrets," Fleming went on. "You don't think I would try to compromise the government, do you?"

"If you did," Lord Broxton said smugly, "there would be immediate repercussions. This Robertson thing has shown us to what depths supposedly loyal Britons may sink."

"And a loyal American. James Hendley was as much a part of the mischief as Robertson." Fleming waited to see what Lord Broxton's response would be.

"You cannot view this as another scandal," said his lordship. "You have allowed yourself to be influenced by the Americans, who have much to answer for in this sad coil." He went to the side-board and opened the upper part of the cabinet, revealing a fully stocked bar. Taking the time to pour himself a single-malt Scotch, he downed the drink, and poured a second. "I will not have such disgraceful doings on my watch, and so I warn you, Mister Fleming."

Keenly aware of the implications of Lord Broxton's lack of hospitality, Fleming kept his tone as neutral as possible. "I have no wish to give any embarrassment, Lord Broxton. But if there is damage being done, I believe the security of the Empire must supersede any worries of discomfiture. I believe I have a duty to do what I can to unearth our enemies."

"Well enough, for you. You are a journalist and you're expected to poke and pry. But when you bring out the hornets, you do not feel their stings, as I do." He drank down his second Scotch and poured a third rather more generous measure than the first two.

"If any part of my investigation redounds to your discredit, I apologize for it now. But consider my situation if you would: I know Sir William is missing, possibly killed, and that other men who worked with him on atomic secrets have been murdered recently. Aside from my experience during the War, I couldn't let something as problematic as this go unaddressed. As a reporter, I have an obligation to pursue my story. As an Englishman, I have a duty to protect my country. How am I to accomplish any of those things if I must reserve my actions in order to maintain your sanction?"

Lord Broxton scowled. "You're a clever chap—newspaper johnnies so often are. You throw words around and make me think that you aren't responsible for anything that happens."

"Lord Broxton, I'm not doing this as an intellectual exercise," said Fleming in a rush of exasperation. "You don't seem to appreciate how much danger we may all be in. You tell me that my hands are tied, and I must accept the limitations you impose for the good of the country. The secrets these dead men worked with have deadly implications, and Robertson is the sole culprit in this case, although how he could instigate the kidnapping of Sir William, I cannot think, nor can I find anything that supports such a supposition." He knew he had stepped over the line, but just at present he didn't care. "I have no reason to do anything to humiliate you—you are the least of my concerns. I want to be certain that the capabilities to build atomic weapons don't spread any further than they have already. And I am very much afraid something of that sort could happen if this situation goes unchecked and undisclosed. It isn't only foreign governments who worry me, but individuals with great fortunes and greater ambitions. Good God, man! The bastard's already got away with killing two—and possibly three—men that we know of. What else is he going to be allowed to do before we are willing to stop him?"

"That is enough," said Lord Broxton with awful hauteur. "You forget where you are, sir. I will overlook your outburst because I see you are laboring under strong emotions. No doubt your journey has exhausted you." He glowered in the direction of the window. "Take a day to gather your thoughts, and give me your report—in writing. I don't think it would be advisable for us to speak face-to-face."

Fleming took a deep breath. "If you insist, m'lord," he said, ducking his head more out of habit than any vestige of respect for Lord Broxton.

"I will not chide you more. I can see you are exercised in—" He stopped. "I'll excuse you now."

"Very well, m'lord," said Fleming stiffly.

"I don't want to hear anything more from you until you can assure me there will not be another lapse in conduct." He tossed off his Scotch. "Lady Broxton and I will be away for a long weekend. If you would prefer to postpone our next interview until my return, that will be satisfactory to me, provided there is any necessity for another meeting between us. You may leave your report with Stowe. He'll put it into my hands." He waved in the direction of the door. "Good day to you, Mister Fleming."

"Good day, Lord Broxton," Fleming said, turning on his heel and leaving the opulent room with long strides that were perilously close to flight. As he walked, he began to realize that in spite of the unpleasantness the meeting had gone fairly well for him. He had not had to reveal more to Lord Broxton than minimal information, and he had not been required to speculate on his discoveries, both of which struck him as fortunate; let Lord Broxton bluster and bully all he liked, he—Ian Fleming—would do his utmost to honor his obligations whether his lordship will or no.

Stowe didn't do more than glance up as Fleming retrieved his bags from the side of his desk. He signaled to the guards to let Fleming pass, and went on reviewing the memos on his desk.

"Don't you have any recreation, Stowe?" Fleming asked as he headed toward the tall doors.

"I play tennis, Mister Fleming," was his disinterested answer.

Fleming uttered a single laugh. "Well, then, carry on," he said as he pushed through the doors.

His Rapier seemed eager to be on the road, as if, machine though it were, it could sense the state of its driver's mind, much as a horse would do with its rider. Fleming drove out of Kingston, impatiently hooting at the slower vehicles around him, and was soon on the open road, bound for his estate.

Cesar was waiting in the kitchen garden when Fleming

drove in. He smiled his greeting. "Mister Fleming, sah," he called. "Welcome home."

"Thank you, Cesar. It's good to be home," he said with feeling as he drove the Lagonda Rapier into the garage and shut off the motor. He got out of the auto, took his bags, and went toward the front door, hoping to have his comfort restored once inside.

Cesar opened the door, a bit short of breath from his rush through the house. "How was your journey, sah?"

"Long," Fleming answered, and went toward the stairs. "Cesar, will you draw me a bath? Heat some water for me? I need a good soak. I fear I smell like old socks." He chuckled, but with a degree of self-deprecation, for he feared it might be true.

"Perhaps a saddle-pad," said Cesar. "Go on up. I'll have the bath ready in half an hour. In the meantime, if you want a bite of luncheon, I can provide that."

Fleming stopped three treads up the stairs. "I am hungry. And I want to have a drink."

"Gin?" Cesar suggested, watching as Fleming considered the possibilities.

"Rum, I think. With mango and a dash of bitters. No ice, but chilled." As he spoke, Fleming's mouth watered.

"Of course," said Cesar. "I'll have it for you by the time you change your clothes."

Fleming took the hint. "They *are* ripe, aren't they?" He resumed his climb to the upper floor, his bags feeling heavier with each step. By the time he reached his bedroom, it seemed he was carrying two sacks of anvils; he set them down and peeled out of his jacket, then emptied the pockets, setting the knife aside on the nightstand. Unbuckling his holster belt, he put the revolver with the knife, glad to be rid of its weight at last. Stretching, he felt relaxed for the first time in days. He skinned off his shirt, wadded it, and tossed it onto the Silent Butler in the corner. Then he removed his singlet and went to get his robe from the closet. As he pulled it on, he felt the familiar caress of the heavy cotton, and at last began to persuade himself that he was safe at last.

Five minutes later he was downstairs, barefoot and tired. He went to the lounge where Cesar met him, a glass in hand.

"Here you are, sah," he said, giving Fleming his drink.

"Thank you." He took a long sip, sighed, and sat down on the sofa. "Oh, by the way, I should mention that Mister Powell is coming out to dine. Do we have something to feed him? He's asked for your chowder, but that won't be enough unless you make a vat of it."

"I'll go into the market and buy a chicken and some fish, if there is something fresh. I know Jared Smith will have conch and clam." He pointed to a stack of envelopes. "Your mail, sah. As you see, there is a letter from Mister Coward."

"Yes, I see," said Fleming. "Thank you, Cesar," he said, motioning Cesar to leave. "Let me know when the bath is ready."

"I will, sah," said Cesar. "While you bathe, I will walk to the market."

"Yes. That seems suitable," said Fleming remotely as he opened his first envelope, a flimsy blue air-letter from Durham, a missive from his cousin. He read through the family news with marginal interest, then opened Noel Coward's letter, entertained by the witty accounts of his recent activities in London, including a sly joke about the new theatre season. By the time Cesar called him to the bathroom, he had finished reading his mail, and was beginning to think life could be ordinary again, a conviction that remained with him all through his bath and the opening of his second bag: on top of his clothes was a half-sheet of paper reading: LEAVE WELL ENOUGH ALONE.

Chapter 33

FLEMING HAD two pages of material to hand over to Merlin Powell when he arrived. He had thrown himself into the task after spending the greater part of an hour trying fruitlessly to deduce who had put that infernal note into his bag; he could not imagine Stowe doing it, and neither of the guards seemed to be likely candidates for such action. Lord Broxton wouldn't stoop to such activities, and if Walter Sissons were a suspect— He could not think who else could have got into his bags without him seeing, and attempts to discern possible suspects gave him a headache, so he concentrated on his writing as much to help him get back a semblance of equanimity as to show any industrious intentions. He handed them over to Powell, saying as he did, "I'll want another go at it before I turn it in."

"Very well," said Powell, taking the sheets of paper and beginning to read. "I see the *u* is still crooked," he added. "You really ought to have someone repair that."

"I will," said Fleming, going into the lounge, where the delicious odors from the kitchen pursued them like enchanting wraiths: conch, clam, cream, shallots, pepper, garlic, and ginger all blended together into the chowder Powell so relished.

Powell continued to read, inhaling conspicuously in anticipation. "Not bad for a first crack at it. You've presented a vast amount of information in relatively few words," he went on. "But I think it may be a bit too dense, if you understand my concerns. I don't think the average reader would be comfortable trying to sort all this out. I think it may be as well to do the pieces on Krandall and Preussin separately, Krandall first, of course. You needn't wrap it all up in a neat package."

"There isn't a neat package to wrap it in," Fleming complained mildly.

"My point precisely," Powell agreed. "Let's use that—*Mystery Surrounding Murdered Mathematician Deepening*—that sort of thing."

"All right," said Fleming, wondering if Powell would say the same thing if he told him about Sir William, and the three notes he had been given, or the tracing device that had been attached to his Packard in America. Something Dunstan had said on the airplane was niggling at the back of his mind, but he didn't take much time to think about it—whatever it was would come later, as he sorted all this out. He went to the bar. "What's your pleasure?"

"Gin, I think, a splash of tonic, no ice." Powell had sat down facing the French windows, and was scrutinizing the pages in front of him. "About your sources—they'll stand up to inquiry, I suppose. This report from Los Alamos—is there any reason we shouldn't quote it?"

"None that I can think of," said Fleming. "I requested it as a journalist, and I was given the photostatic prints by the U.S. Army."

"Then we should have no trouble quoting from the information. I'll have to have the photostats, to make sure the excerpts are accurate. And if we have them to quote from, we can cite them as our source, and not have to bother with a second source, for confirmation." He shrugged a bit apologetically. "I always feel as if I'm asking you to do something awful to your copy-book."

"You're making sure we don't get sued, hardly a copy-book problem," Fleming said as he finished making Powell's drink. "You may want to run it by Whitehall, to be sure it doesn't step on any toes that might not like being stepped on." He said this without a trace of the slyness he was feeling. He had not had much experience of having to skirt around the government instead of having its support, no matter how indirectly given. This position perplexed him and made his work more difficult; he said none of this to Powell, who wouldn't understand.

Powell responded just as Fleming thought he would. "If we have it from the Yanks, and they released it, Whitehall can go bugger itself." His belligerence departed as quickly as it had come. "We can claim innocence, if we have to, and say the Americans are at fault. So long as we stick to the material you were given at Los Alamos, then there can be no objection about our methods."

"Just so," said Fleming as he handed the tall glass to Powell. "Chin-chin."

Hoisting the glass, Powell said, "To the story."

Fleming lifted his thistle of brandy. "To the story," he agreed.

"Now, then, Fleming," Powell went on as he put his glass down, "you say this Canadian chap was murdered. How much official material do you have on that?"

"Nothing official, more's the pity, only what my contact at the FBI reported to me; his information came from the RCMP, and I don't know what, or how much, has been released to the public. We may have to scrounge, as the Americans say, to find a source for this one." Fleming sat down, trying to appear at ease.

"Um," Powell declared.

"If you contact the Canadian office, they should have something to tell you," Fleming continued, as if Powell hadn't mentioned it earlier that day.

"The only news the Toronto office has is that a man was found murdered in a remote hunting lodge. 'Authorities are making inquiries.' " The last was tinged with revulsion.

"Then perhaps: 'sources within the investigation'? " Fleming suggested.

" 'Informed sources' would be safer, since you're not in direct contact with the RCMP, if we can't find anyone to talk to us on the record," said Powell. "Make sure you don't state anything as absolute fact unless the information has been made available."

"In other words, I can say the man was found murdered, not that Mister Maxwell Preussin was found flayed and mutilated," Fleming said, and saw Powell go white. "Oh. Sorry. I thought I'd mentioned how he was killed." He took a cigarette from the brass container on the table and lit it.

Powell took a second, larger sip of gin-and-tonic. "I thought he had been beaten and stabbed, as Krandall was."

"He may have been," Fleming told him. "But what the Mounties found was rather worse than that." His voice dropped as he tried to dismiss his apprehension from his thoughts. "I think it's prudent to keep those details off the page, unless the Canadians release the information to the press."

"We're dealing with very dangerous men here," said Powell, somewhat unnecessarily.

"And desperate, too, I should think," Fleming said softly. Once again he had the impression that he had overlooked something about this investigation, something he had noticed earlier, but that he had relegated to the stack of apparently minor details that was not—the thing continued to elude him. "I'll see what I can determine by tomorrow. And I'll need to make a call to the States in the morning. Will the paper pay for it?"

"Is it necessary?" Powell asked with a fatalistic sigh.

"Very likely. I won't be certain until I make it," said Fleming.

Cesar came to the door with a platter of little thimble-quiches and mushrooms stuffed with cheese-and-crab, all toasty from the broiler. "I thought you might like something to whet your appetites, sah," he announced as he set the platter down on the table.

"Thank you, Cesar," said Fleming, managing a smile, although the juxtaposition of food and the discussion of hideous slaughter did not pique his hunger. "I know we'll enjoy them."

"Thank you, sah," said Cesar, and withdrew.

"You have a wonderful houseman there, Fleming," said Powell around a mouthful of quiche.

"I know," said Fleming. He reached out and took one of the stuffed mushrooms, popped it in his mouth, and let himself enjoy the savor of it.

"I think I'll check with Toronto again tomorrow morning." He chewed on another quiche. "They may have released something more. In a case like this, I'd like to have a hard source we can cite, like the Los Alamos material. Speculation can get us into trouble."

"Attribution instead of supposition," said Fleming with a nod.

"So do you have any recommendations how I might go

about this?" Powell asked with a slight, impish smile.

"Hotchkiss, my FBI contact, mentioned a Captain Mac-Gregor; you might see if you can get him to confirm any of this—officially," Fleming suggested. He looked about uneasily as if he expected someone to appear with more bad news.

"Captain MacGregor," said Powell, committing the name to memory. "Do you happen to know where he's posted?"

"Winnipeg, I should think," said Fleming. "If not, Winnipeg should be able to find him for you."

Powell shook his head. "It could be difficult. The RCMP can be as closed-mouthed as MI5."

"Put Miss Butterly on it. She's the best blood-hound on your floor." Fleming rose and began to pace.

"She's a good filly, no doubt," said Powell.

"Hardly a filly anymore," Fleming said, and chuckled, flicking his ash away as punctuation.

"Point taken." Powell held up the pages and read them again.

When the silence lengthened, Fleming said, "Well?"

"I'm trying to decide how to divide the piece, what sort of lead-in from this to the second article would be most effective." He studied the pages a bit longer. "It'll come to me," he said, and finished his gin-and-tonic. "I agree that this can be a very big story, and we're in a unique position to take full advantage of it. No other paper has put together the information we have." He tossed his head to show his determination and confidence.

"And we might even perform a service to the Empire." Fleming's sardonic note wasn't noticeable to Powell.

"So we might, and a little gratitude in high places can be very worthwhile," said Powell.

"Without doubt," Fleming agreed, and took another long drag on his cigarette.

Powell had another two thimble-quiches, and around the food, he asked, "How much time will you need to finish the story?"

"As it stands now? Perhaps three days. At least the first layer; I'll know more after the weekend, and if there's more to it, then who knows." Fleming stubbed out his cigarette and sipped at his brandy.

"Do you think there *is* more to this story?" Powell asked, so unconcernedly that Fleming knew it was one of his primary considerations.

"I think it's possible. I don't know that it'll be as dramatic as Robertson, but it is enough to light some fires, I'd say." He didn't feel entirely comfortable admitting this, but he knew he owed it to Powell to tell him.

"You sound as if you expect more espionage to be revealed," said Powell. "Surely Robertson is the whole of it."

"I don't know," said Fleming. "I think Churchill has discouraged the remaining Nazis, but there might be more Communists out there."

"Because of the War?" Powell said.

"Yes, in part, and it is a beguiling philosophy for some," said Fleming, then added more crisply, "Of course, if you want to be accurate, the Russians aren't really Communists at all—they're Socialists in an authoritarian, monopolistic state, not that anyone pays any attention to such things. How can anyone reconcile the gulag to the principles of Communism? Marx would find it totally unacceptable. They practice their sort of Socialism in a totalitarian regime, and call it Communism, and the people are too frightened and ignorant to challenge him."

He sighed. "Stalin is the worst enemy his people ever had, if only they knew."

"But they say the people love him," said Powell.

"Because they know he's listening," said Fleming, and shrugged. "We're not going to change that. For what it may be worth, I don't think we're hunting Reds in the name of peace. I haven't come across anything that smells Russian; I would tell you if I had, and I would have handed my information over to MI5. If you want my opinion, the men were not killed out of political differences, but something more dangerous: financial despotism. I think those men were killed so that someone could make profits without being restricted or questioned, or even noticed. I think this man, or men, have made themselves as invisible as anyone of wealth can be, and that he, or they, will do whatever is necessary to remain undetected. So I don't anticipate another out-cry such as Robertson has caused. That would be too much to hope for. At best, I trust we'll find out why those two men died, and who is responsible."

"Have you any theories about that—other than it isn't political?" Powell asked, trying his best to look encouraging.

"Nothing so defined as a theory," said Fleming. "I have an inkling or two, and a hunch, but nothing I can discuss yet."

"Why not, pray?" Powell inquired with extreme politeness.

"Sorry," said Fleming, shaking his head slowly. "There's a lot to review here, and I want to have a careful look at all of it before I commit myself. I need something more to go on. I'm asking you to take a chance on my intuition, although I realize this might not be enough for you." He thought about Sir William for a moment, wondering if he should mention the man to Powell, decided against it, and added, "I think I should keep mum about what I think until I have a better handle on it; I don't want to put anyone at risk inadvertently."

"That's acceptable to me," Powell said, handing Fleming the sheets of type-written paper. "When we've finished eating, I'll decide how to present this." He smiled, adding, "If this goes well, they'll call you back to London."

"Not precisely the result I was hoping for," Fleming said, looking around his lounge as it glowed in the rich light of sunset.

"Oh, yes, Jamaica is a lovely place, and you can find tranquility here that isn't possible in London, but you don't advance here. At best, you have the opportunity to vegetate in comfort. But you're not ready for that. This can be your ticket to recognition and success. Come back here when you've earned your laurels and your fortune so you can live comfortably, with electricity and a better roof, and a second house for Cesar and his wife. You can keep this as your holiday retreat, but don't turn down the advantages only to be had in London." He coughed, suddenly embarrassed. "Sorry. Didn't mean to go on like that."

"Nothing to be sorry for," said Fleming. "I'll think over all you say."

"Your situation is different from mine," said Powell, pressing his point. "I've reached my niche and we all know it. I'm satisfied, but that doesn't mean I don't want my best reporter to get the opportunities he deserves."

Fleming could think of nothing to say and so was doubly grateful when Cesar came to the door and announced that dinner was served.

Chapter 34

As THEY shared port and a ripe Stilton, Fleming said to Powell, "There's some kind of to-do at Walter Sissons's estate this weekend—Lord Broxton is going. It seems to be a very exclusive affair. I was wondering if you could winkle me an invitation, on behalf of the paper, of course." He had been planning all through the meal to ask this favor, and had waited for just the right moment, which this seemed to be.

Powell frowned. "Why? I thought you disliked Lord Broxton."

"Oh, I do. But something he said makes me think that there will be information to be gleaned during the festivities; there's more going on there than meets the eye, if I read this right. If nothing else, I can report on the occasion itself, as a social event." Fleming had a half-smoked cigarette between his fingers, and he used it for emphasis, drawing smoke-sketches in the air. "But I'm convinced that something more than a party will be happening there, or so I have reason to suspect." He thought back to the conversation he had heard between Sissons and Lord Broxton and decided that he was making the right move.

"Something to do with this story?" Powell asked, placing his elbows on the table to demonstrate his obduracy.

"I think it is very possible," said Fleming. "If not, it may point to some garden-variety corruption, but that is still worth a half a column, if I can get solid information." He took a last drag on his cigarette. "There is something going on, and I don't trust it."

"How much more can you tell me?" Powell watched him closely. "I can tell you've been holding something back."

Fleming coughed, chagrined at being caught in his lack of candor. "Well, I can say that there is good reason to be alert to a new development at the harbor. I can also say there is more at risk here than a lucrative contract, although that is probably a factor." He stared at the curtained windows, hoping he could explain his misgivings.

"Which harbor?" Powell demanded.

"I don't know. I don't know what is planned, either, or what it's supposed to accomplish. But I should know after this weekend. I should also know who is bidding on the work, and who is likely to be awarded the work, whatever it is." He drank a little more port. "I'm not setting the Krandall-Preussin-perhaps-Cathcart investigation aside—in fact, I think there could be a connection. Monsieur Soleilsur's name comes up in both contexts." He achieved a tight-mouthed smile.

"If you say so, Fleming," Powell responded with a heavy shake of his head.

"I have it all in the notes. If I can unearth more information about Soleilsur between now and Thursday, I know I can turn it to good use." This last was more hope than certainty, but he spoke confidently, trying to persuade himself as much as Powell.

"I assume this means you want to use our resources?" Powell said, sighing.

"Yours, and others," Fleming said, thinking of Henry Long and Dominique. "I want to be careful; nothing too obvious from any single source. I don't want to send up any flares that might warn Soleilsur I'm looking into him."

"Do you think that could be a problem?" Powell was still not convinced.

"I think Monsieur Soleilsur may be inclined to cause trouble for anyone snooping around his company. He's the sort who doesn't like being under scrutiny. And he's rich as Croesus and has a Midas touch as well, if what I have found out is correct. I haven't hard proof, but I do know that he has a great deal to gain from business expansion, and not all of it is money—he's increasing his influence politically as well." Fleming looked up at the ceiling as if he could discern something in its old plaster medallion or the kerosene chandelier that provided the light for the room.

"Upon what do you base these assumptions?" Powell asked, helping himself to the Stilton.

"I base them on the way in which his name and his company seem to be haunting all the information I have obtained about the dead men; that, and a few remarks I've heard bruited about. Put out on the page, it looks pretty ephemeral, but there's a smell to it, I swear to heaven there is." He wouldn't disclose what he had learned of Dominique and her implied dealings with Monsieur Soleilsur—she was the kind of source Powell would view askance.

"Or you may be curious about a successful industrialist," said Powell. "Not that I blame you. The man's quite a mystery, for what I've been told."

"It's always intriguing to discover someone who is going to such lengths to remain invisible," said Fleming. "I can't help but wonder what he has to hide."

"Now, *there* I'm with you," said Powell. "Is there any more of your port?"

Fleming obliged Powell by pouring him another drink. "I have another bottle, if this won't be enough."

Powell laughed. "I should think this will suffice, thank you."

"Very good," said Fleming, and cleared his throat. "I believe this could become dangerous."

"You mean this weekend party could be hazardous to your well-being?" Powell asked incredulously. "You may be a bit too close to the case, but it's possible you're on to something, as well." He was thinking aloud as he sipped at his port.

"My thought precisely," said Fleming. "I know I'll have to be ready for trouble."

"It isn't that dramatic a situation, is it?" Powell mused.

"I hope not, but it may be," said Fleming.

"Leftover War nerves, I'd reckon," said Powell, having more of the port. He put his hand down flatly. "I'll tell you what I'll do. I'll get you an invitation, and I'll arrange for you to be there officially, for the paper. I'll say you're supposed to get coverage on the men bidding for the harbor expansion project, for profiles. That way you can get interviews without raising eyebrows."

"Thank you," said Fleming, doing his best not to smile.

"So, you will do a few interviews while you're there, and we will print them, so I won't destroy our credibility. We can't have men of Lord Broxton's position thinking ill of us."

"Not here, certainly. In London, it might be a cachet," Fleming remarked, still resisting the urge to smile. "All right. I think I can get three interviews out of it, at least." He thought of the three notes he had received, warning him off, and he suppressed a shudder: he would be going precisely where he was not wanted, and that gave him pause.

"Something the matter?" Powell asked, taking a bit more cheese.

"Goose walked over my grave," said Fleming, and had a bit more port.

Powell nodded. "I know the feeling. It's probably just the travel." He patted the table-top as if to reassure it. "Get some rest tonight, but be sure you've got the first part of your article on my desk by eleven tomorrow."

"I'll do that," said Fleming.

"Very good," said Powell, drinking the rest of his port. "Well, you have a lot of work ahead of you. I won't linger. Come into the office tomorrow, and I'll have your invitation ready for you. I'll also give you a few pounds to spend on something for your hostess. They say Alysa Sissons is a very attractive woman who knows what's due her."

"I should think so," said Fleming. "And she is quite beautiful."

"You've seen her?" Powell asked, surprised in spite of himself.

"We met on the airplane to New Orleans. I'm a little surprised to hear she's already back and planning such a massive party." As he spoke, he decided it was truly peculiar—unless she had been planning this party for some time, and had its preparation well in hand when she went to New Orleans. She hadn't given him that impression at the time, but there was no reason for him to think about such things, and no reason for her to mention her plans, so . . .

"Penny for your thoughts," said Powell.

Fleming shook his head and looked up. "Nothing."

"Missus Sissons must be a real beauty," Powell remarked knowingly.

"She is." Fleming didn't enlarge upon that, preferring to suggest a yawn, his hand over his mouth. "Sorry."

"Nothing to be sorry for. You need your sleep. It's been a demanding few days for you. I'll be on my way." He rose from the table, looking around in the lamplight. "This house could be a showplace, one day, if you choose wisely."

"I take your meaning," said Fleming, getting up to escort his guest from the house.

"Tell Cesar the food was delicious, as always." Powell stepped into the corridor. "Have a good night, Fleming. And have that article on my desk—"

"—by eleven. I will," said Fleming, accompanying him to the door. "Thanks for letting me cover the house-party."

Powell waved the thanks away. "Just do me proud, Fleming. That's all I ask."

"I'll do my humble best," said Fleming as they walked out onto the verandah; it was a cool night, and the sky was filled with scattered clouds hiding patches of stars from view. The weather was turning, Fleming could feel it, and he decided to include a waterproof anorak among his week-end clothing. Perhaps he should have the tear in the Rapier's hood repaired while he was in Kingston, just in case he had to drive in the rain. Surely Henry Long could point him in the direction of an expert sail-maker who could sew up the canvas for him.

Powell was climbing into his auto, his keys rattling against the steering wheel. "Always have to use full choke on this one," he said as the engine sputtered to life. Waving, Powell backed up until he could turn around and drive away, his headlights making two cones of luminescence in the darkness.

Fleming went back into the house, and all but ran into Cesar as he came out of the dining room, his arms laden with crockery and glasses. "Oh! Sorry, Cesar."

"Pardon me, sah," said Cesar.

Watching Cesar maneuver with his burdens, Fleming felt a surge of uncharacteristic gratitude to his houseman. "You do me well, Cesar."

"Thank you, sah," said Cesar, continuing along the hallway. "It's good to have you back, sah."

"And Joshua—how's Joshua?" Fleming asked.

"He's busy with his studies, sah," said Cesar, almost to the kitchen. "He brought the chicken from Bathsheba, then went back home to study."

"Very good. He's a clever lad." Fleming considered the matter, then added, "He could go far, if he puts his mind to it."

"I'll tell him you said so, sah."

Fleming ambled up the stairs, letting his thoughts drift. "You give my remembrances to Bathsheba," he called out as he reached the top of the flight.

Cesar had to raise his voice to reply, "I'll do that, sah, and thank you."

Fleming went to his bedroom, pulling a lighter from his pocket and thumbing it to life, so he could find his lantern. He lifted the glass chimney, set the flame to the wick, and adjusted it to a moderate level. He was about to sit down on his bed when something caught his attention: his revolver and the knife he had taken from the youth in Houston were missing.

Chapter 35

A THOROUGH SEARCH of the room revealed nothing more than that the revolver and knife were not to be found. Sir William's files were still safely stowed in the hidden compartment of his luggage, and Fleming's remaining cash-and-coins were untouched, making it apparent that the weapons had been specifically selected to be taken. Perplexed, Fleming sat on the side of his bed, thinking, and looked up as Cesar tapped on the door. "Come."

"I heard activity. Is something wrong?" Cesar still held a linen towel, testament to his activities in the kitchen.

"I had my revolver on the night-stand, and a knife—you needn't ask how I came by it. They seem to be missing. You didn't remove them, did you?" He was careful not to make the question seem an accusation; he depended on Cesar's good-will more than he knew.

"I haven't been into your room since you came back," said Cesar. "You brought your laundry down to me. I had no reason to come in here."

Fleming nodded. "Who has been in the house?"

"Since you returned? I was out for an hour, at the market and giving the chicken to Bathsheba to draw and dress; you were bathing, and then working. After I returned, only Mister Powell and Joshua have entered the house. I saw Jacinth on the road, but his house is nearby."

"Hum," said Fleming, to indicate he was listening and reserving judgment. It seemed absurd to think he had wakened this morning in the International Waiting Room at Houston Airport. The whole day seemed surreal, like something out of a painting by Dali, and this, just the most recent droopy clock to come along.

"What do you want me to do, sah?" Cesar asked.

"I suppose I should lock all the doors and windows tonight, just in case," said Fleming, only half amused; he tried to make himself take this seriously, to understand the gravity of their situation. "I don't want to find myself in trouble late at night."

"Of course not, sah." Cesar waited a long moment. "Shall I fetch Jacinth and Alphonse?"

"No reason to," said Fleming, though there was a dubious note in his voice. He had a sudden, exhausted urge to laugh, which he stifled.

"Shall I stay the night? I can send word to Bathsheba. She would expect me to remain here if you are in danger." Cesar was clearly worried, and it was apparent he didn't want to go.

"If you think it would be wise," said Fleming, and almost chided himself for giving in to such a funk. "You don't have to."

"I think it may be best," said Cesar. "I'll sleep in the parlor. The couch there will serve as a bed. I've slept there when you've been away." His admission was so forthcoming that it didn't surprise Fleming.

"Very good," said Fleming, nodding. "I'd appreciate the company, no matter what may or may not happen here." It was quite a concession for him to make, but he knew he was too worn-out to protect the house entirely on his own.

"I'll go to Jacinth's and ask him to take a note to Bathsheba.

He'll do this for me." He cocked his head, as if considering what to say next.

"You might advise him to stay with Bathsheba, to protect her if you're going to stay here. If there is danger for you, there may well be danger for her." He wondered as soon as he'd spoken if he'd overstepped and offended Cesar's sense of propriety.

"I may do that; in case anything untoward should occur," said Cesar, whose ready acquiescence told Fleming how very concerned he was. "If you do not mind, I will let him have your shotgun for the night. Jacinth, by himself, is a stalwart fellow, but the shotgun lends him an edge."

"Good Lord, man," said Fleming apprehensively. "What do you think is going on here?"

"I cannot say, and for that reason alone I am troubled," said Cesar. "Will you permit me to lend Jacinth the shotgun?"

"Yes, of course," said Fleming. "But it sounds as if you think we may need weapons ourselves."

"There is the rifle and your forty-five that Colonel Bascom gave you at the end of the War. We have ammunition for it, and the rifle. We can fend off anyone who attempts to break into the house. And I have knives and a cleaver in the kitchen," said Cesar with utmost seriousness.

"What *are* you expecting?" Fleming demanded, his attention wholly on Cesar now.

"I'm not sure, sah," said Cesar, "but I am certain that there is something dangerous to you around this house. You cannot deny it. Perhaps someone has put a curse on you."

"It bloody well seems like," said Fleming, going on in a more matter-of-fact tone, "but that's all superstitious nonsense.

Curses, indeed! You shouldn't embrace such folderol."

"It isn't folderol. Not here, sah, if you will let me say so," Cesar told Fleming.

Fleming shrugged. "Perhaps you're right."

"This isn't Haiti, but still, there are such things done in the night that bring misery or favor to those night people—" He looked around uneasily and stopped talking.

Fleming nodded. "Your point is well-taken. We'll go cautiously, and we'll be armed tonight, but against what, I won't specify."

"Just as well," said Cesar, his nervousness increasing. "I'll have my family gather under my roof. There is safety in numbers."

"I trust you don't think anyone would hurt your family on my account," Fleming said.

"I think there is more at stake here than you know," said Cesar without apology.

"What might that be?" Fleming asked sharply.

It was Cesar's turn to shrug. "I cannot say for sure, sah, but there have been rumors—"

"Rumors!" Fleming burst out. "All this for *rumors?*"

"Your gun and knife are missing," Cesar reminded him. "That is more than a rumor, you will agree. I did not take them, and you did not take them, so we have to suppose that—"

Fleming ducked his head. "You're right." He gestured acceptance. "Very well. What shall we do, you and I, once your family is safe?"

"I think it would be wise to close the house and go to bed. You have the forty-five, and I can take the rifle. As soon as I get back I'll set up empty bottles and tin cans inside the doors

and under the windows so that no one can break in silently."
Cesar produced a humorless smile. "It is one way to provide
us a margin of safety."

"Why not borrow the dogs from Dominique again?" Fleming asked, puzzled by the totality of Cesar's plans.

"Dominique has . . . friends. The dogs might prefer them to
us," said Cesar. "And Dominique is often busy, and does not
like being interrupted."

"Ah," Fleming said, nodding once. "I take your point."

"Cesar Holiday is no fool, sah, to ask the enemy to enter
the house, if you understand me." He motioned toward the
window. "You must suppose you are being watched, sah, and
not by your friends."

Fleming sighed. "What else have I overlooked, Cesar?"

"You have had other things on your mind, sah," said Cesar.
"And the people here are not always candid with—men like
you."

"British men. White men," said Fleming.

"Yes," Cesar agreed. "You mustn't blame us. You are not
always candid yourself, with us."

"I suppose not," said Fleming. "Mutual blindness."

"That, and other things," said Cesar, then changed his tone.
"If we spend an hour preparing the house, we should be safe
enough."

"Indeed," said Fleming, glad for the shift in their discussion. "While you're gone, I'll gather bottles and cans, and I'll
begin to secure windows. You'll come back as soon as you give
your message to Jacinth." It was encouraging to have something to do.

"That I will, sah." He turned on his heel. "If I am not back
in forty minutes, lock the doors and keep everyone out."

"Good Lord, man, you make this sound dire," said Fleming, raising his voice so that Cesar could hear him as he hastened downstairs. The only answer he received was the sound of the pantry door being flung open; Fleming knew Cesar was taking the shotgun. The cold of reality permeated the pleasant tropical night, and Fleming at last shook off his sense of abstraction. As soon as the kitchen door slammed closed, Fleming set to work readying the house for a siege he only half-expected. Taking a dozen empty wine-bottles from the kitchen, he set them up in front of the French doors in the lounge, and the front door, both of which he bolted. Returning to the kitchen, he took tins from the trash and attached twine to them, then hung these in front of several windows, testing them to make sure they would clang together at the least disturbance. He was fixing a metal pail to the back door when Cesar returned.

"I'm troubled," he announced as he came through the door.

"Small wonder," said Fleming, who had regained some of his equilibrium in the last quarter hour. "Is there some particular reason for it?"

"Something Joshua said," Cesar told Fleming as he closed and locked the kitchen door. "I am worried for that lad, no doubt about it."

"Gracious! Why?" Fleming exclaimed.

"He's reached the phase of questioning everything," said Cesar. "I realize all young men—if they're worth anything at all—have such episodes. But Joshua is becoming so angry . . ." He stopped. "No need for this to concern you, sah. There are more important matters to attend to." He looked around the kitchen. "We should lower the lights."

"Yes, we should. I don't want us any more visible than necessary. I've set up most of the house," said Fleming, his purpose lending this simple announcement a weightiness that reassured Cesar.

"I am glad to hear it, sah," he said. "Bathsheba said you are to be careful. She can see things, you know, things that others cannot. She believes you have a mark put on you." He stiffened, prepared for derision.

"What kind of mark does she mean? To what end? Who would do such a thing, and why?" Fleming asked, not wanting to debate the actuality of such concepts just at present, aware that his skepticism would have a hollow ring. He continued to work as Cesar answered.

"I don't know, sah, and neither does my wife. They say Dominique has such skills, but I don't think she would do such a thing to you—not unless she had a very, very good reason." There was a hint of a question in his remark.

"I can't think what that would be," said Fleming.

"No, sah," Cesar declared as he lowered the ceiling lantern to turn down the flames in the lamps hanging there.

"The front of the house is secure. I've left a lantern burning in the dining room, but the flame is low. I don't want to trip over anything," Fleming informed Cesar just as the crack of a rifle sounded, with the splintering of glass and Cesar's sharp cry of pain.

Chapter 36

FLEMING REACHED up to break Cesar's fall, and both of them ended up in a heap on the floor as a second shot splintered the window completely. A clatter of falling pans added to the confusion as the two men sorted themselves out.

"Cesar, how badly are you hurt?" Fleming demanded, just above a whisper.

"I have a wound in my shoulder. It is clean, but it is bleeding and it stings like the devil, sah," said Cesar, only slightly more loudly than Fleming.

"Any broken bones?" Fleming asked as he got to his knees, making himself move slowly and carefully, staying below the level of the counters and the sink.

"Not that I can tell, sah," said Cesar, panting a bit from the pain.

"You'd better stay still," Fleming recommended as he pulled a drying towel off its rail and handed it to Cesar. "Use this to put pressure on the wound. It's not much, but it'll keep you for now."

"Very good, sah," said Cesar with real gratitude.

"Keep low," Fleming muttered. "He's firing from above. He must be in the trees."

"Yes, sah," Cesar agreed, and rolled onto his side behind the butcher-block island in the middle of the kitchen. Above, the kitchen lantern with its five sputtering lamps canted at a dangerous angle, two of the lamps leaking a thin stream of kerosene.

Fleming crawled toward the broken window, taking care to look for broken glass on the floor. He could feel tiny shards dig into his hands and his knees, and he did his best to ignore the discomfort, though he was aware this could end up hurting him badly by driving the glass more deeply into his skin. He thought of his .45 and wondered if he could reach it before the sniper moved around for another, more deadly shot. He kept moving, heading for the unbroken window about three feet beyond the shattered one. His hearing was heightened, so that he thought he could discern the mice skittering in the pantry and the sighing of the slow wind in the trees outside. If only the wind would pick up, he thought, and toss the sniper out of the branches and onto the porch, doing some damage along the way.

"Sah," Cesar whispered from his vantage point behind the island, "there was a flash outside the window. I think he's moving."

"Which way?" Fleming asked, holding still and all but stretching out on the floor.

"Toward the front," Cesar answered.

"Get the forty-five from the pantry," Fleming ordered, and slithered toward the hall, trying to avoid as many of the tiny talons of glass as he could. Once in the hall, he crouched, then slowly rose to his feet, pressing against the wall so as to minimize any shadow he might cast that would give away his place in the house. Without a weapon, he felt worse than naked, but he kept on, determined to find his attacker before he could get into the house and start shooting in earnest.

One of the lamps in the dining room shattered in concert with a small hole punched in the window, leaving a fine array of cracks to mark the event.

Fleming leaned against the wall, waiting for a second shot to be fired. He smelled the sharp odor of kerosene with a hint of acridity that promised smoke: the tablecloth might be charring. This realization made him keenly aware that he needed to act quickly, for if fire took hold in the room, he would have much more to worry about than a sniper in the trees. He bent low and glanced around the door-frame into the room, and saw the fabric of the tablecloth sprouting little bright feathers of flame, all running along the spreading dribble of kerosene.

There was a clunk against the side of the house, and Fleming slipped into the dining room, rushing to the windows to hunker down below the sill, listening. Satisfied, he slipped along to the next window and raised the edge of the drapery, giving himself a narrow slice of the outside to view. Only the lush fronds of the low-growing palms presented themselves, screening the road beyond.

A sharp breaking of a branch among the shrubs at the side of the house sounded as loud as an explosion. A moment later the plants rustled, and then there was a sound of rapid footsteps on the road.

Fleming knew better than to assume this made him safe. During the War he saw how many men got careless and ended up getting hurt or killed as a result of assuming safety when they should have remained on guard. If there was another man watching the house, any move he might make would put him in the second sniper's sights. He crawled over to the table and pulled on the tablecloth, rolling it as it slid to the floor, using his arm to press the flames out. He did his best not to cough on the smoke.

As the waiting dragged on, Fleming began to think he might be all right. He rose very slowly, his back against the wall, and cautiously lifted the edge of the drapery again, this time pulling it back far enough to give a wider look at the road. Nothing happened, and he began to hope that this would be the end of the attack. He used the ruins of the tablecloth to smother the kerosene-fed flames on the dining table, and then righted the lantern, making sure the lamps were firmly in place and the wicks rolled down. Then he made a swift survey of the room, and satisfied that it was secure, he went out into the hall and back to the kitchen to see how Cesar was faring.

"Is he gone, sah?" Cesar asked in a thready voice.

"Someone ran away," Fleming answered as he knelt beside Cesar and looked at the bloody towel pressed against his shoulder. "You need looking at."

"It is a simple wound, sah. It will heal," said Cesar. In the low light, his glossy black skin had a greenish tinge.

"You're going into shock, man," said Fleming, his concern increasing as he saw the towel was saturated and that Cesar's wound was still bleeding. "You must get to hospital."

"That's not necessary," said Cesar, but his voice trailed off.

"Oh, yes it is," said Fleming, getting up and helping Cesar to his feet, feeling him wobble as he tried to stand.

"Sah . . ." Cesar muttered.

"Don't speak," Fleming said as he held Cesar against him. "I'm taking you out to the Rapier and I'll drive you to the clinic in Eastport. You need medical attention." He propped Cesar up against the butcher-block island and went to adjust the canted lantern hanging from the ceiling. A tug or two on the pair of ropes righted it, and the lamps began to burn more evenly.

"You should . . . blow them out." Cesar clung to the butcher-block to keep from falling.

"Too much time," said Fleming, his apprehension about Cesar increasing. He had seen men look as his servant did, during the War, when such a cast to the skin usually meant death.

"The sniper might be waiting," Cesar said faintly.

"Then he'd best get out of my way, or I'll run him down," said Fleming as he took hold of Cesar again and made his way to the back door. He worried briefly about the lamps left burning in the dining room, and decided he couldn't spare the time to blow them out, either; Cesar was hurt and he could not wait for help. The fire in the dining room was out, and he was satisfied that there would be no more mischief at his house, at least not tonight. Still, he was careful to lock the door as he went out, half-carrying Cesar; arriving at his open-sided garage, he pulled back the canvas covering of his auto and flung it aside.

"Don't . . . sah," Cesar mumbled.

"Stow it," said Fleming. Lowering Cesar into the passenger's seat, he had an instant of regret for his leather seats that he quickly dismissed as unworthy. Satisfied that Cesar was secure, Fleming vaulted over the bonnet and climbed into the driver's seat, his ignition key at the ready.

The motor purred to life, the headlamps shone; Fleming engaged the gears and the auto leaped forward. Heading up the road, Fleming pushed the limits of speed, swinging onto the main thoroughfare with squealing tires and a change of gears. Hoping that no one was on the road at this hour, Fleming pressed the accelerator and stared ahead, using his hooter at every bend in the road.

"Hang on, Cesar," Fleming ordered as he raced toward Eastport; he could tell by the way he flopped in the passenger seat that Cesar had lost consciousness. "Hang on."

Ten minutes later, he barreled into Eastport, along the darkened main street toward the clap-board building at the end of the market-square where the clinic was. Passing two bars along the way, he saw business was brisk, but for the most part, the windows of homes showed families were in for the night. A spattering of rain made the dust on the windscreen stand out in runnels, and added to the red stain spreading down Cesar's chest. As he neared the clinic, Fleming began to sound the hooter steadily, hoping to summon assistance. He braked to a halt, turned off the motor, and leaped out.

"Doctor! I need a doctor!" he shouted as he ran around the Rapier to lift Cesar from his seat.

A light came on over the door, and a middle-aged black woman in a nurse's cap looked out. "Doctor is at home with his family, at supper," she said.

"Then fetch him," Fleming ordered as he bore Cesar up the stairs. "Can't you see this man is badly wounded?"

"He is bleeding, sah," the nurse agreed. "I'll send Samson to fetch him."

"At once!" Fleming said, trying to keep the frantic note out of his voice. "He's been shot."

"Oh, sah," said the nurse, either in condemnation or in distress.

"*At once!*" said Fleming, shoving past her into the main room of the clinic. "Where is the examination—"

The nurse pointed to closed double-doors on Fleming's left. She bustled to open them, standing aside to let Fleming carry Cesar into it. "I'll get Samson. The doctor will come quickly."

"Be about it," Fleming said bluntly. He was struggling to get Cesar onto the examination table.

The nurse hurried off, calling for Samson.

Cesar was shaking as if from cold, although the room wasn't chilly. Fleming found a light blanket and wrapped it around him. He took the towel from Cesar's shoulder, and dropped it into the wastebasket near the head of the examination table. Then he looked about for some lengths of gauze he could use to put pressure on the wound. "Cesar," he said. "It should have been I who took that shot."

Cesar made no response. He continued to tremble.

Finding the drawer containing bandages, Fleming took out a roll of gauze and pressed it up against the torn flesh in Cesar's shoulder.

"How did he get shot?" The nurse's question from the door so startled Fleming that he almost dropped the roll of gauze.

"He was working in the kitchen. The shot came through the window," said Fleming, returning to his work of stopping Cesar's bleeding.

"I'll get the antiseptics for cleaning the wound. The doctor will be here in a few minutes." She went about her self-appointed task, gathering a basin, some instruments Fleming didn't like the look of, and a large bottle of tincture of iodine. "I have to get the soap," she said, leaving the examination room for a moment, only to return with a bar of carbolic soap.

Fleming had seen more utilitarian field hospitals during the War, but to his eyes, the clinic's preparedness seemed rudimentary at best. He wondered if he should have taken more time and driven into Kingston to Saint Anne's. But that would have taken at least an hour, and Cesar didn't have sixty minutes to spare. The fifteen minutes he had taken to bring him here might not have left him enough time.

"Keep the pressure going," the nurse recommended. "He's not doing very well, is he, sah?"

"No," said Fleming, whose memory of wounded men in the War was now all too vivid.

"Pity," she exclaimed as she went to bring a flask of boiled water into the examination room.

Fleming stood beside Cesar, feeling desperately frustrated. There had to be something more he could do! He thought it was unfair that Cesar should be in such travail on his account— Cesar, who was his responsibility. "I'll make them pay for this, Cesar. I swear by God I will."

When the nurse returned to the examination room, a young man with a mangled foot and a crutch came with her. He wore a tattered canvas jacket with a medal pinned to it: Fleming recognized the Valor Cross. He wondered briefly what the young man had done to so distinguish himself.

"Do you know his blood type?" The nurse's question abruptly brought him back to the immediate circumstances.

"A," said Fleming. "I think it's A." He had it somewhere back at his house.

"Who in town has A?" Samson asked.

"The baker does," said the nurse. "And Widow Hapgood, I think."

"I'll try the baker first," said Samson, preparing to leave.

"He'll be at Carlo's tavern," said the nurse.

"I'll be back with him," said Samson, going out the front of the clinic.

"Where's the damn doctor?" Fleming insisted.

"He'll be here shortly," the nurse said. "You keep pressure

on the wound. I'll find another blanket. He's still shaking."

"Bring it." Fleming could tell Cesar was slipping away from them. He wanted to find some way to call him back, to stop this ebbing. "Don't let go, Cesar. Hang on. Hang on."

The doctor came through the door, slightly out of breath. He was about Fleming's age, freckle-faced and brindle-haired. "Angus Bethune," he said with a strong Scots burr. "What happened?"

"Cesar Holiday. My houseman. He was shot. About forty minutes ago." Fleming didn't leave off his hold on the gauze.

"I can see that," said Bethune, moving Fleming aside. "I'll take over."

Fleming stepped back two paces. "He passed out half an hour ago."

"Um," said Bethune as he bent over the supine form of Cesar. "Natalie," he said to his nurse without looking up from his examination. "Bring the light nearer, if you would, please."

"Yes, sah," she said, turning on a goose-necked floor-lamp and bringing it up to the side of the examination table.

"There's a deal of torn tissue here," he said.

"Yes," said Fleming.

"I'll do what I can," Bethune told Fleming, "but I don't know how much that will be. This man's gone into shock and his pulse is erratic and thready. He's lost a lot of blood."

"Do everything you can," said Fleming.

Bethune looked at him, a stern expression in his greenish eyes. "That is what I am obliged to do." He motioned toward the door. "Now let me do it."

Chapter 37

DAWN WAS breaking when Doctor Bethune finally came out of the examination room, drawn and exhausted, his head down. He carried a clean linen towel and was wiping his iodine-stained hands.

"Mister Fleming," he said, and the tone of his voice said it all.

"Oh, God," Fleming said as he rose from the uncomfortable chair in which he had passed the night. A few hours ago the nurse, Natalie, had come out to treat his hands and knees—tweezing out the bits of glass in his palms and his legs and bandaging them after spreading stinging iodine on them. He felt oddly guilty at having had such minor injuries looked after when Cesar had been dying.

Bethune made a gesture of helplessness. "I tried everything I knew, but he'd lost too much blood. The baker's transfusion looked as if it might help, but it came too late. I thought that when I'd cleaned the wound and dressed it that he would rally enough for the transfusion to help, but he hadn't enough strength left. It gave out just a few minutes ago. I am very sorry."

Fleming lowered his head, anger and grief roiling through him. "I'm sure you did all you could."

"I don't think a larger hospital or more equipment could have made that much of a difference, not once shock set in," he went on in an attempt to soften the blow. "He wouldn't have made it into the city."

Nodding numbly, Fleming said, "I know you did all anyone could."

"So I hope," said Bethune. "I certainly did all I know how to do."

"I've no doubt of that," said Fleming, looking at the bandages on his hands.

"And you did all a man might to get him the help he required," Bethune said. "You got him here quickly, you put pressure on the wound, you—"

"I got him shot in the first place. It should have been me. It was *supposed* to have been me," Fleming said through his teeth.

"You can't be sure of that, Mister Fleming. There are things that go on among the people here that you and I know nothing of." He turned, about to go back into the examination room. "I've signed the death certificate. I'll have the body ready by mid-afternoon. I'd attend to it now, but I have to get some rest."

Fleming heard him out impassively. "I'll arrange for his family to claim it. His wife's name is Bathsheba. Bathsheba Holiday. If she asks, I will bring her here myself. If she would rather her relatives do, then I will not accompany her. I don't know which it will be yet, so I cannot tell you what or whom to expect. Send me the bill for your care—all of it." Saying her name, he could not imagine how he could face Cesar's wife without being able to present her with the murderer as well, in chains and ready for swift justice. Abruptly his rage grew, like a malign beast within him. He wanted to find those responsible for Cesar's death and smash them to pieces.

"Very good. Will you leave your card with my nurse?" He walked back into the examination room and closed the door, and a moment later, Natalie came out and approached Fleming.

"Doctor wants your card, sah," she said. "And if you don't mind my saying so, you should take something for your pain and rest awhile before you try to drive back. You're in no condition to be on the road."

Fleming had taken one from his wallet and handed it to her. "Thanks for your concern; I'll be all right." He was torn between leaving at once and delaying that moment as long as possible. "I asked the doctor to send me the bill for everything."

"Very good, sah," she said, reading the card. "A journalist. It must be very exciting."

"It's damnable," said Fleming with strong emotion.

There was an awkward silence. "I am sorry about your man, sah."

"No more than I," said Fleming, who was dreading what he would have to tell Bathsheba in a short while, and hoping to find a reason to postpone that terrible moment as long as decently possible.

Natalie ducked her head as if to reassure Fleming that she was aware of his dismay. "We'll get him ready, sah."

"Thank you," Fleming said, and took two ten-pound notes from his wallet. He handed these to Natalie. "This is an initial payment. I know it will be more, but apply this to what I will owe you, if you would."

"I will, and thank you, sah," she said. "The doctor will file the certificate from here. You needn't worry that there will be any questions about it, but you should make a report to the police, sah."

"I know," said Fleming, deciding that he would speak with

Bathsheba before visiting the constabulary. Best to get the worst over with soonest, he told himself, ashamed of his cowardice in facing Bathsheba. He owed it to Cesar's family to inform them as soon as he could; it was what was expected of him, his memory repeated what his nanny had said when he was a little boy: *you must take care of your inferiors.*

"You'll want to change your clothes, sah—they're bloody," Natalie pointed out.

He nodded again. "I will."

"Very good, sah," she said, and left him to attend to her duties.

Fleming stood still for some little time, wondering if he ought to open the examination-room doors for a last look at Cesar, but decided against it. He would see Cesar dead at his funeral. Slowly he left the clinic and went down to his Lagonda Rapier. Cesar's blood had sunk into the leather and dried to a stiff russet-brown; in a remote part of his mind, Fleming made a note to order a new seat-cover, and felt himself a traitor to Cesar for thinking that. He got in and started the motor, his hands feeling mittened in their bandages. He was almost oblivious to the activity behind him in the market-square. Driving slowly—he didn't trust himself to put on speed—he left Eastport behind and headed back for his house, keeping his mind as blank as he could. By the time he arrived at his house, his torpor had faded and he was all but consumed with self-condemnation that only increased as he unlocked the rear door and walked slowly into the kitchen. He looked about, checking the lamps hanging in the lantern: two had guttered completely, but the rest still had small amounts of kerosene in them. He used the two thin ropes to lower it and blew out the remaining lamps, then went into the dining room and did the same thing.

This task done, he went upstairs to wash, shave, and change, projects that proved awkward with his hands wrapped in bandages. Accepting the difficulty as fitting punishment for what had happened, he persevered.

Half an hour later, in a navy blazer and dark trousers, he left the house and once again drove off, this time bound for Cesar's house. Going through the village, he wished he could be invisible, for it seemed to him every eye accused him, and that all blamed him as completely as he blamed himself. As he pulled up in front of the fence in front of Bathsheba's house, he almost lost what courage he had, and he stepped out of the Rapier slowly.

Joshua came out of the door, his school-pack slung over his shoulder. He slowed as he caught sight of Fleming, his clever eyes wary. "Good morning," he said in a carefully neutral tone.

Fleming could not respond in kind. "Will you wait a moment, Joshua?"

"Where's my uncle?" Joshua demanded without apology for his tone. "Has something happened?"

"Come into the house. Bathsheba will want you," said Fleming, coming up the walkway toward the steps. "I'm afraid I have bad news."

Joshua stepped aside, worry and ire building in his face. "What are you saying?"

Fleming tapped on the door. "Bathsheba. It's Ian Fleming. I need to speak to you."

Bathsheba came to the door, her hair still damp from washing. She was in a newly ironed dress of intense turquoise that seemed to upstage the sky. "Mister Fleming, sah. Come in," she said, standing aside to admit him. Her front parlor was small, neat, and ornamented with pictures of saints and other religious figures Fleming wasn't sure he recognized. In one corner stood her precious sewing machine. "If you will sit down, sah," she said, indicating a settee upholstered in a colorful flowered print.

"I think I'd rather stand, thank you, Bathsheba," said Fleming. He heard Joshua close the door behind him.

"What is it, then?" Bathsheba asked, apprehension beginning to color her voice. "What do you want to tell me about my husband?"

Fleming winced. "How did you—"

"You have never come to my house before, and you have come alone. What could it be but something to do with Cesar?" She seemed calm, but there was a shine of tears in her eyes.

"Yes," said Fleming, his voice thickened by sorrow. "I can't tell you how sorry I am. Truly." He took a deep breath. "He . . . He was shot, last night, while trying to ready my house to defend it. There was a sniper in the trees and he—" He paused to swallow twice and take a deep breath. "I took him to the clinic in Eastport. Doctor Bethune worked all night to try to save him."

"But he couldn't," said Bathsheba in a resigned tone. "I thought that must be it." She was weeping silently.

"And what did you do?" Joshua demanded.

"I got him to the best care I could, as quickly as I could," said Fleming. "I know it was little enough—"

"You're damned right it was little enough," Joshua interrupted furiously. "He's dead. Because of you!"

"Yes," Fleming said. "I don't know what I can do to make up for it—there's nothing I can do. I can't make up for it. Ever." He looked at Bathsheba. "I am sorry. I know that sounds inadequate, but believe me, if I had thought this would happen, I would never have let him stay with me. I would have sent him away." He wanted her to believe him so he would have a chance of believing it himself.

"He would not have gone," said Bathsheba.

"And she's supposed to thank you for that?" Joshua stepped around to confront Fleming. "You think we'll just bow down before you, grateful that you gave one of us the chance to get killed for you?"

"Joshua," said Bathsheba. "This isn't the time. Your uncle wouldn't—"

"My uncle is dead! Because of him!" He pointed at Fleming.

Bathsheba reached out and slapped Joshua suddenly. "Have you no respect, boy?" she asked in the full dignity of her mourning. "Cesar wouldn't leave Mister Fleming. He was not one to shirk his duty. You have to respect that, and his death." She paused to wipe her cheeks. "I cannot have you behaving like a spoiled child. My husband is dead. It is for us to arrange for his burial. You will have to talk to the priest, and I will have to arrange to have his body brought home."

"He's still at the clinic in Eastport," said Fleming. "They are expecting you later today." He looked at Joshua. "I share your indignation, little as you may think I do." He gave Bathsheba his full attention again. "I've told the doctor I'll pay his bill. You need not worry on that head. And if you'll send me the accounts for his funeral, I'll be very much obliged."

"You may pay the doctor," said Bathsheba with surprising command of herself. "But I will pay to bury my husband. I have money enough for it, and I will do what I must for him."

"Aunt!" Joshua protested. "Make him pay for it! It's his fault."

"We all die," said Bathsheba. "When we die, we are owed a burial. This is what the living do for the dead. I have money for his funeral," she repeated. "I will not dishonor this family by having Mister Fleming pay for what it is mine to do."

"But he's responsible!"

"So I think." Fleming was feeling embarrassed. "Bathsheba . . . if you change your mind . . ."

"I will remember your offer," said Bathsheba. "Joshua, go to Alphonse and tell him that I will need him, and his delivery lorry, this afternoon. And don't you go raging at him because of what has happened. Just tell him that Cesar is dead and that we must fetch his body home. If I find out you have spoken out against Mister Fleming, you will answer to me." She looked back at Fleming. "You didn't do this to Cesar. Don't you be thinking you did."

"It feels bloody like," said Fleming.

"If it does, then you go and find out who did this. You make him pay for killing my man." Her voice almost broke, but she gathered her will and fought off the tears. "Do this for me, Mister Fleming, and I will be forever in your debt."

"No, you will not," said Fleming. "It is the least I can do."

"You're right about that," Joshua almost spat out the words.

"Don't talk like that," Bathsheba ordered him. "You don't know what you are saying."

Joshua glared. "I know if it weren't for him, my uncle would still be alive."

"I agree with you," said Fleming. "And I want to make recompense."

Bathsheba nodded. "Then you be about your business, Mister Fleming," she told him as she motioned toward the door, adding quietly, "and I will be about mine."

Chapter 38

DRIVING INTO Kingston, Fleming pushed his Rapier to speeds higher than he knew were prudent, given the time of day and his state of mind. Three times he nearly collided with lorries, and once he almost clipped the back of an ox-cart as he raced for Merlin Powell's office, feeling as if he had turned to granite. He hated the sky with its veil of high, thin clouds; he hated the turbulent sea; he hated the frisky wind that slapped at his face as if to bring him out of his funk. It was too uncaring of the world around him to appear as if nothing had happened.

"Watch where you're going!" a pedestrian shouted as Fleming came hurtling around a corner.

Fleming touched his forehead in what could be taken as a salute, then he roared on toward the imposing building where Powell was waiting for him. He parked at the kerb near the entrance to the building and for once he didn't bother to pull the canvas cover over his seats and steering wheel before he bolted through the tall doors and up the stairs.

"You look like death warmed over," Powell said as he caught sight of Fleming striding toward his office. "Up all night on my story?"

"No," said Fleming.

"You aren't going to tell me you don't have it ready," Powell protested as Fleming barreled into his office.

"I don't," Fleming stated.

Exasperated, Powell slapped the top of his desk. "That's

unacceptable. You assured me that—" He stopped. "Good God, man, what happened to your hands?"

Fleming cut him off before he could work into a good tirade. "After you left last night, someone shot Cesar."

Powell stared at him. "Egad! Is he all right?"

"He's dead." Fleming dropped into the wooden chair by the filing cabinets. "I took him to the clinic in Eastport. They worked on him most of the night—even called in a man for a transfusion—but he'd lost too much blood before they . . ." His voice dropped.

"And your hands?" Powell asked.

"I cut them on glass on the floor. You should see my knees, and shins," he said, trying to make light of his misadventure. "Cesar took the full assault. It was terrible."

"Who did it? Do you know?" He had sank back into his chair.

"No." He felt so tired that he was shaky. "I need to make a telephone call to the States again."

Powell glowered in his direction, then shook his head and asked, "About what's happened?"

"Yes," said Fleming. He had decided on the way into town that he had to talk to Hotchkiss one last time, on the off-chance that the FBI agent would have that one missing bit of information he sought.

Powell shoved himself to his feet. "Go ahead. I'll take my elevens now. Do you want a cup of tea?"

Blinking at this very mundane suggestion, Fleming heard himself say, "Yes, please, white, two sugars."

"You'll have it." Powell started out of his office. "Um, Fleming. I'm very sorry about Cesar. You'll express the appropriate sentiments to his family for me, won't you?"

"Of course," said Fleming, reaching for the telephone and asking the operator who answered to be connected to the overseas operator, to whom he gave the number of the Pecos Vista in Roswell, New Mexico, U.S.A. When Bert answered the ring, he greeting Fleming as soon as they were connected.

"Good to hear from you again, Limey," he said with rough cordiality. "I suppose you want to talk to Uel Hotchkiss?"

"Yes; if you would ring me through," said Fleming.

"He's having breakfast. I'll call him." There was a clatter as he put his head-set down and went off to find the FBI agent. Two minutes later he picked up the head-set again and said, "I'll put you through."

"Thanks," said Fleming, and gave his full concentration to what he had to find out.

"Good morning," said Hotchkiss. "I was wondering if I'd hear from you again. I was planning to give you a call later today." He sounded a bit grim. "This isn't a secure line, is it?"

"No. Sorry," said Fleming. "Can't be helped." His tone grew sharper. "Do you have something for me?"

"I think so," said Hotchkiss. "I spoke to the RCMP last night, pretty late. They called me."

"Oh?" Fleming didn't want to throw Hotchkiss off, so he waited for what he had to say.

"They're looking for a man who may have called on Preussin shortly before he was killed. They wanted to know if I had any information about him."

"Soleilsur," Fleming said.

"Nope. They say he's a Brit," Hotchkiss repeated. "But he's also probably in cahoots with Soleilsur, or that's what the Mounties think. They established some kind of link between the two."

"This man, this Brit—do they suspect him in Preussin's murder?" Fleming asked.

"They aren't saying so, but I'd bet on it without a qualm. It smells that way—you know what I mean? I didn't recognize the name, but I thought you might, him being part of Military Intelligence, and all." Hotchkiss coughed gently. "He has some connection to SS Industries, that much is certain."

"Not Cathcart or Krandall?" Fleming asked. "Or Walter Sissons?"

"No," said Hotchkiss. "Who is Walter Sissons? You mean the industrialist? No. Not him, in any case," and shocked Fleming as he went on. "The guy's name is Sir William Potter."

"Potter?" Fleming repeated in disbelief.

"You know him?" Hotchkiss asked with keen intent.

"I . . . yes. He came to my house . . . He was the one who started me on this mad excursion. His name came up in the material I received at Los Alamos, but—" He was grappling with this revelation, wanting to find an explanation for this turn of events, and arriving only at the conclusion that was possible: Potter had set him up. No wonder he hadn't wanted his visit known.

"Great hopping—" Hotchkiss exclaimed. "So you know the guy?"

"I wouldn't say that. He showed up to ask me to undertake some unofficial work for him. He persuaded me to look into this situation. I wonder why he did it?" He began to chide himself inwardly for being so gullible. In his eagerness to make his position clear, he hadn't bothered to question Sir William too closely—he had accepted Potter's claims of covert precautions as an ordinary part of the task. "He called upon me, literally and figuratively, to help him, implying that it wasn't safe to have the investigation carried on within MI5. It was the first time I had met him."

"Pardon me, but shit," said Hotchkiss. "The guy's been chucked out of MI5, very quietly, about a month ago, for conducting a private vendetta and using British agents to do it, or that's what the RCMP was told."

"Good God," Fleming muttered.

"I suppose he didn't mention any of this when he came to see you?" Hotchkiss inquired.

"Nary a word," said Fleming. "Not that one would expect him to."

"Pitched a lot of patriotic guff at you, I suppose?" Hotchkiss asked.

"Precisely," said Fleming. "I have some files he left with me, but they're about three men who worked for him during the War, at Los Alamos, code names Moan, Groan, and Sigh. Krandall, Cathcart, and Preussin, it seems." He knew he was saying too much, but just at present he didn't care.

"Did you have those files with you when you were here?" Hotchkiss asked.

"Yes," Fleming admitted.

"Damn it, Fleming," said Hotchkiss.

"I know; I know," Fleming said. "I still have them. I don't remember seeing anything in them that would implicate Sir William in anything . . . irregular."

"He wouldn't leave that lying around, would he? He probably wants to cover his trail, and you're being used that way. You might not be the only one." Hotchkiss challenged, "Can you get photostats of the files and send them to me, air mail special delivery? Can you do it by tomorrow morning?"

"I'll do it this afternoon. You should have them by Friday."
He knew this was the least he could do, and under the circumstances, he needed to do all that he could to rectify the
wrong he had helped to commit.

"Great. That'll help, I hope."

"I'll include everything I've turned up. It may prove useful
in finding him," said Fleming, wondering who he should talk
to at MI5 about this. "He disappeared."

"Disappeared?" It was Hotchkiss's chance for incredulity.
"Disappeared how?"

"I don't know. We only found his coat—it had been
slashed." Fleming could feel his mind working, the pieces of
this deadly puzzle shifting and combining into new, ominous
patterns. "If he was hurt—"

"So he's got away," said Hotchkiss condemningly.

Fleming thought about it. "I wouldn't say that," he told the
FBI agent. "He may still be here on Jamaica."

"You're kidding," said Hotchkiss.

"No." Fleming could hardly keep up with his thoughts: why
had Potter come to him? Was he the only one Potter had approached? Was it Potter who had been following him all along?
Was Potter responsible for Cesar's death? "When he vanished,
he had to get away in a small open boat."

"Which could take him to a yacht or freighter or who-knows-
what," said Hotchkiss.

"That's possible, but it doesn't feel right." Fleming began
to give his thoughts free rein. "Whatever he's up to, I think
he wants to begin it here on Jamaica. He's probably ready to
make his next move, but before he does, he's got rid of anyone
who could blow the whistle on him, and so he'll want to eliminate anyone who could interfere with his plans."

"Got any ideas about that?" Hotchkiss asked him, curious in spite of himself.

"As a matter of fact, I do: Soleilsur and Sissons are hosting a big occasion, something to do with harbors and harbor expansion. If Potter really is part of this, he'd want to be around for the event." He was guessing now, but he felt he had got it right.

"Harbor expansion," said Hotchkiss speculatively. "I'll get to work on that, see if I can dig up anything on Potter that might—"

"Check out Soleilsur and Sissons while you're at it," Fleming interrupted. "I think it could have something to do with mines."

"Mining?" Hotchkiss asked. "Or bombs?"

"The latter. Mining harbors could effectively control the world's shipping as submarines never could. Think about it." Fleming had been scribbling on a pad, and now tore off the sheet.

"That seems a little far-fetched," said Hotchkiss. "It would take a long time to do, and it would be dangerous."

"Only if anyone bothered to look," said Fleming, remembering what David Dunstan had told him on his flight from Houston.

"How could they get into place?" Hotchkiss asked, dubiety making his question edgy.

"If they had submarines of their own—" Fleming began.

"Submarines are very expensive," said Hotchkiss. "You can't make them and just hide them away under some regular docks. They have to be outfitted and supplied and fueled, and the crew has to—"

"Soleilsur is very rich, and he has the matériel to build and maintain his own private fleet of submarines. He already has more than twenty cargo ships. Who's to say he hasn't a few others he hasn't bothered to register?" As he spoke, Fleming decided that this was likely.

"He has a private island," said Hotchkiss, finally recalling this crucial fact. "There's a maintenance yard on it, for his ships. He might be able to—"

"Have that island checked out," said Fleming.

"On what pretext?" Hotchkiss asked, then went on, "Never mind. I'll think of something."

"Excellent," said Fleming. "Get the CIG on it, if Hoover will allow it. Just be careful how much you tell MI5—who knows what Potter has done to corrupt the intelligence about him." He hated saying this about his own service but he was certain that precautions needed to be taken.

"I get your point," said Hotchkiss. "Okay. I'll do what I can, and I'll get back to you. You have any idea what we're looking for?"

"Submarines, stockpiled ordnance, who knows what else?" Fleming said, anxious to get moving.

"I'll do my best," said Hotchkiss.

"Make sure it's good enough," said Fleming. "If there's as much riding on this as I think may be, you could have the world on your shoulders."

Hotchkiss took a deep breath. "Okay. Talk to you Thursday."

"Until then," said Fleming, and hung up. He paused to scrawl a note to Powell, promising him a story by Thursday, and then he headed out of the office.

Chapter 39

LEAVING POWELL'S office, Fleming encountered the editor returning from his elevens with a cardboard tray holding a mug of tea; he accepted two mouthfuls of it, told Powell he'd be back later in the day, then rushed down to his auto and drove off to Henry Long's chandlery; he parked behind the building next to Henry's ancient Aston Martin, and entered the shop from the rear.

Henry Long was behind his counter, his linen shirt crisply pressed, his churchwarden's pipe curling out a thin wraith of smoke. He did not look around as he said, "Pity about Cesar Holiday."

"It's a crime, not a pity," Fleming responded, unsurprised by Henry's lack of greeting.

"That, too," Henry agreed.

"How did you hear about it?" Fleming asked as he came up to the counter. He looked about to see if any other customers were in the shop and was relieved to discover they were alone.

"You know. One hears things." Henry waved his hand as if to imply that such information came on the breeze. "You took him to Eastport. That was good of you."

"I wasn't about to let him bleed to death on my kitchen floor; he was shot on my account. I have to do something for him," said Fleming with a sudden rush of indignation. "I don't know what more to do. Bathsheba won't let me pay for the funeral."

"Of course she won't. She's a proper woman," said Henry. "And she would rather you bring his killer to justice than give her money to put her husband in the ground."

"Good God, you can be blunt," said Fleming.

"No doubt," Henry agreed. He took a lungful of smoke, blowing it out in rings. "And what did you want me to tell you? Do not tell me that you had no such purpose in coming to me, for I will not believe it—you hear me?"

"I hear you, and you're right," Fleming said, feeling a wave of exhaustion go over him like a storm surge. "I have much to do, and not much time to do it."

"So tell me how I am to help," said Henry Long. "I will do whatever you ask, if it is within my power." He folded his big hands and managed a smile that Ho Tai would be proud of. "I would like to have Cesar avenged, too."

"Very well," said Fleming. "I need to know everything you can tell me about Soleilsur and his business. I want to know what he's doing, with whom he does business, anything. I need the information immediately, but I'll settle for tomorrow morning, if I must."

"I'll tell you what I know. Later I may know more." Henry drew on his pipe again. "You are looking into a snake's nest."

"I'm beginning to agree," said Fleming.

"After you left to go to America, there were those who said you would not come back, that you would die on your hunt." Henry nodded sagely. "The men who said that also said that you were duped."

"Duped," Fleming repeated darkly. "How did that happen, pray? Did they also tell you that?"

"They said you were sent on a fool's errand, so you could be made accountable for the killings done by The Englishman. That's what he's called: The Englishman." Henry shrugged. "I don't think it will work—making it seem you're a former agent turned rogue and assassin. But if The Englishman has done his work well, you could be under a cloud for some time. Questions could be asked that might serve to damage your reputation."

"Henry, how do you find out these things?" Fleming demanded.

Henry shrugged his shoulders. "I listen, and I know men who exchange secrets as currency." He studied Fleming. "What are you going to do?"

"More currency?" Fleming asked.

"No. I want to know so I can misdirect anyone attempting to impede your work." He set his pipe down. "Cesar Holiday was my friend, and my second cousin on my mother's side. I can see that the only chance he has for justice comes from you. I will do everything to help that come about and nothing to hinder your work, so long as it leads to the apprehension of Cesar's killer."

"Very well," said Fleming, accepting his avowal for the moment. "I will need to have some files photostatically copied; I cannot have it done by any usual service. The material is . . . touchy."

"I know someone who will do the work and ask no questions." Henry rubbed his hands together. "What else?"

"I want to borrow your auto," said Fleming. "Mine is too well-known. I don't want to signal my pursuers by giving them such an easy target to follow."

"Ah," said Henry. "A clever move."

"At the same time, I don't want you to drive the Rapier, because it could put you in harm's way, and I've done more than enough of that for my friends already," Fleming went on. "I'm going back to my house to collect a few things. I would appreciate it if you would follow me back in half an hour and let me ride into town with you—concealed, of course."

Henry nodded approval. "I can do this."

"Good." Fleming cocked his head. "Increase my obligation to you: how much do you know about Walter Sissons?"

"He has money and an attractive wife. He fancies himself a power in the world and doesn't realize that he is nothing more than a puppet. He has some sly sense for business and imagines himself a great industrialist. He does everything he is asked to do, because he is willing to think all ideas are his, and those who employ him turn this to their advantage, including his partners." Henry considered what else to say. "He is by nature a bully, and a fool. But he dresses well and spends his money freely enough, so he is indulged."

"Good Lord, Henry; are you truly so strict in your opinions?" Fleming cried.

"You cannot imagine," said Henry in deadly earnest, his eyes glittering.

"Then I hope I never earn your disapprobation—or," he added warily, "have I done so already?"

"If you had, I would not be lending you my auto," said Henry, his smile coming back full force. "I will come after you in half an hour and as we return to town, I will tell you all I know about Gadi Soleilsur. If I say too much here, who knows what might be overheard?" He pointed to the doorway. "Someone could listen in easily. I know. I myself have done just that on any number of occasions."

Fleming managed to accept this gracefully. "I'll assume you'll handle the photostatic copies for me after we return?"

"Yes, indeed," said Henry. "I'll arrange that at once."

"And if I hand you an envelope and address it, will you add to your kindnesses by posting it air mail special delivery for me?" Fleming was beginning to hope that all this might turn out well enough if he was able to keep a step ahead of his pursuers.

"Of course," said Henry blandly. "You have only to ask."

"I have done," Fleming said, studying Henry for a short while. "You're a most perplexing fellow; you know that, don't you?"

"Only to a few, who are clever enough to see it," said Henry. "Off you go, then. I'll come after in thirty minutes."

"Thank you, Henry," said Fleming, going to the rear of the shadowy shop and out into the glary, cloud-streaked sunshine. He drove for home as fast as was prudent, taking care to watch his rear as he went. He suspected he was being followed, but he didn't want to be too obvious in his observations for fear he would put his pursuers on notice.

At his house Fleming pulled the bandages off his hands, then gathered up Sir William's files, slipping them into an accordion file, then he tossed in a large envelope on which he had printed the address of the Pecos Vista in Roswell, New Mexico. He hurried to change into less conspicuous clothes, choosing a loose linen shirt and khaki cotton trousers, canvas-topped deck-shoes, and an anorak of muddy brown. Then he went to the pantry and took out his spare pistol, slipped it into his belt-holster, and settled the weapon against the small of his back, finding its stern, uncomfortable presence reassuring. He sat down at his typewriter and in ten minutes banged out four paragraphs on Geoffrey Krandall's murder with just enough background information upon which to hang his next article, rolled it out of the machine, then hurried down to tack a thin sheet of plywood over the broken window in the kitchen.

By then he could hear Henry Long's auto barreling down his drive. He checked the locks, gathered up his things, and went out to the Aston Martin, slipping into the space behind the seats, uncomfortable though it was, and as Henry dropped a worn woolen blanket of Hunting Stewart plaid over him, said, "Make sure you complain that you couldn't find me."

"I'll stop and tell Dominique," said Henry. "I'll ask if she's seen you."

Fleming knew such a brazen move could be hazardous, but was certain that Dominique was an excellent choice, for anyone seeking information would be likely to come to her. He did his best to lie flat as the auto bounced into the village; the sounds of the market were loud around him as Henry drew up at Dominique's house and parked. Fleming heard him hail Bonsard.

"Have you seen Mister Fleming?" Henry called out.

"I have not," Bonsard exclaimed. "Isn't he with Bathsheba?"

"I don't think so; she would have mentioned it to me," said Henry as he sauntered into the house, leaving Fleming in his awkward hiding place.

For the next ten minutes, Fleming listened to shouts and all the noise of barter, shopping, and village business, then he heard Dominique's dogs bark eagerly as Bonsard opened the door to let Henry out. He listened to Henry laugh, and say, "It may be, it may be," as he got into the Aston Martin, and pressed the starter. The bellow of the engine covered any comment Bonsard might have given. A moment later, Henry drove out of the village, waving to those he knew as he went.

"Well? What did you learn?" Fleming dared to ask as they reached the road into Kingston.

"It was most interesting. Dominique said that she had seen nothing of Soleilsur, but I doubt that was the truth," Henry remarked. "I think she knows precisely where he is."

"What makes you think so?" Fleming stretched as much as the space permitted; he was getting a cramp in the back of his thigh.

"She volunteered too much, and far too specifically, to prove her ignorance." Henry paused to use the hooter. "And she was frightened. Dominique is not a woman who frightens easily."

"No, she doesn't," Fleming said, shocked at the implications of this remark. "Do you have any notion—"

"And Bonsard is carrying a weapon," Henry interrupted. "A neat little pistol in his pocket, I suspect it is a thirty-two, one of those compact guns, not useful at any range, but at close up it could be very effective."

"I've seen him carry a pistol before," Fleming said.

"It is an ominous sign," said Henry with utter certainty.

"I agree," said Fleming.

Henry swerved suddenly amid a tumult of squeals and honks. "Fools!" he shouted out the window. "Man can't keep his pigs and geese together."

"No doubt," said Fleming, his bruised forearms held in front of him.

"Damned fool of a farmer!" Henry fumed.

"So tell me about what you've discovered about Soleilsur," said Fleming, wanting to make the trip into town worthwhile.

"I'll tell you everything," said Henry, and for the next hour as he motored along the road to Kingston, he told Fleming all he knew about Soleilsur, Walter Sissons, and The Englishman, also probably known as Sir William Potter; he talked about SS Industries and the rumors that had been circulating among the fishermen who had seen some distressing things in the last year; he mentioned all that he had gleaned from sailors coming into his chandlery about changes in harbors from the Near East to Panama, from Plymouth to Honolulu. Fleming listened intently, and was increasingly aware that he was in much deeper than he had ever supposed.

Chapter 40

AT HENRY LONG's chandlery, Fleming handed over the accordion file and the large envelope along with a five-pound note. "This envelope is for Merlin Powell. Put it in Miss Butterly's hands and she'll see he gets it." He shook Henry's hand, saying, "Thank you for this."

"Just bring her back to me, as intact as possible," said Henry, his hand on the bonnet of the Aston Martin. "It may be old but it is the best I have and I would prefer not to have to buy another."

"I'll keep that in mind, and do my best to comply," said Fleming, getting into the driver's seat. "I rely upon you to place that call to Hotchkiss in New Mexico. Tell him everything you've told me and inform him of where I'm going, and why. Be sure he knows what you're going to do if I'm not back by Thursday night. And make sure someone goes to Sissons's weekend fete, and finds my body, because if I'm not back by then, I'll be dead. Keep my confidence until that afternoon; speak only to Hotchkiss." He checked the papers in his wallet, and handed his passport to Henry. "Keep this for me, if you will. I have identification enough without it, and you may need something to take to the authorities. I hope it won't come to that. It is dangerous enough with the three of us knowing. If anyone else finds out—"

"Don't assume this will turn out badly," said Henry. "You

have sufficient information now to be able to plan your actions."

"So I hope, and I thank you for all you've told me—it's all been most enlightening, including the faster route to the Sissons estate at Fisher Creek," said Fleming, pressing the ignition and working the clutch, finding it a bit stiff, as Henry had warned it was. "Keep listening to whatever you hear, and be on guard. We must assume that Sir William has duped more men than me."

"I will, upon my honor," said Henry, and stood aside as Fleming roared out of the alley; then he sauntered back into his chandlery and called a distant relation who ran a photography and printing shop.

Fleming put his mind on the journey, deliberately holding his inner doubts at bay. He slipped into the street and headed off toward the road to the mountain lane to Montego Bay, his expression set as if hewn from living rock. He rolled along the gravel surface, doing his best not to speed so that he would not draw attention to himself. As he drove out of the city into the hills, he kept watch on his rearview mirror, doing his utmost to stay alert for anyone who might be following him; eventually he was satisfied that he had got away unnoticed, and he began to focus his attention from what was behind him to what lay ahead, all the while reviewing everything Henry Long had told him, arranging the information in his mind, and piecing together all the intelligence he now had at his disposal.

The road, graded-and-graveled—as so many roads he had been driving on had been, he pointed out to himself, remembering New Mexico—made for slow traffic, producing great clouds of dust sometimes augmented with sprays of pebbles. A half-dozen lorries lumbered up the grade, and a handful of autos, but most of the vehicles that moved on the road were drawn by animals. The high, thin clouds were thickening, turning the sky dull and the world shadowless, dark and light blending in smudges that made distances hard to judge and the lush scenery repetitive as the road angled up the spine of the island.

When he reached the turnoff for Fisher Creek, he took extra care to be sure he was unobserved. He continued up the narrow road, thinking it was in remarkably good condition for a Jamaican country road: no doubt Sissons had sponsored the maintenance. He stepped on the brake as he swung into a steep curve and saw, far below him, the broad shine of Montego Bay; in bright weather the view would have been spectacular, but instead it was ominous, a reminder of how far away Fleming had come from everyone he knew. Shaking off this unpleasant rumination, he went through the village of Fisher Creek, noticing two large whitewashed buildings like warehouses on the east end of the village. There were a number of autos on the street, more and newer than one would expect in such a remote place. The houses all looked to be in fine repair and the schoolhouse was bright with a fresh coat of whitewash. Fleming considered all this as he drove on toward the Sissons estate, thinking that he probably would find the villagers more sympathetic to Walter Sissons than to the government.

Passing the elaborate wrought-iron gateway to the estate, Fleming counted six guards—two carrying shotguns—and saw a sign warning that the grounds were patrolled by dogs, not very encouraging indications. He continued on, going down into the thickening forest and the green gloom of an impending storm. About a mile beyond the limits of the Sissons fence, he pulled to the side of the road, set up the Aston Martin with the bonnet lifted as if because of motor troubles, then took his knapsack and began to walk back in the direction of the estate.

At the chain-link fence, he went away from the road, looking for a tree that might give him access to the inside of the fence. About half a mile from the road he found one, with branches extending well beyond the fence. He set his jaw and began the climb upward, ignoring his bleeding hands as he went. Balancing along the sturdiest limb proved awkward: a clutter of birds took vociferous offense at his presence, and a regiment of spiders and insects—some of remarkable size and texture— accompanied him on his arboreal journey. When he finally dropped into the grounds of the estate, he was prepared to welcome the guard dogs as preferable to the six- and eight- legged companions of his climb.

Making his way carefully up the slope, he paused frequently to listen, trusting to his ears to tell him what his eyes could not. In a quarter hour he reached a great midden that told him the stable was not far ahead. He decided to use the powerful odor of horse dung to help conceal his presence from the dogs in case they were about, and looked for a place near the mid- den where he could wait a bit and do his best to discern the layout of the grounds ahead. He hunkered down on the slope beyond the dung heap and took stock of his situation.

"That mare bites," said a voice on the other side of the midden. His accent was from London's East End, not the mu- sical cadences of the island.

"Too right," agreed another in the same dialect. "Still, she's a treat on the polo field, isn't she?"

"That doesn't mean I want to muck out her stall," said the first. "Give me that roan gelding. Now there's a sweet horse."

"Got a lot of speed on him, does old Wellington," agreed the second voice affectionately. "Nice a horse as any in the stable. Scratch his withers and he'll love you like a brother."

"Not so much speed as Lady Wyndemere, for all that she bites," said the first.

"The game will do them good. They've been in their stalls too long—getting barn-sour, they are." The second clicked his tongue in disapproval.

"They're all ready for a run," the first agreed.

"Yes. Well, then," his companion responded as the aroma of rum-soaked pipe tobacco began to permeate the scent of dung.

"How many more do we got coming in for the weekend?" The first sounded ill-used.

"Eighteen, I think. Six horses each, three more polo players. Yeah. Eighteen. We'll have to put them two to a stall."

"When do they start arriving?" The first was preparing to complain. "It's going to be a hard time with so many to care for."

"Most of 'em'll be here Thursday morning, but Sawyer is arriving tomorrow before noon. Says he wants a day to longe his string and let 'em settle in. The first match is Friday at ten." The second voice laughed. "If it doesn't rain. By the look of the sky, we could have a wet day or two."

"There's a concert in the afternoon on Friday, isn't there? Out on the terrace?" The first grunted and a moment later a stable-rakeful of stall-cleaning struck the pile.

"For that pompous ass Broxton," the second confirmed. "Considering what he's being paid to help Sissons get what he wants, I shouldn't have thought it would be necessary to give him chamber music as well."

"Probably makes it seem less like a bribe," said the first.

"The Missus set it up," said the second. "All hoity-toity, and snooty, for the guests."

"Well, they are supposed to be impressed," said the first. "That's the point of the whole thing."

The second was unimpressed. "If a stable of well-cared-for horses can't do that, I shouldn't think a dozen musicians could."

"They're bringing in more cooks, too," said the first. "We'll dine well."

"If the guests don't bolt it all down. Those people can eat like wolfhounds when they're at a house-party."

"True enough," said the first. "But I don't think we'll lack. We haven't before." Another rakeful of stall-muck hit the heap.

"This is a bit different," said the second. "Time will tell."

"You mean all that hush-hush business?" The first man laughed once as he continued to toss the latest additions to the midden onto it. "It's a lot of show, if you ask me."

"Show?" The second paused. "It may be, but it's more than that: what Sissons expects is more than entertainment." He, too, began to unload his mucking basket. "He's nervous as a rat facing a terrier."

The first man laughed again. "Well, you could be right, Oliver. I still say it's a bubble." He worked in silence, then said, "I'm for having a pint while I can. You care to come with me?"

"Into the village?" Oliver asked.

"No. We're not to go out until after the house-party is over; we're all supposed to stay close at hand, in case we're needed—didn't you see the notice on the bulletin board? I thought I'd run along to the back lodge. There's beer there and no one will begrudge us a pint; we'll have it with cheese and call it high tea. No one will mind. I heard Mister Collins say so."

"Then I'd be glad to join you," said Oliver, completing his task. "We can feed when we're through."

"Plenty of time for that," the first conceded. "The dogs won't be set loose for another three hours, after that gammon caterer comes up with his staff. Right loose in the haft, I'd say."

"May be, but he cooks a treat," said Oliver.

Fleming heard the muck baskets being pulled away as the two grooms prepared to go off for their late afternoon drink. Left on his own, Fleming considered his options, deciding he had two hours to scope out the place before he would have to find a safe haven for the night. If he could discover what was going on here in that time, he might be able to get out before the dogs were turned loose. If not, then he would be hard-pressed to accomplish anything before morning, when more guests would begin to arrive.

He made his way along the side of the stable, taking care to keep in the shadow of the stable-roof. All the stalls had small, fenced paddocks behind them, and in a few of them, the horses stood, occasionally flicking flies with their tails but otherwise moving in that listless way that suggested a storm was building. Fleming found himself encouraged by this, hoping that a good, solid rain would work on his behalf, providing cover, washing away his scent, and furnishing enough confusion to permit him to accomplish everything he intended to do. He wished he had some of those listening devices he'd found on the Packard—he could use them now, or more sophisticated tools that would give him an edge in this dangerous enterprise. A mobile camera about the size of a fly to show him what lay ahead; that would be useful, with a viewing screen built into the face of his wristwatch. At least he had a pistol once again nestled in the holster at the small of his back—little enough if it came to a fight, it was still better than nothing at all. He would have liked to have at least another two of them on his person, and perhaps a hand-grenade, suitably disguised, and a bolt-cutter. He made himself stop yearning for impossibilities and instead to pay attention to his immediate predicament.

Beyond the stable he had to face a broad stretch of lawn to his left, with the north wing of the house rising at the far end of it, and a cluster of various species of palms to his right. He hesitated a moment, then struck off for the trees, anticipating their protection. It would be better, he thought, to have a higher vantage-point so that he might work out the lay of the land rather better than he already had done, but the highest spot for some distance around was the roof of the Sissons house, and that was not only inaccessible, it was very likely patrolled and guarded. He studied the trees above him and decided it was highly unlikely that he could climb any one of them undetected. He decided he would have to take stock some other way. For the time being, he kept to the shade of the fronds and did his best to look about from his concealed position.

After about twenty minutes, his inactivity began to rankle, and he started toward what appeared to be a large garden with a number of paths meandering through carefully laid-out beds of ferns and flowers. He spent half his time bending over various buds and blooms as if he were a gardener, hoping that any casual observer might dismiss him as such. He had worked himself around to the west flank of the house, continuing his pose as a gardener while looking for doors that might give him access to the building when he reached a stretch of slate paving where chairs and tables were set out, large umbrellas ready to be unfurled against the sun when it appeared. Tantalizingly near were two doors, one leading into the main part of the house, the other, less conspicuously, seeming to lead to the servants' sector of the building. Fleming paused, wondering how he might approach it when he heard a soft footfall behind him.

"Ah, Fleming," said Sir William Potter. "I had almost given you up."

Chapter 41

FLEMING TURNED to face a silenced Beretta that was leveled at his head from about eight feet away. "So this was a trap?" He kept his voice cool, though his gut knotted hot within him.

"Ruse would be a better word for it. You were the one who turned it into a trap, for which I thank you. But I have been most fortunate: Henry Long has no notion that the reports he has sent so diligently to MI5 found their way to me instead of the intended recipient. His work has been invaluable to me. One could call it providential, at least from my point of view." He was looking hale and rested, his skin pink from exposure to the tropical sun. No longer in woolen pin-stripes, he sported a linen blazer and slacks in a pale blue-green over a silk shirt of lilac; his tie was pearl-white. "To be candid, I didn't think you'd return from America—in a way it's inconvenient that you did. Still, I'm not adverse to improvisation."

"Was your disappearance an improvisation as well?" Fleming asked.

Sir William used the barrel of his Beretta to gesture to Fleming, indicating he should move away from the house. "No. No, that was very much a part of the plan. Once you were willing to take on the assignment I offered you, it was only a matter of going out to the cove. You made that particularly easy, by the by. I must say I'm grateful for your good manners. Once I reached the far end of the cove, Soleilsur had a cigarette boat standing by to take me aboard."

"And the slashed suit-coat?" Fleming inquired as he began to walk along the path Sir William pointed him toward. "What was the reason for that?"

"Why, it served two purposes: first, it convinced you that my plight was real—it did, didn't it?" He smiled as Fleming nodded. "And it kept you from examining my role in subsequent events, for you assumed I was a victim, not an instigator. That bought me a fair amount of time."

"I'm afraid that much is true, at least until—" He stopped, not wanting to recall the dreary hours of waiting for Doctor Bethune to finish his work on Cesar.

"Yes, until. Well, it had to come: I supposed even you would eventually put an end to my pretense," said Sir William with intensely false sadness. "It's unfortunate that you were so assiduous in your efforts. Had you been more lax, your discoveries would have come too late and none of this would have been necessary."

Fleming decided to do his best to keep Sir William boasting, in the hope that he might find an opportunity to overset him, or to escape. "It was a very tricksy dance you led me."

"I'm sorry it wasn't more so," said Sir William. "Have I been careless?"

Although this was exactly Fleming's opinion, he said, "I wouldn't think so, no. I was lucky. I was able to get a fair amount of information that linked you to the murdered men; I don't imagine I would have made the connection without a little serendipity. If I hadn't got that report at Los Alamos, I don't suppose I would have seen the pattern that linked you to Krandall, Cathcart, and Preussin. Even with that, I assumed at first that you were among the targets."

"I hope you haven't been reckless enough to share your information with anyone?" Sir William shook his head. "I wouldn't want to have to kill too many more of your associates. It would be difficult to implicate you in all of them."

"That is your plan, I assume? To make it appear that I'm responsible for your mischief? That I have done your killings? You need a—what do the Americans call it?—a patsy, a fall-guy. As I've been all along." Fleming wanted to make it seem that he had overreached himself in coming here, that he was without any protection. "You've been planning this for some while, haven't you?"

"No, not for very long," said Sir William with relish. "Hardly more than four weeks. It took me a while to choose you for the goat, however. I wanted to find just the right man."

"Because you can point to my work and travel as the means of my activities? Using my journalism to cover the work of an assassin? Sounds like a Hitchcock film to me; *The Thirty-Nine Steps*. Adventure wrapped up in a riddle?" Fleming inquired, hoping that Sir William would tell him more. "Do you think you can make me responsible for everything you've done?"

"Not all of it. I don't reckon I can lay Preussin's death at your door, but there are ways to link you to a conspiracy that may implicate you in that aspect of his death." Sir William was less willing to delay his work now. "You will see a shed on the path ahead of you. When you reach it, open the door."

Fleming regarded the garden uneasily. "Aren't you taking a bit of a chance? I might escape."

"My dear Fleming, I am *counting* on that. Do escape, please. The dogs haven't had a treat in over a month. It will be un-fortunate that no one was able to reach them in time to keep them from mauling you to death." He stopped walking.

"And if I don't escape, what then?" Fleming asked nonchalantly, trying to cover his growing unease.

"Then I shall have to release you and set you running, after I put a bullet in your thigh to make you ready prey. That reminds me: do give me your handkerchief. I need something for the mastiffs to take your scent." His voice became sharper. "Drop it on the ground. I'll pick it up later." He cleared his throat. "Now, Fleming. Do not make me tell you twice, or I might be forced to put a bullet through your foot."

"Doesn't it worry you that I might scream?" Fleming asked.

"Not a bit of it. Scream away—for all the good it would do you." Sir William was gloating. "The handkerchief?"

"You want something of mine to show the police, to prove I was in the house. You're relying on the laundry mark to provide identification," Fleming guessed, and took Sir William's silence for confirmation. He did as he was told, then continued down the path, and came at last to the shed.

"Stop," said Sir William. "Open the door." When Fleming had done this, he went on, "There are lengths of heavy twine used to bind plants. Take three of them out and toss them toward me. Carefully."

As he did as he was told, Fleming asked, "Is this about mining harbors, and using the mines to blackmail the ships and countries using the harbors? Are you intending to take control of the seas? And are you planning to make an example of Jamaica?"

Sir William laughed. "That's Soleilsur's contribution, and I don't think I'll tell you where we plan to begin. There are so many possibilities, just in the Gulf of Mexico. Consider the ramifications. Think about how thoroughly the world can be brought to its knees, without setting off a single atom bomb. That will give you something to wile away the hours while you're locked in the shed. Incidentally, mine is rather a more political role than that, the second phase of the campaign, if you like. Perhaps you might contemplate the permutations of our plan during your incarceration. There are so many, and some of them will probably be right. Köln. Hamburg. Marseilles. Cadiz. Southampton. Glasgow. Barcelona. Venice. Tunis. Tokyo. Cape Town. Rio de Janeiro. Vladivostok. Baltimore. Hong Kong. Sydney. Bombay. Panama City. Lima. Copenhagen. Singapore. Manila. There are so, so many." He kept far enough away to make it impossible for Fleming to make a successful lunge at him.

"Do you mean to tell me you have mined all those harbors?" Fleming asked, thinking back again to what David Dunstan had said.

"I don't mean to tell you anything," Sir William said bluntly. "I can see you are cleverer than I gave you credit for being. Kneel down if you would."

"So you can shoot me?" Fleming challenged even as he went onto his knees, facing a display of rakes, clippers, pots, soil, and hoses. "There are a fair number of witnesses about, I should think."

"I'm not going to shoot you, not even with the silencer, not unless you compel me to. You would be hard to explain, and there would be blood to deal with. I'll leave your disposal to the dogs. They won't mind the blood." Sir William giggled.

"Does this amuse you?" Fleming asked testily, wondering if he could goad Sir William into an impulsive act that he might turn to his advantage.

"No. You do not." He lost all trace of levity. "I want to tie your hands but I also want to minimize your opportunity to turn on me. You're just temerarious enough to do it. I think, given your training and your service record, you might try that, no matter how foolhardy it may be."

Fleming put his hands behind his back, trying not to rest them on top of his holster. He hoped he might be able to keep the pistol if he didn't do anything to draw Sir William's attention to it. He held his hands out, as if to make the binding easier for his captor. "Be careful not to tie off my circulation," he warned. "You'd be hard-pressed to explain swollen, blackened hands, no matter what the dogs might do."

"You're assuming your death will be investigated," said Sir William with smug satisfaction. "You can't be sure of that, you know." He began to tug on the cord as he spoke, pulling Fleming's hands toward him with each emphasis. "Oh, no *doubt* there'll be an inquiry. And *questions* will be asked. There'll be *speculation*, but it will come to nothing. Who*ever* drove you up here will *have* to tell what he knows. But *no* one here will have seen you. No one." He grunted as he tied the knots, then shoved Fleming between the shoulder-blades, sending him onto his face. "Now for your feet. I shouldn't try anything stupid if I were you."

Fleming felt the twine go around his ankles, once, twice, three times, and then it was pulled tight. He could feel scrapes on his face that he supposed must be bleeding. A moment later, Sir William went to his side and began to roll him the last little distance into the garden shed; Fleming knocked his jaw on the slate flagging and resigned himself to a bad bruising.

"There you go," said Sir William as he closed the shed door. He was breathing hard now, as if he was too excited by his exertions. He went away from the shed quickly, his steps fading rapidly.

Fleming lay on the floor of the shed, his face on the loamy floor, the damp of the ground sinking into him and chilling him in spite of the warmth of the day. Uncomfortable as he was, he made himself think. He wriggled around so that he could reach the knots at the back of his ankle. That was an oversight, he thought, to tie his ankles where he could reach the knots. He worked his hands until he could pull at the cords, pushing the rough hemp back through the knots by fractions of an inch at a time. All the while he thought about what Sir William had said, at the staggering number of harbors he had mentioned. If even half of those had been compromised the blow to world commerce would be catastrophic. Sir William had mentioned over twenty cities, all of them important centers of commerce and politically significant. He had loosened the first part of the knot. He continued his efforts, ignoring the tingling in his fingers that indicated coming numbness. How was he going to continue if he couldn't feel the cord? Would he still be able to get the knots undone if his fingers were insensate? He banished that worry and kept on, refusing to consider defeat.

There was a spurt of water against the shed, and another: the sprinklers had been turned on, even though rain was threatening for the night. Somewhere nearby two gardeners called to one another; Fleming could not make out what they were saying, but he caught the word *supper* and the phrase *enough for today*, and assumed that the day's work was coming to an end. He recalled the grooms had said something about a lodge, and assumed that other members of the staff were bound there. Which meant that the guards might be off duty, but the dogs would soon be patrolling the estate. In a perfect world, he told himself, using his anger to augment his determination, there would be a simple tool he could use to cut through the heavy hempen twine quickly and easily—a fountain pen, a wrist-watch, a cigarette lighter, something. If he had been able to reach one of the clippers or pruners, he could have been out of this quickly, but they were on shelves up above him, so out of reach they might have been on the moon for all the good they could do him.

The second level of the knot gave way; Fleming now began to pull his ankles apart, increasing the play in the cord. He redoubled his efforts, and in a short while his feet were free. At least Sir William hadn't known to tie him in such a way that he couldn't loosen the cords; he had neglected to put a loop around Fleming's neck or to use some other detriment to his escape. He reminded himself that Sir William was planning on his getting free, but he rolled onto his back, his pistol making a hard lump against his spine, pulled his knees up to his chest and worked his arms down and over his rump, then brought his bound wrists to his teeth and began to pull the knots. In forty minutes he was free. He stood up, trying to ignore his numb fingers, but realized he would need to feel in order to escape. Shaking his hands to try to restore sensation to them, he took stock of his situation, knowing with utter certainty that Sir William would be returning within a short while to force him out into the night.

He opened the latch and glanced out into the gloomy dusk. He could hear someone calling for his companions to join him at table; Fleming decided that the dogs would be out soon, and thought he had better not take a chance. He selected a small sickle from the array of tools, thrust it through the front of his belt, and stepped out of the shed into the spray from the sprinklers. Instead of making his way down the path, he managed to climb the shed to the roof, where he lay down, waiting for Sir William's return, shivering in the slow, cool wind. He thought about his pistol and decided against using it for fear of the attention it would attract—after one shot it would be more trouble than it was worth. Perhaps he would want it later, when he had got away from this dreadful place, when he might have to discourage pursuit.

About ten minutes after he had got onto the roof of the shed, Fleming heard steady footsteps coming down the slates of the walkway, pausing, apparently to turn off the sprinklers, for the water stopped spraying over the plants, and the steps resumed their progress toward the shed. Fleming pulled the sickle from his belt and prepared to move.

Chapter 42

SIR WILLIAM pulled open the shed door and stopped still. Then he took a step back, chuckling. "So you've decided to take your chances with the dogs?" he called out, almost merrily. "Well, they have your scent. They'll find you in short order."

Fleming moved to the edge of the roof, gathered his knees under him, and dropped down immediately behind Sir William, the sickle held at the ready as he touched the ground. He wrapped his arm around Sir William's neck, the sickle lying against his throat, and seized his right hand, twisting it and forcing him to drop his Beretta. Fleming kicked this away into the shrubbery and whispered, "If the dogs find me, they also find you."

Sir William went stiff, trying to break away from Fleming's grasp. "Bugger all, you sod."

"Ah, ah," Fleming admonished, "remember how easily I can nick your throat."

"You wouldn't," said Sir William.

"Don't wager on that horse," said Fleming. "You'll lose." He shoved Sir William, forcing him to walk with him down the path.

"You need me to get out of here," said Sir William, his voice rising in pitch.

"What do you think I'm doing now?" Fleming said, and made him walk a little faster. He was going in the general direction of the stable, planning to get out the way he came in.

"You won't make it thirty feet," said Sir William with more bravado than conviction.

"You're wrong, you know," said Fleming. "But I'm willing to put your theory to the test." The blade of the sickle caressed Sir William's neck. "Just hope I remain calm. You wouldn't want me to nick you by accident."

Sir William did his utmost to move slowly, but Fleming kept moving him on. "No matter what you've found, it will come to nothing."

"Do you really think so?" Fleming asked, avoiding the spreading branches of a bougainvillea.

"You have nothing to back up your ludicrous theories," said Sir William defiantly. "Anything I may have said cannot be supported."

"Perhaps, perhaps not," said Fleming, making sure he could see what lay ahead of them across the expanse of lawn between the garden and the stable. "Keep walking. If you try to break away, I will cut your throat."

"Are you willing to take such a chance?" Sir William challenged.

"Do you think I am not?" Fleming countered. "You are the one who has been working to compromise the peace in the world."

Sir William laughed once. "Do you think the dogs will care? Do you think they'll assess your motives before they attack?"

"They will attack you first," said Fleming, feeling oddly petty for arguing with Sir William, particularly now and in this place: his only excuse was that it kept his fear at bay. He glanced about swiftly and uneasily, keenly aware that the most efficient guard dogs wouldn't bark.

"They have your scent," Sir William reminded him. "They know me. They don't know you. Whom do you think they'll go after." He laughed once. "You don't know how soon they'll find you."

Fleming felt his body go tight at the thought, but he banished his fear as best he could. "Keep moving," he said as much to himself as Sir William.

"Someone will see the two of us," Sir William kept on. "You won't get to the stables without detection."

"Take the turn on your left," Fleming said coldly, remembering the way he had come, behind the stable midden. "You'll have to be careful. The footing isn't easy."

"Then we will have to fall together," said Sir William with a confidence that Fleming distrusted.

"You might not like what happens if I trip," he told his captive, pushing the sickle into his neck. "I'm as apt to slit your throat by accident as to release you. Sickles are sharpened on the inside, remember."

Sir William went silent, picking his way stiffly along the edge of the sloping lawn; only a small portion of the upper floor of the house could be seen from here, and Sir William was beginning to fret. "You know you can't get away."

"Then neither can you," said Fleming, all but frog-marching him toward the rear of the stables. "There are empty stalls. I'm going to tie and gag you and leave you in one of them, unless you make it necessary for me to do more." They were at the base of the midden, the odor of horse manure was strong, giving Fleming reason to be encouraged, an emotion that faded as he became aware of the sound of pursuit behind them—dogs running, panting, determined.

"So close and yet so far," Sir William mocked. "They know not to attack me. But they will rip your guts out."

"You had better hope they do not," said Fleming, his grip on the sickle tightening. He looked about quickly, shoving Sir William as he began a desperate rush toward the stable.

The first dog caught up with them just as they staggered into the wide aisle between the box stalls. It launched itself at Fleming, a great brute, half German shepherd, half English mastiff, weighing well over a hundred pounds. The impact of his striking was lessened as Fleming brought up his knee, catching the animal in the chest; he kicked at the dog and thrust Sir William ahead of him. "Open the first stall," he ordered, keeping his grip on Sir William and the sickle.

The dog had recovered enough to attack a second time, and now Fleming kicked it as hard as he could and was rewarded by a yelp of pain. Almost at once, a second dog slammed into Fleming's back, its teeth tearing his jacket. Luckily the holster and pistol kept the dog's teeth from sinking into his flesh. Fleming heard the rattle of the stall door latch as Sir William pulled it open and pressed forward into the stall, Fleming immediately behind him, tugging the door closed as the two dogs hurled themselves at the door from outside.

"Clever," Sir William approved, then screamed as the bad-tempered mare who occupied the stall sank her big square teeth into his shoulder.

Fleming nearly dropped the sickle as Sir William lurched in an attempt to get away; outside the dogs were growling, their claws scrabbling on the wood as they tried to climb. In the next stall, the horse became restless, pacing in the limited confines and chuffing in distress.

"Get her *off* me!" Sir William demanded, his free arm swinging in an attempt to push the mare away.

Fleming dropped the sickle, then reached out and struck the mare sharply on the nose. She shrieked but let go of her prize, half-rearing, her neck snaking out to find another opportunity to strike; Fleming thrust Sir William into the corner of the stall.

"That bloody horse broke my collarbone!" Sir William exclaimed through tightened teeth. There was blood welling over his fine silken shirt. "God *damn* it, Fleming!"

The mare squealed again, her teeth bared. Fleming thought her carrying on would soon attract the attention of the grooms, and decided on a desperate gamble: he drew his pistol, motioning to Sir William to remain where he was, and then threw the stall-door open, whistling to the mare to go, and getting out of her way as she charged out of the stall, directly into the pair of dogs.

Outraged neighing and infuriated barking erupted as the mare kicked and bucked while the dogs leaped at her, their rage turning them against the horse with the pent-up fury of their thwarted hunt.

Fleming knew time was crucial now. He reached out and seized Sir William by his bleeding arm, wrenching him out of the stall. Staying next to the stall, he dragged Sir William along to the next stall, opened it, and stood aside as the horse rushed out. He managed to release another three horses before he saw the outside lights come on. "No time," he muttered, and dragged Sir William with him toward the fence at the bottom of the slope behind the stable.

Sir William was moaning, as much from dread as from pain, and as they got to the chain-link, he began to whimper. "I can't. Fleming, I can't, I can't, I can't."

"Then you can stay here with the dogs," said Fleming, who had no intention of leaving Sir William behind.

"I can't climb." Sir William tried to drop to his knees only to be held up by Fleming's hand on his lapel.

"You'll go up that fence and over it, or I'll shoot you where you stand." Fleming could hear shouting from near the stable and knew he had to go now or risk capture or death. *"Go!"* he cried.

Astonishingly, Sir William did turn and begin to climb. As he neared the top he faltered, and Fleming slid his pistol back into the holster, then hooked his fingers in the chain-link and began to pull himself upward. He was half-way up the fence when Sir William lashed out with his foot in an effort to dislodge Fleming from his precarious hold on the fence. In the next moment, Sir William began to shout for help, calling for Sissons to come to his rescue.

"Stop!" Fleming ordered, moving sideways on the fence to get out of range of Sir William's feet.

"Call the police!" Sir William yelled. "Sissons! *Call the police!* Get them here! Now!"

"Shut up!" Fleming ordered, and climbed higher on the fence.

"Help!" Sir William bellowed. "HELP!"

There was a flurry of excitement near the stables as the grooms struggled to catch the escaped horses and calm the infuriated dogs. The men scrambled amid the animals, the dogs becoming hysterical. A number of voices were raised to order and cajole to end the confusion.

"HELP!" Sir William screamed. His hold on the fence was growing unsteady, and his breathing was shallow. With a look of loathing, he pointed at Fleming. "You did this! Fleming! You!" Although this was little more than a whisper, the intensity of his contempt filled the air between them. His next attempt at shouting was a faint echo of his previous cry.

Fleming continued on up the fence and climbed over it. "Come!" He reached for his pistol, pointing it at Sir William. "You're coming with me. You have a lot to answer for."

"No." Sir William let go of his hold, falling back on the inner side of the fence; he wailed as he landed, and sat for a moment as if winded. "You'll die for this, Fleming."

The sound of sirens announced the arrival of the police—a suspiciously quick arrival—and Fleming knew he was in danger of being caught or killed. He saw four men in the same uniforms as the guards Fleming had seen earlier patrolling the grounds as they came toward the fence, automatic weapons at the ready.

Hesitating no longer, Fleming aimed his pistol and fired, striking two of the men with four shots.

"Over there!" Sir William shouted. "Kill him! *Kill him!*"

Fleming fired toward Sir William, hoping to frighten him to silence, and instead, he saw him waver, then topple, blood spattering from the wreckage of his ear.

There were men on both sides of the wall, most of them shouting. The police were clambering through the undergrowth, their torches showing their way through the darkness. Inside the estate the guards had converged upon Sir William, one of them shouting for medical help. Two of the others began to peer beyond the fence, looking for Fleming.

Just as the guards began to point their weapons in Fleming's general direction, a policeman's torch caught him in its beam, and Fleming raised his hands, his pistol dangling by the trigger-guard from his thumb. He stood very still and completely silent, not wanting to draw any more attention to himself, certain that Sissons's guards would take advantage of any excuse to kill him.

"Hold out your hands!" ordered a police sergeant as he came toward Fleming.

"We have him now," he called toward the fence. "Mister Sissons was right to alert us." He stared at Fleming. "I am going to take your pistol."

"Please do," said Fleming, hoping that the police would not decide to save the Crown the trouble of bringing him to trial. "If you will look in my wallet? I'd appreciate it. You'll find it in my inner jacket pocket." He tried to sound calm, although he was beginning to feel the shock of all that had happened that day. "I'm sorry," he said as his hands began to shake. He reminded himself to maintain a steady demeanor: the situation was far too volatile and would need very little to get out of hand.

"Your wallet?" The sergeant gingerly retrieved the object in question.

"Open it," said Fleming.

The sergeant had three of his men at his side now. "What is it that you want me to see?" He held up Fleming's driving license. "You are Ian Fleming, with a London address, I see."

"There's more," said Fleming as the guards on the other side of the fence came to tend to Sir William.

"Press credentials," said the sergeant. "Four pounds and a half-crown."

"Behind that," said Fleming as he watched the guards put a horse-blanket over Sir William's body.

The sergeant found the folded paper. "Is this it?"

"Open it," said Fleming, a hard note in his voice.

The sergeant whistled as he caught sight of the crest on the fine paper, and the formal heading. "Authorization to use deadly force. Signed by the PM. I've heard of these things, but I've never seen one. Is this authentic?"

"You may check it out. In fact, I ask you to check it out," said Fleming as he glimpsed Walter Sissons striding down to the fence, a shotgun slung in the crook of his arm.

The sergeant made up his mind. "I'm taking you in." He looked toward Walter Sissons. "We've taken him in hand."

Walter Sissons scowled. "He killed Sir William Potter."

"That he did," said the sergeant. "And he may have the authority to do so. We will have to determine this, which may take some time. I'll let you know what we learn."

Fleming moved a little closer to the sergeant, holding out his hands for cuffs. "I am surrendering willingly. I am not resisting." And with that he turned his back on the men on the other side of the fence and went off with the police toward the road.

Epilogue

"YOUR MATERIAL confirms everything we have," Hotchkiss told Fleming that Friday. "Sir William Potter and Gadi Soleilsur have been part of a conspiracy to mine harbors and extort money and influence all over the world. Potter had covered his tracks very well."

From his seat behind Merlin Powell's desk, Fleming heard this out with as much satisfaction as he could summon in the midst of his fatigue and sorrow. "Good work."

"It would never have happened without your inquiry," said Hotchkiss, the connection hissing.

"That's the irony of it, isn't it," said Fleming. "Sir William intended to send me on a wild goose chase so he could make it appear that I was an assassin working to eliminate the men who could have revealed his role in the scheme." He looked up as Powell came through the door with two glasses in his hands. "Have you heard anything more from MI5?"

"Nothing I can tell you on an unsecure line," said Hotchkiss apologetically.

"And somehow I doubt Lord Broxton will be much inclined to let me use his facilities at Government House," said Fleming, almost smiling.

"He's going back to England, I hear," said Hotchkiss, a note of speculation in his words.

"So I understand," said Fleming. "The family have a place in Darbyshire where Lord Broxton can live out his days without embarrassment to the Broxtons."

"It sounds as if this is going to get swept under the rug," said Hotchkiss.

"I suspect it will," said Fleming.

"Too bad. You deserve a lot of credit for what you've done." Hotchkiss cleared his throat. "How are they going to account for Sir William?"

"No doubt they'll think of something," said Fleming, preparing to ring off. "I should think that you, too, won't be given the recognition you deserve for all the help you've provided."

"Maybe not," Hotchkiss conceded. "But I've been told that things may perk up here in Roswell. It *is* an air force base, and security is important."

There was a silence between them, and then Fleming said, "Keep in touch, won't you, Hotchkiss?"

"If they let me," said Hotchkiss with so flat a tone that Fleming knew he had to be in deadly earnest. "You've made enemies, Fleming. You watch your back, okay?"

"Okay," said Fleming, and hung up as Powell went to his liquor cabinet and took out three bottles.

"What's your pleasure? Gin? Scotch? Brandy?" He put his hands on the desk. "You deserve a drink."

"Gin, a bit of tonic, if you don't mind," said Fleming, beginning to rise from Powell's chair.

Powell waved him back into it while he bustled to prepare drinks for the two of them. "Your stories are improving circulation, and you managed to stop an international cadre of criminals from dominating world shipping, saving industry and who knows how many lives in the process." He splashed tonic into the glass that was two-thirds of Gin, then did the same to his glass of Scotch. "And you won't be able to have the praise you so richly deserve."

"I wonder if Cesar would see it that way," said Fleming as he picked up the glass.

"Considering what the stakes were, how could he not?" Powell exclaimed. "I have no doubt he'd approve of all you've done." He sat down in the visitor's chair on the far side of the desk. "I wish we could tell the whole story, but—" He shrugged.

"Exactly," said Fleming, thinking for the first time that he was looking forward to going back to London: he needed some time to lay his ghosts to rest and to regain his sense of perspective.

"Well, here's to your future—may it be filled with successes of all kinds."

Fleming raised his glass to touch the rim of Powell's. "Chin-chin," he said.